UNFORGIVEN

UNFORGIVEN

Jules Hardy

POCKET BOOKS

LONDON • SYDNEY • NEW YORK • TORONTO

First published in Great Britain by Pocket Books, 2007
An imprint of Simon & Schuster UK Ltd
A CBS COMPANY

1 3 5 7 9 10 8 6 4 2

Simon & Schuster UK Ltd
Africa House
64-78 Kingsway
London WC2B 6AH

www.simonsays.co.uk

Simon & Schuster Australia
Sydney

A CIP catalogue record for this book is available from the British Library

ISBN-13: 978-0-7434-9568-4

Typeset in Garamond by M Rules
Printed and bound in Great Britain by
Cox & Wyman Ltd, Reading, Berks

To my mother,
with thanks for not
retiring to Bognor

ACKNOWLEDGEMENTS

The writing of a novel is a curious thing. At the time of writing, the author imagines the creative act is hers alone; it is only when the finished manuscript sits on a table – unloved or otherwise – that the thought dawns that many others have contributed in the process, in ways not always obvious. For example, who'd have thought that the concoction and sampling of cocktails ranging from MD49s, through Lovelies and Princess Punches, to arrive at Is It Tuesday Yet?, would have involved so many bartenders? Thanks to Marie, Moosey, Mark and Mater for those (the paracetamol are in the post . . .). Paula must be mentioned, both for the magnificence of her lime fish and the ragged beauty of her restaurant. I had never appreciated the extraordinary vitality and versatility of West Indian language (sadly fading) until I visited Mr Washington's First Historical Café, and read Mark Abley's *Spoken Here* and John Mendes' *Cote ci, Cote la* (thanks, Viv and Trina, for the long, long loan). Thanks, too, to Naurice for losing his teeth, and to Audrey for providing the Girdle which has exercised us so much over the years. So many people come to mind: Clydie, Pigeon, Pirate, Salt, Bap, Doc, Pearl . . . the list goes on and on. How did they unwittingly contribute? Simply by living their lives. And, of course, Redman, who used to bring bags of limes, and then one day fell out of a tall, tall tree.

Ultimately, however, I must acknowledge one other without which this book would never have been written – but how to thank an island? Thanks anyway. Mih nable string bury dere.

DIANA

Obviously, I've been thinking about him, thinking about Sammy, ever since the news came through, but I have to say I never really knew my brother, even though he was only two years older than me. When I was born, it was as if a . . . a . . . as if something, something like a wall, slid down between us. Thinking about it, maybe it wasn't a wall, maybe it was more like a one-way mirror, because I always felt I could watch him forever and he'd never notice me; as if he could lead his life with me watching him and he'd never look at me, never be aware of me. Even when we were very young I felt like that. He never really noticed me, he just lived out his life on the other side of the mirror. Anyway, that's what I used to think, how I used to feel when I was young. I used to feel lonely, I suppose. But, of course, that was before I accepted Jesus into my life. *Diana shrugs, tugs at the worn crucifix dangling on a thin, gold chain. She leans forward, picks up a plastic beaker and sips at still water.* Now I know that Sammy was just self-absorbed, he was just vain. He *was* vain. Some people might think I was jealous because I wasn't beautiful, because I wasn't part of his life but I wasn't jealous, I'm *not* jealous, because I know beauty comes from within. Purity of heart is beauty; faith is beauty; the will to duty and fidelity is beauty; chastity and temperance are beautiful. Some people may laugh, may think these words are old-fashioned, but they are eternal. Those same people only want to know about Sammy just because of who he knew, who he brushed up against. Who he . . . slept with. How vacuous is that? Because I'm his sister, because I share his blood, I care about what has happened to his soul: is he numbered among the damned? *Diana looks away, lowers her eyes, as if to speak of damnation is not her prerogative.* But I suppose Sammy was beautiful, he was so handsome. Even the thing with his ear was, in its own way, beautiful. As if that single flaw, that imperfection, made him more desirable. When I was a little girl I always felt alone, as if I had been left on the wrong side of the mirror. Like I was looking through it watching my family living out their lives and I wasn't a part of that. But I'm not bitter. *Diana sucks her lips as if they have been dipped in citrus juice.* I remember very little about our childhood, when we lived in Cyprus. I know I was always left out of the games. Sammy used to ask school friends over and they'd play in the garden, well, it wasn't really a garden, but anyway, they'd play games and he never asked me to join in. I'd sit on the back doorstep and watch them. But you don't want to know about me . . . Sometimes I knew my mother was standing behind me as I sat on the step and I'd look up at her and she was always looking at Sammy. I'd tug at her trousers and she'd look down at me as if she didn't know who I was, and then look back to Sammy. Sorry, I'm sorry. So . . . Sammy . . . Sammy, Sammy. I don't know. I knew nothing about his life once we came back to England. I went to a local school and he boarded at Redpath. You'll have to ask other people about that time, about when he was at school. I do remember that trouble always followed him around. He nearly killed my grandparents with worry. I visit my grandmother once a week, now she's in the Home, and she's told me about what a tearaway Sammy was, how much trouble he caused. I can remember sitting at the dinner table every night and the talk was always about Sammy and never about me, no matter how good I was, or how well I'd done at school. Even though he wasn't even there, the talk was still all about him. Not that I'm bitter, you understand. I have a wonderful husband and four lovely children; I am blessed. We all are. All apart from poor Sammy. *Again, Diana sips at the water, fingering the cross at her throat.* There were those parties, of course, the parties at the cottage in Cyprus. Fortunately, I was too young to be able to recollect them clearly. I've heard some of the accounts of those who were there and I am appalled. I can't believe that my parents would subject me to that. But perhaps things were different then? Perhaps parents were different then? I remember that I had terrible arguments with my mother every Friday because she wouldn't let me wear my school uniform for the weekend. She used to call me 'the little Nazi'. 'The little Nazi.' And my father laughed. I remember he always laughed when she called me that. My mother could speak Greek and sometimes I wondered when she spoke, what she was saying about me. Maybe it was difficult for them. They were all so tall and tanned and . . . and *relaxed* about themselves, living on the other side of the mirror. I never worked out why I wasn't like them. But I'm not lonely now. *Diana shifts in the chair, rubs at her neck, rolls her rounded shoulders.* I'm not used to talking like this. I'd really rather not do this. There are many things I'd rather not remember. I'd certainly rather not remember the weekends in the fisherman's cottage. They were . . . they were . . . decadent, licentious. The smell of woodsmoke, which my husband adores, makes me feel unwell.

Even a hint of alcohol makes me nauseous, reminds me of my mother and her filthy cocktails. But you don't want to know about this, do you? You want to know about Sammy. Always Sammy. He loved those weekends. He revelled in them because, of course, he was always the centre of attention. I do have a memory, perhaps it's more of a feeling, about one time at the cottage when Sammy had been to see his friend, a local boy. I can't remember his name. He was an ugly boy and – God forgive me – I liked him because of that. Anyway, Sammy went to play with him one day and when he came back, he was different. Sammy was different. I know it's not right to speak ill of the dead or disappeared, but Sammy had been arrogant and when he came back that day he wasn't any more. He wasn't arrogant. I remember that. Sammy came limping back to the cottage and, of course, my mother abandoned the game she was playing with me and went to look after him. Sammy had a graze on his knee but he couldn't stop crying, which I thought was odd. But after that he was different. He was quieter, he spent more time on his own. He didn't pick arguments with me so often. *A string of rosaries appears in Diana's hands and she begins to fondle the beads, move them around.* One summer, years ago, when I was training to be a nurse, I visited my father with Alistair, who was my fiancé at the time, and Sammy turned up. I think he'd finished his exams and he turned up in Cyprus for a holiday. Before he arrived we'd all been having a lovely time, visiting the sights and ruins, but once Sammy was there everything changed. There were parties every night and drinking until the early hours. My father even suggested that Sammy slept with some girl in the house which, of course, I tried to stop. But my father just laughed at me. *A shuddering breath as the rosaries click.* I think this is all wrong.

I don't understand it. All the fuss. Sammy wasn't important, he wasn't well-known, he wasn't famous, so I can't understand what all the fuss is about. Why so many people care about what happened to him. I can only think it's because of that woman. That Jezebel. She reminded me of my mother. Poor Sammy. He went away and he was out of his depth. He didn't belong there, amongst those sorts of people. I know you want to know about Sammy and what he was like and how he met the people he met and what those people were like but I can't tell you. He used to phone me sometimes, in the middle of the night. Perhaps he felt guilty about ignoring me, but the calls were always drunken, he never made any sense. Alistair, my husband, thinks Sammy was trying to apologize for something, but that's Alistair for you — always seeing the best in people. I don't think that. I think it's a case of the sins of the father being visited on the son. Which is curious because he was a real mummy's boy. Of course, after that terrible Christmas, you know, what happened at Aspen, the phone calls dried up. I never heard from him again — it must be more than twelve years now since I heard from him. Sammy just disappeared and I barely thought about him until a couple of days ago. *Again, Diana looks away, looks into the neutral distance.* My clearest memory of Sammy, if you really want to know, isn't the most recent. I can remember him fighting in the jeep, fighting the soldiers who were taking us to the airport when the Turks came. He must have only been about eleven but it took three of them as well as my father to keep him in the jeep and then get him on the plane. I was scared of him, then, the way he was fighting, like he didn't care whether he lived or died. *Diana sighs, places her hands together as if in prayer, as if closing a book.* What's terrible . . . perhaps

I shouldn't say this . . . what's terrible, is that I find I can't grieve.
I can't grieve because I don't know what's happened to him, if
he's . . . if he's dead or not. And anyway, I hardly knew him. It
would be like grieving for a stranger. I always thought Sammy led
a charmed life. Sometimes I'd see his picture in a magazine or in
a newspaper, you know, once he went to Hollywood with her.
And I remember thinking that he led a charmed life – no matter
what Sammy did, he always came out of it smelling of roses. But
I don't think that now. Now I think he was charmed but he was
also damned. Charmed and damned in equal measure.

1963–1974

Samuel Harold Andrew Knight was born in a cottage hospital on the outskirts of a dull market town in Surrey, England. His parents had been married for six months to the day; it was 1963 so no one much cared about the brevity of their marital relationship. Sammy must have been cramped in his sanguine waiting room because when he emerged, face rumpled with red, leathery welts, mouth working soundlessly, his ears were folded over, the skin scored, almost, by a fold. It was as if Sammy had no desire to hear the music of life. The midwife tutted when she saw evidence of such indifference and teased back the flaps of skin, announcing to the exhausted mother that Sammy's ear canals did exist and that they would be fine. For the seven days Sammy stayed in the hospital, his ears were taped back against his skull and at the end of his cot his mother taped a small, handwritten cardboard note: PLEASE LAY ME DOWN WITH EARS FLAT! For months, Sammy wore the tape on his ears and still his mother lay him down carefully, ensuring the soft flaps were as flat as they could be. The baby's right auricle opened like a flower and nestled against the tiny, pulsing skull. The left auricle, however, drooped a little, its rounded tip tipping over, and along its edge was a serried line of tiny bumps. These, the midwife informed Sammy's mother, were the result of his ear being dragged against the wall of the birth canal. When he was older, Sammy would sometimes run his little finger along these bumps; they reassured him.

Sammy had no memories of the small, rented maisonette

where he spent his first two years. Had no memory of his tall, long-haired mother pushing him in a pram from shop to shop, buying each day what the small family needed. Had no memory of the sounds of his parents' love-making, although he slept in a cot in the same room. No memory of being taken to parties and left on a bed in a room with the door ajar should he begin to cry. He slept through his parents' discussions of what they should do with their lives, lying on his front in his cot, snoring quietly, aden-oidally, as they searched through classifieds and adverts in newspapers, drinking endless cups of tea and eating Marmite sandwiches. The farewell party his parents threw – when the maisonette filled with people they barely knew and the neigh-bours complained, first to his drunk father and then to the police – had no resonances for Sammy. Even the month-long canter across Europe, in a battered VW Camper van, driven with bravado and uncertainty in turn by both his mother and his father, was lost to him. But sometimes he thought he could remember something of the ferry journey from Greece to Cyprus. Sometimes, when he lay in his hammock, years later, one hand on his heart, the other flung above his head, he thought he remembered travelling across the Aegean, thought he ran across the deck of a ferry in the sun as his father chased him, pretend-ing to be a tiger as he, Sammy, squealed, tripped and fell, and the tiger caught him. But he couldn't be sure; couldn't be sure if he remembered this, the feeling of falling and the exquisite fear of being caught and snatched up, or if he simply remembered the sound of his father telling him it was so.

Donald Knight, Sammy's father, was an engineer. He could look into empty space and imagine bridging it, taming it, even moulding it. He spent his working days worrying about pin-jointed trusses and bending moments, torsion and normal force. Donald specialized in fracture mechanics, most particularly, stress analysis. When he wasn't visiting the sites where he was employed, he sat at the dining room table and scrawled notations on paper, calculating the balance to be struck between the decrease in potential energy and the increase in surface energy resulting from the presence of a crack. Often he would take his notes and rolls of blueprint back to the Knight's house on the ever-spreading outskirts of Limassol, and Sammy would peer at the pieces of paper weighted down with lumps of rock and wonder at what he saw:

$$\sigma = \sqrt{\frac{2'E\gamma s}{\pi\alpha}}$$

$$\sigma = \sqrt{\frac{2'E\gamma s}{\pi\alpha\,(1\nu 2)}}$$

These notations confused Sammy, because he knew the letters were real letters, Greek letters, so why were they behaving like numbers? Sammy found out over time that when his father wrote in pencil, he was unsure of the outcome of his calculations; but when his father calculated in his flowing, striking hand with his Cross fountain pen, then he knew, even before he put that pen to paper, that he was in control of his materials.

'Physics,' Donald would say, sitting back from pages and pages of calculus, rubbing his eyes and then pulling Sammy to him. 'Everything is physics.'

'Everything?' asked Sammy, every time.

'Yes – even you.' And Donald would laugh, go on to explain why sweat made Sammy feel cooler, why blood from cut knees flowed down and not up, why his eyeballs were wet. 'They'll tell you it's biology, but it's not – it's physics.'

Donald's own father was Canadian and he had instilled in his son at an early age an appreciation of the value of callisthenics, and so each morning, before he left for work, Donald performed a series of odd jerks and stretching movements, leaping around in the small, scrubby garden, then slowly unwinding, unfurling like a sunflower, like a weaving cobra – bending moments indeed. Sammy often stood in the open kitchen doorway, chewing on a hunk of bread smeared with honey, and watched Donald, puzzled. No one else's father did this. Sometimes Sammy thought he caught a glitter in the air around his father, as if sparks were showering from his arcing body, like the welding machines his daddy had pointed out to him. Donald, who thought of the world in terms of physics rather than poetry, was unaware that the word callisthenics derived from the Greek for beauty and strength. Was unaware that others had moved in the same way, in the same spot, hundreds of years before.

The young Knight family lived in a modern house, one of thousands of new homes which had been built after Cypriot independence from Great Britain. It boasted electricity, running water, main drains, tiled floors and a fully-equipped bathroom, with bidet. The walls were white, the garden beige with dust and chalk. Beatrice, Sammy's mother, tried to tame this dustbowl, tried to decorate it, annotate it, almost, with colour, but few flowers grew there. Once Donald had sluiced off the sweat occasioned by his leaping and bending, he dressed and drove away down the unmetalled road to other outlying areas of Limassol, where he oversaw the development of roads and bridges which would link thousands of houses identical to his own. In the neat white house, Beatrice cajoled Sammy into his school uniform. Then she walked with him down to the main road and waited with him at a bus stop. Once the green and white bus had stopped, opened its doors and swallowed Sammy, Beatrice walked back to the little house, finding the pushing of the pram bearing Sammy's increasingly heavy sister, Diana, harder as it moved up the gradient. Donald had once calculated the difference in calorie expenditure in a normal, healthy adult on the walks to and from the road. For Donald, everything was indeed physics.

St Augustine's was a small, private English school in Limassol. It had cypress and cedar trees planted in the playground, shading a sandpit and an area marked out for hopscotch and jacks, as well as a small football pitch. The classrooms were presided over by a succession of English teachers, all of them seduced, made lazy, by the climate, by the food, by the unexpected experience of living on an island that was neither European nor Persian but, rather, a fusion of both. These couples and adventurous bachelors were among the first of the English diaspora who travelled with the intention not to colonize but, rather, to assimilate. Sammy fell in love time and again with the succession of young, tanned women who appeared at the school to teach for a term, for a year, before moving on in an attempt, as they confided to Beatrice, 'to find themselves'.

Sammy's friends at St Augustine's were the sons and daughters of the ex-patriate community in Cyprus – an increasingly endangered species. The girls and boys he played with were the children of businessmen and the upper echelons of the military; or the sons and daughters of consulate and embassy staff, named Janet and John, Peter and Edward and Wendy. These names echoed in the playground before school began, rolled out over the walls, across the town and out over orchards of citrus fruit and olive groves. Colonial names, short and stout and safe. Each morning Sammy, and, later, his sister Diana, sang the National Anthem, asking God to save their Queen, who was, as Donald often pointed out, a German married to a Greek. There were a few Chinese, a few Turks, some French and German children, but everyone spoke English. Sammy's lessons involved, first, cats sitting on mats. Sleek, fat cats, well-fed and well-bred, cats which had nothing to do with the animals he saw scavenging in garbage, thin bodies like graters slinking through bars. Later, he drew and counted clowns and stripy balls, read stories about Noddy and his friends, learned about the seasons and how acorns grew. Sammy's history book had pictures of men in tights and puffy waistcoats, or tall black hats and long frock coats. A man called Henry had, apparently, had six wives. Sammy and his friends tittered about the Virgin Queen and swapped sherbert lemons, fruit salads and black jacks at playtime. And all the while, beyond St Augustine's walls, grapes were grown and fermented on the foothills of Olympia, as carts pulled by donkeys creaked along glittering, chalk roads and Makarios plotted his return. The children of St Augustine's were unaware that there was a deep faultline of tension stretched across the island of Arcadia; they could recite the alphabet and illustrate it with apples, balls and cats, but they did not know that it was the Phoenicians who had realized the idea of making signs for sounds and that those signs could denote more than sounds. Sammy Knight could have been plucked from the shade of the cedar which shadowed the main school house and set down in a classroom in England and he would not have been out of place.

Sometimes Sammy invited his friends to the house after school and there they would play Cowboys and Indians in the yard, or Grandmother's Footsteps followed by Tag, watched sullenly from the doorstep by the roly-poly Diana. When they were done, Beatrice fed them corned beef and tomato sandwiches and poured them glasses of Ribena, which the Chinese children sipped shyly as the English boys shouted and tussled, spilling the ruby drink on the ground, which sucked it up without trace.

The reason the young, nubile women who passed through the school, stopping to teach desultorily for a term or two, felt able to confide in Beatrice Knight, was because they considered her to be hip. The Knights led respectable, productive lives from Monday mornings to early Friday afternoons, but then, at three o'clock, a transformation took place. Donald returned to the small, modern house and stripped off his suit and tie, dressed in baggy Chinos and an open-necked shirt, rolling up his sleeves. He often left his brown feet bare, proud of their length and elegance. He thought of them as Jesus feet, feet that might have walked the shores of Galilee. As Donald changed, Beatrice would pack away the messily annotated theses and articles she translated for students and lecturers at the university, and then the family would pile into the rusty Fiat 600 for which they had swapped the Camper van, and drive west out of Limassol, past miles of white and grey pebbled beaches, until they reached the isolated fisherman's cottage they rented for six pounds sterling a month.

The cottage was a two-storey, whitewashed building with stable doors in front and back and faded blue shutters covering tiny windows, set in thick walls. Blood red geraniums and wild poppies scattered themselves prettily around the cottage, and within the walled, rocky garden a few stunted olive trees grew. Upstairs there were two small bedrooms in the eaves, with sloping ceilings, and downstairs was a single room with a large chimney breast and open grate, an old oak table with six chairs, a tall dresser and a sink. The well pump was out the back, as was the privy. The cottage stood on a low cliff, looking out over the Mediterranean, raised above the sea so the winter storms and high neap tides left it untouched. From the small kitchen window, Beatrice could watch high cirrus cloud snag on the peaks of the Troödos mountains whilst keeping an eye on Sammy as he played.

The Knights always broke their journey to the cottage at the nearest village, where they bought bottles of rough, oily retsina plugged with hand-shaved corks, bags of figs, lemons and potatoes, small boxes of grapes, a few of the long, flat local loaves of bread. Donald favoured a particular shop which sat beside the small harbour, and he would leave Beatrice to buy the staples and take Sammy with him to watch as he made signs to the old woman who sat behind barrels in the dark doorway. The woman's hands were stubby and gnarled but looked strong enough to snap a neck. Sammy remembered those hands all his life; could remember the sight of the woman's arms dipping into a barrel and hauling out blocks of wet feta cheese, white and pocked, dripping with brine, the scent mingling with the smell of the harbour. As if the cheese had been birthed by a sea cow. Then the hands dipped into another barrel and drew out wooden ladles heaped with olives, some green as seaweed, some the texture of brown velvet, like donkeys' eyes. There was something so ugly yet so beautiful about the old woman's hands, that Sammy often looked away, overwhelmed, and reached for his father's hand, squeezed it tightly. Always the old woman reached out with her horny, oiled hand to touch his talc-fine, downy cheeks and Sammy would recoil, shuffle behind the defensive wall of his father's legs. The shopkeeper would smile then, her shattered, brown teeth glistening in the bronze evening light, and she would offer Sammy an olive, but each time he shook his head and looked away. Once his father had given the shopkeeper a handful of drachma, he'd load Sammy's arms with the bags and the two of them walked over to the harbour, to look at the day's catch as the scent of rosemary and garlic leaked from the olives, sometimes sluggishly staining Sammy's T-shirt with oil. Donald strolled along the harbour wall, peering at bloodstained boards covered with sardines and buckets filled with shellfish, as Sammy walked behind, staring at glassy eyes and finny sequins. Again, Sammy would stand squinting in sunlight as Donald sketched a notion in the air with his hands. When they were done and Donald's fish had been gutted and cleaned, Sammy would turn and there, across the harbour square, standing by the Fiat in the shade of a stunted pine, was Beatrice, smiling and waving, her blouse impossibly white against her tanned skin. (That was how he thought of his mother when he pictured Beatrice – standing in shadows, lighting them, diffusing them, her hand raised, frozen, in salutation, smiling in such a way he knew that smile was for him alone. Lying in his hammock in the shade of a jacaranda tree, thousands of miles from that Cypriot fishing village and tens of thousands of days away from those late Friday afternoons, he could still conjure Beatrice's distant smile.)

The family piled back into the tiny car, the children balancing boxes and trays on their knees in the minuscule back seat, Beatrice hunched in the passenger seat, oozing bags at her feet, and Donald would drive the remaining ten miles or so, singing 'Sweet Molly Malone' at the top of his voice.

In summer, Donald and Beatrice would unpack the car as Sammy ran around the garden, reacquainting himself with the rope swing and the tree house Donald had built. Diana sat in the darkened kitchen, pulling at the hem of her blouse, sulking as she watched the images she saw through her one-way mirror. Donald would set a fire in the barbecue pit he had designed, snug against the stone wall, as Beatrice swept the windblown sand from the floors and made up the beds, and the four of them would eat late, sitting around an oil- and wine-stained table beneath a pergola, watching the stars light one after another. The children became adept at flipping open sardines and stripping the bones out, fine and toothy as a zip; they could prise apart oyster shells, snap open mussels and tiny clams. Once they had eaten their bowls of honey and yoghurt, or slices of grainy halva, Beatrice took them to bed, and brother and sister fell asleep in moments, their beds separated by mere inches, lulled by the sound of sea water dragging through pebbles, rolling them back and forth across the beach below the bedroom window. In winter, when the evenings were shorter and the people living in the mountains to the north woke to sharp frosts every morning, Beatrice served soup or her own version of cassoulet – good peasant food, thickened with rice, potatoes or beans – and the Knights ate their Friday meal in the kitchen, a fire burning in the grate.

No matter what the season, the weekend started in earnest on Saturday mornings, when the first of the visitors arrived – perhaps on foot, walking down the track having been dropped at the coast road; or perhaps a group arrived by car, van or truck, spilling out with backpacks and sleeping rolls. The military men sometimes commandeered an army jeep to travel in, and Sammy loved it when this happened because he knew that he would be taken out on a ride across dry river beds and along cliff edges, places no other vehicles could reach. Some visitors even arrived by boat, hauling the vessels up on the shingle and then climbing the cliff face up to the cottage. No invitations were sent, no formal notification went out, but somehow the news spread like bush talk about the weekends at the Knights' cottage. It was as if only listeners who were the right type could hear this bush talk, the hippies, the beatniks, the drifting teachers, the disaffected military. These last were tolerated because they brought with them the cheap, duty-free spoils from the NAAFI – cartons of No. 6, Embassy and Rothmans; bottles of gin, whisky, rum and brandy. Other visitors brought with them food and wine, marijuana and, occasionally, LSD. Some of the soldiers, who had families, who had sons, brought with them footballs and bats. Donald and Beatrice sat in their sun-blasted garden like Roman senators, like Greek Gods, and accepted these offerings, always graciously to be sure, but there was an air of inevitability about this ceremony. The Knights – all except Diana, who would be in her dark, pokey bedroom, reading, trying to ignore the shouts and cries floating on the scorched air – waited in the sun every Saturday morning, anticipating largesse.

As the day wore on, tents were erected in the garden, or people simply rolled out thin mats and sleeping bags under a cloudless sky. The barbecue pit smoked all weekend and there was always someone in the kitchen, scrubbing potatoes or slicing tomatoes and chunks of feta, cutting bread, skewering lamb and washing grapes. Joints were rolled and corks popped before lunchtime, and the garden would be dotted with groups of men and women lying in the Mediterranean sun, lazing on their backs, made garrulous or mute by one drug or another. The livelier amongst them, those who drank beer and wine, clambered down to the beach and began scratch games of football, cheering Sammy's every move, every kick. By mid-afternoon some would be sleeping, whilst others had disappeared to find some privacy, a shady spot where they could make love surrounded by the scented mist of crushed lemons. Eventually, as the sun began to fall, someone would inevitably bring out a guitar and ragged choruses broke out, formless, almost tuneless. Couples clambered down to the beach, to strip and swim naked, or simply to float in the saline water, pale buttocks and ivory breasts looking vulnerable in the moonlight.

And over all this presided Donald Knight, with his elegant, bare feet and tanned, equine face. He sat at the table, in the shade of the makeshift pergola covered with grapevines' curling lime green tendrils, a cigarette smoking between his fingers, long, thin legs crossed, and he watched. The visitors looked up to him, literally, from their vantage point as they lolled on blankets and sheets of tarpaulin, and listened to every word he said. Sammy, who might be playing with one of the drifters' children, or sitting in the tree house, legs swinging, or lying in a stranger's lap, watched his father talking, and sometimes he thought he caught a glint of the glitter that shimmered around his father as he moved his hands to illustrate a point. Sometimes he wondered if other people saw it.

The women, with their long, braided hair, bronzed skin and broken nails, were all of them in love with Donald. Each thought, although she never shared this thought, that he looked as if he had travelled the road with Kerouac, thought that Donald knew all that it was important to know. Donald talked about the stars in terms of light rays, about the heat retention of the earth that the women could feel in their thighs and buttocks, about the motion of the ocean. 'Physics,' he would say, 'everything is physics.' And the women believed him. The men were all a little in love with and a little in awe of Beatrice. Even the army officers, always slightly awkward in their movements, unconvincing in their cheesecloth and tie-dyed shirts, fell for Sammy's mother. Beatrice was then, in the late sixties, in her prime. She was earth mother and amateur archaeologist, she spoke Greek, she fished, she sang. She cooked, she danced and she mixed the meanest cocktails. Donald, sitting at the head of the table, looked out over his disciples and noticed the way the men followed his wife's every movement, the way their lips parted slightly when Beatrice knelt to stoke the embers or turn a rack of fish. And then he would reach out for her, reach out and curl his arm around her hips, pulling her close, and smile at his seated acolytes.

When he was older, Sammy recalled these weekends with startling clarity, trapped in his study at Redpath College, a master patrolling the corridor outside, he closed his eyes and imagined those lost summer evenings – the splashy hiss of fish oil falling on glowing embers, the sweet scent of marijuana, the vivid green and velvet mauve of a woman's dirndl skirt, the exquisite faint scratch of an unknown woman's hand stroking his dark hair as he fell asleep in her lap. But more than any of these was the memory of his mother mixing the cocktails. As the sun began to slip away behind the headland, Beatrice would set up her bar on the table, reading the labels of the bottles brought by the soldiers, smiling occasionally as she came across an exotic liqueur presented to her by a traveller: Pölstar cucumber vodka, Sisca crème de cassis, Alvada Marsala, or perhaps Giffard Orgeat Sirop de Gomme. Beatrice built, she muddled, she shook and churned, she tried to blend as best as she was able without electricity. The ice was supplied in blocks by a fisherman in the nearest town, and Beatrice shaved and picked at it, creating a shower of glitter of her own. When she was done, his mother called for Sammy, who would break off from a card game, or an arm wrestling match and trot over as silence fell. Donald would solemnly place the official taster's hat – a jester's hat with bells at each of its points, which had been left behind by a traveller – on Sammy's head. Beatrice handed Sammy the official taster's cup – a thick, scratched glass tumbler, marked with a dollop of red paint to show that no one but Sammy might sup from it – with a tiny puddle of liquid in the bottom. Sammy, aware of all eyes on him, would sniff and hold the glass up to the firelight, before drinking the cocktail. Sometimes he near-choked, sometimes he swallowed and smiled; always he turned his thumb up, because he wanted the crowd to laugh, because he needed to be loved, because his mother had concocted the drink and he needed her to be loved too. The pitchers were then emptied into the mélange of mismatched vessels and Sammy could tell by the expressions of the visitors whether his mother's alcoholic alchemy had worked; whether she had wrought gold from liquid.

Sammy, sitting in the oppressive silence of his Redpath study, could remember how, every Saturday night without fail, as the moon rose and the heat fell, his mother would lament the fact that she had never tasted Havana Club rum – not the Silver Dry nor the Añejo Reserva, none of them. Beatrice had been an admirer of the Latin American concept of *demos* ever since she had first seen a picture of Guevara's chiselled features. It was, she would say, her ambition to find a bottle of Havana Club Tres Años and make a genuine daiquiri; as it was she had to make do with Navy dark rum and the drink was muddy and overly sweet.

When she had finished experimenting with mixtures, conferring on each an outlandish name, Beatrice settled herself with one group or another, lit a joint and Sammy would go to her, to snuggle against her long, soft body and fall asleep as she rubbed his feet or arms, or stroked the tiny bumps on his ear, whichever part of him was nearest. And his sister watched all this from the vantage point of the bedroom window.

On Sunday mornings the party woke slowly, over hours, the soldiers departing first, needing to be back at base. The sound of the jeep engine woke some of the campers but most turned over in their flimsy tents, or burrowed deeper into sleeping bags, trying to block out the morning sun, and fell asleep again. Sammy always woke in his own bed, listening to the sea making waves, and he never knew how he got there, never knew who had carried him up the stairs. When he appeared in the kitchen it was to find Beatrice already up, washing plates and cups in the sink, and she would ask him to fetch water from the pump. As mother and son laboured, the party stretched, yawned and scratched itself, wondering what to do with the day. Some of the men went swimming, some fished along the surf line, others went walking along the coast, all of them leaving the women to clear up the debris of the night before. Breakfast and lunch were cheese, honey, bread, olives and retsina. The visitors were always subdued, until their hangovers melted in the sun as the amber wine settled in them. Gradually they drifted away, leaving nothing but scuffed earth and singed roaches. Once they were alone, Donald and Beatrice would send Sammy and Diana off on a mission – to find seaweed, to collect firewood, to do anything at all that would allow husband and wife time alone in their tiny bedroom. Sammy and his sister always argued as they walked away and – unknown to Donald and Beatrice – spent their time separately, Diana sitting on the cliff head, pulling at grassy clumps as Sammy skittered down the cliff face and searched the beach alone. They returned to find their parents sitting at the table, fingers touching, talking in a murmur. Sunday night was quiet, the four of them playing cards after they had eaten and the children went to bed early, as they had to leave before dawn to drive back to their boxy house outside Limassol and resume their other, very controlled, very English lives.

*

During the school holidays, Beatrice usually took the children to the cottage and Donald would join them when he could. The weekend parties were different then, as the drifting teachers moved on and away and the soldiers went home on leave. During the week Sammy spent his time swimming and playing, building lizard traps and inventing other worlds in his mind. He had a few toys – Dinky models of Morris Minors and Bedford Vans, an old wooden tennis racket and four flat, fluffy balls, a home-made cricket bat and stumps. Sammy's holiday friend was a local boy called Adonis, who lived on a smallholding just a mile away from the cottage. Beatrice had laughed when she was told Adonis' name for he was a short, ugly boy, with a squat, stocky body and full, wet lips. When he was ten, Sammy was allowed to walk alone to Adonis' house, as long as he stuck to the road and didn't venture farther afield. Sammy enjoyed the long dawdles he made when he went to fetch his friend, along a stony, hard road, olive and citrus orchards spreading north to the mountains, their peaks a hazy blue-green. Sammy walked always with a stick so he could swipe at stones, imagining the sound of leather on willow as he hit a six at the Oval. Occasionally a truck would pass, heading for the main road to Limassol, coating his shorts and T-shirt with fine, white dust. He had a hat which his mother insisted he take but he snatched it off the moment he was out of sight of the cottage. Sammy's skin was brown, the rich shades of oiled teak; he looked as if he belonged in Arcadia, with his dark hair and loose limbs. Only his grey-green eyes gave him away, spoke of a gene pool which spread further than the Adriatic.

Sammy liked going to Adonis' house because there were sheep and goats, and the family owned a dog, a shaggy cur with a cast in one eye. Sammy and Adonis teased the dog and chased the sheep, which ran helter-skelter with no definite plan for escape, tails twitching, ears drooping. The boys pelted each other with the rotten windfall from the orchard and played hide and seek in the outhouses, hiding themselves in dark shadows behind rusting ploughs and burying themselves in straw bought in for the horses. Sometimes Adonis walked over to the Knights' cottage where he would insist on playing cricket or marking out a race track in the dust on which they raced the Dinky cars. Adonis was jealous of Sammy, of his height, his leanness, his toys and the fact he had another life he lived when he was not with Adonis. He had seen a photograph of Sammy in his school uniform, white shirt startling against a scarlet blazer and red and blue tie. Adonis attended a local village school, dressed in clean, but worn shorts and a fraying, collarless shirt.

Perhaps it was this jealousy which, one hot, airless afternoon in August, prompted Adonis to persuade Sammy to leave the safety of the road and venture north, into the countryside which was criss-crossed by tracks and dry river beds. Sammy, heart pounding, followed Adonis through the brush, ignoring the scratches of the thorny ground cover, slapping at the insects which crawled on his skin, drawn by the lactose-loaded smell of his sweat. Adonis, shading his dark, squinting eyes against the sun announced they would play hide and seek in that desolate, awful place and that Sammy had thirty seconds to conceal himself. Sammy, driven by the desire not to lose face, recognizing (although he could not have put a name to it) the punchy challenge in Adonis' posture, in his voice – the challenge of a boy who had been born on that land, who belonged to it – began to run as Adonis closed his eyes and counted out loud. Sammy ran across uneven, stony ground, bending low to avoid branches of trees, tripping on ruts left by cart tracks, trying not to think of the scorpions and snakes his mother had warned him about. Panting, knees cut by a fall, he found a deep, dry river bed, carved over years by the flashing winter rains that cascaded from Olympian peaks, with loose gravel and stones lining it. Sammy spotted the shadow thrown by the crown of a toppled, gnarled olive tree and crawled beneath it. He crouched in the shade, licking at his fingers and wiping the blood from his knee, careful not to make a sound. His ankles began to ache and sweat tickled his curved spine. If he closed his eyes, burgundy circles bloomed beneath the lids, flowering outwards until they were replaced by other circles.

Sammy's eyes slammed open when he heard the sound, odd clanking-iron music, accompanied by hollow scuffles. His eyes hurt as his pupils contracted and he recognized the rustic rhythm – a donkey-drawn cart, a sound he had heard many times, all around the cottage. Sammy smiled as he calculated how long Adonis had been searching for him – soon he could stand up and yell, having won the game. But then came the sounds which cut his world in two: a crack like a rifle, like the air being rent, a dull, chalky thud, a minor, discordant scream and the crunching of wood. The scream, he later realized, had been the donkey braying madly as its back was broken. Sammy's breath came suddenly quick and shallow, and then he jumped, banged his head on the trunk of the dead tree, as a woman screamed. The quality of this scream was different from the first; it was a yowl of desolation, a sound followed by unearthly grunts, like a cougar retching. Sammy felt cold. He edged his way up the bank of the river bed, careful not to make yet another noise to add to the cacophony, and he peered over the bed's lip. At his eye level, only feet away, was an overturned cart, its axle jagged-snapped, one wheel lying askew, the other flat on the road. A woman, dressed in a long, faded red skirt, olive shirt and head scarf, was grunting gutterally as she tried to heave the cart, pushing at it, trying to flip a dead weight of weathered oak. The donkey began to bray once more, its front legs twitching frantically as blood oozed from its slack, wet-gummed mouth, thick yellow teeth being stained red. But what Sammy was looking at, what he couldn't look away from, was the little boy who was staring straight back at him, the soft white skin of his cheek pressed against the razor-edged gravel. Sammy knew of this boy, had seen him once as his father drove to the cottage. He was an albino, covered with flour-white skin, eyelids red-rimmed and wet from squinting in the sun, his hair translucent as rain-free clouds. He always wore trousers and long-sleeved shirts to cover his colourless, tiny frame, and a wide-brimmed straw hat, which Sammy could see was lying near the broken axle, lifting now and then in the light breeze. But Sammy knew it didn't matter that the little albino boy had lost his hat; Sammy knew the little white boy would never need it again because he was dead. His breath still shallow, beginning to burn red and dusty in his chest, Sammy slipped cautiously back down the river bank and crept away from the shelter of the tree. He crabbed along awkwardly in a crouch, his knees aching, still bleeding, until he was far enough away from the sound of grief to stand up and pump his arms and legs as hard as he could. Sammy flew through the dust and brush and snakes and scorpions until he reached the road, which was bland and safe and familiar. He wanted to slow down, to walk, a stitch was puckering at his side, but he found he couldn't stop running, he tried but he couldn't stop, and he half-limped, half-trotted all the way back to the cottage and when he got there his mother asked him what was wrong and it was only then that he realized he was crying, that there were dirty dust-tracks on his face, and he lied and said he'd fallen and hurt himself, pointed to his knees and he saw the puzzled look that crossed his mother's face because Sammy didn't cry over cuts and scrapes and he tried to stop crying then, began to hiccup, said he felt bad and Beatrice took him to his bedroom and stayed with him, stroking his hair, pushing it away from his forehead, scratching the skin there lightly with her long nails until the hiccups grew faint, mere stirrings of his belly, and Sammy closed his eyes, feigned sleep so he wouldn't have to talk to his mother, who slipped off the bed and closed the thin curtains, tip-toed out of the room, leaving him to try to forget how the little boy's dead eyes had looked.

They had looked heavenly blue, a blue like the sky, a blue like the thin shell of a broken bird's egg, blue and empty. And the little boy's white hair had moved with the light breeze, as if it were still alive, as if it wanted the comfort of the straw hat. For the rest of that day and all the night that followed, Sammy lay in his bed, telling himself that there was nothing he could have done, that he could not have lifted the cart, that he could not have saved the boy. The boy was dead. He could not have changed things because the boy was dead. Besides, he should not have been there. His mother had been right; he should not have left the road, he should not have gone where he should not be.

*

The Christmas after the accident – about which Sammy never told anyone until years later – Beatrice took the children back to England to see their grandparents, and Sammy was grateful for this, grateful to break away from the memory of dust, scorpions and open, empty eyes. Beatrice's parents lived in a large, unimaginative redbrick house in a respectable area of a Surrey town. They were an unimaginative, self-satisfied couple who had never understood their only child; never understood why she had not stayed in England and settled down nearby to have a family. Instead, she had fallen pregnant – the shame! – and then married Donald, who was obviously a very bright boy but very, well . . . unreliable. Donald had always made them feel a little uncomfortable, with his languid body movements and upper-class drawl. He drank and smoked, listened to popular music and wore his hair unnecessarily long. Beatrice's parents always made sure they stressed the fact that their son-in-law was an engineer when asked how their daughter was doing; an engineer involved in important work which had taken Beatrice abroad.

Beatrice, for her part, found these visits to her parents' home near-insufferable. She had grown up in the smug, bumptious town, with its neat lawns, clipped rose bushes, cars washed every Sunday morning, nannies who pushed prams, women who dressed to shop, who dressed to clean their teeth, who probably dressed to have sex. Beatrice spent most of her time sitting in a wing chair in the lounge, her legs pulled up beneath her, a book in her lap, getting up only to heap more coals on the fire. By her side was a small pie-crust table on which was a glass, a bottle of Harvey's Bristol Cream Sherry, a pack of Bensons and an ashtray. Occasionally she emptied the ashtray and wiped the glossy veneer of the table with her palm, leaving grey smears like clouds, smears like the forgotten past, which her mother dutifully polished away each morning.

Sammy and Diana, who were unaware of the tensions, who did not notice the pursing of lips, the almost imperceptible shaking of greying heads, had a wonderful time, their arguments forgotten. They found the biting winds and swirling flurries of snow exciting, relished walking sleek pavements, looking behind to check the footprints they left in the thin white cover. Diana, smitten by the glitter of Christmas trees, would stop and point with pointless, mittened fingers, as Sammy tried unsuccessfully to gather slush into snowballs. They pressed themselves against shop windows, noses cold and bloodless on the glass, stunned by the choice of toys on offer – Airfix models, Scalextric, Sindy Doll and Action Man, Spacehoppers, Pogo sticks, portable record players, Spirograph, Meccano, Lego, compendia of board games, chemistry sets and paint sets and and and. Such an abundance of *things* – Sammy would stand in the musty corner shop at the end of his grandparents' road, turning a shilling coin in his fingers as Grandpa bought his papers, scanning sweeties, calculating how many flying saucers, gobstoppers, liquorice wheels and Lucky Dabs he could buy, a choice made more difficult by the shelf of jars behind the till, jars full of wine gums, cough candy, pear drops and sherbet lemons, dolly mixture, jelly beans. Or perhaps he should buy a single tube of Smarties, Spangles, Refreshers or Toffos? Choice was an agony for Sammy, made him want to pee.

Not only did the children encounter choice in all its guises, they also encountered a new medium; each day they watched the clock, willing the hands to turn, to reach the moment when the television was switched on. *Doctor Who*, *Daktari*, *Skippy* and *Blue Peter* – they watched them all open-mouthed, sitting on cushions in front of the screen, Diana squealing when the Daleks appeared, clapping when Skippy bounded across the bush. Sammy watched intently because he liked to slip away into the monochrome world where all eyes were grey. And behind them, in the wing chair, sat Beatrice, sozzled on sweet sherry, dreaming of finding Havana Club Tres Años.

The only time Sammy was aware of the tension in the air, quivering like a taut wire waiting to trip the conversationally unwary, was when he overheard his mother and Grandma talking in the kitchen, behind a closed door. There was something about the quality of their voices, which sounded sleek as metal, hard and shiny, that made him want to move away.

'Beatrice, I have already said that your father and I are willing to pay the fees.'

'For the last time, Mother, my kids are *not* going to public school in England. They're quite happy where they are. They get a good education and they're happy.'

'I grant you that the primary school there may be quite adequate, but we think that Sammy should have a good secondary education—'

'He will have one – in Limassol.'

'We understand that you don't want to leave your husband on his own, and that's why we're prepared to pay the boarding fees. There's Redpath College just up the road. Sammy could be near us and you could come home to visit him during the holidays, or, I suppose, he could go out to that island.'

'Cyprus. It has a name. It's called Cyprus. And *that's* my home, not this place.'

'Well, whatever. Although why you live in such a place, I don't know. No doubt it's filthy and the water will be undrinkable.'

'Why don't you visit us and find out what it's like?'

Beatrice's mother rolled her shoulders in a way that Sammy couldn't see but could imagine. 'Your father wouldn't like that.'

'How do you know? Have you asked him?'

'I don't need to. Beatrice, Sammy had a bad start in life, we simply want to make up for that.'

'A bad start in life? What are you talking about?'

'You know perfectly well.'

'Oh God – we're not back to that, are we? Mother, I don't think Sammy knew his parents weren't married when he was conceived. He was a foetus so I doubt it bothered him much.'

'You're drunk again, as usual. I don't know what's happened to you. When you left school you were such a nice girl. We were so proud of you.'

'And now you're not? Even though I'm happily married, with a job and a home, a good degree and two lovely kids . . . that's not enough?'

'The children look like urchins.'

'No, Mother, they look healthy and fit, not like the pasty kids here. They live in the sun, they swim, they play sport, they go sailing and walking. They eat good food and sleep like babies. They are *not* coming back here. And neither am I.'

Sammy bolted up the stairs as he heard the door handle turn, scooting into his bed, where he lay itching in nylon sheets as he wondered what an urchin was.

By the time Beatrice, Sammy and Diana left, three days later, the cracks had been plastered over with food and false bonhomie. There was no more mention of boarding school, no mention of lost pride and urchins. Instead, as the taxi's diesel engine rumbled, dry kisses and tense, awkward hugs were exchanged. Sammy knelt on the back seat and waved until the taxi turned a corner and then he sat and thought about the bag of presents he was taking back – Action Man, a yo-yo, Etch-a-sketch and Twister. It wasn't until he was skating across the rink of almost-sleep, his head on his mother's shoulder, that he realized, dozily, in a fragmented way, that he hadn't thought of broken-bird's-egg-eyes for weeks. Sammy had built his first fence and outside it lay a tiny, broken, albino-white body.

When Donald and the headmaster appeared in the doorway of the classroom, Sammy was doodling in the margins of his rough book, trying to draw a perfect circle but the ends never met, no matter how careful he was. Each time he had to bend the line, ruin the curve. The air in the room was being boiled by July sun; the heat seemed elastic, seemed to relax and stretch synapses, making thought baggy and impossible. Sammy drew his circles and ached to be gone, knowing his days at St Augustine's were dwindling to nothing, that he was merely marking time, which itself seemed elastic in the heat. The summer holidays filled his mind, pushed out all other thoughts. The Knights were going sailing for a week with a colleague of Donald's who owned a yacht. Sammy had seen the yacht, with its arcing, billowing sails and varnished deck and he wanted to be on board, sailing away. It was when the young, blonde teacher, Miss McConney, fell silent as the headmaster muttered something to her, that Sammy looked up and saw his father, dressed in a crumpled suit, his tie undone. Sammy began to sketch a wave in the air but stopped. He never knew when he knew. Could never recall the moment when he knew. Was it then? As his fingers closed on his fist? Or was it when he noticed that there was no glitter cascading around his father? Or was it when the teacher sat very slowly at her desk, sat and laced her fingers, chewed her lip. Sammy watched the headmaster walk towards him and he found the man's manner menacing, not because the head looked surly as he normally did, rather, because he looked as if his face had changed. The headmaster touched Sammy's arm.

'We need to have a word with you, Samuel.'

And Sammy swallowed, stood up and followed the man, avoiding the stares of his friends, keeping his eyes on a crease in the head's dark jacket. When they reached the door, the head nodded to the teacher. 'Apologies for the interruption. Please carry on, Miss McConney,' he said but Sammy noticed that she didn't move, didn't seem to hear.

Once they were standing in the corridor, Donald stood still, touched his lips with his fingertips. Sammy thought his father had forgotten he was there.

'Would you like to go to my office?' asked the headmaster.

Donald said nothing, so the head gently guided him down the corridor to a heavy, oak door and opened it, waved father and son in and closed the door behind them. Was it *then* that Sammy knew? He looked at his father and he waited. After a long time, a time that smelled of dust motes and leather, a time tasting of copper and heat, Donald spoke.

That morning Donald had taken a lift into work because he was going to visit a site near Vasilikos and the yacht-owning friend had suggested that they travel together. Beatrice, who had been reading about the new discoveries of mosaics at the House of Dionysus in Paphos, decided to take the Fiat and see for herself what had been unearthed. She knew a few of the professors and team leaders, had translated papers for them, and they would allow her beyond the barriers, would take her around the site. After seeing Sammy and Diana onto the bus, Beatrice had packed a lunch and taken a few water bottles – a couple for herself, and one for the Fiat, which had a tendency to overheat on long journeys. Beatrice travelled alone along the coast road, so no one could say what exactly happened; no one could describe the minutiae of the accident, could not say whether the Fiat had blown a tyre, or a cat had flung itself into the road, or a bird had swooped low and struck the windscreen. The fact was – the *fact*, which Donald held onto, dealing as he did with facts – was that the tiny car had swerved violently, crossed the road and crashed into a heavy truck carrying rubble across the island to act as hardcore for the road-building Donald was overseeing. A lot of physics had taken place in those moments, involving velocity, mass and gradient. There had also been kinetic and potential energies to consider, as well as the tensile strength of the materials involved. There had been a *vast* amount of physics taking place but even Donald had to admit that there had been a lot of biology involved too.

Donald Knight, fracture mechanics engineer, fell apart over the next few days. He knew that there must exist an energy balance between strain energy released as a crack extends but he was unable to achieve that balance. A Charpy or Izod test conducted on Donald at that time would have discovered that his shear stress had reached a critical point and could not be resolved. Miss McConney, the young teacher, came to stay in the modern house outside Limassol, with its bidet and cool tiled floor, metalled and surfaced road passing in front of it. She fussed over Sammy and Diana, trying to console them, cooking and cleaning, trying to establish order even as chaos approached. Donald sat at the table, unmoving; occasionally he slept with his head on his arms. Miss McConney didn't know what to do with him. She was twenty-two years old, how could she have known it would have been a good thing if she had held him and stroked his hair? If she had gently pulled him into the bedroom and held him through the night? Instead she dusted and baked, worrying all the time about what would happen to the children. As Miss McConney worried and Donald dimmed, the travellers, drifters and visitors arrived at the fisherman's cottage on the coast to find it locked, the garden empty, the barbecue pit brushed clean.

As it turned out, Miss McConney did not have to worry over-long about the children; on the morning of Beatrice's funeral she found that she was worrying, instead, about herself, as Turkish troops landed in the north and rolled across the island. Donald stirred himself, then, from his trance and called in favours from his army friends at the base. Within an hour he was bundling his children, dressed still in solemn greys and black, into the back of a jeep. Diana sat on the rough plank and wept quietly, overawed by the presence, the size, of the soldiers. Eleven-year-old Sammy, whose sense of danger, of the unexpected, had been honed to a fine, sharp point when he looked into a pair of sky-blue eyes, asked what was happening. Once Sammy realized his farewell to his mother was being denied him, that he was leaving his mother behind, Sammy fought with Donald, with the soldiers. He lashed out with small, ink-stained fists, kicked at the khaki-clad giants with newly polished, tightly laced shoes and he would not stop. Every time Donald thought he had a grip on his son, Sammy slithered out of his grasp, once shaking off his jacket and trying to jump from the speeding jeep, only to be caught and trapped by a soldier. The jeep bounced onto the tarmac of the apron with Sammy still fighting as Diana cowered in a corner, listening to her brother panting and grunting. Donald, his heart already broken, dragged Sammy up the clanking, metal steps, hauled him by his wrist and gave him to a stranger.

Sammy and Diana flew out of Cyprus with nothing but the clothes they wore. Sammy slumped on the bench, ignoring the sting of grazed knuckles and the whimpers of his sister, and he began to build another fence, a very high, near-insurmountable fence, outside which now lay the small albino body and the bloodied remains of his mother.

GRANDMOTHER

You can't expect me to remember much, not at my age. I'm ninety-seven, you know. Surprised? Yes, I can see you are. Everybody is. Everybody congratulates me on my well-being. Oh yes, my mind is still sharp as a razor. Why, there are other women in the Home who are twenty years younger and they're practically at death's door. I'm not saying I'm in perfect health but I have always looked after myself. Never smoked and restricted myself to a few glasses of sherry at Christmas. Harvey's Bristol Cream, that was my favourite. In that lovely blue bottle. *The old woman closes her eyes and rests her head in her hand for a moment. Her teeth click as she swallows.* What did you want to know? Not that I've forgotten but I do get a little absent-minded, especially in the afternoons. It is the afternoon, isn't it? *She twists a watch strap on her sinew-wrist and the silver skin creases as she squints at the enormous black and white hands and face.* Three o'clock. I normally have my nap about three o'clock. Why have you come? Oh, yes, you want to know about Sammy. Sammy. My grandson. Sammy, my grandson. Well, I'm not sure why you're asking me. I haven't seen him for years. Must be twenty years or more. He just upped sticks and went and we never saw him again. He never visited me, never even came to his grandfather's funeral. And now he won't be coming to mine. *Falling suddenly asleep, her heads drops, her chin resting on her sternum, which seems to have risen up, puffed up as the remainder of her body has shrunk. Her arthritic, knobbled fingers quiver and flinch as she sleeps, as if conducting a tiny, private symphony. She jolts awake, touches the lapel of her blouse, straightens it, unaware that the buttons are set awry.* Of course, if she hadn't gone to that island, my daughter, Beatrice, that is, if she hadn't gone out there, everything would have been different. When she was a little girl she was lovely. Neat and tidy, never a hair out of place, always top of the class. A girl you could be proud of, a girl you could love. Not that I'm saying I didn't love her later, just that she made it so . . . difficult. Beatrice should never have married that man Donald. She should have stayed here and married, raised her children in their own country. Where they belonged. Not in that filthy place. She drank Harvey's Bristol Cream too, you know. When she came to visit, she drank Harvey's. *The memory of a hand sweeping across a table, transforming fortified sweet wine and ash into a cloud.* Funny, isn't it? To think Sammy would be older now than Beatrice was when she . . . had the accident. If she'd been here she would never have been driving in that silly car on her own. Sometimes I get a little depressed about it all. Sometimes I wonder if we were all cursed in some way, what with Beatrice being taken from us and then Dad having his cancer. Two years he took to die, poor man, in pain all the while. And now Sammy . . . but Diana is a rock to me. She visits and we pray together. She tells me it's not a curse but God's wish. There's a time when we are chosen, she says. *She sighs, as if she wishes now to be chosen, as if fearful that the time of her choosing has passed and she will spin out eternity in the grubby, beige confines of the Home.* Of course, after the accident we took the children in, Dad and I. We could have done nothing else. After all, it was the Christian thing to do.

I remember there was some trouble out on that island and they had to come back anyway. Is that right? There was some trouble and they flew back alone, Sammy and Diana. Typical of Donald to be so thoughtless, to be so selfish. To send two wee children alone on an aeroplane. As I said, I'm ninety-seven and I can't be expected to remember much but I do remember going to an army base to collect the children. I remember it like yesterday. A beautiful summer's day, the sky so clear and the hedgerows full of flowers, not all thin and bare like they are now, just full of flowers. And Beatrice being buried thousands of miles away, not here, not buried here. And I looked at the flowers and I didn't know whether to be happy or sad. We parked the car, the Morris Oxford, a lovely car, and walked across a big field to a Nissen hut and I could feel the sun on my arms and I still didn't know whether to feel happy or sad. And then a young soldier opened the door of the hut and beckoned to someone behind him and Diana and Sammy came out into the bright light. It was so clear and bright. We walked towards them, towards the children, and as I drew close I could see Sammy's face and I knew that nothing would be right again. *Her nails scratch at the faux leather of the wheelchair as she recalls the moment of realizing nothing would be right again.* A while before the accident I had suggested to Beatrice that Dad and I pay for Sammy to go to Redpath College. A very nice school, not far from us. Perhaps not in the same league as Harrow and the like, but a *nice* public school, with a sound reputation. But Beatrice was, frankly, rude to me. Snubbed me, almost. Laughed at the idea. Where was I? Sammy. He had changed. I remember that much. We sent him to Redpath and he caused us nothing but trouble. Trouble was all he was good for. Defiant little bastard! *A scraggy fist thumps the arm of the chair, as spittle flies.* Little bastard! There, I've always wanted to say it and now I have. Ungrateful little bastard. He killed Dad, I know that. Killed him with worry. Sammy was always running away, being brought back by the police and us having to apologize and say sorry and it will never happen again, knowing all the time it would. *On the old woman's mottled-tissue cheeks have appeared two scarlet spots; her breathing is laboured and she reaches tremulously for the pale green oxygen mask.* And the neighbours watching all the time. It was the worry that killed Dad. That and Sammy's mess and his music and his hidden packets of cigarettes. Coming in stinking of smoke and never a word. Never a thank you for the sacrifices we had made. I know it was difficult, losing his mother like that, but so did Diana and she was a model child. She didn't go off the rails like Sammy. Of course, the worst thing was his friends. The neighbours watching as he met his friends at the gate. We'd never invite them in – why would we? In their leather jackets and filthy T-shirts. But what finished us, both me and Dad, were the wogs and the darkies. He had wogs for friends and his best friend was a Paki or something. *Her lips pucker, close like a well-worn sphincter over pearly, ill-fitting teeth.* Well, he's had his comeuppance now, hasn't he? We told him to stick to his own, mix with his own but no, he had to go off and upset us. And look where it's got him. I'm ninety-seven, you know. And I didn't get to be this age by mixing with wogs. *She takes a long, stuttering toke of pure oxygen and grins, skull-like, before settling her blanket around her and drifting into a self-righteous sleep.*

1974–1978

So, Sammy's grandmother got what she wanted in the end; the price for being granted that wish was high – too high – but she and her husband did send Sammy to board at an English public school. She no longer thought that she could make up for Sammy's bad start in life, a start which seemed to be getting worse year by year, but she could think of nothing else to do. So Sammy was despatched to Redpath College and his sister, Diana, lived with her grandparents and attended the local primary school.

Redpath College was an unremarkable, rather worn public school in Surrey, with the usual number of old boys who returned to teach and live out their lives there. At any given time there were a few dynamic young turks who thought they could drag the school into the 1970s but they soon became dispirited and left. There was a cricket pavilion, there was a refectory, there was a chapel; there was no freedom, there were no girls. The drab buildings of the college were constructed from red bricks, the grounds were tame, the gates sturdy and the marshal fearsome. The science labs had not been refurbished since the 1940s, the sloping, wooden desks in the classrooms had pendant ceramic inkwells in the corner, the gym was bare but for ropes, ladders and medicine balls. The teachers wore academic gowns and mortar boards and wrote in cursive script on worn blackboards; the pupils were expected to write their work with fountain pens, using only blue ink. The dorms smelled of sweat and young skin, dust and disinfectant. Redpath College had managed to ignore the ripples running through the fabric of society and contrived to maintain an even keel as it sailed serenely down the years. The atmosphere was one of quiet resignation, an undramatic male domain where displays of emotion were frowned upon, where the teachers kept an eye open for hanky-panky whilst ignoring the bullying, a place where creative thought was frowned upon. Redpath College managed to attract a sufficient number of able pupils to ensure its Oxbridge entrance count was acceptable; the remainder of the students went on to redbrick universities. The college could muster a quorum of sports teams and finished every year in mid-table, no matter what the sport. Redpath College was the product of the labour of men with no imagination – as such, it was unprepared for the arrival of Samuel Harold Andrew Knight.

When Sammy arrived at the college, spruce in a new uniform, he was angry and he stayed angry for the next three years. As he was shown his bed in the dorm, given his timetable, told the rules and regulations – so many fucking rules – he seethed. As he sat in chapel listening to the headmaster, Dr Simon, intone homilies about hard work and its rewards, Sammy seethed. When prefects – or praeps, as they were known – castigated him, which was often, he seethed. When teachers disciplined him, sending him out with a yellow slip, setting him detentions, imposing menial tasks during his free time on Saturday afternoons, he raged. Sammy swore in class, wore his tie loose, did no prep, talked when the teachers did. Sammy Knight was tall and tanned, lean and fit, bitter and lonely. He escaped the grounds often and was tracked down by the marshal, who would find him at the train station in the nearest town, or in a coffee shop or sitting on a bench in the park. For the marshal, an ex-Army man with a pronounced limp and handlebar moustache, the hunting down of Sammy Knight became a fine sport, a *raison d'être*. He prided himself on the fact that Sammy Knight never managed to get further than the station or the town limits; he always caught him before Sammy could spread his wings and fly. He'd pounce on the boy and drag him or drive him back to the college where he delivered him to the head-master, Dr Simon, with a smile of quiet satisfaction. Always the marshal pounced on Sammy and bore him off; he never thought to ask the boy where he was going, and he certainly never thought to ask why he was running. If he had, Sammy could not have told him. Because Sammy could not have told anyone why he escaped, could not have explained why he slipped out of the college grounds and began to search for something. All Sammy knew was that he hated being confined; the only fences he could tolerate were those he built for himself. Dr Simon, dressed always in his gown, tried to be even-handed with the boy during their inter-views, tried to be fair and non-judgmental. But the fact was, even if he had lost his mother, the boy was rude and uncommunicative, and he wore his tie loose, his top button undone – the cardinal sin. So Sammy was grounded, made to learn poetry, forced to write pages of lines, stripped of his sporting cups, and eventually rusticated. This last was nearly unbearable, as he had to spend the week in his grandparents' house, where he could see the wing chair his mother had sat in every Christmas and, next to it, the pie-crust table she had wiped with the soft palm of her hand. Sammy escaped from school because he missed his mother, because his father had replaced her (Miss McConney, the young teacher who had been told about the death of the first Mrs Knight in a hot Cypriot classroom, became the second); because his last memory of Cyprus, which was his home, which was where his mother had danced and cooked, lived and died, was of being dragged across tarmac, as engines screamed and soldiers in battle dress waved them on, shouting.

The holidays were purgatory. In the summers, Sammy and Diana returned to Cyprus, to stay with Donald and his wife in the boxy, featureless house outside Limassol. Donald, of course, had to work, so it was left to the young Mrs Knight to entertain them. She took them to the beach, where Sammy walked the sands alone, or tramped along the cliff path, as Diana sat silently and read. Mrs Knight tried to arrange children's parties, inviting pupils from St Augustine's, where she still worked in term time, but these events were a disaster. Sammy would start fights with the timid Chinese or argue with the Italian girls; he'd ruin any games she organized and refused to apologize for his behaviour. Eventually even Donald realized that Sammy was disruptive and tried to punish him but he was always left with the sense that his son didn't care. Donald also tried to talk to Sammy about his school reports, which were atrocious, but Sammy didn't care much about those either. Every summer's morning Sammy would stand in the kitchen door, as he always had, eating his breakfast and watching his father performing his callisthenics, prolonging his bending moments, and Sammy realized that his father's glitter had disappeared forever. Realized that Donald was stiff where once he had been flexible. It didn't occur to Sammy that his father found his presence disturbing.

At Christmas, Donald and his wife returned to England and the fractured, jigsaw family convened at the grandparents' house for the festive season. No one enjoyed these occasions; nothing — no amount of presents, no amount of food — could alleviate the atmosphere of edgy tedium. No amount of empty chatter masked the storm cloud of furious silence that hovered wherever Sammy was. He would slip away from the house and walk bland, empty suburban streets for hours, stealing magazines, drinks and sweets from shops to swap them for cigarettes with the louts who hung out in the park. They laughed at his accent, at his clothes, but they did give him cigarettes and matches. Sammy returned home late at night, his jumper and hair smelling of acrid smoke, to find his father pacing in the hallway, waiting for him. Twice the police were sent out to look for him but Sammy didn't care. Late at night he lay in his room and listened to pirate radio stations fading in and out on the ether, heard the new nihilistic music of the Damned, the Clash and the Stranglers. He stole copies of *NME* and *Melody Maker* and emulated the look of the time as well as he was able — torn shirts, spiky hair and chains. His grandmother began to wonder if the thousands of pounds invested in making up for Sammy's poor start in life was, in fact, money wisely spent. She even went so far as to mention this to Sammy, but he didn't care.

On the first day of term of Sammy's fourth year at Redpath College, when he was fourteen, he was summoned to Dr Simon's office and read the riot act. Sammy was, apparently, treading a knife edge — one step out of place and he would be expelled. Dr Simon spoke at some length about the need for socks to be pulled up, for shoulders to be put to the wheel and hands to man the pump, as Sammy leaned against a chair and looked about himself at the familiar room.

'This is an important year for you, Knight. You begin your O level studies and the quality of the rest of your life will depend on your results. We know from the few occasions when you have made an effort that you can work well, that you have the intellectual capacity to make something of yourself. Over the years I have become aware that you think the world owes you something. Quite what that is, I can't imagine. Just remember – there are many worse off than you. Of course, I lament the passing of your mother but that was a long time ago, Knight, and it's time you put it behind you and concentrated on the future.'

Sammy stood straight, stopped staring through the window at distant clouds, stared instead at Dr Simon. 'Don't talk about my mother,' he said, almost conversationally.

'Be quiet, Knight, I've had enough of your insolence. I don't want to see you in my office again this term. Just knuckle down and concentrate on your studies. And good luck.' Dr Simon watched the boy saunter out, leaving the door open, and he wondered about Sammy. One of the few boys he didn't seem able to get through to, as if the boy had an impenetrable wall around him. He wondered how long Sammy would last. Wondered – as he sometimes did about a few of his charges – what Samuel Harold Andrew Knight would be like when he was an adult. Dr Simon couldn't imagine.

Sammy walked over to his shared room in D House and found a slight, beautiful Indian boy unpacking his case, filling one of the two cupboards with his clothes. Sammy flung himself on his bed and watched the meticulous folding of jumpers and socks, the careful hanging of pressed trousers and shirts. Watched the Indian lay out his books and pens on his desk, the one over by the window, each of them at exact right angles to one plane or another. When he was finished, the boy turned round and approached Sammy as he lay on his bed, held out his dusky hand.

'You must be Samuel. My name is Rajiv Samaroo.'

Sammy ignored Rajiv's outstretched hand. 'Where you from? I've never seen you before.'

'Today is my first day at Redpath. I have been living in Berlin for three years, with my family, attending a gymnasium there. But I am originally from Sansobella.'

'Where the fuck's that?'

Rajiv dropped his hand. 'I believe that geography is taught here. You should know where Sansobella is.' And the beautiful boy turned away, straightened the counterpane on his immaculate bed and left the room.

Sammy stared at the ceiling, thought of the Michelmas term stretching before him, filled with rugby and cold showers, Latin and CCF. Evenings spent in this room, the corridor outside being patrolled by the house master, Mr Leonard, as prep ticked away. Sammy promised himself that this term, this time, he would make it to London. He would evade the marshal and make it to London. He wasn't sure what he'd do when he got there, but he wanted to see the Rainbow and Hammersmith Odeon. He wanted to go to a concert at the Roundhouse in Chalk Farm — the Ramones were playing later that month and Sammy would be there. He rolled off the bed and yanked sheets and blankets into an untidy mess to cover it. Opening his case he threw the clothes on the shelves, stuffed underwear into a drawer. The only item he treated with any care was a Sony music cassette player, which he kept in a drawstring bag when he wasn't using it, along with a set of headphones.

Sammy slipped the headphones on that evening, as he and Rajiv sat at their respective desks, books open, expected to do prep for the next two hours. Sammy slipped a tape of Patti Smith's *Horses* into the deck and began to tap the desk with a ruler. Sat back in his chair, tie loose, feet on the desk, eyes closed, and slapped out the rhythm, moaning about Redondo Beach as he thought of long-gone parties. Rajiv, who was trying to make sense of Browning's 'My Last Duchess', tolerated the noise for a while and then stood up, walked over to Sammy, lifted one of the half-orange-sized headphones and whispered in Sammy's ear that if he didn't turn off the tape then he, Rajiv, would make Sammy's life unbearable. Sammy laughed, looked at Rajiv and stopped laughing.

'I want to work. You do not want to work and I do not care about that. But I do care if your not working makes me not able to. We have a problem.' Rajiv, who looked pensive, who looked gorgeous, who looked as if he could wield a knife, sat on his bed and stared at the anguished English boy. 'What is the problem? Why do you not want to work? What else is there to do? We are young – we can be sad later. But at this moment what else is there to do but work?'

Sammy frowned. 'There're lots of other things to do.'

'What? What else is there?'

'Well, run away for a start. Get the fuck out of here for a start.'

'That is not a start. That is doing nothing, running away. The way you speak of it is as an end and it is not. Running away is not an end. You think if you run then everything will be alright?' Rajiv pushed his raven-black hair back from his forehead.

Sammy snapped the headphone back onto his ear and began to shout about jet planes and free money. Rajiv watched him for a moment and then returned to the issue of the guilt or otherwise of Alfonso II.

Over the next few weeks Sammy studied Rajiv as Rajiv studied his books. He was fascinated by Rajiv's attention to detail, by his fastidiousness, his ability to concentrate on the task in hand. Sammy handed in prep that was half-completed, written on crumpled paper in an untidy scrawl, as Rajiv submitted reams of tidy text. Sammy sat at the back of classrooms, picking at the stripes of his house tie with the point of a compass, and watched Rajiv's black-haired head bend over his notes, his brown hand being raised to answer a question. Sammy watched him in class, on the sports pitches, in the refectory and noticed that Rajiv managed to get along with everybody: teachers, younger pupils, prefects, even Dr Simon. He was never condescending, never fawning. One Friday afternoon, when he should have been running cross-country, Sammy took himself to the library and consulted *The Times Atlas*, poring over the pages, imagining himself crossing inland seas and mountain ranges. He looked at the map of Cyprus, tried to find the local town near the cottage on the coast, but the map was not detailed enough. Eventually he turned to the maps of the Caribbean.

That night Sammy sat in his chair in their shared study, looked at Rajiv's back and said, 'So, where do you live in Sansobella?'

'I thought you did not know where Sansobella is. Why should you care where I live there?' Rajiv did not turn round to address Sammy, his voice bouncing off a page of quadratic equations.

'Sure I know where it is – in the Caribbean. Way down south, a republic in the Windward Island chain, south of Grenada, north-west of Trinidad, comprised of three islands, Sansobella, St George and Dorado.' Sammy had done his research – the first time he'd done any since he'd been sent to Redpath College.

Rajiv's back was turned, so Sammy didn't see him smile.

Rajiv Samaroo saved Sammy Knight. First, having seen Sammy's initials stencilled on his sports' gear, he conferred upon Sammy the nickname Shake, and then he saved him. It was an unlikely coupling, the friendship between Rajiv Samaroo and Shake and it took the teachers by surprise. Sammy Knight, troublemaker, loner, compulsive escapologist, faded away to be replaced by, if not a model pupil, then at least by a boy who attempted to do his prep, who answered questions, who was where he should be most of the time. Still Shake smoked, still he wore his tie loose and spiked his too-long hair, but he stopped trying to run having discovered it was more interesting to stay and spend time with Rajiv because Rajiv had so many stories to tell, such a different world view. Rajiv talked to him about islands where snakes slept in trees as caiman slithered into the rivers, where the days were always twelve hours long, where fires burned in sugar cane fields and the moon was upside down. He helped Shake with his prep, coached him for his exams, reminded him about times of house meetings, CCF and call-overs; reminded Shake to go to his detentions, which were still frequent.

The teachers at Redpath were nonplussed by the relationship.

Over tea and biscuits in the staff room some wondered if Knight was paying Samaroo for his help; some, over pints of beer in the local pub, speculated about the precise nature of the friendship, bristling with indignation, their occasional, slowly nodding silences pregnant with meaning. More than a few of the teachers were worried about what they perceived as platonic miscegenation; after all, whilst the school was content to accept foreigners, this acceptance should not transmit the wrong signals. What, they all wondered, was in it for Samaroo?

Rajiv had never met anyone like Shake. His childhood school in Sansobella had been peopled with others like himself. In Berlin he had been isolated first by language and then by colour. Rajiv had never encountered disregard for authority, had never encountered anger unmoderated by respect and so he was intrigued. Shake always chose Rajiv to be on his side in sports, played squash and tennis with him, taught him how to bowl a googly. He bought Rajiv chocolate and cakes to satisfy the Sanso sweet tooth and left the unexpected gifts on his desk. Shake tried to educate Rajiv – whose tastes ran to soca and the Carpenters – about the wilder side of music. Whilst other boys in Redpath were listening to the Eagles and David Bowie, Rajiv was subjected to lectures on Television's 'Marquee Moon' and Patti Smith's 'Radio Ethiopia', the Stranglers, the Damned, the Sex Pistols, the Clash, all lectures accompanied by soundtracks. Rajiv, who was determined to immerse himself in English culture, whether it be the English public school system or the English gutter, sat speechless through Shake's bedlam-punctured monologues, wondering why these bands didn't have pleasanter names. The teachers who passed the study door and heard the cacophony that was the Dead Kennedy's announcing they were too drunk to fuck, wondered yet again about the relationship between the Paki and the Rebel, as they were now described in the staff room.

Donald, Shake's father, would have configured the friendship of the polar opposites which were his son and Rajiv as a Venn diagram. To be sure, there were many differences between the two boys but there was also a shared prejudice: both found the thespians and ersatz literati of the sixth form laughable. Those boys who walked the corridors of Redpath carrying the works of Grass, Mann and Huxley, who watched the films of Fellini and Truffaut at Film Society meetings, who auditioned for parts in the school plays (*Equus* and *Rosencrantz and Guildenstern*), who wore their hair straight and long, were all objects of fascination. Shake – who was protected from ridicule by his sporting achievements, by his aura of indifference – had only to walk into their shared study and say, 'I think you're tho *right*, Timothy,' to reduce Rajiv – who was protected from ridicule by his academic achievements and his friendship with Shake – to giggles which soon became heel-beating guffaws.

The staff at Redpath were unaware of the confectionery Shake left on Rajiv's desk, did not realize that Rajiv did not merely tell Shake the answers to his many questions but that he tried to explain the answers, would spend hours talking Shake through plate tectonics, titration, diffusion, the meaning of hubris and its effects. The teachers did not know that Shake could lie on his bed as Rajiv studied and not feel the need to talk, to make noise, not feel the need to impress or intimidate. But above all of this, the teachers who asked themselves what was in the friendship for Samaroo, did not even consider the possibility that the Paki had met the first white boy who was colour-blind, the first white person who didn't give a damn what colour Rajiv was. And none of the staff, even in their cups, even halfway down the sixth pint, when their imaginations had been unleashed, made the connection: Rajiv and Shake were both island boys.

It was Rajiv Samaroo who cajoled Sammy Knight into studying for his O levels, by the simple method of bribery, which no one else had thought to try. If Sammy studied hard in an attempt to pass all his O levels, he could spend the summer in Sansobella – where the moon hung upside down, where surf pounded on endless beaches, where caiman lurked – if he did not, he would spend the time in Cyprus with the second Mrs Knight.

RAJIV

This is not the best time for me to be doing this. I have many things to be doing, many commitments to fulfil. My family and I have been here less than three weeks and there is still so much to do. A consignment of containers is arriving in the port this afternoon and I intend to be there, so I cannot speak for long. *Rajiv Samaroo sits behind the long, littered desk in his office and pulls at his pristine shirt cuffs, the diamond signet ring on his little finger catching and trapping the weak sunlight, throwing it back as a rainbow.* You want to know about Sammy? Well, I did not really know him – by which I mean, I did not know him as Sammy. Or rather, only for a short while. I knew him as Shake, to me he was always Shake. Indeed, I gave him the name and then everyone called him Shake. I met him many years ago, when I went to school in England. We shared a room in a boarding house. At first he made me very angry because he would not work. I had to study in the same room as Shake and he would play music or lie on his bed, talking, trying to distract me. As I say, I was at first very angry. My father had always told me that it was my job to work, to study and I was not able to. But eventually Sammy and I came to an arrangement. I cannot remember now how we did this, it is all a very long time ago. *A knock at the door; a young Indian woman enters, hands Rajiv a sheaf of papers. He reaches into the breast pocket of his suit and pulls out a gold-plated fountain pen, with which he signs the papers. When the young woman has left the room, Rajiv stands and looks at the view from his window, looks out over grey streets and scrapers, the polluted waters of the river Main glittering dully in the distance.* Did you know Anne Frank was born here? In Frankfurt? She lived here until she was eleven, until she was . . . displaced. My children now attend the gymnasium here and they will be visiting the Jewish Museum next week where they will learn all about Anne Frank and her life. Where they will learn all about her family's escape. Their eventual capture. Perhaps they did not run far enough? *Rajiv sighs, smoothes his thinning hair across his coffee-skinned scalp and it is possible to catch a glimpse of the beautiful boy he must have been.* What you have to understand about Shake is that he lived for years being what other people wanted him to be. He read magazines about the . . . fashion of the time and he would adopt it, whatever it was. He was fallerfash. It was as if he had no identity of his own. I remember one day becoming furious with him because he was so untidy, so *disorganized*, and I shouted at him. Shake was very upset then. He did not know how much I minded and after that he was better, he would try to put his things away, try to keep order. I think he thought it was how young men behaved. Do you understand? He thought it – his lack of organization – was in some way charming. And perhaps it was? Because everyone always tried to accommodate Shake, tried to help him. He should have been expelled many times but the school was reluctant to do this. I wonder now if that was because of his mother's death. I was told about it one day and I was very shocked. I had not realized that Shake had grandparents who lived close to the school, and a sister living with them. This I did not agree with. They were his family; he should have been with them. What is there but family? But I realized that Shake did not think of them as family, not in the way I thought of my tanties and nanas and nanis and parents thousands of miles away in Sansobella. *Rajiv turns from the window, sits once more at his cluttered desk, picks up a thick folder of invoices and flicks through it, unseeing, drops it amongst other papers.* What you have to understand is that Shake was an island boy. *Rajiv taps his chest, leaving dimpled impressions on the starched shirt.* Shake was an island boy here, in his heart. He liked his worlds to be small, to be manageable. *Rajiv smiles.* I remember the summer we spent in Sansobella, when we were boys. We must have been sixteen, seventeen. I always loved Sansobella – the land of opportunity. I still love it now, and wish I could have stayed there. But Shake, he liked St George, tiny, sleepy St George. Where nothing happens and the sky is always blue. I worry for him. I miss my Danny Kyow. *Biting his lip, Rajiv stands and buttons his jacket, fussing again with his cuffs.* It is late and I must go.

1978

The Samaroo estate in Queenstown, the capital of Sansobella, was unlike anything Shake had ever seen. The main house, built up high in the hills behind the city, was a rambling affair of balconies, porches and canopies, slung seemingly randomly from the eaves. Inside, the house was cool and dark, decorated in East Indian style, with vivid wall hangings, chandeliers, low, over-stuffed sofas covered in red brocade or orange velvet. The floors were tiled, covered with ornate rugs, and fans spun in every room. From the kitchens came the pungent, sharp scent of spices which permeated the lower floor. Rajiv and Shake were given a shabby bungalow in the grounds, which was simply decorated and had its own small pool. The bungalow was shaded by travellers' palms and towering bougainvillea bushes, and on the porch was a set of rattan furniture. Shake sat on the rattan sofa on his first evening in Sansobella, looked around himself and said, 'I can't believe they've put us down here. We could do anything and they wouldn't know.'

'Like what?'

'Like have parties or smoke dope. You know.'

'They know I would not do these things, that is why we are here.'

Shake lit a cigarette, began to prowl around the pool, investigating his surroundings. Pulled back a set of louvred doors and found behind them a tiled bar area with a fridge.

'Hey – this is cool.' He opened the fridge and found a stack of S&G beers. 'Want one?'

'No, thank you. My religion does not permit me to drink. But please help yourself.'

Shake opened the freezing bottle and rejoined his friend by the pool. He put his feet on the table, sipped the beer and watched the sun set as he sweated. He watched the herringbone clouds turn from a pink as pale as oleander flowers to a deep crimson, and then night fell, suddenly. He began to slap at mosquitoes, drawn to him by the alien, sweet smell of his white sweat. Rajiv lit a coil beneath the table and for the first time Shake smelled the acrid odour of compressed wood pulp and citronella, a smell he grew very used to during his life. He looked over at his friend in the light spilling from the bungalow, thought how different he looked in his own place. Looser maybe, older definitely. Rajiv drew a cigarette from Shake's pack and, to Shake's amazement, lit it.

'I do not smoke at school because it is not allowed but I smoke at home.' Rajiv settled back.

'You never told me that.'

Rajiv shrugged. 'We will have a wonderful summer,' he said.

And they did. Rajiv and Shake went to Parlavu Beach, which was a drive away, up over the peaks of the hills and down to the rugged northern coastline, where racing, spume-spitting waves curled and hurled themselves along miles of sand. The currents and rip tides were jagged and unpredictable as sharks' teeth and Rajiv – who swam like a dolphin, dark, arcing, sure of himself – kept an eye on Shake as he tried to impress the girls watching from the beach. Sometimes they were driven to the east coast, where towering but ordered waves rolled in and Shake learned to surf there, taught by Rajiv and his older brother, Vijay; they were taken to the largest of the inland lakes and there they would waterski, or take sailing lessons in one of the Hobies lining the water's edge. And always they were collected from the door of the main house and driven in a limousine with tinted windows, the chauffeur locking the doors before setting off down the driveway, lined with royal palms. The doors were not unlocked until the car had come to a halt by the sailing club, or the beach house, or the restaurant. Even when the boys took a trip to the Eboni swamp, where they paddled shallow canoes along the still waterways of the mangrove swamps, in search of caiman, fresh-water turtles and the black skimmer, they were accompanied into the swamp by two taciturn, broad-shouldered men. Shake thought nothing of this, was too concerned with having the time of his life to wonder why he and Rajiv never walked anywhere, why they were never left alone. Even when they went to pool parties or house parties for the night, the chauffeur – a tall, illiterate Gujarat warrior – stayed, sleeping in his car until the boys had had enough fun.

Shake spent that summer sitting in the back of the air-conditioned limousine, staring out at a world that could not look in, and sometimes he wondered at what he saw. Queenstown scared him, with its old, rusting American cars, rattling trucks and dented dumpsters racing along the boulevards, not braking for pedestrians, not braking for red lights, just winging each other, mirrors flying as jaywalkers beat their chests and yelled 'bounce mih nuh!' at drivers. The crowds of dogs, ribs moving like piano keys playing macabre, unheard music as they breathed and gulped at the corpse of one of their own, lying by a storm drain. And each boulevard, each street, each trace lined with stalls lit by burning flames, cooking up aloo pies, doubles, fried shrimp, fried chicken, the vendors made shadowy by blue haze. And the men who walked the streets, bandannas marking their allegiances, their jerky, limping hustle marking them as hard men, waving their hands, spitting in the street, dipping their hips at passing women – they scared Shake too. Even the women unsettled him, lounging on their faded galleries circling crumbling Spanish-style mansions, lifting thick, blue-black hair from the napes of their necks, lazily scratching naked ankles. Or the proud black women, dressed in immaculate long, white skirts and turbans, brandishing tightly rolled black umbrellas at drivers as they crossed busy roads, stately and inviolate. Or the young, leggy girl-women, lounging on walls, on street corners, on pavements, their breasts high, their thighs never-ending, watching the limo pass with narrowed eyes. Sometimes Shake felt uneasy, as the limo paused at a junction or stopped at a light, and he found himself staring at a young woman, sitting on a hard plastic chair, her knees vulnerable in the harsh light, waiting patiently as a sister or friend plaited cornrows. He felt uneasy because the girl was staring right back at him and she didn't know it. Outside the city, on the sugar cane flats crisscrossed by tarmac, Shake found other things to be fearful of: old black men who rode cycles festooned with pans, dulled cutlasses and cloth, howling at the moon as the limo slid past; mangled dogs hairless with mange; cars burning on embankments; the mad, black, angular bulk of cattle looming out of darkness; the glutinous bubbling of pitch lakes; the flare of distant oil refineries sketching plans on the night sky; the great, stinking mounds of garbage by the roadside; the vultures which cruised on ugly, tattered wings. All of this playing out like a silent movie beyond the closed, tinted windows.

If Shake did not wonder about the fact he and Rajiv were guarded every moment of their lives, neither did he wonder about who was paying for these days and nights of endless entertainment. He and Rajiv simply spun out their lives on sun and surf, like an ever-growing pod of candyfloss on a stick, spun sugar, fine, sweet crystals. It was only at night, when he lay down to sleep that Shake remembered the baying, cycle-riding man or the scar running down the face of a young girl, twisting her lips into a never-fading smile.

It took Shake a long time to adjust to the fact that the beat at the heart of Rajiv's life was his family. Always there were sisters and brothers with them, and Rajiv talked to them, laughed with them as Shake tried to remember what his sister, Diana, was like. Throughout the summer, the family took trips together, Mr Samaroo being absent at work. The children were expected to sit quietly through interminable afternoons spent visiting other East Indian families in their spicy, exotic mansions. In the evenings Shake and Rajiv were expected to dress and eat with the Samaroo family, in a long, richly decorated room at the back of the main house which overlooked a man-made lake. At first Shake was shy, made nervous by his lack of understanding of the correct etiquette. Rajiv had three brothers and four sisters, countless aunts and uncles, grandparents and family friends who came together to eat and Shake – used to Marmite sandwiches eaten standing up in the Cypriot kitchen, over-cooked meals wolfed down in the refectory of Redpath, and stiff, wordless suppers with his grandparents in Surrey – was unsure what to do when confronted by the long table, centrepiece of a lunacy of colour, peopled by women in sequinned saris and men in Nehru suits. He watched Rajiv, mirrored his every move, said nothing. The first night, he spooned onto his plate the same as his friend, a muddy looking mixture of vegetables, forked a mouthful and ate. Shake chewed and thought he was going to die as his tender cheeks combusted and his throat closed. Somehow he swallowed the burning bolus and followed its path down into his guts as his eyes watered. Rajiv, who was talking to his sister, Sunita, did not notice this but his mother did. Mrs Samaroo beckoned over a maid, spoke to her and within minutes Shake was given a bowl of yoghurt and a pitcher of water, some naan and mild chutney.

Mr Samaroo presided over the table, urbane and commanding, plump hands, nails shaped and shiny as a young girl's, protruding from the cuffs of tailored suits, pinky ring flashing in the light of the chandeliers. He sat at the head of the table, made soft by luxury, his dark eyes, ringed by giraffe lashes, sliding from face to face, as peacocks strutted the springy lawns beyond the window shrieking their off-key calls. If madness had a sound, Shake thought, it would be the peacock's cracked yell, and it unsettled him. Shake would watch Mr Samaroo when he thought himself unwatched, glanced at the other men as they listened to the patriarch. Mr Samaroo leaned back in his chair, crossed his legs and played with a knife or a glass, as he spoke, uninterrupted. Shake was reminded of his own father, Donald, sitting in a chair on a different island, in a different time, his Jesus feet bare, his long face lit by a Mediterranean sun as he spoke about physics, and women sat at his feet, listening. Mr Samaroo did not have glitter dancing around him but he had something, something perhaps weightier, more substantial than a cascade of falling stars. Chewing on chapatti, chana and bhaji Shake considered this, as peacocks screamed and sweat ran down his spine.

Every late evening the boys went back to their bungalow and sat in the pool, Shake drinking beers, Rajiv sipping Pepsi and smoking, delicately tapping his ash into an ashtray balanced on the tiled edge. They lay back, their legs floating, arms akimbo, elbows gripping the tiles, and stared up at the night sky as they talked, of school and girls, cars and surfing, CCF and food. The underlighting flushed the pool a white-turquoise and the pumped water rippled, gurgling a little as they spoke. Shake's skin, when he first arrived, had looked luminous in the water, silver almost. One night, when weeks had passed, when his skin seemed as black beneath the water as Rajiv's, Shake asked, 'What does your father do?'

Rajiv shrugged and the ripples bounced. 'Import and export.'

'What?'

'What what?'

'What does he import and export?'

'Anything.'

'How can it be anything? I mean, how can he import anything? He must have some kind of . . . of business.'

'Yes. Import and export, that is his business.'

The sound of a distant ambulance siren swirled around the palm leaves. Shake looked at his friend in the shifting, pale shadows of the pool lights and knew Rajiv would say no more, thought how like his father Rajiv looked.

'It's funny, he reminds me of my father, a bit. Dunno why.'

Rajiv thought of the lathe-thin, uncomfortable man he had

met once, when Donald had collected Shake from school, and he frowned slightly but said nothing.

Shake slid away from the pool's edge, floated into the middle of the pool and spread his arms and legs, starfish-like, his dark hair, long now, moving like kelp, and as he spoke he could hear only his own voice, locked inside his head, knocking against his ears. Shake swallowed and he could hear soft tissues closing tackily against each other. 'My mother was killed in a car accident. When I was eleven. She was in a car on her own and it crashed into a truck going the other way.'

Rajiv, who already knew this, having been told by others, nodded, unseen. 'I am sorry,' he said, unheard.

'She was . . .' Shake pushed gently against the edge of the pool and began to spin slowly, watching the half-moon describe a circle. 'She was fun. Not like laughing aloud fun, but always just fun. She was very tall.' Rajiv watched Shake's hair move in lazy swirls and nodded again. 'She was very tall and she had long hair. We used to have parties every weekend. In a cottage on the coast. Loads of people used to turn up and give us things. And my father used to sit at the table looking over everyone. Like he was looking out *for* them or something. Like he was God. And my mother used to make drinks.' Shake drifted into the middle of the pool and came to rest, and there he was turned slightly by the pumped water. 'She used to make cocktails. There were all these bottles that people brought. I can remember some of them. There was a tall one with a red cap and a blue one with the picture of a mountain on it and a weird kind of clay one, you know, like tiles or something, with some kind of gin in it. And there were always lemons everywhere, slices of lemons because they grew everywhere. I remember the smell of lemon and booze and smoke. Like I can imagine it if I try hard enough. And a big block of ice which she used to smash with some kind of knife and it was always melting. Weird, isn't it, how you remember something like the label on a bottle? You can remember that but you can't remember other things. I mean, I can remember my dad sitting there with the glitter all around him and my mother holding up a jug and pouring lemon juice in it but I can't remember things I want to remember.' Shake thought how strange it was that he was looking at the same moon that his father was looking at in Cyprus – only it would be day there, or maybe early morning. His father wouldn't be looking at the moon. Maybe he was still asleep, sharing his bed with the second Mrs Knight. 'Sometimes I think it's because we left so quickly. Because we left and ran to England and I didn't have time to remember.'

Rajiv waited in the silence and then slid over to Shake, touched his arm. Shake flinched. 'It is late. I am going to bed.'

'I'll come in a minute.'

Shake lay in the water and stared at the moon, willing himself to remember, but instead he found himself measuring the moon's path against the dark outline of the main house as he heard the creaking of a donkey-drawn cart. Shake began to shiver, climbed out and towelled himself dry, felt sweat prickling at his temple but still he shivered. He stood outside Rajiv's room, shivering, wishing he could open the door, cross the wooden floor and climb into Rajiv's bed so Rajiv could hold him and stroke his head, scratch his scalp with his fingers, lull him to sleep. Shake pushed open the door, pushed it open silently, and looked at his friend, black against pale sheets in the gloom, imagined climbing in beside his friend, imagined how he would be misunderstood. So Shake took his shivers and his night fright into his own room, stripped off his damp trunks and threw himself on the bed, pulled the sheet tightly around him and lay staring at the slat-lines of light coming through the shutters. Eventually he turned, lay on his back, placed one hand on his heart and the other above his head and finally he drifted into darkness.

Each morning a house boy brought chilled water, tea and plates of fresh pineapple, papaya with lime and slabs of grinning, bloody watermelon to the bungalow. The boys would wake, each in his room, to find it cleaned of dirty clothes, the bathroom spotless, fresh towels on a chair, the fruit on a table. Meeting on the gallery, yawning and stretching, they'd swim, shower and make their way up to the main house, where they would find the day ahead of them already shaped, moulded by the dictates of Mr Samaroo.

On a few occasions, Shake would wake to find Rajiv already gone, or standing on the bungalow's gallery, gulping too-hot tea, dressed in a linen suit, close-shaved, his hair slicked back.

'What're you doing?' Shake asked, the first time he saw Rajiv tying his laces, then polishing the toes of black leather shoes.

'I have to go with my father to his offices. He wishes me to see how the business runs.'

'Eh?'

'I have to go out for the morning. I shall be back for lunch.' Rajiv straightened his tie, stared at his reflection in a mirror. 'Perhaps you could go into Queenstown?'

Shake thought of the blue-hazy traces, the mangled dogs, the

Chinese men yelling strange, blunt syllables as they shoved over-stacked barrows across choked streets, thought of the length of the women's thighs. 'I think I'll just stay here. Read or something.'

Shake rummaged through the canvas bag he had brought with him, pulled out a paperback copy of *One Flew over the Cuckoo's Nest*, and lay on a sunbed by the pool. He smoked, he fidgeted, he flexed his arms in the sun, watching the muscles bunch and slither under the skin. He listened to the gardeners talking, trying to unravel the patois, trying to remember things they said so he could ask Rajiv the meanings later. Thick words, like fudge, like half-frozen cream, dropped over the fence, studded with shiny pearls of intonation: a boy who was 'true true fatigue', a woman who was 'well tie, like a paime', a 'monkey who doh climb grou-grou boeuf tree'. Shake read about Nurse Ratched and wondered about her, he picked his toenails, he lifted the waistband of his trunks and looked at his pale, limp prick lying against dark skin. Rajiv had looked so old, so sure of himself when he left to go to work with his father. Had looked as if there was a sheet of glass between them. As if had he, Shake, reached out a hand towards Rajiv, it would have smacked against something unseen.

Since that day, Rajiv had disappeared often in the morning, returning at lunchtime, his tie still snug against a snow-white collar, his slim frame moving like silk in the creasless suit. Always Shake felt uneasy, until Rajiv had changed his clothes, sloughing off years and gravitas and assurance, until Rajiv thundered out of the bungalow, yodelling, and crashed into the still waters of the pool.

*

At the end of the August of that kaleidoscope summer, the Samaroos flew to the island of St George for the week of the Great Boat Race, taking the English boy with them. Mr Samaroo chartered a small plane for the family to fly from Queenstown to the airstrip outside Bridgewater, the capital of St George. Four jeeps were waiting for them, rag tops down, and the family piled into them, the women and girls giggling, hitching up saris and pushing the boys aside to jostle for places on the hard seats. Shake hung back until last, when the jeeps were full and he was told to stand on the fender board at the back and hang on to the frame of the roof. As the jeep bounced out of Bridgewater on the rutted road that ran north to Grand Anse, Mr Samaroo gestured at the building works and new houses being thrown up along the main street, shouting to be heard above the grinding of gears and the groaning suspension. Shake didn't listen, instead he hung on as hard as he could, his body shaken by each thumping pothole and sunken drain, shutting out the laughter and yells of the party as he looked about himself at the yellow and blue rum shops, the pan theatres, the goats tethered at the roadside, the grasses and trees flowing down to the kerb, lianas trailing. Schoolchildren, already back from summer recess, ran alongside the jeeps, dressed in immaculate uniforms, waving, shouting and grinning. Shake wanted to wave back but dared not, his sweating hands already slipping on the roof frame. Bridgewater petered out in a trail of pastel-painted shacks and the road smoothed itself into hard-packed dirt. The convoy followed the old coast road, and if he stood on tiptoe, Shake could make out flashes of the lime-blue shallow waters around a reef. They headed towards Coral Strand, the tyres of the jeeps grinding through sand laid over ground coral, and finally reached the gates of the Samaroo residence. The jeeps crawled up the drive, coming to a halt in front of a dilapidated plantation house, the paint rusted by salt spray, the galleries and interior made dark and cool by the shade of yellow pouis, cassia and mango trees. It was only as the jeep came to rest that Shake realized that it was the first time he had travelled in a car without tinted windows and locked doors, the first time he had looked up to see a moving sky slashed by banana plant leaves.

The boys were given a room under the eaves, and when the louvred door was pushed open, the heat was like a wall of oil into which they walked and emerged the other side covered in a slick. Rajiv waved his slim hands around, began to throw open the jalousies and demararas, cursed as he switched on the ceiling fan and nothing happened. The house was set back from the sea, on a small rise, and the breeze heaved at the wall of oil, shunting it back little by little, until the room began to cool. But still the shingled walls felt hot, even the bare floorboards were warm underfoot.

'Let's go,' said Rajiv, grabbing two musty towels from a wooden wardrobe.

Rajiv led the way along an overgrown track, pushing back the mimi-may, stinking susan and long grasses, stamping on half-collapsed banana plants and yanking at strangling morning glory. At the foot of the rise ficus grew tall and palm trees, undermined by high storm tides, leaned towards the sea, their trunks running level with sand then rising in a crown of yellowed leaves. Coconuts, fronds and brown aerated bubbles of seaweed were the only litter at the shoreline. The beach opened up left and right, bounded by rocky headlands, shallow reef crops visible just beyond the breaking waves. Beyond the eastern headland Shake could see another headland, made misty by spray, and beyond that another and if he squinted, shaded his eyes against the late afternoon sun, he could make out buildings dotted on the green slopes of the farthest horizon. He sat on the sand, a dark gold, coarse sand, scooped a handful and saw the gold was an illusion. Each speck was white, grey, brown or black, minuscule and cuboid. He dropped the sand, brushed his hands clean and watched Rajiv wade into the waves, watched him lift his shoulders and hands as the water curvetted around his hips and waist, then the startling pink-white soles of Rajiv's feet flashed as he dived. Shake wrapped his arms around his knees, rocked a little as he noticed pirogues gathering on the skyline, watched them funnel in towards a common goal, prows high, the fishermen invisible in the glare from the water. Silence. No sirens, no purring of water pumps or pool pumps, no distant roar of planes landing and leaving from Queenstown, no shouts from the street, no blare of megaphones strapped to car roofs bawling about jumps-up. Other than the metronomic shush and gurgle of wavelets bursting on and bubbling through coarse sand there was no sound. The rhythmic soughing of the water seemed to grow louder and Shake lay back, unmindful of the sand in his hair, the slight grating on his shoulder blades, and closed his eyes – the lids magenta, arterioles pulsing – and dozed until Rajiv spattered him with cold spray. Shake smiled lazily, raised himself on his elbows and looked about.

'What's this beach called?'

'It should be called Samaroo Beach,' said Rajiv, rubbing at his ears with the towel and shaking his head. 'But it is not. They call it Heavenly Cove.'

Shake nodded. Pointed to the racing pirogues, dark now, against the falling sun. 'Where are they going?'

Rajiv pointed west, jabbed a finger around the headland. 'Just around there is a fishing village called Zabico. And look,' he pointed into the glare on the horizon, 'can you see the sandbanks there?'

'Yeah.'

'That's the beginning of Coral Strand. Everyone who visits St George goes to Coral Strand, to spend a day or a week. White sand, pale blue waters and palms – a small paradise. And that way,' Rajiv swivelled, pointed east, 'is Grackle Bay and if the headland was not there it would be possible to see Bridgewater. That is where the boats will come in on race day.'

'How long have you had a house here?'

Rajiv shrugged, wrapped the towel around his shoulders and sat next to Shake, pulled at the sand. 'Maybe three years.'

'I'd live here, on St George. I wouldn't live in Sansobella, I'd live here.'

Laughing, Rajiv pushed at Shake's shoulder. 'And what would you do here? There is no business! There is nothing to do. It is fine for times like this, but there is nothing to do.'

'Oh yes!' said Shake, laughing. 'I forgot.' Shake imitates Rajiv's accented English, 'At this moment what else is there to do but work?' He shoves at Rajiv's shoulder. Often Shake makes fun of his friend's seriousness, of his friend's assertion that they were young and could be unhappy later.

A small plane cruised along the horizon, banked lazily and

turned full circle, heading for Bridgewater airport. Rajiv nudged Shake and pointed. 'You see? This weekend hundred of Sansos come here and fill the hotels and the villas. We will all meet at Grackle and Coral Strand, and it will be good. But when we are not here,' Rajiv sucked his teeth, 'nothing happens. They are lazy and when we go they count the money and fall asleep until we come again.'

'Who's lazy?'

Rajiv glanced left and right, leaned forward as if examining a small pebble in his hand. 'The blacks.'

Shake thought of the gardeners and the pool men in the Sansobella house, thought of the drivers who had collected them from the airport. Remembered the baggage handlers and the cleaners at the airports, the beach clubs, the shopping malls. Thought of the garbage men, neckerchiefs wrapped around their faces, who bounced at the back of the stinking dumpster trucks, the men driving the Cats and diggers as roads rolled out behind them, black asphalt spread by black men in shorts, bandannas soaking up their sweat. Could picture the men swinging the scythes at the roadside, clearing grasses, ebony hands turning the oiled handles easily, over and over, as their backs bent. Thought of the Samaroos climbing into their air-conditioned cars, before sweeping through the gates of their mansion to be taken to their offices in downtown Queenstown, by the docks. And from the windows of those offices they could sit in their swivel chairs and watch the stained T-shirts of the black stevedores grow darker as pallets and containers were unloaded portside.

'They are lazy,' muttered Rajiv again, aware of his friend's doubts.

'Mmm,' hummed Shake, not knowing what to say.

'Look, everyone has been a slave. All of us. My ancestors came from India as indentured labour for the plantations, working for the white English. The Chinese, they came as indentured labour too. The blacks, the Indians, the Chinese, all of us. Even your people have been slaves.' Rajiv shrugged.

'But that doesn't mean they're lazy. How can you say that?'

'Look at the place!' Rajiv spread his arms wide, swept them over the island. 'Look at the roads and the houses! They do not bother with anything. They do not paint, they do not build, they do not even fill in the potholes. They sit in the sun or sleep in the shade and wait for the Sansos to come with money. The only place that is civilized is Grand Anse, where Sansos are building hotels and pools and putting up villas and walls. There they have hot and cold water, electricity and telephones. In other places they have nothing. They are lazy.'

That week, as the Samaroos and their white guest went to the beaches and ate in the cavernous air-conditioned hotel restaurants, Shake thought about what his friend had said. He hadn't argued with Rajiv because he wasn't sure he had understood. So he watched the Samaroos sniggering at the locals, watched the way Mr Samaroo – looking odd in shorts and polo shirt, effeminate and plump – snapped his fingers for waiters, noticed he never looked at anyone as he gave his orders. Even Mrs Samaroo was surly, rude almost, when she spoke to the locals. She glowered and then smiled as she turned to her children and sisters. Shake watched and he tried to understand.

The party spent a day at Coral Strand, dragging huge iceboxes over to a cabana and hauling sunbeds for the women so they could lie in its shade. Vijay put a boom box on the table and turned up the volume, the music fighting with other boom boxes up and down the sands. Reggae, calypso and soca bounced off the trunks of the palm trees and scattered over the lagoon. The waters were filled with children screaming and fighting and around them groups of white Sanso men, bulky and bearded, wearing bush hats, sank down in the water up to their necks, holding fluorescent plastic beakers full of neat rum and ice, cigars burning between their thick fingers. In the distance waves broke on the reef, frothed in a virgin-white band, and rippled demurely to shore. Glass-bottomed boats chugged through the crowds of swimmers, adding to the bedlam with their own reggae sounds pulsing, scattering shoals of ghostly white fish. Silver, blunt-snouted flying fish, wings gossamer-thin, flew in shallow arcs through the crowds, fleeing the racket and commotion. Women in saris waded into water, magenta, cyan and daffodil-yellow silk blooming around them like sodden, wild petals. Local women carrying trays of peanut brittle, coconut cake and benay balls walked slowly among the crowds, dabbing at their temples with sweat rags. Mrs Samaroo waved away a beautiful, sad-eyed young woman, without looking at her wares, without looking at the woman. Shake noticed the black vendor was missing two fingers on her left hand, saw Mrs Samaroo pointing to the absence and turning to an aunt to say something. Shake wanted to go to the sad-eyed woman and touch her arm, wanted to buy everything she had and send her away from the beach, away from these people who were ignoring her. But he was scared he would be doing something wrong, so he sat rock-still, in the shade of the cabana roof, and followed the cake seller's trek around the beach.

She sold nothing. Rajiv pulled at his arm, trying to drag him out into the lagoon, where Vijay and Sanjay were throwing a frisbee. Shake shook his head. 'In a minute.'

Mr Samaroo and his brothers came dripping to the table. They towelled down, talking in thick, Sanso accents, and sat as Mrs Samaroo dug a bottle of rum out of the ice and placed mugs in front of the men. Shake knew, by that time, that the men would talk in patois for the frivolous matters of life, switching to Queen's English for the serious matter of business.

Mr Samaroo downed his rum, argued for a while about the various merits of Trinidadian, Guyanan and Jamaican rum, ended the debate by slamming his hand on the table, laughing, and yelling, 'If snake come outa bush and say "snake dey" – *he dey*!'

'Yuh beatin' yuh own drum and dancin'!'

'We offah dis gol' – dis Huggins! – and yuh wan' babash!'

The men laughed, poured another round. Mr Samaroo straightened his shoulders and leaned forward. 'Hear me now – there are rumours that Kouranis is going to buy.'

'Buy what?' Baboo pressed down his wet, dense silver hair, smoothed it over his crown.

'This.' Mr Samaroo tapped the table. 'Kouranis is going to buy Coral Strand.' Shake, who was pretending not to listen, heard the name Kouranis for the first but not the last time.

The men sat back, shifted on the wooden bench and looked around themselves.

'Buy Coral Strand? Yuh lie!' Baboo screwed up his eyes. Squinted at his nephew. 'Can he do that?'

Mr Samaroo nodded. 'It is said that the lease is up for sale. It is said that the government has put the lease up for sale.'

'Who is Kouranis anyway? Where is he from? What is his family? I hear the name but I don' see any family.'

'He is Greek. How would we know his family? He is from an island in Greece where his family own oil tankers. That's what I hear. He came to Sanso perhaps two years ago and began to spend money.'

Baboo leaned over and spat in the sand.

Mr Samaroo kicked sand over the spittle puddle. 'Hear me now! Kouranis is planning to buy the ferry, a chain of chop-chop shops and maybe the brewery.' He sipped more rum. 'And Coral Strand. That is what I hear.'

Baboo laughed, smoothed his hair again, set his hands on skinny, brown thighs and laughed. 'What are you saying? Him got more money dan God?'

'I am beginning to think so. He has more palm oil than God.' Mr Samaroo rubbed fingers and thumbs together.

'Who him coining?' asked Baboo.

'Anyone who holds out their hands.'

'Yuh holdin' out yours?'

Mr Samaroo motioned to his wife to bring a fresh bottle of rum. 'Every day fuh t'ief, one day fuh watchman.' And he tapped the table, signalling the end of the talking. The men sat staring at the children splashing in the lagoon as Shake slipped away to join Rajiv and the frisbee.

For two days that week, Mrs Samaroo had teams of local women come in and clean the Samaroo holiday home. Carpets and rugs were taken up and beaten, the dust and sand of months, grey and fine, bursting out of them, drifting in sour-smelling clouds. Local women on ladders with buckets of warm soapy water wiped the thousands of louvres in the house, as others, on their knees, scraped the wax from floorboards and scrubbed the pale wood clean before laying and buffing another layer of wax. The blades of ceiling fans were lifted down and cleaned, as were the hundreds of crystal teardrops on the chandeliers. The boys were told to go out, told to take their towels and disappear. Shake waited for Rajiv on the porch the first morning, sitting in an old cane chair, foot swinging, looking at the women climbing ladders in the hallway, listening to them talk, the words obscure but that hardly mattered as the rising cadences and high-pitched yelps of laughter told him all he needed to know. As did the silence that fell whenever Mrs Samaroo appeared, short and bustling, to run a finger along a rail, or point to a corner on the staircase. Then the women became sullen and slow, pushed their sweat rags down in their pockets, leaned on their brooms, hips jutting out, and sighed deep and low. Once Mrs Samaroo had gone, the younger women yanked the sweat rags out and stuffed them in their mouths, their eyes watering, cotton dresses shifting against slim bodies. The older women rolled their shoulders and their eyes, grunted as they reached for yet another crystal teardrop.

Rajiv, when he eventually appeared, led the way down the rutted track on an old, maroon sit-up-and-beg bike, its brake blocks worn, its saddle cracked, the front wheel slightly buckled, describing an unlikely ellipse. Shake followed on an old Raleigh, the Sturmey Archer gears slipping, causing him occasionally to lurch forward into the handlebars. They pedalled east on the old coast road, lined with palms and cassia, crushing hibiscus flowers and the long, brown pods of the flamboyant tree beneath worn

tyres. Passing Grackle Bay, they skirted a row of yellow-, green-
and red-painted makeshift stalls, men sitting on stools outside,
carving and whittling. Beyond them, on the sands, lay the white
bodies of tourists on brightly coloured towels, the paraphernalia
of the tropics all around them: straw hats, sun lotion bottles,
paperback books, spines cracking in the sun, T-shirts and sunglasses, rush mats and beach bags. Groups of East Indian Sansos
sat on loungers, using iceboxes for tables, the women immaculate,
gold jewellery flashing. Past Grackle Bay they came to the outskirts of Bridgewater, where small shacks stood on pilings,
amidst long grasses. Net curtains billowed in the windows as
washed clothes dried on bushes in the yard. Beneath the shacks,
yardie hens pecked at bare ground and goats knelt, at the ends of
their tethers, straining to reach the furthest blades of grass. Dogs
barked at the boys, some chasing them down the road a ways
before stopping and wagging their tails, as if at a job well done.
Children squatted by the gravelled roadside, pitching marbles,
looking up when they heard the hissing of tyres; seeing Shake,
white boy, they'd stand and wave, shout garbled greetings. They
passed the abattoir, a dour, concrete block, with a red tin galvanize roof, a few cattle tethered outside, chewing at the rampant
verge. Cars began to pass them, all of them either vivid pink, blue
or yellow, Asian and boxy, all of them the same, crawling along,
the drivers jouncing in and out of potholes. Freewheeling down
into Bridgewater, the capital of St George, they passed through
an endless avenue of palm trees, the trunks playing a strobe light
over Shake's face as the shadows flew past. They stopped at a
shack by the docks and bought shrimp rotis, ate them sitting on
a verge, watching the traffic bunching up in the car park as a ferry

loaded. Shake recognized the old Bedford trucks from his child-hood Dinky toys, frog-eyed and blunt nosed, their exhausts belching blue fumes as the drivers argued over who should embark first. Reggae rolled faintly across the scrubland between the dock and the market.

'Where are we going?' asked Shake. 'I mean, are we going somewhere in particular?'

Rajiv, who had a sweet tooth, finished his bottle of Miss Tubby root beer and tossed the bottle in the river. 'We are going to a place past Plymouth. I want to show you something. Come on.'

They cycled out of Bridgewater and began to climb a steep hill, eventually walking the bikes up a winding road.

'Fucking hell.' Shake plucked at the nape of his T-shirt which was soaking, rucked in wet folds. 'How much further? Why can't we just go to a beach?'

Rajiv smiled. 'We will.'

'Thank fuck for that.'

'Here,' said Rajiv ten minutes later. 'Here.' He dropped his bike on its side and stepped off the track, pushing into the bush.

Shake watched him, eyes narrowed against the sting of salt sweat. Rajiv disappeared, screened by curtains of balisier, thorn bush and wild pepper. Shake thought of snakes, of scorpions. Of a chalky landscape and the creak of a wheel. 'Hey! Wait a minute.' He stood at the edge of the bush, could feel the heat rising through his trainers, could see the blackness at the heart of the bush. Hear Rajiv grunting as he pushed at something. 'Wait!' Shake shoved into the foliage, not feeling the scratches on his arms and face, wanting to see Rajiv's slender back. The bush was dense, tangled; impossible to see where his feet were stepping.

Shake panicked, thrashed at paddle leaves which tilted at him as if asking a question. He stopped suddenly, sure he could hear movement. An invisible wetness flopped onto his ankle and Shake shook it off, roared with fear and pushed through the bush to find Rajiv on the other side, laughing at him, and at Rajiv's back was the wide wide world – or so it seemed.

'Shit,' murmured Shake, encountering the view of the northern ranges of Sansobella for the first time. Hundreds of feet below him the waters churned blue-black, unsettled, unhappy, almost, turning this way and that, trying to find a way out of the narrow Sansobella Passage. In the middle of the maelstrom was Frigate Island, which, according to Rajiv, was covered in bird shit. Behind the island were the blue-grey mountains, which fell away to the west. Shake shaded his eyes as Rajiv talked, pointing out the places they had been on Sansobella – where Chachalaca National Park was, where they had swum and surfed at Guachara. Explained the morphology of what they were looking at, the fact that Sansobella and St George existed at the peripheries of two tectonic plates, that the mountains of Sansobella were the result of subduction; that the Sansobella passage was a trench, a vast, near-vertical marine chasm.

'Look,' Rajiv said, and fished out the sullied napkin which had been wrapped around his roti. 'Look.' He tore the paper with his brown hands, yanked it apart. 'That is what happened at some time. The earth stopped pushing and opened up and that is why there is Sansobella and St George. Dorado is just a volcano on the fault line.'

But Shake hadn't listened to any of this; Shake was watching the clouds, watching the maddened water below him.

'It is beautiful, isn't it?' asked Rajiv, staring at Sansobella.

Shake looked at his friend, then, looked at his face, at his eyes. 'You mean Sansobella?'

'Yes. Of course.'

'Would you rather be there now? Right now?'

Rajiv sucked his teeth, shrugged. 'Maybe any other time. Yes.'

'I like it here,' said Shake. 'I like it here. On St George.'

'I know.'

Shake watched the local women again the next morning, as they climbed and hefted and yelped with laughter. He sat in the cane chair and watched them as they bent and stretched, watched the way their worn, washed-out dresses, soft as air, pale as dreams, folded around their thighs. Oblivious of the white boy, the women talked in gentle murmurs, or called out to their men, who were swinging scythes outside, clearing the encroaching scrub. Shake slumped in the chair, unmoving, the sounds washing over him, and perhaps it was the heat that made him feel sleepy, made him want to lie down and listen to the crooning voices. Women's talk, women's movements – the arc of an arm, the long curve of a hip – lulled him.

'Come, let us go now,' said Rajiv sharply. Shake's head snapped up and he saw his angular, skinny friend silhouetted in the door-way.

Again, they set off with towels and bottles of water, on the decrepit bikes, heading north, this time, to the drag-out, banana-shaped Grande Anse beach. This time the ride was level, and Rajiv had breath enough to shout to Shake as they cycled lazily, shoulder to shoulder.

'See? Here they are building what will be a fine hotel, the Oriole. It is being built with Sanso money. See the tower? That will have the best penthouse suite in the Caribbean. And down there,' they slowed for a backdigger, brakes squealing, as Rajiv pointed, his wheel wobbled and the two of them catspraddled on the track.

'Shit,' said Shake, rubbing an elbow. 'You arse.'

Rajiv laughed, remounted his bike and rode on, leading Shake along the sweep of Grand Anse beach, pointing again and again to plots where building was taking place. 'These beaches are close to Coral Strand and that is where people wish to spend their time. So Sansos are investing for the future. My father is considering buying some land and building on it. Or perhaps he will convert our summer house.'

Shake nodded as he slowed for another backhoe and a truck passed, loaded with sand and cement bags. After a couple of miles they came to Pillikin beach and the traffic disappeared. Shake cycled slowly, weaving a little on the deteriorating road, watching the pelicans flying in to settle on the pirogues in great crowds, rocking the boats. Eventually they came to the village of Sangaree, where Rajiv bought cold, cut coconuts and cake.

'This is the turn off to Killdevill. Over there,' Rajiv's voice sounded wet as he chewed the yellow jelly. He wiped his lips with the back of his hand, nodded across the road to a sweep of land, covered with coconut trees planted in rows, cattle grazing beneath the swaying, lean trunks, 'is the Huggins Estate, Pillikin Division. Look, can you see the estate house – up there, in the hills?'

'Oh yeah. What kind of estate is it?'

'A rich one. The Huggins family make rum, good rum. It is my father's favourite. They are white. The Huggins are white.'

'White?' Shake frowned.

'My father says they live as if time stands still. Every evening at five-thirty they have cocktails on their verandah, and someone plays the grand piano. They dress for it – you know, long dresses and tuxedos. Anyone can go as long as they are white. A lot of the ex-pats in Killdevill go every evening. My father says he cannot imagine what they can talk about. Seeing the same people all the time, what do they talk about?'

Shake stared up at the house, trying to imagine what went on there. Maybe it was like that film *Casablanca* or something?

'This is not their only estate – they have three others. My father says they are so rich it makes his eyes water. What is strange is that the first Huggins was a criminal. He was deported from England for stealing land and rebelling against the king. He was nothing but a common thief and yet he ended up a wealthy man.'

Shake frowned. 'Didn't we do something about this? In history? We did something last term about the Atlantic triangle. I can't remember.'

'No, I do not suppose you can. Come on.'

Again, the boys followed the coast road, nothing more than a wide, dirt track, heading to Gilbey beach. Shake saw huge villas and wooden shacks, sitting on neighbouring plots, cars driven by white men lolled towards them, dipping in and out of potholes, as local men strolled by the roadside, carrying cut-lasses, waving lazily to the boys as they passed. They pedalled through the villages of Polonaise, Fleischmanns, Vampiro and

Myers, arriving at Gilbey beach at midday. After a long swim and soak they lay in the shade and dozed. Shake woke up first, drank some water, lit a cigarette and sat in silence looking about himself. It seemed to him that the colours – the talc-white of the sandbanks on the horizon, the trees climbing the hills behind, the sand on which he was sitting – were more vivid than any he had ever seen. The only other people around were two fishermen, way down the beach, looping rope. Shake didn't know it then, but one of them was Mister Jeremiah, still young enough to haul in fish to feed his family. Behind the fishermen was a settlement of small houses, faded pink, powder blue and daffodil yellow, tended gardens dotted with bursts of flowers. A hand-painted sign tacked to a tree announced the name of the village: Tom Collins. Shake sat and watched the fishermen as he listened to waves breaking and thought he never been anywhere so fine, so complete.

Later that afternoon Rajiv led the way back to the Samaroo house, down the eastern side of the peninsula, which was scored with pocked crags, the coast battered by the waves of converging oceans. Through St Croix, Caipirinha, Craddock and Du Bouchett they cycled, and as they passed Tanager Bay, Rajiv pointed to the horizon. 'That's Dorado, the third island. As I said, it is a volcano.'

'Is it live? I mean, does it erupt?'

Rajiv wiggled his wide, slim shoulders, began to freewheel down a slight incline, his front wheel describing its odd ellipse. 'I believe it is active but it has not erupted for hundreds of years. There are many volcanoes in the Caribbean, Kick-em Jenny is not far, over in Grenada.'

'Who lives there? Who lives on Dorado?' Shake shouted as Rajiv flew down the slope.

'Film stars. Famous people.'

Film stars? Shake shrugged, stepped on the pedals and yelped as the chain slipped and the bike stuttered, throwing him forward.

The town on the southeast side of the peninsula, which marked Killdevill's limit, was Paria. Shake arrived at the crossroads sweating, his hip bone bruised by the handlebar. He lifted the hem of his T-shirt, wiped the sweat from his face, could feel salt crystals rasping against his nascent beard.

'We should hurry now, it will soon be dark and we have no lights.' Rajiv turned right, back onto the Pillikin Road which would take them home.

Shake, who was tired, who felt lazy, who wanted to be back on Gilbey beach, lying in the last of the late afternoon sun, began reluctantly to pedal, his back aching. He watched Rajiv pulling away from him, his friend's thin, wiry brown legs working. It must be about five-thirty, Shake thought, and he looked up to the hills on his left, where the Huggins' estate house sat, saw lights snapping on, tried to imagine men and women dressed in tuxes and dresses in this heat and it was then that he smelled it.

Shake squeezed the brakes, put his feet to the tarmac, flip-flops snagging, to stop himself. The smell. He turned and saw a stall across the road, snug in the shade of the trees, built of wood, near-invisible. Shake dropped his bike, walked across to the stall as if in a trance. He was confused because he was on another island, a dusty, arid island with a different sky, where olives grew and women drove donkey carts. He could hear singing and a woman with long hair laughing. Shake stood by the stall, his mouth open as the scent of wood smoke, salt and lemons enveloped him. More than that; something else. The woman behind the stall was sitting on a low stool, plaiting corn-rows in a baby's hair, her fingers moving slowly and surely. She glanced up at Shake, raised her eyebrows. Shake looked at the fruit and bottles of juice; picked up a bottle and opened it, smelt the pink liquid and he could hear his mother talking about Havana Club Tres Años.

'What is this?'

The woman looked at him sideways, her head cocked, lips unsmiling. The white boy looked strange, as if he had been at the weed. 'Is passion fruit with a little bit o' rum to lift it.'

'Passion fruit.' Shake sniffed at the bottle again.

'Is five dollah a bottle if yuh wan' it.'

Shake sniffed and he could see gnarled hands dipping into a barrel of feta, could feel oil spreading on his T-shirt.

'Hey – yuh wan' it, is five dollah.'

'Um – I don't have any money.' Shake looked up the road, into gathering darkness but Rajiv had gone.

The woman leaned over slowly, took the bottle gently from his hands and screwed the top back on, shrugged and opened her hands.

'I'll come back tomorrow – will you be here?'

'I here every day, baby, every day,' the woman crooned, return-ing to her tight plaiting.

'I'll be back.' But Shake never did visit the stall again; he had forgotten that the next day was Boat Race Day.

Shake was woken at dawn by the sound of rain lashing on the galvanize, beating out a rushing sound across the tin. He burrowed down in the sheets, tried to dampen the racket by pulling the pillow tight over his ears but still it rolled out a bass tattoo. He sat up, saw Rajiv still slept and wondered how. Crossing to the doors which opened on the gallery, he stepped in a puddle oozing across the floorboards, noticed the rain forcing its way between the slats of the shutters. Opening the louvres a crack, ignoring the sting of wind-driven drops, Shake looked out over Heavenly Cove below, barely able to make it out in the storm. Low, bullet-grey, near-black clouds careened across the headlands, the fronds of palm trees streaming in their wake, as sea-spray rose like steam from the beach. Shake stood and watched the storm pass, deafened and shivering as the wind chilled his damp skin. Eventually the noise changed to a minor, staccato drumming as the wind dropped and a pale grey strip appeared on the horizon. Shake skipped back to his bed, trying to avoid the long, slim rivulets of water which were inching along the worn boards, shook the rain from his long hair and lay down.

As water dripped from leaves and the racket on the roof became strangely syncopated music, Shake lay on his back, feeling the lumpy pillow growing damp. He felt alone, suddenly, and knew this was a thought he had been trying not to think for a long time. Felt the distance between himself and his family as a weight, felt the thousands of miles pushing on his chest, pinning him against the damp mattress. What was he doing here? On a tiny island in the middle of an ocean? No one knew he was there. His father and grandparents would think he was in Sansobella because he hadn't told them he wouldn't be. Shake began to breathe shallow, rippling breaths, as his skin prickled. No one knew he was there. The bare boards, the slatted windows, made him think of prison cells, of cages. He turned his head, his neck creaking, and stared at the sleeping Rajiv, whose hands were curled like petals beneath his chin. The sun slammed into the room as the wind dropped and rags of torn clouds drifted away. The temperature rose and Shake began to sweat, felt sodden, waterlogged. He threw the sheet back, walked around the room, opening the shutters, slamming them against the wall, watched steam rise as leaves fried, and then kicked the frame of Rajiv's bed.

'Hey! C'mon! It's Boat Race Day.' He tore Rajiv's sheet away, saw his friend's hard on and backed away. Backed away to the door, opened it and slipped out.

Vijay had to park the car more than a mile from Grackle Bay and the three of them walked to the public beach. Vijay and Rajiv walked ahead, shoving each other, shouting and laughing as Shake tagged along behind. The rest of the Samaroos were following later, to watch the boats from Queenstown come in. Shake was too busy monitoring his breathing to join the brothers; his ribs were falling and rising easy now, his lungs, those bloody air-filled sacs, gnarled with mushroom-like alveoli, were drawing in salty air without faltering. Nearing the beach the three of them felt the bass beat before they heard it, as they joined the crowd heading for the sands.

'Dey some bram,' said Vijay, who had stopped slapping at his younger brother, who stood tall, who stretched his shoulders. Vijay watched a Sanso girl glide by, passing white, Latin, almost, with olive skin, her long, tawny hair covering her naked back. 'Yuh got blues?' he asked Rajiv.

'Yes,' said Rajiv, whose eyes were also locked on the gentle curve of the girl's back, on the flat muscles on either side of her spine, noting the way they moved laterally with each step. Rajiv, his eyes still locked, felt in his pocket, pulled out a clump of ragged blue notes, each of them worth a hundred Essangee dollars. 'I got blues.'

'H'bout Danny Kyow?' Vijay swung his chin, unnoticed, at Shake.

'Him OK.'

'I see yuh by the snackette at what o'clock?' Vijay asked the question but barely listened to the answer, so busy was he with checking the line of his T-shirt, the lie of his thick, black hair.

'Tree o'clock. Us meeting mammy en, nuh?'

'Yuh be der.' Vijay moved away, tucking a comb into his back pocket, shimmying his hips a little, drifting after the Sanso girl, like a disinterested dog tracing a half-scent.

'Where's he going?' asked Shake, lurching as he was jostled by men with dreads, women suckling babies, girls with high breasts bunched beneath tight cotton blouses tied at the waist. He felt a hand pass over his buttocks, turned to see a young black woman, hair pulled back so tight it made her almond eyes cat-like, smile and then suck her teeth with a high, minor note. 'I thought Vijay was going to stay with us?' Shake glanced at the woman with the cat's eyes, who had stopped to lean against a thick bamboo pole, noticed she was missing two fingers on her left hand.

Rajiv laughed. 'Vijay stay with us? Yuh makin' joke? Him seekin' canal conch.'

'Eh?' Shake frowned – he had never heard Rajiv talk so.

Rajiv unravelled some blue notes from the ball of crumpled

money in his pocket. Flattened them and held them out to Shake. 'Here.'

'What's that?'

'It is called money.'

'Why are you giving me money?'

Rajiv smiled as if he knew more than Shake. Which he did. 'Two dog get daub.'

Shake, whose breathing was still troubling him, who had the horn, who was being shoved and banged about, who didn't want to look into cat's eyes, who did want to feel three fingers trace the line of his buttocks again, who felt marooned, said 'What's that mean?'

Rajiv laughed, glanced at faces in the crowd. 'All I am saying is you should look around for a while. There is a lot happening and if we try to stay together we will lose each other anyway. Come here.' Rajiv dragged Shake to a low wall, pointed down to Grackle Bay, the beach covered with bodies and tents and stalls. 'See that green and white striped tent over there?' Shake nodded. 'I shall meet you there at three o'clock. We will all be meeting there, to watch the boats come in.'

'I don't have a watch.'

'No one here has a watch.' Rajiv was exasperated. 'Ask a tourist, or look at the sun. You should know what o'clock it is in the day by now.'

Shake looked at Rajiv, saw in his friend's face an emotion he couldn't recognize, one he hadn't seen before. 'What time is it now?'

Rajiv shrugged. 'Maybe eleven o'clock.' He glanced at the crowds again, moved away, moved back towards Shake.

'OK,' said Shake. 'See you later.' He turned and pushed through the crowds, fighting against the flow of sweat-sleek bodies, pushed until he reached the periphery of the beach, where the belt of the crush was looser. He circled around the back of the crowd and came back to the low wall, where he sat, feet swinging, watching Rajiv with a crowd of boys. All of them Sanso, all of them Sanso East Indian. Shake could tell this by their clothes, their jewellery, their haircuts, the way they moved. Shake watched Rajiv change, change the way he walked and stood, the way he turned his body, arms folded, to talk to the sisters of the boys, as his toes curled and bit into sand.

'Yuh sure look t'irsty.'

Shake swivelled as the three-fingered woman slid onto the wall next to him, her hips coming to rest against his.

'Yuh buy I a beer,' she said, not looking at him.

'Uh, yes, of course. Where from?'

She jerked her thumb over her shoulder, pointing out a man standing by a dustbin filled with slush, ice and bottles of S&G beer. Shake clambered to his feet and joined the mêlée around the bin, all of them black and Shake felt fine; he'd been in Essangee for weeks, he knew how things worked, he could even understand some of what was being said. He compared his skin colour to those around him and it wasn't so different. Shake was pressed against the back of the young man ahead of him and he noticed for the first time the fine, endless tight spirals of short black hair, the dry-blue smoothness of the man's skin, the way beads of water sat on the skin. He focused on the hands of the vendor as they rummaged in the icy bin, pulling out dripping brown bottles, the labels slipping, sitting askew on the curved glass. Saw how big the man's hands were, the thumbs bending back from huge knuckles, scars running across the back of them. Scars everywhere, on all the men crowding him, pushing him backwards, elbows in his ribs, forcing him to the edge of the circle around the bin. Long, almost pink keloid scars on shoulders, a man with a healed welt on his arm, a slash above another's eye, running across his forehead. Why so many? Shake looked down and noticed wide, splayed, bare feet, the toes flat on the sand, spongy, almost. Yam foot, Rajiv disparagingly called them. And on the legs which were shuffling and flexing, yet more scars, flesh scooped out of shins by bamboo, slashed by glass or raked by coral. Shake was tall but he was no match for the men around him, who yelled at each other, at the vendor, at passers-by, and Shake didn't understand a word. In the distance, under the shade of a yellow poui, he could see a stall surrounded by tourists, their faces puce, burned, sucking at plastic glasses of beer, whose hands constantly checked the wallets in their pockets, or the money belts at their waists. Even from a distance Shake could see that their nervousness outweighed their happiness and he smirked, tried to stand in the loose, marionette manner of the men around him. Suddenly Shake found himself, he didn't know how, standing right by the vendor, a towering blue-black man, with thick, tangled dreads and wide shoulders. As he bent to pull out three beers with one of his vast hands, Shake was reminded of the chart in the biology lab in Redpath which showed the tendons and musculature of the human body. A man buying the beers counted out five ragged green notes, singles, taped together, browned at the edges, followed by a handful of coins, then pushed his way to freedom.

The vendor turned to Shake, said something.

'Uh, two beers, please.'

The scarred hand fished in the water, came up with a brace of bottles. 'Ten dollah.' The other hand was held out even as the vendor looked at the man behind, lifting his chin.

Shake knew this was wrong. The beers were two dollars each. 'Sorry?'

The vendor didn't even look. Clicked his fingers. Repeated 'ten dollah'.

Sweat was running down Shake's face and he wiped at it with his hand. 'I thought it was four dollars. I thought the beers were two dollars each.'

The vendor stood up tall, shoulders like boulders, as the men around Shake passed the story between themselves, like a biscuit tin, each man dipping in, each man having something to chew on, something to say.

'White price,' said the vendor.

Shake wanted to run, felt loneliness wrap itself around him once more. He wanted Rajiv there but knew Rajiv would never be there, at a local stall, would never allow himself to be served by a Rasta. And sitting on the wall was the woman with three skittering fingers, waiting for a beer. Shake pushed his hand into his pocket, tried to separate one note from the rest, but they were stuck together with sweat. He turned slightly only to find a wall of black skin and was forced to peel a blue note away from other blue notes as black and brown eyes watched. A rumble went through the crowd as Shake pushed two hundred dollars back into his shorts and held out a hundred. The vendor stared at him, took the note and held out the beers. Began to serve another man as the woman on the wall turned and searched for Shake with her almond eyes.

'Um,' Shake couldn't hear his own voice for the rushing in his ears, 'where's my change?'

'Huh?' The vendor cupped a pink palm around his black ear.

'Um, I think you owe me some change.' Shake didn't know why he was doing this; he had more money. He could walk away and hand the young woman a bottle, sit on the wall and watch the crowds and drink his beer. It wasn't even his own money.

The vendor looked at Shake. 'Yuh know what t'ought make ah man do?'

'Hey!' A bony man waved a skinny arm at the vendor. 'Him give yuh hundred, ent! Yuh pick out dey eye!'

'Is say yuh sayin' dey? Yuh playin' mad?'

The men began to yell, tendons standing proud on their necks, fingers jabbing hot air. All around Shake voices were rising, taking one side or the other. Some seemed to be saying Shake shouldn't be there – 'cockroach have no right in fowl party!' – that he should be with the other whiteys; others were bawling about the money, passing judgement on whether he should be paid his change. The vendor, who stood taller than anyone, fell silent, eased back his dreads, folded them in one of his enormous hands and gently coiled them back on his crown. He licked a thumb and finger, flashed notes swiftly from one hand to another and held out a bundle of red and green rusted notes to Shake, who took them and jogged away from the stall.

Sitting on the wall Shake could still hear the row rumbling on, rolling across the sands, across the ocean. His bare back felt vulnerable, as if words could scurry across the sands and lash him, make welts. The woman sipped at her beer, the froth making a tiny semicircle on her upper lip, as Shake checked the change the vendor had given him. Sixty-seven dollars. The two beers, which should have cost four dollars, had cost thirty-three. He shoved the notes into his pocket, discovered that the remaining two hundred dollars were missing and he lowered his head.

'Yuh okay fine, baby?' asked the woman, mussing his hair with her three-fingered hand.

Shake didn't know what to say. He chugged down his beer and stared at the waves coming in. Something had happened, was still happening, and he didn't understand it. His beer bottle was empty, white froth sliding down the brown glass and he wished he'd bought more. The pots and pans in the stalls on the beach were beginning to cook, belching out the scents of bhaji rice, salt fish choka, patchoi cheese, cascadura curry and cassava pone.

'What yuh call, baby?'

'Shake.'

'Shake, nuh? Der's a name. I call Ruby. Shake, baby, I tink yuh should hand me dollah and I fetch we beer.'

Shake dragged the tatty paper ball from his pocket and handed it over. Ruby delicately unravelled the knot of notes and straightened out four red singles, returning the rest.

'Dey only two dollah.'

A black hand slapped on Shake's thigh and he looked up to see the skinny man holding out a bottle filled with clear liquid.

'Doh min' Bluebottle. Is so he stop. Always him anger in two twos. Yuh got yuh dollah? Heah.' The man sat by Shake on the wall, handed over the bottle and motioned for Shake to drink. 'Bluebottle got problem with whiteys. Me? I no care. All people de same, yuh all is folks too. Heah.' The skinny man touched the bottle and smiled. Shake drank and his eyes watered as the puncheon rum, ninety per cent proof, clear as air, hot as fire, wormed its way to his stomach. 'Yuh heah on yuh own?'

'Nuh, him heah wid me,' said Ruby, handing Shake a beer. 'What yuh sayin, Bones? What yuh doin' getting' yuh hungry-lookin' self heah?'

'I jus' sayin' how's t'ings. Dis boy treat bad by Bluebottle. Him no get dollah change and dat hook me chile.'

Ruby laughed, threw back her head and laughed, showing white teeth, translucent as porcelain in the midday sun, stark against her lipstick. 'Oh hey? What yuh do, Bones? Yuh t'in like a horse whip and yuh holin' a few ever day, Rum Boo. Yuh hittin' for Bluebottle, nuh? How yuh could *talk* so?'

'T'iefin' from young boy is de wus.' Bones took the bottle back from Shake and swigged, the joints of his elbows slithering like marbles beneath his skin. 'Is dat I say.'

'Is whey yuh is?' asked another man as he joined them, touching knuckles with Bones, making Shake do the same. Behind him were two other beach boys, dressed in hot shirts and shorts, each holding a half-bottle of firewater. Bones made the introductions and soon Shake was surrounded by a press of black bodies, beers and rum being passed around as comments were made about Bluebottle and what they'd like to do to him: 'him in more trouble dan brong, wid his face set in beas'.' Shake sucked down burning balls of rum and tried to follow what was said.

'Whey yuh from, Shake?' asked Ruby.

'England.'

'Englan'? Maybe yuh know Baggy? Him a brudder of me.'

'Baggy? No, no I don't.'

'OK.'

Bones waved his empty bottle in the air. 'Hear dis talk. Bluebottle, him got hard ears but I tole he. Der been commesse and boderation but in dis heatment I say forgive he and less lime.'

'For dat!' shouted a beach boy, dumping his own empty bottle in the sand.

Shake found himself being watched by a circle of brown eyes; hooded or bloodshot, they were focused on him. A white couple, wearing straw hats and tightly cinched money belts, sandals strapped on their feet, edged past, looked at Shake and began to whisper to each other, shaking their heads slightly. Ruby sat with her hands in her lap, working her depleted fingers, staring out to sea.

'What?' asked Shake.

'Dey need drink,' said Ruby. 'Dey all working in idle hall and dey need more beer.'

Slowly, Shake understood, his mind crawled belly-first to an understanding and he stood up, swayed and staggered a few steps as he yanked the notes from his pocket. Ruby snatched them from him and handed out a few to Bones.

'Das dat,' she said.

'Yuh makin' joke, baby!' Bones licked a thumb and greased his pink palm with a swipe. 'Him drinkin' me rum.'

'Das dat,' said Ruby.

Bones took the notes, spat in the sand. 'In time, baby.'

'No hurry.' Ruby dragged Shake back on to the wall as the men wandered away, the beach boys grinding their hips, scuffing in the sand as they moved through the dancers on the beach, headed for a beer stall at the water's edge.

'So baby, how yuh doin'?' asked Ruby. 'Yuh want maybe to dance or go somewhere?' She ran a scarlet nail the length of Shake's thigh.

'I think I need to walk a bit.' The puncheon rum had punched a hole in Shake's guts, seemed to be leaking into his legs and chest.

Ruby helped him to his feet, looped an arm through his and propelled Shake away from the beach, away from the thudding bass notes and the smell of bubbling fat. Each step of the way, Ruby waved to friends, called out greetings, making sure people saw her with the handsome, young white man. Ivory trophy. On the south side of the worn, low headland, behind rows of cars, was an abandoned sugar storehouse, its coral walls still standing, rusted and pitted by spume. Ruby drew Shake into the shade, kicked a clearing out in the ground covered with bottles, tins and plastic bags, as Shake leaned against the wall, fighting the sense that his brain had separated into two deserted storeys, like an abandoned house.

'Come here, baby,' crooned Ruby, turning the young man round, looking at his tanned white skin, his grey-green eyes. 'Less have we some fun.'

Shake swallowed repeatedly as she pressed his palms hard against her breasts. He was still swallowing as she moved her hips against his, swinging them gently, brushing against him. It was the sensation of her three fingers wrapping around his cock that made him heave suddenly. Ruby, feeling the convulsion running through Shake's belly and ribs, jumped back, tripping on a snaggle of ground vine. Shake, bent double, hands on his knees, threw up a mess of raw alcohol and half-digested papaya as Ruby shouted, her bare feet spattered. His throat felt bloodied, as if it had been raked with a fork, as if it wanted to close but still Shake heaved. He was left hawking acid drool as Ruby walked out into the blinding sun, in search of a tap. Shake was oblivious to her leaving, his blurred mind concentrating on the act of ceasing to retch. He stumbled to a boulder, sat and rubbed at his eyes with the heels of his hands, swallowing yet again. The stench of his sick made him feel nauseous again and he stood gingerly, rubbing his stomach, walked out, squinted in the glare and saw a rocky cove blasted out of the headland by restless waves. Scrambling down to the water, he grazed his knee, scraped his knuckles, felt the sting as he waded into the murky water and sank beneath the waves. After scrubbing himself with damp sand, as he'd seen the old boys do, he sluiced himself and climbed back up the jagged slope, lay on a shadowy patch of the broad-leaved, scrubby grass and fell into a deep sleep.

It was the thunderous roar of a shark-prowed motorboat skimming into Grackle Bay that woke him, the prow beating out a boom as it slapped every wave head. Shake was confused, took moments to reassemble the facts of his existence, as cheers and blaring music rose from the beach. He had fallen asleep in the shade but the sun had dropped down the sky and now he was dripping with sweat, his hair and skin stiff with dried salt. Shake felt as if his body would creak and crack if he tried to sit. His mouth was filled with acid glue but his head and guts had cleared. He was ravenous but unable to move. Slowly, like hands of autumnal chestnut leaves drifting in a breeze, floating down to settle on dark soil, he remembered the argument with the beer man, the drinking of puncheon rum, the shame that followed. He remembered, too, sneering at the herds of pale people milling about with their white-price beer. Eyes still closed, Shake thought, pieced together, *stitched* together, a picture of what had happened. Realized, suddenly, too late, that Rajiv had not wanted him to meet his Sanso friends. At this realization, Shake opened his eyes, took in the fact of the sun having slipped. He turned on his back and stared at the choreographed wind-dance of palm leaves against a cerulean sky. Rajiv was embarrassed by him, even though he was white. Shake lay beneath the palms and tried to accommodate the idea that Rajiv didn't want to be English, or German or American. Rajiv wanted to be East Indian Sanso. Rajiv didn't want white skin and Shake realized, then, that he had always assumed Rajiv did.

Shake followed a sandy track down to Grackle Bay, passing families picnicking, stopping a tourist to ask the time, dreaming of a bottle of ice-cold water. Motorboats began to converge on the bay, engines screaming, as they fought for second place and Shake could see the Samaroos setting up their table by the green and white tent. A tall man with the muscles of a man in a poster hanging in Redpath College, dreads tied in a mad knot, leaned against a palm, a thick joint billowing smoke at his lips, a man who turned to look at him. Shake recognized Bluebottle and began to jog, jogged down the beach and forced his way through the mass of jigging, dancing bodies, jogged all the way back to the safety of the pale-skinned Samaroos.

'Hello – are you OK?' asked Rajiv.

'Fine.'

'Here.' Rajiv handed Shake a frozen beer.

'Is there any water?'

Rajiv looked at him and smiled. 'You want water? What happened to you?'

Shake shrugged. 'Nothing. I'm thirsty, that's all. I'm just thirsty.' He swigged at the beer, nearly gagged, gestured towards the shoreline. 'Who won the race?'

Rajiv frowned. 'A boat sponsored by someone called Kouranis. My uncle came second.'

The afternoon dragged on, Shake willing the sun to fall beneath the horizon as he sipped at water and watched the crowd for the minefields that were his new friends, but none appeared – no bones and no rubies.

That night, as the two boys lay in darkness, listening to the sloughing of the wavelets on Heavenly Cove, Shake asked, 'You awake?'

'Yes.'

'Can I ask you something?'

'Mmmm.'

'This morning, on the way to the beach, after Vijay had parked?'

'Mmmm.'

'He called me Danny Kyow. I heard him call me that. What's it mean?'

Shake heard Rajiv's bed creak as he turned over, heard Rajiv breathe, imagined he could hear Rajiv think, come to a decision. A Sanso decision as it turned out: 'Albino. "Danny Kyow" means albino.'

RAJIV

Rajiv walks, smiling, into his office, dapper as ever, and sets his briefcase carefully on his now-cleared desk. Already this morning I have conducted two meetings – here it is possible to arrange such things. To the minute. I walk out of my house and the car and driver are waiting for me; I say I will see someone at twelve thirty-five and at that time there is a knock on my door. This attention to . . . detail, to time, makes business easy. In Sansobella and St George? *Rajiv raises his shoulders, turns his dainty hands back and forth.* I arrive for a meeting only to be told that the manager has gone out, to come back. When? I might ask. When will he be back? Thursday, I am told, but without certainty. *Rajiv laughs but there is a tiny grating edge to this laugh, which suggests that this attention to detail might make business easy but life itself a little more difficult.* So – where was I? I have been thinking about my friend a great deal. You say you want a picture of Shake, but he is not an easy man to sketch. Perhaps none of us is. After that summer, the one I mentioned, when Shake and I went to Essangee, as Sansobella and St George is called, our friendship changed a little. I think he learned a great deal that summer. You may think it fanciful, but I think Shake began to learn a little about privilege, learned a little about poverty. He fell in love with island life; learned to watch out for snakes and scorpions and caiman, learned to be wary of rip tides.

I also think he learned, too, when to be silent and how to be vain. You see? I warned you I might become fanciful and yet I am not a fanciful man. When we returned to Redpath College, Shake was more . . . likeable, less brittle. As I said, our friendship changed because he did not need me any longer; he had learned how to make friends with other people. But he knew I was always there. That he could come to my study, in his messy uniform, tie undone, hair too long, and I would always be there. I was there because I was always working. I would have preferred to take the baccalaureate but in Redpath we could only take A levels. Shake did enough work – just enough – to pass his exams and we went to the same university. It was there that he began to work for me and our relationship changed yet again. *He pours himself a glass of jasmine-scented green tea, sips at it.* Shake knew what he was doing when he became chameleon island boy – he changed to become whatever people wanted him to be and so he was popular. I was not popular because I worked hard, because I was admired by the teaching staff. At school it had not mattered but at university the students were different. More judgemental. They had different values. And I was not popular because I was not white. It was a long time ago and attitudes have changed, not enough, certainly, but in those days I was too dark for most students' taste. Shake would come often to my room in halls, to talk, or simply to lie on the bed and drift away. He had these quiet times when he would drift away, as if he had gone somewhere else. He told me once that he was building fences in his head, told me some strange tale about a little boy who had died in Cyprus. I could never make sense of it. Many people thought Shake was like an open book, as the English say. As if he were lying open on a table, waiting to be read and understood, but they were wrong. When we went to university, as far as I was concerned my childhood was over. For Shake, I think it had just begun. Once we had graduated Shake worked for me. For a while I think he entertained notions of becoming a writer, a journalist. *Again, Rajiv smiles.* Imagine it: Shake as investigative journalist. I remember that he went to visit his father when the exams were over – I had to lend him the money for the airfare. *Rajiv touches his chin with manicured fingertips.* He never repaid me and now I am pleased that he did not. When Shake came back, I remember him telling me that his father had laughed when Shake told him he wanted to be a journalist. I hardly knew his father and I knew he did not like me. *Rajiv shrugs.* But I laughed too. He could never plan, Shake could never project into the future. Every day he earned what he needed for that night when I was planning for the next week, the next year. But it hardly mattered because then he met Emma. I liked her but sometimes I wonder what would have happened if he had not met her. I wonder what would have happened if I had not had to return to Sansobella and assume responsibility for the family and then Shake would not have met Emma. There is a saying in Sansobella. 'If shit was sugar, farmer wouldn'-a plant cane'. There is no point in me asking 'what if' of something that happened so long ago that it no longer has meaning. Emma and I had much in common: we both planned, looked forward to the future, thinking we could shape it. Emma's misfortune was that she fell in love with a boy, not a man. She bought cat in a bag. Shake's childhood went on for ever. Or, rather, it would have done but for what happened in Aspen. *Rajiv falls silent, fingers the knot of his tie, staring at the papers on his desk.* Shake arrived one day at my house in Sansobella. I returned from work to find him sitting at the gate. I had not seen him for many years, perhaps ten years, and he looked old and worn, what we call qualebay. He was proppin' sorrow and need help, as we say, so I took him in and then I took him to St George, set him up there. My wife, she never understood Shake, she judged his book by his cover. She thought he was a bum, a scrunter, but she never knew him. I visited Shake often, spent weekends on St George with him but I always went alone. I would not take my wife or children, and I would not stay with Shake, I always booked a hotel room. I could not stay with him because he was still too . . . messy. Everything was always unfinished. Maybe it will stay that way now, for Shake. Forever unfinished. We spent the days fishing, or sometimes we took towels and an icebox down to Heavenly Cove and watched the pirogues coming in. My wife, she always maintained that Shake asked for money; she could not understand that I offered it, that I forced him to take it, so he could plan, so he could make something of himself. *His tea finished, Rajiv puts the glass back on the tray. Walks to the window, looks out.* Here they call Frankfurt the American city. They say it is more like America than Germany. When I was planning to emigrate, planning to leave Sansobella, I considered moving to America, taking my family there. But remembering how I have been treated there, in airports, in restaurants, by people who think I must be carrying a bomb rather than a laptop, I decided to come back here. I have always believed that leaders should lead by example and not exception. I look at America and I think about that, which is why I am here. I wish Shake had come with us. I asked him to come with us. I met him for breakfast at the Kiskadee just before we left and I asked him to come with us to Frankfurt. *The cityscape of scrapers fades and Rajiv can see a reef with waves breaking, frothing, in the distance, pirogues bouncing in the swell.* I warned him what was happening but Shake did not listen because he did not want to hear. He did not want to hear about his little paradise falling apart. I watch the television every night now, I watch BBC World News and I see Queenstown burning, see the blood of my people being spilled. I am fortunate, my family is fine, is safe. But I wonder if my country will survive? How long is it now? Since Shake disappeared? It must be a week. *Rajiv folds his dainty hands together, as he thinks of distant sirens and strobe lights.* Last night I felt something slip away from me as I tried to sleep. As if something had ceased to exist.

1980–1984

In the late summer of his eighteenth year, Shake was stunned when he called his grandparents from a public phone box in a pub in Cornwall, where he was camping with friends from school, to discover that he had managed to achieve grades which allowed him to study at the same university as Rajiv. Rajiv was in Sansobella with his family, and Shake had to wait until he returned to his grandparents to make the long-distance call to share the news, his grandfather pacing in the hall, pointing at his watch as the boys talked. Eventually, overcome by the thought of the cost of Shake's voice travelling thousands of miles, his grandfather cut the connection.

At the end of September, Shake travelled down to Exeter by bus, with a rucksack crammed with clothes, a Sony Walkman and a cheque from his grandmother to see him through the first term. Rajiv was driven down by an uncle and aunt, arriving at the halls of residence with three bulging cases.

'What've you got in those?' asked Shake, as he lay on Rajiv's bed, smoking, brushing ash off the ornate bedspread given to Rajiv by the aunt, watching his friend unpack.

'Books. We were given a long reading list for the summer.'

'Oh, OK.'

'Did you have a good summer?' Rajiv began to place the books on shelves, switching them around, arranging them alphabetically.

'Yeah, it was great. I lived with Oli and his family in Wimbledon. We got jobs in a make-up factory for a month, to get some money together, and then went down to Padstow with Henry. Y'know? From D House? We were down there for three weeks, camping. It was bloody brilliant. Got pissed every night and went to the beach every day. And there were girls everywhere, crawling out of the woodwork.'

'What was the factory like?'

Shake looked at Rajiv, who was bent over the desk, trying to plug in a worklamp. He thought that Rajiv had put on weight, looked soft at the edges. 'The factory?'

'Yes.'

Shake shrugged. 'It was alright. I got thirty-five quid a week for eight to five, Monday to Friday. But Oli and me were the only guys there, which made it OK.'

'Was it automated?'

'What?'

'Was the assembly line automated?'

'I don't know. Yeah, I suppose so. There were hoppers. What difference does it make?'

'I have been reading about the developments in automation.' Rajiv was taking a degree in economics and business studies, a course chosen by Mr Samaroo, when in fact he should have been reading English, his understanding of cadence and sub-text being finer than most. Instead it was Shake who was the English student.

'Gripping stuff. How was Sansobella? What did you do?' Shake had wanted to return to the islands but his father had refused to pay the fare, claiming not to have enough money.

'Vijay was married in August, and we went to St George for Boat Race Week. I studied at home a lot and worked with my father. It was a quiet summer.'

'What was Boat Race Day like?'

'My cousin won the race by two and a half minutes, followed by one of Kouranis' boats.'

Shake lay on the bed and stared at the small, white ceiling of the modern room. For the first time he had the sense that whilst he and his best friend were talking about the same subject they were saying different things. Rajiv checked his watch.

'We should go. The vice principal is talking to us all at four o'clock, in the sports hall.'

'Is he?'

'Yes.'

Shake rolled off the bed. 'Shitty little rooms, aren't they?'

Rajiv looked around himself, raised his eyebrows. 'They are clean, functional. There is a communal kitchen down the hall and we each have our own shower. I think it is alright.'

Shake spent the time of the vice principal's speech looking at the other students, scanning the rows of fresh-faced first-years, trying to work out what they were like, as Rajiv took notes. As the hundreds of hopefuls poured out onto the hockey pitches when the vice principal was done, Shake asked Rajiv if he wanted to come to the union bar.

'There's a couple of blokes I met last night. They're a real laugh and we arranged to meet in the Ram at six to play pool.'

'But,' Rajiv fished in his pocket and pulled out a sheet of A4, 'at six o'clock we have been invited to meet our lecturers and fellow students. Look.' Rajiv pointed to the timetable.

'Yeah, but, well. I mean, we'll meet them soon enough, won't we?'

Rajiv looked at Shake. 'It is your decision. If you change your mind, the English faculty is over there.' He pointed to a distant, redbrick building. 'I am going to my meeting.'

'Well, I'll see you later. I'll come by your room.'

Shake didn't see Rajiv for four days, didn't see him until they bumped into each other in the coffee bar at Cornwall House.

The summer break had been three months long, not long enough for the motherless Shake and the East Indian Sanso to grow apart, rather it was long enough for each to become more of that which they had always been.

The terms rolled by and became years. Shake, within a few weeks of arriving at Exeter, worked out the person he wanted everyone to think he was: he was surfer boy before they existed. His black hair was long and tousled, in winter he wore old Levi's, torn at the knee, his always-tanned skin showing through, long, baggy jumpers or faded sweatshirts, with ragged cuffs. In summer he wore denim shorts and thin white T-shirts to emphasize the colour of his skin and often walked barefoot. Shake remembered the cool Sanso boys, and he wore bracelets, wore his shorts low on his hips. He carried one pen in his back pocket, one folder with paper and one book when he could be bothered. These he would leave on the shelves of pubs, or by a girl's bed, or in friends' rooms. And Shake had plenty of friends; people he knew, or who wished they knew him, waved to him in lecture theatres, called to him across the street, yelled from passing cars. Because Shake could be whatever anyone wanted; he joined a crowd and fitted right in. He could get along with the Wellies, the rugger buggers, the public school crowd, the artists, the hippies, the small bands of punks and drunks, and he could do this because they all wanted him to like them. Because Shake was cool, hip. He reinvented himself over and over, folding in on himself like a petal, closing as one flower and opening as another. He was invited to dinner parties with the wealthy students living in rented houses in Topsham, or cottages in the villages around Exeter. He went to parties in the shabby student houses around Springfield Road and Heavitree, and he would find himself rolling a cigarette, sitting on a chair, legs crossed, barefoot, drinking cans of Carlsberg Special, with women sitting on the filthy carpet, gazing up at him and he'd wonder if he had glitter cascading around him. Shake lost his virginity during his first week at university, at one of these parties, lying on a young woman who was herself lying on a pile of coats, his foot jammed against the door as his new-found friends hammered at it, yelling obscenities. Sex became another recreation, like pool and darts, or surfing at Newquay. Shake had girlfriends for a night, a week, a month at most, and then moved on. Often he would have to sit in the Ram or DH or the Queen Vic, and look concerned as he listened to the friends of an ex-girlfriend trying to persuade him to just talk to Sarah or Jane or Maddy, to just explain what went wrong. Often, Shake ended up in bed with these friends.

At the start of the second year, Shake moved out of halls and into a room in a shared house, where he lived in squalor because he had never had to cook or clean or wash his own clothes. At Redpath the boys were catered for, at home his grandmother cared for him, so he had no experience of caring for himself. He lived on Marmite sandwiches and tea drunk from tannin-stained mugs. In the evenings he would buy a pasty in the pub, wash it down with beer. Girlfriends would take his clothes to the laundrette, or sometimes try to impress him by asking him over and serving up pasta or vegetable rice and always he slept in their rooms.

Shake spent three years partying, playing pool, drinking and having sex. Often he was called up to speak with his professor or the director of studies, but always he managed to churn out just enough under-researched work to get by under threat. Girlfriends would lend him essays to rewrite, or dictate essays for him as he scribbled. The pints of beer, the trips to London for weekends, the tickets for gigs in the Pit, the late-night burgers in Banana's, were expensive and every term Shake ran out of his grand-mother's money within weeks. Then he would go to see Rajiv.

Rajiv Samaroo was a model student, industrious and driven. Rajiv never moved out of the halls of residence because they were near the library and faculty buildings and he went to every lecture, every seminar, as Shake slept his mornings away in one bed or another. He assisted the department with its research and attended every talk given by doctoral research students. Most evenings during the week he sat in the library until it closed at nine o'clock, reading and making notes. He still did not drink and he had given up smoking, having calculated the cost of doing so. He never went out at weekends, instead he holed up in his room, poring over balance sheets. Sometimes he saw Shake, walking up Prince of Wales Drive, or sitting on the grass outside DH, or lining up a shot over a pool table in the Ram as he, Rajiv, sipped orange juice and read the *Telegraph* and the *FT*. Rajiv played squash three times a week in an attempt to reduce his ever-expanding waistline, wrote letters to his mother in Sansobella, played bridge on Friday nights with a group of like-minded students, learned chess and joined the Young Conservatives, who were not as welcoming as they might be; Rajiv was, after all, a little on the dark side.

Rajiv knew why Shake came to his room in halls to see him, knew that Shake needed money but Rajiv also knew that Shake could come to visit and be himself, that Shake didn't have to try to be anyone he was not. Sometimes they would go out for a walk down by the derelict, deserted docks and walk along the river, and all the time Shake could be himself. If Shake needed a tenner, for a bus ticket to London or to repay a personal debt, Rajiv would give him the money. If his friend needed more than that, a hundred pounds to clear an overdraft perhaps, or the next month's rent, then Rajiv made him work for the money. On one occasion, Rajiv was woken by the warden of the halls and had to take himself to the police station to fetch Shake, who had been charged with being drunk and disorderly (he had been drunk as a skunk, and arrested for throwing light bulbs at passing buses). Rajiv posted bail, took Shake back to halls and tidied him up, returned him to court the next morning and paid the fine of fifty pounds. And then he told Shake he had to work off the debt.

On the evening of his son's departure for Exeter for his first year's study, Mr Samaroo, in his wisdom, had given him, first, ten thousand pounds, and, then, a challenge. If Rajiv could double or more than double the ten thousand during his undergraduate years, he could keep whatever sum he made. If, however, he failed, he would be obliged to repay the full ten thousand. Rajiv accepted both the money and the challenge. On his arrival in Exeter, Rajiv, instead of meeting people in the Ram to play pool, spent a day examining the properties on offer in the estate agents' windows. He then spent a further day scanning the ads in the local paper for rooms to rent. He studied the message boards in CH and DH, where students pinned sad slips of paper, torn from A4 lined pads, written in biro or pencil, pleading for the opportunity to live in a room somewhere in the city and offering to pay good money for the privilege. Rajiv opened two bank accounts, invested the money and waited, and whilst he waited his fingers flew over the pad of his calculator. When the Falklands hostilities began to fizzle and spark, property prices fell and Rajiv dressed in a bespoke suit, tailored in the traces of Snake Alley in Queenstown, went to one of the four high street banks and lied through his teeth. Within two months Rajiv was a landlord, although none of his fellow students knew it. His mortgage repayments were two hundred and twenty pounds a month, his income from the three-storey, dilapidated Victorian terraced house was three hundred and ninety. Rajiv revisited the bank at the beginning of his second year and this time he did not have to dissemble. He had already arranged a loan through his uncle with an Indian co-operative mutual company, a loan running at 5.2 per cent as compared to the base rate of 8.25 dictated by the Bank of England. With the loan, raised against the collateral from his first house, he bought another property. With the overdraft authorized by the bank, also raised against the collateral from his first house, Rajiv started his first – but not his last – business. This was why Rajiv never went out at weekends. As Shake was dancing to Siouxie and the Banshees' 'Christine' in a bar somewhere, shimmying his slim hips to the beat, drinking beer and waving a pool cue, or jumping about to Echo and the Bunnymen in the Pit, Rajiv was in his small, white cuboid room, crunching numbers as he tried to second guess first Geoffrey Howe and then Nigel Lawson, the Chancellors of the Exchequer.

Rajiv Samaroo was not white, nor was he passing white, but he had lived in England for long enough as a student, reading the papers, walking the streets, watching the privileged students of Exeter University at play, to understand a little of their mind-set. The English, he decided, liked to party – not like Sansos at Carnival or *Mas*, not like Sansos at Boat Race Week or Long Weekend, or Spring Bling or Easter on St George, when everyone came together in a celebration of wealth and music and sun and surf. No. The aim of the English was to reward themselves at birthdays or weddings, graduations or funerals by getting drunk. They even rewarded themselves for experiencing good fortune – pay rises, bonuses, share dividends from privatization – which seemed to Rajiv absurd. But nevertheless, they did this, they rewarded themselves by throwing parties. About the display of ostentatious wealth, Rajiv knew a lot; he was, after all, East Indian Sanso. Midway through his second year at Exeter, Rajiv used his loan to buy two vans, arranged a subcontract agreement with a firm renting marquees and he set himself up as an events organizer and it was Shake who drove the vans, Shake who erected the frames for the canvas and laid the duckboards for the birthday parties and graduation ceremonies of the wealthy students. For these days of humping poles and wood, setting up trestle tables and cable for lighting, manoeuvring Portaloos in place, Shake was paid between fifteen and twenty pounds. Usually he didn't see the money as it was owed to Rajiv. He didn't see Rajiv either, as his friend was still sitting in the white cuboid room in halls, working out how much money he had amassed that week.

Rajiv Samaroo doubled the ten thousand, on paper, within months of flying out of Queenstown. He left Exeter with a first-class degree in economics, a citation and a glowing reference from the department, three houses in Exeter, two in Bristol, a flat in a shabby area of Fulham and a balance of two hundred pounds in his bank account and thirty pounds on his no-longer slim frame. His net worth, however, was in excess of two hundred thousand pounds. On paper. Because his actual cash assets were merely two hundred pounds, Mr Samaroo insisted that Rajiv pay him back the ten thousand. Rajiv sold the first house he had bought for twenty-one and a half thousand pounds, the crumbling three-storey Victorian terrace in Exeter, and made a profit of twelve thousand, which he handed over to his father with a smile, explaining the extra two thousand was interest paid.

Shake left Exeter University with a hangover, a third-class degree, an overdraft of twelve hundred pounds and a dose of the clap.

Shake had not seen his father for more than two years, and he was shocked when he saw his father waiting at the arrivals gate in Larnaka airport, because Donald looked so much older than his forty-eight years. His father looked emaciated, his face scored by sun and time and smoke. The shirt he wore hung on scarecrow shoulders and his hair was too long. Father and son hugged briefly, and Shake could feel his father's scapulae moving beneath thin skin like bat wings. Again, he was reminded of the biology lab in Redpath, where a yellowed skeleton hung in the corner. The skeleton, Shake remembered, was called Charlie and wore a school scarf around the horny vertebrae of its neck, grinning insanely the meanwhile. Walking out into the arid, dust-blasted heat of the Cypriot summer, Shake followed his father to the car, noticing the angularity of the movement of his father's frame. The inside of the small Honda was baking and Shake hung his hand out of the open window as they made their way west along the rutted highway, swooping his fingers up and down in waves.

'How long are you staying?' asked Donald.

'A month.'

'Diana is here.'

'Is she?' Shake hadn't spoken to his sister for months.

'Yes. With some drip of a boyfriend called Alistair or Alex or something. She's taken Jesus into her life and I blame him. Alistair, I mean, not the good Lord.'

'Oh shit.' A God-squadder in the family.

'So you managed, after three years, to get a third-class degree?'

'Hmm.'

'Hardly impressive.' Donald threw the car to the right and swerved around a truck, as he said, 'It's a shame you couldn't get a flight into Paphos because I've moved. I'm renting a house in Lemba now because I couldn't stand living in Limassol any more.'

'I didn't know you'd moved.'

'I wrote to you about it.'

'Don't think I got the letter.'

Donald slowed to join a long tailback of cars, halted by massive roadbuilding and earthworks, and a film of dust began to settle on the car. The queue inched along, orchestrated by ill-timed light changes, as Donald explained that he now worked on a development outside Paphos, where the English were buying time-share homes in their thousands. Shake looked at the glaring streaks of white concrete slashing the hills to the north, one concrete box being bolted onto another.

The journey to Lemba took four hours, what with roadworks, funded by the EU, scarring the coast, and a stop to buy bottles of water and skewers of rosemary-scented lamb on the way. It wasn't until they turned off the main road to drop down into the small village, the Mediterranean glittering on the horizon, that Donald announced that the second Mrs Knight had left him and was filing for divorce.

'On the grounds of unreasonable behaviour apparently, which comes as something of a surprise to me. I was going to write to tell you but I didn't want to disrupt your studies for your finals. It would seem the concern was wasted.' Donald stopped the car by a high white wall, slid open a heavy iron gate and parked the car in the shade of a lemon tree.

'You're getting divorced?' Shake pulled his rucksack off the rear seat and shouldered it.

'So it would seem. Diana is, of course, very distraught about the whole thing. She wants to get in touch with my soon-to-be ex-wife and effect a reconciliation. I haven't the heart to tell your sister that she's living in sin with a local plumber. Unreasonable behaviour, my backside. So Diana prays for us instead.'

The house in Lemba was an old single-storey building, with extensions that appeared to have been added randomly, with no thought to comfort. The room Donald gave Shake had been built on the outside wall and no door had been knocked through to the interior of the house, so Shake had to go outside and round to the sliding doors at the back whenever he wanted to use the bathroom or fetch a beer from the kitchen. Shake threw his rucksack on the bed and went to find his father, who was pouring a glass of ice-cold retsina for himself.

'Diana and the Wimp have gone into Paphos to visit the museum.' Donald looked his son up and down, took in the long hair, the single hoop earring and the tatty jeans and sneakers. 'I can't imagine you'll be spending your days quite so productively. What will you do whilst you're here?'

Shake shrugged. 'Can I have a beer?'

'You're twenty-one now. You can do what you damn well like.'

Having opened a large bottle of Kēo, Shake went outside to join his father, sat at the table and looked around himself. The house, Shake thought, was a great improvement on the soulless box in Limassol. There was a view over the sea and no neighbours. The garden ran down to a dry river bed, and from the gallery, shaded by a riot of grapevines, he could see the site of some kind of archaeological remains.

'I take the car to work every day so if you want to go to Paphos, there's a bus service from the main road. It's only a few miles but please don't hitchhike. There are two bars here in the village, one down by the crossroads and one a little further on the left, heading down to the sea. There's a small shop up the road on the right, where you can buy beer and cigarettes. Do you have any money, Sammy?'

The sound of his childhood name surprised Shake. Sammy was the boy who went where he wasn't supposed to, the boy who looked over a river bank and saw a pair of pale blue eyes. Shake built fences. 'I've got a little bit, about a hundred quid. I did some work for Rajiv last week.'

'Ah, Rajiv. An example to us all,' said Donald, pouring himself another retsina from the bottle he had brought to the table. 'Bloody Thatcherite,' he remarked mildly.

Sammy could think of no reply and so he slowly drank his beer as he watched his father reading the newspapers Shake had brought from London, wondering if the decision to visit Cyprus had been mistaken.

The next day, when his father had gone to work and Diana and the Wimp had taken a local bus to Kourion, Shake prowled around the house, checking out all the rooms (Diana and her boyfriend were, it appeared, sleeping separately), looking in cupboards and drawers. His father, it would seem, lived like a monk – bar the drinking. In the living room he found Donald's old gramophone, a Bush turntable and speakers of which he was very proud. Still working twenty-five years after it was bought in England and shipped out. Next to it, leaning against the wall, were the vinyl albums Shake remembered from his youth: Chet Baker, Cannonball Adderly, T-Bone Walker, Ella Fitzgerald, Etta James, the covers dog-eared and peeling. On a scratched, battered sideboard he saw the framed pictures of his mother. Beatrice leaning out of the stable door in the little fisherman's cottage, laughing, pointing at the photographer. Beatrice asleep in the grass, her arms around both of her children, who were snuggled into her side. Beatrice smiling into the sun, sitting on the eroded capital of a toppled column in the midst of an earthquake-shaken site, the distant sea a dull grey in the photograph, so old it was black and white. Oddly, it was this monochrome image that triggered in Shake memories of broiling Sundays spent fossicking in unmanned, unguarded sites along the south coast. Diana and he squatting on the dusty ground, picking amongst the stones and debris, unearthing small, broken figurines, as Beatrice gently brushed and dug away at the compacted soil, hoping to reveal mosaics. Donald lying on a blanket in the shade, sleeping as his family dug out fragments of history. And the spoils of those days fossicking, Shake saw, were scattered about on the shelves above the photographs. Small, primitive terracotta fertility goddesses, patches of fragile mosaic, the lip of an urn, traces of black and white pigment still visible. The brushes and trowels Beatrice had used were stacked in a wooden box by the radio. Of the second Mrs Knight there was no trace in the house. Against the opposite wall Donald had put a bookcase, and in the silent, isolated heat of the morning, Shake began to take the books down, one by one, to examine them. He found work by Mann, Orwell, Kafka and Camus, Ginsberg, Bellow, Updike and Salinger, many of them with his mother's name written and dated on the inside cover. On the bottom shelf he unearthed a battered copy of the *Savoy Cocktail Book*, its cover torn, the pages stained with splashes and teardrops of juice and alcohol, all the stains brown now, sepia, as if the past had become entirely monochrome. He saw from the inscription that it had been a wedding present from his father to his mother: 'To my beloved Beatrice on our wedding day. Perhaps by the time we are old and grey we shall have had enough time to sample each and every one? Je t'aime. Donald, 17 March 1963.' The book fell open at a page where a limp, discoloured bookmark had adhered to drops of a sugar-laden liquor: PLEASE LAY ME DOWN WITH EARS FLAT! Shake closed the book and put it back on the shelf, walked out of the house, out through the gate and into the village of Lemba.

The village was small, the houses shuttered against the heat, turning blind eyes to the road. Shake walked the streets slowly, walking in shade when he could. Dropping down the road, he found the ruins he had noticed from the gallery, a few low walls and stone gullies. A phalanx of people were kneeling in a row, scraping gently at the top soil, within sections marked off with wooden pegs and string. Others were over on the other side of the site, poring over blueprints, arguing quietly amongst themselves. Shake stopped at the edge of the site, reading notices pinned on a pole. It transpired that the project was being run by the University of Edinburgh, the aim being to unearth what they could about the earliest known settlements on the island, from the Chalcolithic period, whatever that was. Also, they were trying to recreate the strange roundhouses the settlers had lived in, using foundations and fragments of artwork as guides. A small group was sitting in the shade, drinking water, and Shake went over to introduce himself. It turned out that they all knew Donald, who had been helping the project leader with the physics of engineering a round dwelling. The students were from all over Europe, volunteers spending a month helping excavate the site in exchange for food and a tent and free weekends. This discovery saved Shake from boredom – not to mention the company of his sister. He'd stroll down in the afternoons and help them carry bags of debris to the edge of the site, or lift the long, seasoned logs which would comprise the roof. He learned about the rudiments of building and the history of tilemaking and setting; he became involved in the act of building the roundhouse, and at the end of the day he would stand back, as the sun slowly lowered itself to the horizon, and scan the results of his labour. Occasionally in the evenings he sat with the volunteers in the bar on the crossroads, where the group spilled out onto the street, drinking cold beers, watching the activity in the village. Inevitably, there was a woman who fell for him, a tall, black-haired student of classical civilization, called Joan, and Shake woke up next to her some mornings, wondering where he was as he looked at the green, billowing walls of her tiny tent.

During that month at the end of his university days, Shake found himself soon following a routine. He woke long after his father had gone to work, usually to find his sister had already left on a mission of self-improvement, shoulder bag packed the night before, the Wimp trailing in her wake. Shake showered, made himself coffee and then sat out on the gallery for a few hours, his feet up on a chair, reading. Perversely, having just finished his English degree, Shake developed the habit of reading that late summer. He'd make himself some lunch and then walk down to join the students at the dig, making sure he was back by five-thirty, because he had also developed a taste for making cocktails, which his father adored. Donald brought back from shopping trips on the way home from work increasingly exotic and undrinkable liqueurs and Shake would select a drink from the *Savoy Cocktail Book*, mixing and muddling the ingredients in order to make sense of them. Sometimes Diana and the Wimp joined them, if they had returned from their day trip, to sit at the table drinking water or juice as neither of them touched alcohol. Donald, whose memories of the fisherman's cottage, of life in London with Beatrice, were stimulated by the drinks, would turn on the gramophone and select some jazz or blues to play. Noticing that Shake had spent a couple of nights out, and guessing where his son had been, he suggested to Shake that he bring the students to the house if he wanted, suggested that he sleep with whoever he was sleeping with in the comfort of his room. Diana, shocked by this suggestion, took a stand and said she objected to this.

'Why?' asked Donald, downing a Nose Dive.

'The church is very clear on the matter of the sanctity of marriage. Besides,' she said with a sniff, 'there is the danger of herpes.' It was 1984, the Orwellian apocalypse was about to begin, but Diana, a nineteen-year-old virgin who was training to be a nurse, was unaware of the plague of AIDS spreading from the heart of Africa.

'Bollocks,' said Donald and motioned for a refill.

Shake smiled and took his father's glass into the kitchen. There, he placed an olive in a shot glass, filled the glass with gin and dropped it into a tumbler. He slowly poured in ginger ale to the lip of the shot glass, picturing his sister's plump, pale, earnest face as he did. Diana came out in hives if her skin was exposed to the sun, and she took her trips wearing linen trousers, long-sleeved shirt and a wide-brimmed hat. Shake wondered, as he carefully carried the Nose Dive out to his father, why they were so different, brother and sister. Was it because Diana had been snared by his grandparents? As Shake had boarded at Redpath, trying to make his escape, or spent the summer around Sansobella with Rajiv, Diana had been living with their grandparents. Shake loved Diana in some vague, amorphous way, because he felt he had to, but he didn't like her. Was that wrong?

Shake took his father up on the offer to invite the students back to the house, which made his father happy because he could re-enact his long-gone weekends in the cottage. Donald sat in the tall chair on the gallery, legs crossed, barefoot, a drink in one hand and held court. He talked about physics and astronomy, pointing out the constellations to the students who sat on the wooden boards at his feet. He ranted about the miners' strike in England, heaping opprobrium equally on Thatcher, who was a bitch from hell, scourge of the working man, and Scargill, who should never have taken the miners out when coal was stockpiled in towering mounds. Thatcher, apparently, was the reason Donald would not return to England. Donald discoursed about enosis, EOKA and the Attila Line which divided the Turk Cypriots from the Greek Cypriots.

'The Turks,' Donald remarked, 'will one day have to make up their minds if they are going to look east or west. Are they Asian or European?'

Donald argued with the project director about the ancient history of Cyprus, as Shake sat in a chair stroking Joan's black hair as she leaned against his legs.

'It was the Phoenicians who wiped out or displaced the early settlers,' announced Donald. 'The Phoenicians, bright buggers that they were, ran around the Mediterranean working out the best trading routes. This island, situated as it is near the ports of Alexandria and Constantinople, must have been the jewel in the Phoenicians' crown.'

'But—' interjected the expert on the ancient history of Cyprus.

'I'm not saying they ransacked, raped and pillaged, rather they *displaced* the early settlers.'

Shake watched his father, who may no longer have had glitter cascading around him but who was still a live wire, sparking, dangerous to the touch, and he thought that whilst his father's behaviour might not have been unreasonable, it was certainly adversarial. He couldn't imagine the second Mrs Knight withstanding the onslaught. On the other hand, Donald might have been adversarial but he was never boring. (Donald declaimed on any subject, appeared to be an expert on any topic under discussion. Unless that topic was his dead wife, Shake's mother, about whom he would say nothing. Shake asked one Saturday morning if he could have the cocktail book, take it back to England, and Donald nodded. Shake asked about the giving of the present, where they had been living when they were married and Donald stood up and left the table.)

The evenings would ramble on, cocktails and bottles of cheap retsina and crates of Kéo disappearing slowly. The volume of the music would be turned up and some of the students danced on the scrubby grass, crushing lemons underfoot, until Diana appeared in her nightdress and demanded the music finish, pointing to the watch she wore even in her sleep. And there was something about the bulk of Shake's sister, the force of her genuine disapproval, such that the music was turned off and the party disintegrated. Once Diana and her ethereal Wimp had departed for England, having had their fortnight holiday, the evenings stretched out until dawn.

The Sunday morning before his departure, Shake asked if he could borrow the car and Donald, who was lying in his bare, whitewashed bedroom, nursing a hangover, said he could. Shake drove along the old coast road, past Paphos, past the emergent, brutal highway, past the Rocks of Aphrodite, eventually reaching the turn-off to the fisherman's cottage, and the hamlet where Adonis and his mangy cur had lived. Shake could recognize no landmarks, the landscape being essentially the same everywhere – arid, scrubby flatlands and foothills. As he turned left, frowning, trying to get his bearings, he saw the tumbledown ruin that was what Adonis' family small-holding had become. Turning left again, knowing, now, where he was, Shake drove for a mile or so, and saw that the cottage had been bulldozed, the land levelled, and in its place stood six boxy, whitewashed time-share houses. He stopped the car and looked at the development, noticed a communal swimming pool had been built in front of it, an attempt at landscaping made. Beyond the pool the Mediterranean shifted, catching sunlight. Shake reversed the car, turned and drove back to the main road.

He didn't want to drive straight back to Lemba, so he set off north, following a rutted road along a wide, braided dry river bed. Shake began to climb, slowly, inexorably, grateful that he had to concentrate on negotiating the road, avoiding speeding cars and motorbikes because that concentration ensured he did not think of the demolition of the cottage. Shake twisted and turned the car through cramped villages, hairpin bends, around blind corners, aware, always, of the rumble of trucks approaching, carrying cargo from the quarries. Hours later, past midday, he drove into the car park by the ski resort at the summit of Mount Olympus, closed at the height of summer. He stepped out of the car and stretched, arcing his back, then walked through the trees to the viewpoint from where he could see the northern coastal towns, thousands of feet below, and he knew, because his father had explained it all to him one night, that he could see both the Turkish and the Greek Cyprus. Somewhere down there was a line, to the north of which lived the Turks and to the south of which lived those Cypriots who wished to become part of Greece. The line was invisible, but as his father said, it was no different from those lines drawn between France and Belgium, Spain and Portugal. Shake knew he had to leave soon, it was a long drive back to Paphos; he had gone to Olympus on a whim, driven by a desire to see something of his childhood island before he left, and his father would be worried as the hours passed. As he walked back to the car, Shake remembered a trip to the mountain the family must have made when he was eight or nine, at Christmas. They had braved the winter snows near the summit because Donald had wanted to ski the thin snow lying on hazardous runs. Diana, Shake and their mother had tried to build a snowman but the snow was too thin, too watery. Shake remembered that, strangely, there had been ladybirds everywhere, the tiny scarlet beads of their carapace looking like drops of blood on the thawing, refreezing, fluxing cover of snow.

Three days later, Donald took a day off work to drive Shake to Larnaka to catch his flight back to Gatwick. Shake was, by then, used to his father's driving, knew, somehow, that Donald was daring oncoming trucks and cars to have the temerity to visit upon him the overload of physics and biology that would leave his children orphans.

'So, Sammy, what are your plans for the rest of your life? Do you intend to simply be a sponging beach bum or will you at some point have a career?' Donald smiled as he said this, drawing the sting from the words.

'I quite fancy going into journalism or publishing or something.'

'You've obviously researched your options well.'

This time, it was Shake who smiled. 'At this moment what else is there to do but work?' he said, and laughed.

At the airport, as Shake stood by passport control, his father fussed with the *Savoy Cocktail Book*, wrapping and rewrapping it in a plastic bag before pushing it carefully into a pouch in Shake's backpack.

'Look after it,' Donald said.

'I will. Bye Dad.'

Father and son hugged, and this time Shake did not notice the sharp edge of Donald's shoulder blades, did not think of Charlie the Skeleton. Instead, he thought how wonderful the month had been in the odd house in Lemba, how unexpected the pleasure had been, thought how much he liked his father.

Over the next few years, Shake made sure he visited Donald every now and then, spent a week or two each year with him but they never managed, father and son, to recapture the bonhomie, the *surprise* of that summer. Donald died, one cool winter night as he lay in bed in his randomly arranged house, surrounded by images of Beatrice, forever smiling and pointing, forever lying in the sun with her children in her arms. He went to sleep nursing a headache, a headache which was, in fact, an incipient aneurysm. As Donald dreamed of buttresses arcing across chasms and gorges, a blood-filled blister, bulging on the fork of a cerebral artery, burst, flooding his brain and that finely tuned organ drowned, taking with it all the knowledge and opinions and memories that Donald had acquired over decades. As Donald would have noted, the event occurred because the pressure exerted by the fluid exceeded the tensile strength of the artery wall. Everything, after all, had indeed been physics for Donald.

EMMA

The first thing I ever noticed about Shake were his hands. He was wiping pink sauce off the hem of my dress and I noticed his hands. They were tanned and they looked strong, capable. I remember thinking he had very shiny, clean nails. *Emma's voice is surprisingly deep, deeper even than it sounds on screen. Her face – so familiar – is more dynamic stripped of the deceptions of make-up. Behind her, the Pacific Ocean spreads like sluggish oil to the horizon, flat and dull. On the boulevard the traffic, too, is sluggish, inching through wavering heat clouds. Emma turns the wedding ring on her finger, glances at it, as if she is not yet used to the feeling of metal on skin.* We met on 19 March, 1989. I remember the date because it was Oscar night and I was going out with some guy called Chris, who'd been on the sound production team for *A Fish Called Wanda*. We went to the London party and, of course, I spilled wine on my dress. I went to the kitchens to clean up and there was Shake. I thought he was beautiful, exotic almost, with his tan and his ponytail. He didn't look like anyone else there. Funny, I'd been looking forward to the party for so long but I spent the night making up any excuse to go to the kitchens so I could see Shake. I behaved incredibly badly – I went home with him, just left Chris drinking and schmoozing. I'd never done that before – gone home with a man I'd just met. I know now that the reason I did was because he was so . . .

unknowing, so innocent. He didn't know who I was. I'm not saying that I was famous then – I wasn't. But I was well-known and he hadn't got a clue who I was. I liked that. *Emma toys with the bulgar wheat and rocket on her plate, puts her fork down, grimacing. Pushes the plate away from her.* Bloody muck – can't stand the stuff but my nutritionist says I should eat it three times a week. We went back to his flat that night – well, it wasn't night, it was early morning – and it was a dump somewhere on Wandsworth Bridge Road. He rented it from his friend Rajiv, and he'd lived there for years, five years I think. I don't think he'd ever vacuumed the place. After that, I always insisted he came to my house. I must have been living in Chiswick then. God, it's all so long ago, it's difficult to remember. It was a different time, a different life. I met Shake at a time when things were changing for me. *Fire Before Dawn* had been released and I'd just won the Globe. For years I'd been a bit player, a small-part actor, but that movie changed all that. You have to understand the power that Hollywood has – a wand is waved and your life changes. Only later do you realize that the leaving of your old life – your friends, familiar places, favourite pubs and restaurants – is part of the deal. Perhaps because I met Shake then, at the point of that leaving, that departure, I didn't notice it. The metamorphosis doesn't happen overnight whatever people say. You don't become a star overnight, it takes time. But I had Shake with me, so I didn't notice. *Emma motions to a waiter for the check.* Can we walk for a while? I need a cigarette and the beach is about the only place left in the entire bloody state where you can have a fag. *Emma signs for lunch, ties her hair back and slips on a pair of shades.* Shake moved in with me after a few weeks, which sounds crazy, but it felt right. I knew the moment I met him, the moment I saw his hands move, that I wanted him. I'd never felt that before. Or since, come to that. *Emma shoulders her bag, negotiates her way between the tables and pushes her way out of the door. The heat is stifling, the carbon in the air palpable, it seems to coat the skin with a processed slick. She lights a cigarette and drags the smoke into her lungs, as if there were not enough in the air.* Shake was working for Rajiv then. Corporate entertainment and all that crap – big company parties, society weddings, events like the Oscars, Wimbledon, Henley. You know the sort of thing. He didn't earn much but he didn't care. He'd get his wages and call them drink tokens. I suppose it didn't matter because I was raking it in. In winter, when the parties died down a bit, he'd oversee Rajiv's properties. Rajiv owned a lot of houses which he rented out and Shake did the maintenance. Always annoyed me – Shake would never do his washing or clean up, or do the washing up, but he'd go to Rajiv's places to decorate and fix things, or unblock toilets and drains. *The breeze from the ocean is whipping Emma's voice away, sending it bowling down the sands. She takes a baseball cap from her bag and slips it on, kicks off her shoes and carries them as she walks, looking down at her bare feet.* Sometimes we'd visit Rajiv and his family when they were England, staying in their pile in Notting Hill – God, what Rajiv must be worth now. He's probably richer than me. Anyway, we'd go there and I never enjoyed those evenings but I went because Shake wanted me to. I never understood why they were friends, they were so different. But they *were* friends, good friends. They were very close. Shake was easy with Rajiv, he was very quiet when he was with him. Which made a change, because the rest of the time it was like living on a demolition site, there was so much mess and noise around Shake. *She laughs suddenly and her face opens, unfurls.* He always woke up early – like six o'clock or something – and he'd put on the same bloody record every bloody morning. By the Stranglers – shit, what was it called? 'Just get a grip on yourself' or something. *She begins to sing, unfolds her arms and waves them frantically, her voice cracking with the effort of singing loudly.* Every bloody morning that's what he did. Said it got him going. In his van he'd always have the radio on, or he'd play tapes at top volume. Shake always made out he was so cool but he liked the worst music – the Eagles, the Stones, Springsteen. He made me promise never to tell anyone and if people came round to supper or for drinks, he'd play all this obscure crap. To be fair, he did listen to jazz and blues, said his father had always played it when he was a boy and he grew up with it. *Emma wraps her arms around herself again, lowers her head.* He told me about the parties his parents had, in a cottage somewhere in Cyprus. Funny, I can remember that conversation very clearly. Odd, isn't it, how we can conjure up the most inconsequential, tiny slices of the past with complete clarity? Shake and I were lying on the sofa in the Chiswick house, and I even remember we were drinking bottles of Beck's beer, and he told me about how every Saturday he and his parents would sit in their garden looking over the sea, and people would arrive and shower them with gifts. And he told me how his father once said to him, 'This is life. The rest is just for money.' *Emma frowns, gently chews her lower lip.* Perhaps it wasn't so inconsequential. Shake was forever throwing parties. I'd come back from the set, or from weeks on location and I'd walk into a party. Any excuse, and Shake would throw a party. He was always meeting people and asking them round, because of his work. He mixed a mean cocktail, knocked up the best daquiri I've ever had.

It was my money he spent but I didn't care because I always had such fun. He'd hire a pool hall for the night, or a house in Devon for a weekend and we'd all drive down and party. *Lighting another cigarette, Emma sits on the sand and scoops a handful, lets it trickle away between her fingers.* One night, many years ago, when Shake was still living in Fulham and I was in Chiswick, he walked over to my place. He often walked rather than drove, he loved walking the streets, watching what was going on, looking into people's lit rooms. Anyway, he arrived very late and I was asleep. He let himself in and climbed into bed, woke me up. And as I was swimming out of sleep, all I could smell was rum, woodsmoke and lemons. There was a firemen's strike on and he'd stopped by Putney Bridge where the men had lit a fire in an oil drum to keep warm. He'd stayed and talked to them, had a drink with them, and they were drinking rum toddies and when he came to me he smelled of smoke and rum and lemons. He smelled of outside and . . . safety. That was when I fell in love with him. I can point to that moment, when I was waking up, and say that was when I felt love. *Her deep, beautiful voice stills and she stops sifting sand, stares at the horizon.* He wasn't always noisy. Sometimes he'd have quiet moments, times when he'd sit and do nothing, just stare into space. And he used to read a lot. I'd come home and he'd be lying on the sofa, reading. I never seemed to have time but he always had a book on the go. There was something very sexy about finding him, my loud, cool, brash Shake, lying on the sofa, just reading. And he used to like cuddling – really cuddling. Every morning, when we slept together, before he put the bloody Stranglers on, he'd cuddle me up. All day, if I was there, he'd insist on regular cuddles. I've never met another man who did that. And

I've never met another man who giggled. Shake had this weird giggle and it took me a while to work it out but I realized that he only did it when he was embarrassed. Like the time I finally asked him why he always had a tan – it had been bothering me, I mean we lived in Chiswick, not the bloody Caribbean and he was always tanned. And Shake giggled. It really shocked me. Turned out he used sunbeds. I ask you. Vain bugger. *Emma smiles, then shrugs, scoops at the sand again.* I haven't thought of these things for years. Like I said, little things, tiny slices of life we forget and remember. It all seems a long time ago, as if it happened to other people. And perhaps it did. Of course, then I won the Oscar and that was the end of London and pool halls and football on a Saturday. No more curries on a Friday down the Shish Mahal, no more pints of Pride by the river, or gigs at the Marquee. Because I had to move here and I brought Shake with me. Maybe I shouldn't have? Maybe I should have left him in London, in the place he knew? But I couldn't leave him and I couldn't stay. So I asked him to marry me, and off we went. Full of hope, full of ourselves. What you have to understand is that when we lived in London I knew Shake was faithful, I knew he never even flirted with another woman. He was a one-woman man. And I knew he was proud of me, that he admired me. The night I won the Oscar, when my name was read aloud, I turned to him and the look on his face was like nothing I'd ever seen; as if no moment would ever be as good again and that the moment was mine and mine alone. He smiled and stood up, held his hand out to me and helped me up because I didn't know what to do. But Shake did. Shake knew what to do. *Emma closes her eyes for a moment, perhaps replaying the memory of Shake knowing what to do, as the sun begins to dip and shadows grow long.*

1983–1990

Shake was listening to Frankie telling him to relax, his knee jigging, fingers tapping, when the plane dropped through the thin cloud cover and, squinting through the window, shading his eyes against the sun, Shake could see London, could see the curves of the Thames, the dun-coloured estates in the east. The plane tracked west, and Shake, his forehead pressed against the glass, Sony Walkman switched off, saw the scrapers of the City loom and fall away, could make out the Palace and Hyde Park, the museums and bridges. As the plane passed over reservoirs and the undercarriage dropped and locked, Shake sat back in his seat and frowned, realizing at last that it was all over. University, finals, Cyprus – it was all over. The summer was at an end. As the plane wheels thudded on tarmac, bounced and settled, Shake wondered what he should do, where he should go.

Standing in the terminal, surrounded by families worn by travel and worry, fathers pushing teetering trolleys as mothers shouted at toddlers, yanked them by their wrists, Shake checked his wallet. He had three pounds and twelve pence. Hitching his rucksack on to a shoulder, he made his way to a bank of public phones, dialled the only number he knew by heart and watched the departure display board flick-flack: Daar es Salaam, Tokyo, Colombo, Rangoon, Bangkok, San Francisco, Los Angeles.

'Hello?'

Shake had forgotten how Rajiv always sounded surprised when he answered the phone. He shoved a ten pence piece into the box, covered his ear with a hand to deafen himself to the cries of young children. 'Raj?'

'It is Rajiv Samaroo.'

'It's Shake.'

'Hello, my friend. How are you?'

'I'm in Heathrow and I'm coming into town.'

'How was your summer?'

'Fine, fine, thing is, I was wondering if—'

'I cannot hear you, my friend. It is very noisy where you are.'

'I'm in Heathrow and I'm coming to town and I was wondering if I could crash at one of your places?'

'Pardon me?'

Shake dropped the rucksack, yelled into the mouthpiece. 'I'm coming into London and I don't have anywhere to stay.'

'You must, of course, come here.'

The line died as Rajiv replaced his phone.

For the first month he stayed in Rajiv's flat in Wandsworth Bridge Road, Shake woke every early morning, on the sofa in the front room, and promised himself that he would buy *Media*, the *Guardian*, *Time Out*, the *Evening Standard* and spend the evening poring over the job section and classifieds. He also promised himself he would not go to the pub that night, would not buy a kebab from the takeaway on North End Road. Then he would bounce from his makeshift bed, snap on Capital Radio, shower, and dance around the galley kitchen as the kettle boiled. He made Rajiv tea, took it to his bedroom and woke his friend by gently shaking his shoulder. Rajiv, hair tousled, silk pyjamas askew, sat up, rested against the bed head and, after a cursory greeting, talked business as Shake listened and jotted down notes.

'Twelve crates of Tattinger are to be delivered by Marshall's to the Taylors' house on Putney Heath. However, I wish you to go to the distributor's warehouse and collect the champagne because I do not entirely trust him. He is a cockney chap and I suspect his morals. The marquee in Limpsfield was broken down last night and I have told them you will be picking it up before midday. The caterers for the NatWest convention are fools. But what can I do? I would like you to go Patel's in Hounslow and collect the meat for the event. Mr Patel had kindly said that he will loan us a refrigerated van for the journey but this means you will have to return it. There are no helium balloons to be had. It is a gloomy picture. However, flowers are always a fine substitute. Indeed, I wonder why more people do not select fresh blooms in the first instance. Perhaps you could make a detour soon to Vauxhall to see what is on offer? An overview is all I need – price per dozen. Tomorrow morning, as I am remembering, it will be necessary for you to go to Billingsgate and buy,' Rajiv leaned over, picked up a slip of paper on his bedside table, 'fourteen pounds of plaice, five stone of oysters, twenty pounds each of mussels, six fresh salmon weighing no less than seven pounds each and a crate of crevettes. Make that seven salmon.' Rajiv finished his tea, smoothed his hair prior to the pantomime. 'I am assuming that you are available?'

Shake mimed opening a Filofax, flipping through pages and scanning a diary. 'Looks that way.'

'That is good. One thing, though, before you leave. Can you please remove the wetsuit from the kitchen?'

'OK. I was just drying it off. Sorry.'

After three months, Shake was working five days a week for Rajiv; after six he was working seven days and all notions of journalism had evaporated. Rajiv had, by then, put Shake on the payroll; there were no more bundles of banknotes handed over each evening to be spent in the pubs on North End Road. It was Rajiv who suggested that Shake rent the flat, as he, Rajiv, was buying a house in Notting Hill, and Shake finally had a place of his own in which he lived out the years.

Shake began to learn the city he had seen from the plane – endless and infuriating, a maze of streets and cultures and dispositions. In the van, driving through the clogged streets, Capital Radio blaring in the cab, warning him of traffic jams, feeling himself to be part of the city, part of the filthy, noisy, crowded, uncontrollable mess, Shake felt, sometimes, that he belonged. After a few months spent collecting packages and catering supplies from the outposts of the city – Peckham, Clapton, Ealing, Kensal Rise, Dalston, Blackheath – Shake felt the city in some way belonged to him. As the traffic grew heavier, grinding to a halt time and again on the Mall, down Brompton Road, on the North Circular, he began to prefer the days spent driving out to the estates and mansions in Surrey, Hampshire and Kent, rolling down driveways cut across immaculate lawns, to arrive at the doors of some vast pile or other. There were times when he had to stay for the event because the marquee needed to be broken down that night, and Shake drifted at the edges of the party, retaping cables, fixing broken lights, clearing bottles and stacking them in crates, ready to be taken away. He'd help the bands set up and he'd be given backstage passes to gigs in town, at Wembley, Hammersmith and The Marquee in Camden.

Shake rubbed along with everyone: the merchant bankers who hosted lavish affairs in corporate offices in the City, the catering staff, the Surrey bankers, the cleaners, the Essex barrow boys made good, the subcontractors, the Hampshire housewives. Shake: still closing as one flower and opening as another. When he wasn't working, Shake partied; he drank with the men who set up the marquees, picked up women as he mixed cocktails, watched Chelsea at Stamford Bridge, went to gigs all over the city, arrived at parties carrying bottles of Bollinger, surplus given to him by futures' traders who couldn't be bothered to deal with the excess stock at the end of the party – the party that, it seemed, was never going to end.

It was the 1980s, and there was excess everywhere, an excess of everything, or so it felt to Shake. There was money flying on the breeze, people were making thousands in a day, selling houses, buying more, selling them on immediately. Advertisers sold a mistaken idea, a fallacious image and made millions, city boys undermined sterling and bought grams of coke, the coke dealers bought houses, and so it went. Gordon Gecko announced that greed was good and it seemed everyone agreed with him. But still Shake's outgoings exceeded his income; by the time Rajiv had persuaded Shake to invest money in bricks and mortar, the moment had passed. Shake looked at the price of property, flinched and went out to party.

For five years Shake drove his van and watched the street life, for five years he watched the urban landscape change from the vantage point of his cab. He leaned his elbows on the worn steering wheel as he waited at traffic lights, smoking a B&H, chewing gum, imagining he could feel the tarmac tremble with the weight of traffic, and he watched. He saw dark-suited men braying on the pavements, hailing taxis as they drunkenly tottered after three-hour lunches; bag ladies digging daintily in bins, picking out the half-eaten sandwiches of those who were too full, too busy, too indifferent to finish them; he watched frail, well-groomed, blue-rinsed widows standing aside to allow raucous crowds of American students push past before stepping through the doors of Fortnum's; he closed the cab window against the dust and roar of construction; he watched the ageing punks and new romantics jostle for pavement space on the King's Road, watched the Indians working the pavements of East Ham.

And all the time he was doing this the radio chattered, fulminated and sang. Frankie sang about two tribes as news came in about hotel bombings in Brighton and Shake imagined the bricks and mortar flying, wondered if Donald would have approved. The further Shake drove, the more he saw and the more he heard. He spent his days driving, his evenings drinking and his nights in Rajiv's flat building his fences, as football stadiums collapsed or burned, as pickets were beaten by police on horseback. Rajiv praised Thatcher for facing down the rioters in Brixton but it was Shake who had to drive through the edgy streets, Shake who had to negotiate the broken glass and shattered bricks littering the streets. 'They are on welfare,' Rajiv said of the blacks who smashed their own neighbourhoods. 'They are lazy.' And still Shake didn't know what to say to this. The space shuttle exploded on television as journalists and printmen gathered at the fortress that was Wapping, and still Shake drove the van, collecting and delivering, his elbows resting on the steering wheel, listening to the radio crackle and spit. He tried, sometimes, to drown out the news of the world by shoving a tape in the player and turning up the volume. Grace Jones' demand that he pull up to the bumper distracted him from thoughts of the cloud from Chernobyl drifting and settling across Europe but when the tape finished he found himself looking at the sky. Many nights he spent in rented rooms and cluttered studios with brazen, lusty women, who themselves seemed to be seeking oblivion, who helped him to forget, for a while, the bodies lying in the streets of Hungerford, the rusting carcass of a car ferry capsized in the shallows of the North Sea. Shake drew breath, imagined it could get no worse, this mismanagement of lives, of the woof and weft of existence, but then a lit match was dropped and the fire at King's Cross razed another thirty personal histories.

Shake tried to explain to Rajiv, one frost-cracked night as they sat in the over-heated, humid conservatory of the house in Notting Hill, that he felt his country was damned in some way, as if it were being punished but Rajiv simply smiled and began to list tasks for the following day, pushing his plump little fingers down with each point.

'Raj, I'm talking to you.'

'And I am talking to you.'

'Why is it happening?'

'Why is what happening?'

'All the things I've just said – Bradford, Heysel, Brixton, Hungerford, *Herald of Free Enterprise*, Clapham, King's Cross – why are they happening?'

'I do not know.' Rajiv shrugged. 'I think you want someone to blame and there is no one. It is unfortunate. But, then, many things are unfortunate. You say nothing of the earthquakes in

Armenia, the mudslides in Guatemala, the poisonous gases escaping from the lakes in Cameroon. Why, I wonder, do you not mention these things? Instead you talk of small-town trouble. If it troubles you, do not listen.'

'But I *can't* not listen, I can't get away from it.'

'I wasn' at the weddin'; don' invite me to the funeral.' Rajiv's voice was his father's voice, the voice of a man used to being heard, the voice of a man who slipped into patois when discussing unimportant events.

Shake walked back to Fulham that night, his hands deep in his pockets, collar turned up against the freezing wind, and for once he did not look into the lit rooms of the terraces of Earls Court, did not watch drinkers spilling out of pubs nor did he try to imagine conversations between couples eating in restaurants. He walked with his head down, watching his feet pound out the miles on filthy, slush-coated pavements and he decided that perhaps Rajiv was right. No one was to blame; it was all simply unfortunate. There was no need to feel fearful, no need to fear punishment even if that punishment seemed random, casual almost. Shake looked up then, looked at the river of steel running through the streets as cars headed out of town, looked up at the low, orange cloud, at the gaudy Christmas lights flashing in the smeared, smut-marked windows of a pub on Eel Brook Common and he stepped inside.

Months later, a gas leak snaked from a rusted pipe in the North Sea, a spark arced into its midst and the Piper Alpha oil platform blew apart as men jumped, hair and skin alight, into the inferno the sea had become. A year after Shake had noticed the Christmas lights in the Duke, the remnants of a shattered jumbo jet exploded in a Scottish town, the impact registering on the Richter scale, and Shake decided that, for once, Rajiv had been wrong and he had been right. This was no small-town trouble. Shake crossed the jumbled wasteland of his living room and switched off the news, lay on the sofa and put one hand on his heart, touched the bumps running down the length of his ear. He remembered, a few years before, his first summer in London, watching Live Aid, seeing the montage of shots that accompanied the Cars' 'Drive', one child's face after another, some looking at the camera as they chewed on pap, some unable to look, too weak to breathe, almost too weak to live, black and brown skin fly-speckled, black and brown eyes gummed closed, and he remembered crying, just as everyone around him did, remembered being shamed into sending a cheque for fifty pounds which he did not have. But nothing had changed. Those children may have lived or died, but there were millions to take their place and still the images of toppling cattle, flapping, torn makeshift shelters and withered maize collapsing into dustbowls appeared again and again. Shake had learned, years before, when he stared into a pair of robin's-egg-blue eyes, that he couldn't change things and he lay on the sofa and wondered when he had forgotten that lesson. He imagined he could hear, in the rare silence that surrounded him, the turning of a cart's wheel on chalky gravel.

Shake might have carried on in this way for years, hanging onto Rajiv's coat-tails, flying on the magic carpet of his friend's success, living in his rented, untidy flat in Fulham, the fridge empty but for old eggs and bottles of champagne. He might have become a middle-aged bachelor of the sort who considers

London the epicentre of the universe, who walks the same paths to the same football grounds, pubs and Indian restaurants so often that those paths indeed become ruts, deep furrows. Or he would perhaps have married the daughter of a Surrey banker and moved out to the suburbs, where he might have attempted to run a similar business which would have eventually failed. It would have failed because Shake had to be told what to do, had to have his life strapped down by others, otherwise the friction between what he ought to do and what he wanted to do, between where he ought to be and where he wanted to be, dragged at him and brought him to a halt.

As the decade of freewheeling and money-spinning slowed, moved towards its conclusion, as Thatcher's revolution ground down, Rajiv's mother, the plump, diminutive Mrs Samaroo, fell ill, and Rajiv returned to Sansobella, leaving Shake to run the business for a few months. Despite the transatlantic phone calls and the chattering of the fax machine, Shake was overwhelmed. He spent evenings sitting in the office, worrying at the proposals for future events and the logistics of current jobs. Deliveries were missed, employees called in sick, the mothers of soon-to-be eighteen-year-olds changed the numbers, the menus, the locations. Shake discovered that an easy charm solved none of these problems.

The *Fish Called Wanda* party began at midnight and Shake, already exhausted by a fifteen hour day, deliberated whether to send a deputy to oversee, but a phone call from Rajiv aborted that plan and Shake dragged himself to the venue. It was, at first, a sedate affair, as guests smothered yawns and drank juice and sparkling water. Shake, having checked the bar stock and décor, dreading the night ahead, went to the kitchens. He poured a coffee and slumped on a chair in the corner, smoking, watching the caterers go about their business. A difficult one, this, with breakfast scheduled for six in the morning. A television flickered in the corner, showing the arrivals stepping out on the red carpet, long dresses and tuxes looking out of place on a sunny, March afternoon in Los Angeles. Shake was admiring Jodie Foster, hoping she'd win for *The Accused*, when the kitchen door swung open, slammed against an aluminium counter, sending a tray of canapes crashing to the floor.

'Did I do that? God, I'm sorry.' The woman bent down and began to collect shards of crockery in her palm.

'I'll do that.' Shake began to sweep up the mess. 'You better be careful, you're getting muck on your dress.'

The woman's hem was smeared with lurid seafood sauce. 'Oh for God's sake.' She stood up and Shake could see a livid red wine stain on her ivory-silk-clad left breast. 'I came in here to see if I could clean myself up. Now look at me, covered in gubbins.'

Shake looked. The woman had an arresting face; her eyes were too small, her nose too large and lips too full for perfection but he wanted to keep looking at her. A cheer went up from the party as Jamie Lee Curtis stepped out of a limo thousands of miles away.

'I'll get you sorted.'

'I'm Emma,' she said as Shake returned with a bottle of white wine, some soapy water and a linen napkin. 'Thanks for this. I'm astonishingly clumsy.'

Shake watched as she dabbed at the wine stain, could not look away despite the intimacy of the moment. 'I'll clean up the rest if you want.' Shake knelt and began to wipe at her hem with a damp cloth.

'We're moving to LA,' Shake told Rajiv over lunch. 'Emma's contracted for three parts over the next year, with some others in negotiation.'

Rajiv, plumper than ever but nevertheless elegant in a bespoke, tailored suit, tapped the linen tablecloth of the table in Bertolucci's with the tip of his breadknife. 'So, Emma will be fine, she will be busy. But what will you do?'

Shake shrugged. 'I like it there.'

'But there is nothing for you to do. What will you do for work?'

'We are young – we can be unhappy later,' said Shake but neither man smiled.

And both of them, although they said nothing, thought of sitting on the beach at Heavenly Cove, when they were boys, when Rajiv had laughed at Shake's notion of living in St George.

EMMA

The late afternoon sun has begun to dim, a haze has gathered around it, transforms into an insubstantial rainbow nimbus. Emma unknots the sleeves of the sweatshirt tied at her waist, slips it on, as people along the shoreline pack their bags and fold their towels. I'm not going to talk about Aspen. I am not going to discuss those events. Enough was said and written at the time and I have said and thought everything I can ever say about it. Like I said, perhaps we shouldn't have moved to LA, perhaps we should have stayed in Shake's beloved London. Because there are so many seductions here, so many blandishments. There's always a party going on somewhere, always spongers and sycophants who want to move into your orbit, who will say and do anything to be a part of it. And, you see, Shake's life changed. We have a saying in England – to be on the other side of the bar – and that's what happened to Shake. All his life he'd been working for other people's parties and then suddenly he had other people waiting on him hand and foot. I was working like a dog when we first arrived and I'd be driven home late at night and he wouldn't be there, he'd be out, living it up. I never came back to find him reading or mixing me up a cocktail any more because he was out having cocktails made for him. He kept saying he'd start looking for work but what, really, could he have done? He knew how much I was earning – the trades print the details. It was no secret. What I said about the deal with Hollywood? About leaving your old life? There's another part of that deal which is difficult to understand. It's that there are very few secrets it's possible to keep. I know it's much worse now and I'm glad I'm out of it, you know, just an uptight, ageing English actress, hardly worth bothering with. But some of the stuff that's printed now – photographs, editorials, blogs and all that. Shocking. Grief, conception, abortion, addiction, divorce – it's all out there for public consumption. Shake was unprepared for it all. Because of the way he looked, the paps loved him. Like I said, he had always been vain and the attention fed that vanity. He made the mistake of thinking that they were just interested, he didn't realize that they were waiting. I should have seen it happening, should have tried to do something, but I was too busy. After a while Shake stopped talking about work, he just went surfing and cruising the bars. Sometimes he'd slow down and we'd spend time together and then it was fine. If we were together somewhere else, not in LA, we were fine. We spent weekends up in the hills sometimes, in a lodge, and we went sailing and fishing down in Mexico. And we were fine, happy. There were cuddles, there were some beers, there were no drugs. The drugs. I should have known, really. But I was working on location for months in some ghastly place in Kentucky and I wasn't around to see it. I was so bloody glad to get home at weekends, I didn't notice anything. When the filming was over – and you know, I can't remember anything about that movie, can't even remember the name of it – we went to Dorado. It was like spending a holiday with a stranger. I thought Dorado would be a good place to go and blow the bluegrass roots of Kentucky out of my hair because everyone in Dorado was a someone, so it would be a level playing field. But the week we went, there was some rock group who'd rented a villa. So I spent days on the beach as Shake slept off yet another hangover in our villa, and then he'd be out at night sampling everything on offer. And I mean everything. And he was so out of it, he didn't realize that I knew what he was doing. *Emma shivers, lights another cigarette, begins to turn the ring on her fourth finger.* It's unsettling to think I must have been one of the last people to see him. You see, I went to St George for a few days a couple of weeks ago and there he was. Captain Shake, Dream Chaser. For twelve years I'd been wondering where he was and I stumbled across him on that speck of an island. We spent the day together, not doing much, mainly talking. We had quite a lot to say, as you can imagine, or, at least, I did. *The smoke from her cigarette swirls before being whipped away by the breeze which has kicked up. Along the boulevard the streetlights flicker.* I'm doing some stagework now, just like everyone else. *Death and the Maiden*, opening off Broadway in October. I was in New York a while ago for pre-rehearsal, and we were discussing the themes – justice, truth, guilt and all that. And forgiveness. Forgiveness. We were talking about whether Paulina should be merciful, whether she should forgive Dr Miranda, given there is uncertainty about his guilt. It was odd listening to the others talking, musing almost, about returning good for evil, about leniency and forebearance. And all the while, I'm sitting there thinking about Shake. Mike, the guy who's cast as Gerardo, is a bloody born again, a fine actor, but a religious nut. And he's talking about forgiveness and grace and I'm thinking that there are some things that can't be forgiven. But I didn't say anything. *She buries the butt of her cigarette in the sand, smoothes it with her palm.* When I was a girl we had an old black labrador called Buster. I'd known him all my life but, of course, Buster grew up and grew old before I realized it. I must have been about twelve or thirteen when his back legs went and we had to lift him so he could stand. Then he developed a problem with his kidneys and he began to fade away. He'd always slept on a cushion in front of the Aga in the kitchen and I can remember every time I saw him then, I'd stop and look at him, to see if he was still breathing. I'd check to see his ribs were still moving. We all did. After Aspen, I found myself doing the same with Shake. He didn't go out any more. He sat by the pool or in a chair by the window in the den, and he was so still, so frozen, I'd have to look at him to check he was still breathing. But I still couldn't forgive him. It never goes away, you know, it never goes away. It's the first thing you think of every morning when you wake up, even now, all these years later, it's the first thing. *Emma jumps as a fountain of glittering sparks explodes from the flat roof of a hotel on the strip, cascades to earth in a rainbow of scarlet droplets. Soon to be followed by another and another, as cracks and thuds echo and roll along the wide, packed streets.* Bloody hell, I'd forgotten it's Independence Day. *She watches as the sky is etched by trails of tinsel and erratic glowing golden orbs.* Shake was really trying, when I saw him in St George, he was really trying. He was living in a shit hole, trying to build a house for himself. It would have been lovely when it was finished. Sure, it would have been small, but it would have been Shake-size, Shake-shaped. He was working hard, working for himself, by himself. And he had changed. He was quiet; there was no music, no tapes or CDs blaring. He didn't jig about like he used to, getting up all the time to fiddle with things. I'm not saying he was at peace because I don't think he ever would have been. He had too many demons to deal with. But he was quiet. And he was . . . I don't know. Not vain, humble almost. I met a few people who knew him and they genuinely seemed to like him, for who he was. As if he was . . . respected, in a way. And you know, I would have stayed the night with him, if he had asked. I would have stayed with him but he didn't ask, and that was the biggest difference of all. *Emma stands up, brushes the sand from her hands, shoulders her bag. The fireworks are exploding all over the horizon, from backyards, from the jetty, from hotels. A celebration of liberation.* Seeing his picture on the news, nothing but a thumbnail amongst so many, was a shock. They used an old one, from the archives, of when we were married. It was a shock because it wasn't the man I'd just met again. It was someone else, someone I used to know so well. I tried to pull strings with the English embassy to get information but even I couldn't get anywhere. My kind of fame is only useful for the trivial things in life, for fripperies. It's been more than a week now, ten, eleven days. *Emma shrugs and shakes her head a little.* Thing is, the Shake in the thumbnail was no hero and for him I would have hope. But Captain Shake, Dream Chaser, seemed like a man who might have tried to be heroic. Who might have tried to change things. *Emma turns and walks away, a silhouette against a crazed, electric storm of cordite as the oompa-oompa of the Independence Day Parade grows louder.*

Between the boundaries which denote the tropics of Cancer and Capricorn, the palette used to paint the land and sky is not the same palette as that used elsewhere in the hemispheres. The sunlight, its source closer to the earth than elsewhere, burns fiercely, burns the colours themselves, flushes them, traps them in a tropical prism. There, the clock governing time and life works differently; the days and nights are near-twinned, at the equator they are identical. The equator — where the world turns upside down and winter can become summer — the imaginary line with which the earth is girdled, marks the point at which the winds are dragged west to the north and east to the south as the earth spins. This dragging, this hauling of the air itself, is known as the Coriolis force and this force creates the trade winds — which have nothing to do with merchants, nothing to do with Phoenician mariners plying their trade across the globe, 'trade' meaning constant — bringing with them clouds. These, too, move always in the same direction, unable to break away from the cycle. Stratocumulus, altostrata, lens clouds, cirrus, cirrostratus and lofty cumulonimbus, towering up to six miles, pearl-white and stretched, tumble reluctantly in the wake of the trade winds, unable to change course, unable to dictate their own destiny. These clouds are dragged over oceans, deserts and landlocked lakes, drift over archipelagos, peninsulas, the horn of Africa, the isthmus of Panama, and the island chain of the Caribbean. Some of these Caribbean islands are mere shelves of dead coral and uplifted limestone smothered in white sands, others, to the south, nearing the equator, are the remnants of mountain ranges, the worn stubs of volcanoes, some of which still belch ash and steam, which rise up to meet the passing clouds.

St George, an island to the south of the Windwards, is such a volcanic outcrop, its cone eroded, dead now, covered in cloud forest and epiphytes. The land slopes away from this scene of former violence, slopes away, first, as rainforest, and then in plateaux and hills, down to the long, sweeping beaches of the coast. To the west, there are the lowlands, and there it is possible, still, to see the vague outlines of the old plantations and estates – a collapsing sugar mill, a corroded water wheel, boiling pots abandoned in backyards, pots which had swung over fires, heating water, molasses and dunder. Dilapidated estate houses sit high above the plantations, houses which are being entombed and devoured, now, by the forest which had given them shade. Up in the hills, where few people live, this forest flourishes in wet season, the rains and waterfalls feeding silk cotton, mahogany, poui, immortelles, and casuarina trees, orchids, grasses and bromeliads. To the east of the island, the coastline is jagged, vicious, the rocks ocean-pounded, populated by seabirds. To the south, the forested hills drop down steeply to inaccessible beaches, small coves protected by towering, bare headlands. The coastline here has no shelf, the waves break on a steep wall of rock which drops down into a trench, a trench populated by thousands of species of marine life. Every day, in the early morning and as dusk falls, boats scour these waters, dropping nets and lines. To the north of the island are the finest beaches, impossibly golden and white, collared by palms and sea grapes, crescents of reef protecting the sands, ensuring the waters of the Caribbean Sea flash turquoise and pale emerald. Seagulls and white terns flying low over the reef boast blue breasts, are transformed from the mundane to the otherworldly by the reflection of the water burned by the sun. Along this stretch of coast there are hotels, guest houses and apartments, all built for the visitors who have escaped their pale *dun and beige landscapes to the north, who come to marvel at blue-breasted seabirds.*

The coastline is broken by a bulge of land, the Killdevill Peninsula, which juts out into the Caribbean, a ridge of hills running along its spine. Here the villas and houses are hidden behind fences and walls, huge bougainvillea arch over the grass verges, royal palms line gravelled drives. Swimming pools glitter between the trunks of trees as hot tubs steam and jacuzzis bubble. Sprawled on sun loungers, white bodies turn pink and copper and bronze. Small villages and hamlets are scattered like boozy jewels along the beaches and bays: Polonaise, Vampiro, Myers and Tom Collins. Images of this last settlement, the houses and villas painted in a pastel rainbow, ornate galleries and decks looking out over the waters, appear in lustrous, glossy magazines lying on glass-topped coffee tables all over the world. Tom Collins is not so moneyed as to be daunting but sufficiently beautiful to be arresting. The beach is a perfect sweep, as if an arm has extended itself, spilling sand, and the sands are lined by palms, sea grape, sea almond and sea cherries. Nets are strung in the branches, pirogues move lazily in the shallows, their gunwales swamped by pelicans at dusk. Tourists drive there at dawn to walk the sands and watch the sun rise over the headland. They walk barefoot, hand in hand, occasionally remarking on a swooping bird, or the sound of a coconut crashing to ground, as wavelets froth bubbles over their pale toes. If they arrive early enough, they might catch sight of the fishermen setting out, ghostly in the dawn's light despite their dark skin. The beach at Tom Collins is favoured by the locals for taking the salt, that is, the sand is just the right consistency to give the body a sea bath, and sometimes the tourists catch sight of an old local, his skin black, his hair grey, scrubbing himself down before dipping into the waves. Unknown to them, Mister Jeremiah takes the salt every morning, always has, during his seventy-two years. Further along, nearing the easterly headland, where the houses are gathered, the tourists might see a white man – who is no longer white, who is a dark, walnut brown; only his hair, tied in a short ponytail, gives him away – trotting down a long flight of uneven, wooden steps, and crossing to a cage at the back of the beach. Perhaps they slow a little, as they watch him pull a surfboard from the cage and then paddle out to a gleaming, white powerboat, watch as he climbs onboard. As the sun clears the headland and slams into their eyes, they squint at the boat, shading their eyes, and pick out the name stencilled on the side: Ribailagua. The strangeness of this name occupies them until they reach the end of the beach and turn to retrace their steps. And then, as they begin to think about the breakfast that will be awaiting them in their all-inclusive resort, they may talk about the white man, speculate about his origins, wonder how he has contrived – when they have not – to live in paradise.

These tourists, who daydream about standing on the gallery of a house in Tom Collins, sipping coffee and watching the changing shades of dawn, are unaware of many things. Unaware of the animals in the bush, which has been cut back to create a cordon sanitaire around the hotels and resorts, untamed bush which encroaches, which has to be butchered daily. The tourists do not consider how it might be to live amongst snapping turtles and caiman, snakes, peccaries, manicou, rats and dengue-carrying mosquitos. They do not know that praedial larceny, poaching, theft and the slaughter of leatherbacks, iguana and bush meat are rife; that there are bands of nowhereians – the homeless, the outcast, who live nowhere, who belong nowhere – who smoke crack and run tasks for the boatmen who drift into coves under cover of darkness. They are oblivious of the fact that there exist, even on the small island of St George, worlds within worlds.

The tourists return to their pale, milky landscapes after a week, after a month, and take with them memories of baking in the sun, eating kingfish and river lobster, drinking ice-cold beers and weak punches. As they stand in their cold, grey houses, brushing sand from their shoes and bags, they remind *each other of the walk along Tom Collins, how the clouds drifted along the horizon between sea and sky, flushing deep crimson and pink, before turning silver. They are careless of the fact that these same clouds herald wet season, dragging with them thunder and lightning, sheets of electricity which leech the colours from the land and render everything in shades of lavender and violet. They choose not to remember images they have seen of tropical storms, cyclones and hurricanes, images of tattered palms uprooting as galvanized tin roofs flutter and fly, of walls of muddied water carrying away walls and cars and cattle. Folding their clothes and putting them away in drawers and cupboards, the tourists choose instead to remember the trains of pink cotton-wool puffs of cloud. Some imagine it is the hand of God that is responsible for this display, others imagine it a daily display of ethereal magic, when it is neither of these. It is simply physics, the cause and effect of the interplay between pressure and temperature, which dictate the extent of wet and dry seasons, the occurrence of violent, unexpected tropical storms.*

14 June

The woman wearing the stetson, Cuban heels and bootlace tie taps her pinkie finger on the long, mahogany bartop; tick-tick, tick-tick sings the signature ring. She watches closely as he builds the Mint Julep: mint, sugar, water. Muddle. Bourbon. Crushed ice. Stir. Garnish with mint leaves, add straw. He places the slippery, iced glass on a silver salver and offers it to the elegant cowgirl, the glinting tray balanced surely on five fingertips. She doesn't look at him as she tosses a twenty on the bar. Instead she focuses on the cocktail. Closing her eyes, she, first, sniffs and then inhales deeply over the lip of the heavy, curved old-fashioned. Only then does she glance at him, her face empty, and nods slightly. Then she drinks, drinks long and hard. Half the julep is gone.

He can't help himself. 'The name comes from an Arabic word, they say. *Julab*, which means "rose water".'

The cowgirl ignores him. Swills a little of the drink in her mouth. 'Too much sugar.' She downs the remainder, puts the now empty old-fashioned on the bar. 'Not bad. Had a better one in New Orleans few years back. But not bad.' She turns on her heel, runs a finger along the brim of the stetson and she's gone.

He places the glass carefully in a sink, wipes the bar with a soft cloth. Too much sugar. He checks the cleanliness of the zester, the spiral-handled spoon and Hawthorn strainer, wipes the already gleaming bases of the Waring blenders. Too much sugar. He tugs at the tips of his waistcoat, adjusts his black dickie bow and then he senses it. The arrival. Like a bulge of air wallowing at the door. He swallows and pulls needlessly at his cuffs. A stool creaks as Papa Dobles sits at the bar, foot resting on the brass rail.

Turning back to the bar, he sees the beard, the wild, blue eyes, a white shirt pulled snug against the belly. 'Yes sir?'

'Daiquiri.' Papa Dobles lights a cigarette, unfolds a newspaper. 'No sugar.'

His hands are trembling. But then, he's about to make a daiquiri for Ernest Hemingway – he *should* be trembling. He pours a double measure of Havana Club, a single of grapefruit juice, a third ounce of maraschino liqueur and crushed ice into a shaker. Then he drops a lime into boiling water and waits the longest half minute of his life, watching his fingers pulse, before twitching the fruit from the bowl and rolling it beneath his palm, pressing it down on the marble board. Selecting a knife, the sharpest, cruellest knife, he slices the fruit, squeezes the juice of one half into the shaker and agitates the shaker in a short, violent burst. He strains the drink into a double martini glass, pouring it over a sparkling mound of crushed ice. The silver salver is held out once more, and Hemingway's meaty fingers grip the delicate stem. Resting his palms on the brass rim of the bar, he watches the glass travel to the lips hidden in the beard.

It's the gravel shriek of a cocrico that wakes Shake from his dream of tending the bar at El Floridita. He is hauled south across the Caribbean Sea, dragged from Havana to his bed in St George, by the raucous, disgruntled call of the birds outside his shuttered window. Shake lies in the gloom of pre-dawn and wonders what Papa Dobles would have made of his effort, wonders if he'd have smiled or spat it out. The cocrico shrieks again and Shake pushes away his early morning thoughts. He climbs out of bed and throws open the rotting shutters. There are the birds, long brown tails hanging uselessly as they scramble and squabble in an allemanda bush, tearing ravenously at the golden petals, which look pale grey in the still-sunless early morning. He claps his hands and the cocricos stare at him a moment, heads held high, bright red throats looking as if they have been cut, before returning to their ravening. Shake shrugs, scratches a heel with the horny ball of a foot, yawns. He looks at the pit beyond the allemanda bush where his swimming pool will be, a pit which will collapse if it's not lined before wet season. Shake imagines diving into cool turquoise water, lapping for half an hour before climbing out, towelling himself and drinking a fresh, cold smoothie. Pushing aside a bead curtain he walks into the shambles of his galley kitchen, fills a kettle with purified water from a plastic bottle, balances it carefully on the slanting gas hob. Saltbag, his old black and tan dog, pushes into the kitchen, tail wagging, and Shake fills a bowl with chow, takes it outside and strokes her head as she begins to crunch the biscuits. Back in the kitchen, he tears open a pack of Chief coffee with his teeth as he switches on his laptop, hits a favourite site and scans the meteorological charts for the Lesser Antilles; Hurricane Zorro has sheared north, heading for Florida, predicted to rip through Haiti on the way. He zooms in on the Republic of Sansobella, St George and Dorado. Zooms in again – should be OK. One metre swell, winds ten to fifteen. He'll skirt west of the island, pick up the customers from the Oriole Hotel's jetty and then through Grackle Bay and fish off Torpoint, on the trench lip.

Dressed in tatty, stained T-shirt and shorts, Shake stands for a moment, drinking coffee on his makeshift, creaking porch, cobbled together from the ends of sawn timber lengths, and he watches the sun clear Rickey Point, sees the palms and pouis swamping the village of Vampiro opposite as they turn a rich, deep green. Then the clamber down sixty-seven steps to Gilbey beach, where he collects his surfboard from a padlocked cage beneath a sea grape, and paddles out to *Ribailagua*. He ties up the board before hauling himself on deck, water sluicing from him, staining the wooden slats dark. Shake fires the engines, watches blue smoke coil and fade from the exhaust, checks the electrics and radio. *Ribailagua* cruises slowly to shore, Shake barely revving, aware of people sleeping in the fan-spun bedrooms of Myers, Vampiro and Tom Collins, the village and villas dotted around the bay. He feels the hull bump and nestle into sand and tosses the anchor, checks back, before cutting the engines. It takes five trips to load the iceboxes, spare can of diesel, crates of beer and soda. Shake checks his watch, looks along the beach and sees a sauntering Bap, T-shirt pulled up to his armpits, scuffing the sand.

'Hey – you're late!' Shake taps his watch.

'I thorry.' Bap jogs the last few metres, takes the last icebox from Shake. 'Climbed the macaroni tree lath night. Many time.' And Bap smiles.

'Jesus! What happened to your teeth?'

There is a long, blank space where Bap's teeth had been two days before.

'I eating thouth an' drivin' when de thtorm come Tuethday night. Tunder came right here,' Bap drops the icebox and waves a black hand over his head, 'juth here. I thpit out pig foot and trow it in de drain. When I get home, no teeth. I thpit dey out too by mithtake. I wen' back, but de thtorm washed dey away.'

Shake thinks of the American he's collecting, a merchant banker or something from New York; all Regatta and Polo and Armani, the kind of man who'd be wearing Calvin Klein boxers and Givenchy aftershave to go deep sea fishing. Not to mention his wife and daughter, both mall minxes. The daughter in blonde cornrows and toe rings, belly like a washboard, tits barely covered in six hundred dollars of Versace. Shake watches Bap wade through the water and heave the box onboard.

'When can you get some more?' he shouts.

'More wha'?'

'Teeth. When can you get some more teeth?'

Bap shrugs. 'When me haf money. Next trip to Thanthobella, maybe.'

Shake mounts the steps back to his shack, showers in cold water, shaves as best he can. He ties his dark hair in a tight, short ponytail, slips on clean shorts and T-shirt – decorated with his logo, Dream Chaser – collects his cell phone, cap, sunglasses and log book before jogging back down to the beach and joining Bap on *Ribailagua*. The boat chugs out around the small headland, Midori Reef breaking turquoise waves to the north, shattering the swell, reducing it to foam and confused water. Once past Vampiro, the swell picks up again and the hull thuds as it rises and falls. Shake opens up the throttle, dancing across the crests, sliding sideways and correcting the slew. Bap barely notices, busies himself with bait and tackle.

'We got three,' yells Shake above the engine's roar.

Bap nods, sucks at the gap in his gum.

The American family are waiting on the jetty of the Oriole Hotel, and Shake can tell they're trouble even before he nudges the pilings and Bap ties up.

'Morning.'

The man checks his watch before ignoring Shake's helping hand and climbing aboard and Shake catches the scent of Ralph Lauren's 'Polo'. The wife, tall and pale, does take Shake's hand and as she steps in clumsily, he notices the angry rash of pus-tipped bites on her ankles and shins. She lurches with the swell as she sits, and her bony hip thuds against the corner of the bait box. She closes her eyes slowly and breathes deeply, lowering her head. Shake hasn't seen such a display of long-suffering for quite a while. He's irritated with her already and he's only known her thirty seconds.

'You OK?' he asks

The woman nods quickly, almost imperceptibly, compressing her lips. Bap gurns behind her.

When Shake turns to help the daughter on board he finds himself to be the object of frank, liquefying sexual interest. The girl, who is wearing nothing but a pussy pelmet and crop top, the number 69 picked out in sequins across her breasts, grasps Shake's hand as if she'll never let it go, and steps, slowly, achingly slowly, stretching toes, calves and thighs, opening her legs, over the gunwale of *Ribailagua*.

'Thank you,' she says, then she settles on the bench opposite her parents and begins to examine her painted nails.

'OK.' Shakes claps his hands – a gesture that irritates even him but which is habitual. He reaches behind the wheel and pulls out a laminated map of the island of St George glued on hardboard. 'Well, welcome aboard. My name's Shake, and this is Bap, who's crewing today. Given the forecast this morning we're going to head round the west side of the island, along Pillikin, here, then south through Grackle Bay. We'll cast some lines then, see if we get something along the way, and then we'll be trolling off Torpoint, near the Three Sisters. Just a bit of background info so you can appreciate what you'll be doing and what you'll be seeing. As you can see from the map, the republic is actually three islands, the main one, Sansobella, is due south and you'll be able to see the mountains on the north of Sansobella once we've cleared the west coast of St George. St George, as you can see, is much smaller than Sansobella, and much prettier you'll be glad to know. The third island, Dorado, here, is smaller again. It's actually a volcano and before you ask it's not extinct but it is, apparently, dormant. Which is good news for all the film stars and rock stars who live there. There's a deep trench between Sanso and St George, and that's why the fishing is so good. Let's get going and check it out. Life jackets are under here, just lift this buckle . . .' Shake talks the safety patter without thought. 'We should be back at the hotel by about half past eleven, with something for supper.'

Shake looks up to see the wife fiddling in her shoulder bag, as her daughter stares into the middle distance. And he knows, he just knows, the guy – what's his name? Mr Westmore? – is going to ask a pointless technical question. Shake gets the impression Mr Westmore hasn't climbed the macaroni tree for some time.

'I was wondering, Mr Shake, what horsepower d'you have here?'

'Two diesel Yanmar engines, two hundred and forty hp.'

'Oh, I see.' Mr Westmore looks saddened by this fact and Shake wonders why he asked.

'Anyway – let's get going. Make sure you put on lots of sun-block and wear a hat if you have one. I've got some spare. Help yourself to beer, coke, water, whatever you want from the icebox. It'll take about thirty minutes to reach Torpoint. If you need any-thing, ask Bap.'

Bap smiles alarmingly and lisps a greeting.

Shake climbs up onto the flybridge as Bap casts off the bow line, and *Ribailagua* eases away from the jetty. Out in open water, the swell increases and Shake powers up, begins to plane the waves, reducing the pitch. Mr Westmore hauls himself up the ladder and comes to stand by Shake, legs braced, feet splayed, arms crossed.

'Everything OK?' asks Shake.

'Fine.' Mr Westmore nods his pale ginger head. 'I was won-dering where the name comes from?'

'What name?'

'The name of your boat. It's a strange name.'

'It's named in honour of Constante Ribailagua, the head barman of El Floridita in Havana, 1912 to 1952.'

'Oh, OK.' Mr Westmore frowns. 'You're English, aren't you?'

'Yes.'

'My great-grandmother came from an English village called Frithelstock Stone, in Devon. Maybe you know it?'

'Afraid not.'

'No. No one ever does.' Mr Westmore looks even more despondent than before.

'I was born in England but I left when I was two and I haven't lived there for a long time.' Shake feels compelled to apologize for his ignorance. 'But it's interesting, because if you look at a map of St George a lot of the names are from Devon. Some of the sailors who landed here must have been from the area. There's Exeter, Torpoint, Plymouth and Tamar for a start.'

'How long you been doing this?'

'About ten years now.'

'Hmm. Must be a great life. I work on Wall Street in hedge funds.' Mr Westmore grips the grab rail. 'I have a seven bedroom house in Greenwich, a son at Yale and a beautiful daughter. I drive a Jaguar or my Maserati if I want a change. Sometimes I drive out to our summer house at Sag Harbor on Long Island, where I own a bar and restaurant, where I have a sixty-foot yacht moored. I also have a duodenal ulcer, hypertension and haemorrhoids.'

Not surprising he looks so sad, thinks Shake. But when he glances at Mr Westmore, it's to find the man smiling slightly.

'Well,' says Shake, 'I have a one room wooden shack on a piece of land that looks like a clearing in a jungle with an empty swimming pool pit in the middle. There's one tap with cold water and the power cuts out twice a day usually, sometimes more. The phone line goes dead most days. I drive a fifteen-year-old Land Rover, when it allows me. I'm building a concrete house and I have more outgoings than income. I also have a crocked left knee.'

'Last year we went to Puerto Rico, year before to Nassau.'

'Nice.'

'No, not nice.' Mr Westmore mops the sweat from his temples. 'Just more of the same. Went looking for something different and they weren't it. It's not the same – Wall Street. It's not the same. I've worked there more than twenty years and it's not the same. The whole city is different. Everyone I know has been looking for something ever since and I don't know anyone who's found it.'

Shake always has a problem with this, does not know what to say.

He'd been out deep sea fishing with four young, English guys early that morning, around Jacamar Island, and he didn't get back to dock until nearly nine. The Englishmen had been disgruntled and sunburned by the time they returned, and walked off to the Oriole Palm Bar with barely a thank you. Shake remembers looking round and the grounds were deserted, no security, no gardeners, no guests around the pool. He'd cleaned up the boat and then walked across the manicured lawns to the beach bar, puzzled by the set of the shoulders of the men there, puzzled by their immobility, their silence. Shake arrived in time to see a replay of the second plane coming in, argent and curving, arcing like a scimitar as it sliced through the tower. Shake stared as the clip replayed, frame by frame, each frame matching the slamming of his eyelids. His hands and thighs felt suddenly cold and he'd sat on a stool, looking up at the screen, waiting to believe what he was seeing over and over and over again. The bartender poured him a straight whisky, unasked, and Shake – who never touched anything stronger than an occasional beer when he had the boat – drank it and the glass was refilled. He sat there for hours, with the same men, building yet another fence, fighting the sense of mute panic. The world kept showing itself to Shake its awful immensity and he kept trying to draw it back in, pull it back in, reduce it once again to an unimportant, sunlit Caribbean island. No one spoke. Sometimes the men glanced at each other, sometimes they cried and no one said anything. When the near-atomic dust clouds began to race along the concrete canyons, burgeoning florets of breathlessness, a heavy-set blond man stood, set his stool carefully against the bar, wiped his eyes with the heels of hands, and said, 'That's it, then.' And everyone knew exactly what he meant.

'That's why I came here, to St George,' says Mr Westmore. 'I don't want just another slice of America with white sand. I want . . . shoot, I don't know what I want. To live a little, maybe. To not feel safe. Because anyway, I don't feel safe. I never feel safe. So why pretend it's all the same? My duodenal ulcer? I got that *since* nine eleven. It's not the work, it's not the dealing and the commuting and the parties. It's not that.'

'No.'

'Don't know why I'm telling you all this. Never told anyone before.'

'It's because you'll never see me again.' Shake slows the Bertram 31, and the bow drops a little. 'You should put some cream on your face. The wind makes it feel like you're OK but you're burning all the same. Here.' Shake ferrets in a box and digs out a tube of SPF 30.

'Thank you.' Mr Westmore takes off his baseball cap and slathers his face with the white cream, which smells of coconut and banana. He looks at Shake, face clown-like, his pale eyes made yellow by contrast. 'I have to tell you, I never fished before.

Not even when I was a kid and I always wanted to. That was another reason for coming here – a colleague told me you got some of the best fishing in the world around St George. So I told Marcia, my wife, to sort it out and she did. Got a week at the Oriole, with a driver. My income,' says Mr Westmore with another of his quiet smiles, 'exceeds my outgoings, however hard I try to spend it.'

'I mean, like, what is *hap*pening here?' Lolita steps onto the tiny flybridge, has little choice but to nestle herself against Shake. 'I mean – that guy downstairs, with the teeth? Gross. God, Daddy, what's with you?'

'My daughter, Leanne.'

'Hello, Leanne.'

The pressure of her breasts against his back increases slightly. 'Hi there, Captain Shake. When do we get to kill us some fish?'

'Um, pretty soon. If you could both go down on deck, we'll drift for a while here, see how we do.'

Ribailagua begins to rock gently in the swell as father and daughter climb down to the deck and Shake follows them. In the cockpit, he switches on the occasionally functioning fish-finder, curses as the five-inch screen wavers and breaks up. Bap looks over his shoulder. Whispers.

'What yuh doin'? Us never uthe dat.'

'I know, I know. Shit.' Shake hits the consol and the screen flickers green and red. 'Bap – can you look after the women? I'm going to work with Mr Westmore.'

'Can I look after de women? Can *I* look after de women? Watch me now.' Bap dances across the deck, his body fluid as warm oil.

As it happens, the Westmore family doesn't return to the

Oriole until past midday. Marcia Westmore, her stomach empty, having heaved her breakfast over the side, is near-delirious with sunstroke and lust. She has watched Bap for hours, watched the way his body moves: the sharp, scallop-edged torso of the black man as it bends over the gunwale, manoeuvring the gaff; the length of his thigh; the long, loose knot of his calf muscles, higher than she has ever seen before; the balance, the ballet of his moving around the deck. Leanne, who is seventeen, who is half-naked, who is baked through with heat, yeast rising, has watched Shake's every move. Has watched his arms and hands, tanned a colour she didn't know existed on the spectrum of white bodies, as they conjure an instrument from hooks, filaments and weights. Has watched jealously as Shake's tall, lightweight body wraps itself around her father's, showing him how to reel in and release. Has watched as Shake takes off his baseball cap and shades, revealing strange grey-green eyes, to reset his ponytail, shot through, Leanne notices, with grey hair. And then there is Mr Westmore, ginger and pink, awkward and proud, weaving a little as he follows his family down the jetty. Dangling from his right hand, which is raised, which is bloodied, is a brace of kingfish. Vicious fish, silver as fuselages, ancient as coelcanth, difficult to lure as a spurned woman, tasty as an experienced whore. Mr Westmore, manager of hedge funds on Wall Street, father of arrogant, over-privileged children; worn, inadequate husband of the now-swooning Marcia, reaches the end of the pier and turns in the blaze of red-hot sun, waves with his unbloodied hand. The hunter's farewell. But *Ribailagua* is already motoring away, churning the plankton-rich waters, heading for Gilbey beach.

*

Shake and Bap clean the snapper and grouper caught by Leanne and her mother, slicing and yanking out guts on the deck of *Ribailagua,* Shake half-listening to Bap lisping what, exactly, he would like to do to the seventeen-year-old American girl, sketching curves with his scale-crusted pink palms. Bap laughs as he remembers how Leanne had screamed when her fish came up, hook snagged through a gill, how she had cannoned around the deck, as the grouper gasped and flapped, flicking her bare belly with pale, bloody water.

When they're done, Shake bags the catch and gives it to Bap. 'There you go.'

'Yuh no wan'?' Bap takes the bag, points to the pack of du Maurier in Shake's pocket. 'Gimme one.'

Shake gives him a cigarette, lights one for himself, then pulls a wad of bills from his pocket; Mr Westmore had paid cash for the trip. Shake flicks the bills, counting. Whistles. 'The guy gave us a tip. Some tip. Said he had the time of his life.'

Bap smokes and watches closely. 'Yuh wath good to him, man.'

'Here.' Shake gives Bap an American hundred dollar bill. 'I want you to go to Sansobella and get your teeth fixed. You spend it on anything else and you ain't working for me again.'

Bap grins and kisses the note. 'I go on ferry to Thanthobella dith evenin'. Nex time yuh ketch me, I beautiful again.'

'Can you tell Stumpy to come by me on Monday? I've got a booking early morning. It's an all-day Dorado trip.'

Bap frowns. 'Thtumpy? Him a pithintail – him no like work.'

'Maybe not, but he likes money. Just make sure you get your teeth.'

Bap jumps into the water and wades ashore, yelling to a driver who's pulling away from the beach, wanting a drop back home.

The routine of Shake's morning is reversed; the boat is emptied and tied up, the board paddled ashore and he climbs the steps to his shack. The door is – as always – unlocked and he pushes it open with his elbow, drops log book and cell phone on the rickety table, dumps an icebox in the corner. He changes back into the tatty T-shirt and shorts, which have dried salt-stiff, and takes the last of his beastly cold S&G beers down to his hammock beneath the pink poui at the edge of his property. Swinging gently in the shade, beer finished, Shake sleeps, one hand on his heart, the other flung above his head. He wakes two hours later, when the sting has gone out of the sun, and labours a while in his plot, slashing vines and uprooting brush with a cutlass, setting a fire which burns the sap and dry coconut husks in a sweet-smelling, drifting blue cloud. Shake lights a du Maurier and sits on the ground, wiping his face with a sweat rag, admiring his work. Slowly, over the months, he's cleared most of the back of the property. Around the front, by the gate, there are piles of breeze blocks, plywood spots for concrete, distorted buckets, broken tiles, long lengths of rusty steels waiting to be angled by heavy spanners to support the walls. But out here, round the back, he can begin to picture the garden – he'll plant ixora and double oleander, ginger lilies and banks of heliconia, maybe some crotons? Against the walls he'll have the dark salmon bougainvillea he likes, with a few of the blood-red variety thrown in. Maybe a path running across there? Or should it curve in front of the Tuff tanks, with trellis covered in blue pea? Should he have air bricks across the south wall of the utility room, or just a square of them? Should he be doing any of this? Should he be building in concrete? Shake falls back, bareback, on the stony, earthy ground, lies there unmoving, compressed by panic, and he drifts away, drifts to the place, which he cannot name, where he retreats to escape this compression. Shake is not sleeping, his eyes are shut and his ribs are moving, but he is not sleeping. When the weight – which never diminishes, which never changes – is finally lifted from him, he finds the fire is smoking, nearly dead, and the Saltbag is lying next to him, keeping him warm.

Dragon the builder has knocked Shake up a makeshift shower – a small wooden enclosure with three fixed walls, a half door and no roof. The water runs off the single mains tap and it's always hot at first and then freezing, sluicing away down to the main drain. As Shake soaps his body he considers which cocktail to mix himself that evening, decides on a vampiro since the only spirit he has is silver tequila. But later, when he comes to add the tequila to the orange and tomato juice, honey, Worcester Sauce, onion and chilli, he finds the Sauza bottle has gone.

'Shit.' The bottle had only been half full but all the same.

Shake whistles and Saltbag, who he'd found as a puppy in the bush behind Grand Anse beach on the day he arrived in St George, starving, her skull suppurating from a cutlass chop, the dog who'd been with him for ten years, hauls herself to her feet and follows Shake down the steps to Gilbey beach. The two of them slowly walk the length of the sands and back, Saltbag sniffing in the brush, snuffling amongst the palm fronds, lilies and driftwood as Shake watches the frigate birds spiralling on the thermals, some so high they're like floaters in his eyes, moving against a sky which is paling before sunset. A line of pelicans, rising and dipping, near-skimming the water, lazily flapping wings in synchrony, head west towards Pillikin. A customer, some guy from a college in Wales, had once told him that a group of pelicans was called a scoop. A scoop of pelicans. Shake likes that. Looking up, he sees Mister Jeremiah sitting on the smooth rock at the end of the beach, hands on knees, feet splayed. Shake calls Saltbag to heel and he sits on the sand at Mister Jeremiah's feet.

'Good night,' says Mister Jeremiah.

'Good night. How're you doing?'

The old man shrugs. 'I t'irsty.'

'So'm I. Looks like Bones has been in my place today. Took a bottle of tequila.'

'I see him on the road looking for a drop. Him look happy.'

'That'll be the tequila.'

Mister Jeremiah frowns, looks down at the white man. 'Why you no lock yo' door? Yuh crazy man? Or jus' a sweet hand Dan?'

Shake shrugs, strokes Saltbag's greying muzzle. 'I've known Bones a long time. He's always thought I owe him a drink.'

'I got me no cuchuments an' I lock *mih* door.' Mister Jeremiah blows out his cheeks, watches the tide retreating.

'Why are you thirsty then? Bones steal your beer too?'

'No. The Essangee beer strike in Sansobella – it bite. No beer making now for two month. We runnin' out. In Sansobella dey got themselves some and dey keepin' it. It said the hotels here have some but we not. Soon be nuttin' but Miss Tubby and rainwater.'

Shake considers this. He's not read the papers, does not have a television and his radio is broken. His laptop he uses only for business. He relies on bush talk, on the fishermen, on friends to tell him what he needs to know – which isn't much. 'But it will be OK, won't it? I mean, Kouranis can't keep it up.'

'Kouranis?' Mister Jeremiah hawks mightily and spits in the sand. 'Why him care? Him got money, him own Essangee brewery, him own Miss Tubby factory. He own damn near ever'ting. He can sit an' wait and we go t'irsty. Or we drink Miss Tubby. Either way him still get money.' The old man sucks his teeth. 'Or someone maybe kidnap him. Kill him.'

Even Shake knows that Kouranis owns more than the brewery and the soft drinks factory. He also owns a daily newspaper, the Chunky Chick fried chicken company, KupKake fast-food outlets and a construction business. And not only in St George; he owns all the outlets in Sansobella too, as well as malls across the main island. Property, transport, restaurants, the brewery, a haulage firm, the ferry company. He also owns Coral Strand, and every time Shake hears Kouranis' name, he pictures Rajiv's father sitting in a cabanah twenty-five years before, drinking rum, telling Baboo that Kouranis may be richer than God. Kouranis is Greek, the people of Sansobella are East Indian, Venezuelan, Chinese, Brazilian, Hispanic, Korean and Black; the people of St George are nearly all West African black, the few people living in Dorado are wealthy white. A heady mix. A dangerous cocktail. Shake watches a pirogue heading into the bay, outboards roaring, elegant, curved prow riding high, the lashed bamboo outriggers sketching the outline of a heart.

'I'm sure they'll sort something out. I mean, we can't live without Essangee beer.'

'Who dis "dey?" nuh? Who dis "dey" doin' de sortin'? Kouranis – him can live widout beer. Man drinks champagne for breakfast.' Mister Jeremiah stands, very slowly, rubbing his back.

'I'm driving round to Wrexall on Sunday – can I pick up anything for you?'

'I begin to t'ink some commanding powders be a good idea.' Mister Jeremiah laughs. 'Yuh could fetch me mih goat. It bein' held in Exeter for me. Yuh know Cussbud Perky?'

Shake looks up at the old man, shades his eyes. '*Who?*' Even by the standards of St George, this is a name to conjure with.

'He drive a liddle vehicle, a liddle red English vehicle.'

'A red Mini?'

'Dat de one.'

'I've seen it. I think I know the guy.'

'If yuh can trouble dat would be good.'

'Sure, I'll get it.'

'What o'clock you come by?'

'I guess about five. Is that OK?'

Mister Jeremiah nods, waves an arthritic hand and makes his way down to the water's edge for a sea bath. Shake watches the old man rubbing down with damp sand before rinsing himself. Jeremiah Roberts is one of the few locals left on the Killdevill peninsula. He owns a plot of land further down the beach, on a sandstone bluff, looking out over Myers and the sea. It's a steep plot and the old man's house is a three-room wooden structure, built in the old style, with a corrugated tin roof and six-pane wooden casement windows, the porch framed with elaborate batchboard. It stands on four, slender concrete pilings, two thirty-feet high, two ten-feet high. When the storms come through, Shake worries for the Roberts family. There is a tap at the front of the house, but no water inside, there are chicken coops and yardie hens running round. The yard is terraced in places, and the family grows lettuce and peppers, tomatoes and bodie beans. Washing is strewn on the fencing to dry and there are stacks of sawn timber in the uncultivated front garden. Mister Jeremiah has been variously offered one, two and three million US dollars for his fine plot and each time he laughs and the other occupants of Killdevill sigh. His great-granddaddy slaved on the old Huggins estate and bought himself out come emancipation, then he bought a parcel of the land he'd slaved on. Jeremiah Roberts isn't about to sell the only thing he has, where his family have lived for generations. Each time he scythes the grasses or tills the soil he imagines he can smell sugar cane and rum and molasses, imagines he can hear the crack of whips, the clank of shackles, and he's right. Mister Jeremiah and his wife, Miss Avarice (now, *there's* a misnomer, thinks Shake), raised eleven children in the teetering house. Eleven children, who have borne more than fifty grandchildren and they, in turn, have multiplied. Mister Jeremiah is proud of them and so he should be; with a couple of exceptions, they have all married and made lives that have spread from the freed slave's smallholding to Sansobella, to Trinidad, Barbados, New York, Miami, London, Toronto. They have become teachers, architects, factory-line managers, firemen, psychiatric nurses, chefs. And Mister Jeremiah is proud of them all. Shake has met many of them, is sometimes invited to eat with the family when curried goat is cooked up, and he is humbled. Because he looks around the house where they were raised and he remembers some of the grandchildren spilling off the porch in the mornings, ready for school, immaculate in dark blue gymslips, shirts whiter than surf with bright red ribbons tied around their pigtails, or crisp beige shorts with a black belt and spotless pale blue shirts, leather satchels buffed to a high sheen. How did Mister Jeremiah and Miss Avarice manage that? How did any of them manage it? But they did. Mister Jeremiah is an elder in his church; he believes in a god. He prays to his god and he thanks him. Shake remembers when he met Mister Jeremiah and the first question he'd asked was about Shake's wife, about their children. When Shake replied he had neither, Mister Jeremiah had shaken his head and said he would pray for Shake. Mr Jeremiah may believe in a god, but when the times demanded it, the commanding powders supplied by the Obeah man came in handy. Voodoo, Hoodoo, Obeah, the black arts of revenge practised in hot, dark, stolen lands.

Saltbag shifts, moves her paws in the sand and begins to pant. The dog needs feeding. Shake stands, brushes the sand from his shorts and waves a farewell to Mister Jeremiah, who is too busy scratching and rubbing his thick, greying hair to reply. When Shake and Saltbag arrive back home on the porch, Shake sees there's a fly infestation around the light. Thousands of winged ants, flying, spasming, crawling. He gives Saltbag a bowl of chow and boiled, flaked snapper and watches the arrival of frogs, tongues flicking, picking off the flies as they fall. An hour later the porch is littered with a carpet of dead flies. Shake sweeps it clean, smokes a last cigarette and takes himself to bed.

15 June

Shake spends the next day, a broiling Saturday, visiting the hotel complexes around Grand Anse and the airport, checking they have his leaflets, flyers and cards, talking to the receptionists and managers, drinking Bentleys in the bars, acting smooth and easy, making sure they remember him. Flyers distributed, he drives the short stretch of highway to Bridgewater, parks by the ferry terminal and visits the S&G Post Office to collect a parcel. He queues for twenty minutes at one of three booths; the other two have bored women slumped in them, heads in hands, doodling on pads, refusing to look up at the customers. Eventually he reaches the head of the queue, hands over ID and asks for a delivery from the US. The woman disappears into a back room and Shake, shivering a little in the air-conditioned air, retreats into the white space he keeps empty and pristine for times just like these. He replays *Spartacus* in his mind as he waits for the woman to reappear. When she does, shoe heels scuffing the tiled floor, she is empty-handed. She sits once more, with a sigh, and motions for the man behind Shake to step forward.

'Excuse me.' Shake leans forward. 'I know the parcel was sent more than a month ago. I'm sure it must be here.'

The woman sighs again, sucks her teeth. 'It been hot.'

'What?'

'The girls no like carrying when it hot.'

'Fine. Well, anyway, that's why I've come here, so the girls don't have to carry the post in the heat. I've come to collect it.'

'We having troubles here. Since last two months.'

The tender for the management of S&G Post had been put up six months before and, rather surprisingly, New Zealand Post had secured it. The odyssey of Shake's parcel is being orchestrated by someone who works ten thousand miles away from the point of posting and nine thousand from the point of delivery. More than that, this person is now living a different day, tomorrow, whilst Shake is struggling to get through today.

'Is dis it?' The security guard places a parcel in front of the woman.

She scans it, matches the name on the ID and nods. Looks up at the security guard and frowns, annoyed that her incompetence has been undermined. She punches the pad of a calculator, pushes the parcel across to Shake and holds out her hand. 'Dat two hundred dollah.'

'What?'

'You pay tax on it. Ten per cent and the value of goods stated at tree hundred US. So dat's two hundred dollah Essangee.'

'But look – it's got "urgent" written all over it, plus it's stamped right there. It arrived in Sansobella on May nineteenth. That's more than three weeks ago.'

'Two hundred Essangee dollah or I can' release it.'

Shake pays up and fumes as he walks back out into blinding sunlight, freezing sweat inching down his spine. He needs to visit the hardware store and he decides to walk there. Bridgewater is not an attractive town. Occasionally cruise ships venture into Grackle Bay and drop anchor, and dinghies bring curious tourists ashore. If they're expecting to be greeted with ready smiles before being led along dusty streets lined with gingerbread mansions, built in the shade of flamboyants and jacarandas, boasting porches where iced tea and fresh mango juice is served beneath whispering fans, they're in for a disappointment. Shake walks along the promenade, now devoid of palms, which have been cut down to make way for thatched concrete huts, where vendors set out T-shirts made in China, sporting the familiar, smudged face of Bob Marley, along with carvings imported from Guyana and Mexico. He stops by the wide river, the reason for the town's name, and buys a double with hot sauce from an Indian serving from a polystyrene Eskie strapped in the basket of his pushbike. Shake stands in the shade of a furniture store by the river and eats, watching the sluggish snake of filthy water make its way to the harbour, a flotilla of small Miss Tubby bottles drifting amongst the plastic bags and beer bottles. Finishing the last mouthful of chana and bake, he wipes his fingers and sets off to cut through the market, a concrete rotunda, with concrete floor and concrete stalls. The market sparks thoughts of communism and sickles for Shake, makes him think of Russia. But, of course, it's sweltering, the air trapped beneath the roof is fetid and unmoving, flies zooming in random, electric blue triangles, drunk with excess, overjoyed by the abundance of rot. And behind each stall there sits, not a babushka but an old woman from the hills. Each early morning they come, carrying their panniers of green oranges, shadon benet, scythe, cristophene, mangoes, plantain, lettuces, callaloo, bodie beans, tomatoes, pawpaw, breadfruit, pigeon peas, portugals, rough lemons and limes the size of mar-bles – whatever's in season. The women sit, hands crossed in their laps, dressed in long skirts and shirts, working men's boots or barefoot. They are unmoving – having long ago learned not to move unless the cavalry is coming – apart from their dark brown, dark-blue tinged eyes, which follow Shake everywhere. But the produce is good, freshly harvested, grown in deep, dark volcanic earth, watered by hilltop rain. Shake stops long enough to buy a handful of oranges, some lemons and limes.

'Twenny et dollah.' The crone holds out her hand.

'How are you, Miss Lizbeth?' Shake listens hard as she answers; Miss Lizbeth is more than eighty years old, she doesn't know how much more exactly. She has lived in the hill village of Beaulieu all her life. At the end of every night she climbs down to the road, in the still-dark, where she waits for a drop to Bridgewater, because now she needs cash when she used only to need goods to barter. Miss Lizbeth eats yardie chicken or fish, pig foot and rice most days, sits on her porch at night, sucking chenet, and watches the moon pass. Miss Lizbeth still corrugates her clothes on a washboard, still collects water from a pump, still talks the old way.

'Yuh nuh know whey win' a-come from fuh blow fowl tail. Summer han' Curtis a jacket. Aiyee – what carryin' ons and Curtis him since been drinkin' rum. Her nuttin' but a goat mout, Marie-salope. Yeh Curtis? Him a big mou mou man yet so him let she res'. But I say him in trey-trey,' and Miss Lizbeth leans forward, points an improbably bony, brown finger at Shake, 'who do good fuh jumbie is dem self jumbie do fright.'

'Right.' Shake waves a hand and moves on, leaving Miss Lizbeth to jabber at the world. He can still hear her as he walks out of the market. He has no idea what she's talking about.

In the hardware store, Shake finds the shackles and pliers he needs, walks to the counter, and waits as a tall, heavy woman in a dazzling fuchsia skirt, white shirt and white turban argues over a padlock. Shake is fascinated, at first, by the scars on her hands and upper arms, but this interest fades after a while. The woman is talking fast and thick and the storekeeper looks bored. It would seem the woman wants some copies of the key which opens the lock, but the store owner refuses to cut them, saying it's cheaper for her simply to buy a new one. Eventually he pushes the padlock back across the counter. 'Yuh haf to buy another.'

Incensed, the woman grabs the lock, announces 'Dis is a lost nation!' and sweeps out.

Susannah Huggins' villa, Mojito, stands alone on a peak, the highest point on the peninsula of Killdevill, where she can look out over Midori Reef, Gilbey beach and Tom Collins. On clear days she can see the distant peak of Mt St Catherine in Grenada. As Shake backwashes the pump basket of her infinity pool, he looks north, and he can just make out his own place by the beach, can see the white dot that is *Ribailagua* in the bay, dimming now, in the fading sunlight. As he drops two fresh tablets in the basket and resets the cover, Susannah appears at the gallery railing above him.

'How long you going to be?' she calls.

'I've finished,' Shake shouts. 'Anything else you want doing?'

'Just a lightbulb up here.'

Shake fetches a ladder and changes the bulb, accepts a cold S&G beer (Susannah, of course, has a stash of crates) and takes it with him to one of the guest bathrooms, where he has a long, hot soak. He shaves, changes into fresh shirt and shorts, and joins

Susannah by the pool. Shake performs this routine every Saturday evening.

'What're you making tonight?' Susannah asks.

'Have you got any absinthe?'

'Yes, of course.'

'In that case I'm going to knock you up a Rattle Snake. Found the recipe the other day in an old book.' Susannah has a bar behind her jacuzzi, and Shake busies himself as he talks. 'Recipe's for six, but I figure we'll manage it. Apparently, either cures snakebite or kills snakes.' Shake mixes the rye whisky, egg whites, absinthe and sweetened lemon juice, blends them, and serves the cocktail strained through a sieve.

'Well?' he asks.

'Shit,' says Susannah. 'Kicks like a mule.'

Shake sips and frowns. 'Too much absinthe. It said a few dashes but I never really know what that means.' Shake sits, drinks and tells Susannah about his day, about the woman in the hardware store with the scarred hands and the fact that the two of them were, apparently, living in a lost nation.

'I know that woman,' says Susannah. 'She was born in Sansobella and married a man from here. They lived in Toronto for nineteen years and they both lectured at the university, apparently. As far as I know, they had a big house in the suburbs and the kids went to a good high school. They came back, must be last Christmas. I hate that. I *hate* that. Y'know, when they come back here, dress themselves up like market mammies and start talking about "we heritage, we culture", rev-ol-u-*shun* and e-man-ci-pa-*shun*. And they've just spent two decades living abroad, bringing up their kids to be well-educated, with good health care and then they come back here and when they're not going on about lib-er-a-*shun* they're complaining about the roads, the gardener, the outages, the water. And I'll tell you what else – she got the scars in Toronto, not here. Fucks me off.'

Shake smiles. Susannah is many things – judgmental and abrasive, intolerant and far too rich for her own good, but never dull. Susannah is seventh-generation St Georgian; the Huggins family had owned the flatlands between Pillikin and Grand Anse, all the way round to Exeter, as well as the Killdevill peninsula, where Mister Jeremiah's ancestors had slaved. The estate had thrived on the backs of slaves, indentured labour and stolen land, and around the walls of Susannah's villa hang old maps of the sugar cane fields in the Pillikin division, engravings of the distillery houses, boiling huts and racks of oak ageing barrels in the Killdevill division. Huggins' rum, sanguine and smoky, blended by masters and aged for at least seven years, was considered one of the finest single marks in the world; perhaps that was why Seagrams bought the Huggins' label in the late eighties. Susannah waited until her father died before she sold the remains of the estate lands, and fine estate houses, to developers. Then she had Mojito built, the villa on the hill, a state of the art glass, wood and marble affair without a jalousie, demarara, shingle or length of batchboard in sight. The towering atrium around which the house is built, has a retractable glass roof to deflect the tropical storms. Susannah employs a team of gardeners, a housekeeper and security at the gate; she also has a handyman and poolman, but she likes Shake to check the pools and Jacuzzi.

Susannah Huggins speaks Queen's English until the rum in her blood turns to blackstrap molasses and then her language becomes pure pidgin patois; even now, after ten years or more, Shake still finds it shocking when Susannah, who is not passing white but Cambridge-educated white-white, cusses out a local in their own terms, in their own voice. Susannah is not an average white woman; she is caught betwixt and between: she has no mother tongue.

Susannah's wealth has ensured she has never worked, never had to be employed by others. She reads and writes, surfs the net and watches cable television. She travels when she feels the urge, telling no one where she has been, what she has been doing on these travels. Shake happens to know but he says nothing. Susannah is occasionally overwhelmed by the desire to cook, and she will order ingredients from Sansobella and Trinidad, have Maine lobsters or French *paté de foie gras* shipped in. She once, famously, had a half dozen wild Cornish seabass flown in from England and spent a day preparing a twenty-seat dinner party, simply to prove that the local kingfish could be matched for flavour. When she throws these parties, Shake always finds that he is previously engaged. He did once accept an invitation to a cocktail party at the villa, attended by the great and good of St George, the ex-pats, the old families, the politicians, and he watched Susannah drinking rum until she felt the time had come to say something interesting if not complimentary about each of her guests. Yet all of them had accepted invitations since; Susannah Huggins is too rich to ignore. She is too bold, too angry, too unloved to ignore. Her wealth has ensured not only that she never has to work; it has also ensured that she is universally loathed.

'See the news today?' she asks Shake.

'No.' He knows where this is going, same place it always does.

'No change there, then.' She refills her glass from the shaker. 'Couple more of these and I'll be speaking with forked tongue. Twelve more US marines killed in Iraq. More photos from Abu Graihib. Genocide expected in Darfur.'

Shake senses the fence he began to build many years before grow a little taller, a little thicker. Sometimes things get over the fence, no matter how high he builds – the sight of a naked man cowering before a slavering dog as an American soldier laughs; a child, wearing only a vest, staring wide-eyed at the camera, pale face emptied of emotion, as a Russian policeman sprints with her in his arms, carrying her from the carnage that was her school; the distinct silver silence of falling snow.

'You don't give a shit, do you?' says Susannah conversationally.

'It's not that. I just . . . I just can't think about it. I can't stop it. I can't *change* any of it. It's too hard.'

'So you're happy to live in your little world, cruising around an island thirty miles long and seven wide, for the rest of your life? Having your fortnight in Florida once a year?'

'Oh, c'mon, Susannah. We've said all this a million times.'

'You need to find yourself a good woman, Shake. Wouldn't mind the love of a good woman myself, but I'm too old and too ugly. But I'm told you're considered quite a catch. What's stopping you?'

Shake knows Susannah's turned the corner, her blood is beginning to thicken and soon she'll be vex. He met a lover of Susannah's once, caught them by surprise in a bar on Collins in South Miami Beach. The lover had been young and Latvian, a tall, dour woman who spoke immaculate English. The three of them had a drink, talked of nothing and Shake had left the couple alone, walked on to the next bar. He wonders sometimes if Susannah has ever forgiven him that chance encounter.

'How's the fishing business? Still chasing dreams?' Susannah asks and this is why Shake comes back every Saturday. Susannah knows when to move on, when to shift the conversational focus.

'It's OK. It's good. Took an American family out yesterday – three of them. Got a Dorado trip on Monday.' Shake lights a du Maurier, fights the desire for another Rattle Snake. 'But I really need a new fish-finder. They sell these packages now – GPS/fish-finder combos but they're not cheap. Plus I need a new anchor, my VHF Ni-cad battery's knackered, outriggers are beginning to rust. I could go on: chafe guards, windlass, trolling combo, downrigger, trolling blocks, Morse controls. But, shit, I can't afford all that. And the mount of the fighting chair's beginning to look dodgy. I looked on the net for a Pompanette Tournament, and I couldn't believe it – they're over four thousand US bucks. So I guess I'll have to make do with a Todd sportfishing, they're only three-sixty.'

'How's the house coming along? Did you get the doors delivered?'

'Yeah, and I managed to fix the lintels and hang a couple of doors downstairs. But Dragon really needs to brick up and render upstairs. I mean, I work on it whenever I can but when I'm busy? The trouble is, it sucks up any profit I make.' Shake chews the inside of his cheek. 'I sometimes wonder if I'm doing the right thing. I mean, I can't really afford to live in Killdevill. Buying the land nearly wiped me out even eight years ago. I could sell it and walk away with a bundle of money. Maybe I should.'

'Don't do that. Build your concrete house, Shake. You know I can always help you out.'

Rum money. Blood money. 'Thanks but no thanks. Anyway, Rajiv's visiting soon. I'll talk to him.'

Susannah pours the last of the cocktail into her glass, diluted now by melted ice. 'You going to Jungle Jam?'

'Yeah. Ought to make a move, really.' But Shake just sits there, by the infinite waters, blowing smoke into the silence. The lights in the villages below them flick on and off as palm fronds move in the breeze and car headlights light the tracks, flaring and dying as they bump into potholes.

'Shake, I know you'll think I'm paranoid and I know you're not interested, or you pretend you're not. But I think something's happening.'

'What d'you mean?'

'Here. And on Sansobella: And maybe Dorado. The whole country. I think something's happening. I think it's something to do with Kouranis and the Indians. I've overheard a few people talking, read some articles and blogs. But it's more than that.'

'Like what?'

Susannah sighs, shifts in her chair. 'I can't explain it. It's a feeling more than anything else. Like a change in temperature. As if I've put my hand out the vehicle window and the temperature's suddenly dropped.'

'That's crazy.' But Shake is listening hard.

'I know, I know. But I think something's afoot, as you English would say.' Susannah finishes her drink and stares at the lip of her pool, which has no lip, which becomes the Caribbean Sea. 'It's about power. Power and money.'

'Isn't everything?'

'Now you're just being glib. You're not stupid, Shake, you just pretend to be. Think about what's going on.'

'It's just a strike – the usual shit about automation. It will be resolved.'

'This isn't about beer and you know it. It's about the colour of your skin.' Susannah thumps her chest. 'It's about the colour of your heart. The colour of your money.'

Shake stands up, pockets his cigarettes. 'It's wet season coming. People always get jumpy around now. Dragon was telling me the other day his bouchette has dropped.'

Susannah flicks this away with an angry hand. 'Fuck Dragon. Him jus' a bushboy who talk too much. Fucking dog amongst doctors.'

'I'd better get going. You OK? Do you want to go in and I'll let the dogs out?'

'No. I going to sit heah all on mih own an' admire mih view.' Susannah's voice is changing, rising and falling, changing shape.

'I'll call you.'

Susannah doesn't answer so Shake leaves her by her pool, collects his dirty clothes and walks through the exquisite, empty house. As he reaches his jeep, he hears a thick, deep voice.

'Shake, yuh be wary o' mashin'.' It's Susannah, leaning over a gallery, looking down at him. In the shadowy light of a hidden photocell she could be a soucoyant, a ghost.

Driving down one of the many tracks tracing the hills, jeep rolling and bouncing, heading for the coast road, Shake tries not to think of what Susannah has said. Instead he tries to measure her paranoia, tries to calibrate the extent of it. God knows, she has good reason to be paranoid, bitter old white slaver, sitting in her hard-edged, glass-lined castle on the hill, gated and guarded; rich as Croesus and queer to boot. Billy-bloody-no-mates, as an old teacher of his would have said.

He drives through Polonaise and Sangaree, down to the highway, which peters out at that point, becomes a rutted, narrow two-lane road, because the tourists rarely venture any farther from Pillikin and Grand Anse. He picks up two locals, who are also heading for the village of Paria and the Jungle Jam Bow Wow there. The boys are wearing muscle shirts and baggy pants, laceless high-tops and dreads. They offer him a toke of weed but Shake declines. They sit silently passing the joint back and forth until it's done. Turning off the road heading into Paria and the beach there, Shake can hear the music already – the inimitable chain-link, broken-glass sound-mesh of steel pan. He parks on a verge and the two locals saunter off, with a wave of their hands.

Paria is heaving, as it does every Saturday night, the population more than doubling. Saturday night is the big night in St George, Jungle Jam Bow Wow, where tourists, hustlers, locals, ex-pats, sex boys mingle as sweat flows. There are stalls on the track-side, generators throbbing as pirate CDs blare and barbecues flare with the oil dripping from chicken and sweet pork chop, burgers and fish. Roti and chana pie vendors ply their trade from the boots of cars. Crowds of pale tourists nervously touch their money belts as they walk, most avoiding eye contact. As Shake strolls down towards the beach, acknowledging the people he knows with a wave, a high five, or a knuckle knock, exchanging a few words, the pan stops and for a few minutes it is possible to make out the jumble of music spilling from the bars. Shake checks his watch – eleven o'clock – and almost immediately the ground begins to shake as the jump-up real baggai begins. He reaches the small, teeming strip, each bar proclaiming itself to be the original home of Jungle Jam Bow Wow, and there on the sand is a stack of speakers the size of a container truck, blasting the opening frenetic bars of what sounds like indie garage or garbage rap or ragga or whatever the fuck it is they call it. And on the sand, which is already filthy with napkins and plastic glasses and polystyrene boxes and shards of glass and empty half-bottles of rum and dented coke cans, a beast is dancing, a beast composed of hundreds of bodies. The beast, Shake thinks, looks savage tonight.

Shake likes to drink in the Bananaquit, a bar which looks like an engine repair shop, which *was* an engine repair shop until a couple of years before. Bald tyres and spanners are still the only decoration. Shake asks for an S&G.

'Yuh funny man.'

'You haven't got any?'

The barman sucks his teeth, shakes his head.

'Arawak?'

He shakes his head again.

'Wild Boar?' Shake doesn't like Wild Boar beer, but it doesn't look like he has much choice.

'I got Mauby and rum. Dat's it.'

'You really haven't got any beer?'

'Yuh want rum or what?'

'Where's Clydie?' Shake knows the guy who owns the Bananaquit – if there is any beer, Clydie will sell it to him. The barman tilts his chin at the beach, and there's Clydie, dancing like a duppy, sweating and shuffling his hips. Clydie never usually leaves the bar during Jungle Jam. 'I'll have a rum and water.'

Shake stands and watches the ruckus on the beach. The bass beat is running up his legs, he can feel it in his chest. An exodus of older tourists is taking place; they're running the gauntlet of rum-fuelled locals, who are asking for money, touching up the women, offering drugs, a ride, asking for a drop. The beat changes and the beast dances even faster. There are a few ex-pat white women drinking in the bars around, women who know how to handle themselves, women who've been around for a long, long time, but Shake notices even they are picking up their bags and choosing their moments to sidle out, head for their cars. The unintelligible, baying yells get louder, and Shake sees the flash of a cutlass outside the Red Light bar. There'll be some choppings tonight. Jungle Jam doesn't finish until dawn, so plenty of time yet for commotions. An overweight, sunburned white woman, maybe in her fifties, hair wet with sweat, plastered around her neck like a noose, showing blue-veined legs and sil-very stretch marks around her bare belly, staggers into the Bananaquit, breathing heavily, rests her head on her arms on the bar. A young man, tall and black, stands behind her, rubbing his crotch against her back.

'Hey beau-ti-ful, we have a rum and den we dance. You beau-ti-ful. I wan' yuh to have my babies.'

The woman hiccups and looks up with bleary eyes, turns awk-wardly and smiles up at him. 'Jus' one more.' Rocking with the effort, she forces a hand into tight shorts and pulls out some notes. Shake looks at the man, who looks straight back at him before running his hands over the woman's breasts. Two plastic glasses of neat, white rum appear and the two of them take off, the woman stumbling.

A tumult of shouts, the sound of breaking glass and Shake decides it's time to head home. He pushes through the crowds, grateful for being tall and relatively sober, and he sees Bap at the Red Light. Bap is stroking Leanne's face, crooning to her, as she weaves with the effort of standing. Bap tugs at Leanne's crop top, then wraps a huge hand around her waist, pulls her close to him, grinds his hips against hers.

Shake forces his way over to the bar and grabs Bap's arm, yanks it away. Bap reels back, steadies himself against another man, who shoves him. Bap's eyes are bloodshot, the lids droop-ing. On his shirt there's a red stain where he has dribbled hot sauce. Between his fingers he holds a burned-out cigarette butt. The neck of a half-bottle of puncheon rum sticks out of his jean's pocket.

'What the fuck are you doing here? You're supposed to be in Sansobella.'

Bap doesn't know who Shake is; all he knows is that he does-n't like him, doesn't like the white man. He's spent the hundred American dollars unwisely – on puncheon rum, roti and a few hits of crack cocaine. He swings at Shake and misses, falls against a group of drinkers, who close around him, shouting, waving fists and bottles. In the mêlée, Shake sees another man reach for the young American girl and he shoves him away, grabs Leanne and pulls her away from the bar, drags her down the track to his jeep, pushes her in the passenger seat and reverses quickly all the way down to the road, glancing back, expecting to see a river of black bodies chasing him, expecting to see the beast made fluid.

The journey to the Oriole is punctuated by Leanne's vomiting fits. When he finally arrives at the hotel's guarded barrier, Shake is glad that his skin colour means there is no questioning, no delay. He half-carries the limp Leanne into the hotel and tells the night receptionist to ring her parents' room and he leaves.

It's gone two in the morning before he sits on the step of his rotting porch, looking out over the black waters of Gilbey beach, moonlight scattering and regrouping over and over as *Ribailagua* bobs in the water below him. Saltbag slumps next to him, panting, and Shake buries his fingers in the old dog's tan and black fur, needing comfort. He can make out the rafters and breeze block walls of his incomplete concrete house and he thinks of the love of a good woman. Shake lies back on the sandy floorboards to stare at the sky and, as Saltbag rolls over and nestles against him, he notices how much the temperature has dropped.

16 June

After he's checked *Ribailagua* and then showered, Shake sets off in his jeep the next morning, Saltbag sitting in the passenger seat, seemingly smiling, content to watch the world go by. Shake drives down the east side of the Killdevill peninsula, through the villages of St Croix, Caipirinha, Craddock and Du Bouchett, to join the coast road at Paria. He sees men asleep in their cars, some young men staggering along the verge, trying to flag him down, still drunk or out of it from the excesses of Jungle Jam. Driving through Paria, Shake sees the village is wrecked, as if it has been plundered and pillaged, and he wonders if he'll ever go to Jungle Jam Bow Wow again. Ten years before, Saturday night in Paria was a celebration of pan, calypso and soca on the beach. Calypso Rose and Lord Kitchener would come over from Trinidad to sing there in front of an appreciative audience of locals, with tourists made welcome. There were bars serving S&G, Wild Boar and Arawak beers, and maybe a few bottles of rum were passed around. The only food then was roti, curried goat and doubles. People talked, they clapped, they danced, they went home. It was a good night, an easy night, a time to lime, a chance to ease up and relax yourself. But now the bass beat roared, the sand jumped and the beast cavorted on the beach as bashment crews made noise and drugs were bought, sold or stolen.

East of Paria, the island changes; the further he drives from Pillikin, Grand Anse and Coral Strand, the deeper he drives into the past. Through John Dory, Liberty and Exeter, tidy villages

with communal greens, small, shingled churches and grey, concrete emergency shelters, built to survive earthquakes. The land
through which the potholed road is carved, rising and falling, following the coast, is lush and untamed. Goats and cattle graze at
the roadside, and the jeep's tyres crush windfalls of papaya, avo-
cados, breadfruit and oranges. The land is so fertile, so fecund
there is not time, or energy, to harvest all it gives up. Shake stops
in New Georgia, the only large town other than Bridgewater,
buys diesel for the containers in the back of the jeep and fills the
vehicle's tank. It costs next to nothing and it's still flowing, unlike
the beer. Kouranis the Greek may own a great deal, may control
the lives of too many people, but he doesn't own the oilfields of
Sansobella. Shake stops at a place he knows south of New
Georgia and has some eggs and coffee, gives Saltbag water. He
looks down at the natural harbour below, around which the town
is spread, and notices how few yachts are moored there. This
time of year there are usually fifteen, maybe twenty, some sailors
staying over for the hurricane season. But he can only see six. He
fetches his binoculars from the jeep and scans the names: none
from the US, all French and Venezuelan.

Driving south through Lebe Lebe towards Wrexall, the land
changes again as the hills grow steeper and the road is shattered
in places as he approaches the southern range. On distant ridges,
peaks and cliff edges Shake can see houses perched, built away
from the traffic, electricity and mains water which runs along the
road. Houses which can only be reached by steep climbs through
bush and forest, houses where life is lived as it has been for
decades. Somewhere up there, Miss Lizbeth is killing her chick-
ens, pumping her well and cursing her daughter-in-law, Summer.

There are old estate houses set out in clearings, some dilapidated beyond repair, near strangled, some maintained by the island's House of Congress. Shake sees a couple of hunters out, swinging their cutlasses, wearing trousers tucked into high rubber boots and long sleeved shirts, bag slung across their chests. They're hunting iguana and Sally Painter in the bush, the boots stop the serpents and scorpions in the ballesai getting through the skin, the stick may stave off a caiman. And always they have with them their dogs, lean, pointy-eared, long-tailed, semi-feral. The hunters look at Shake with dead eyes, follow his passing without acknowledgement. It's illegal to take the iguana but bush meat sells. So does turtle meat.

The sun slips behind a bank of grey cloud as Shake drops down to the fishing town of Wrexall. He doesn't like the town, never has; if there was anywhere he could buy Mister Jeremiah some commanding powders it would be here. Obeah land. The local men sit on stumps of walls which have been near washed away by incoming tides, the houses seem to be giving up in despair, rusted galvanize peeling from rafters, piles of garbage rotting on the roadside, filthy, torn netting hanging in salt-etched casements. The place looks abandoned, derelict, but behind smashed panes of glass there are signs of life – a television blaring, a child crying, a man drinking rum from a bottle. Shake pulls up outside a carpenter's shop, steps out as a brown puppy with a mashed leg dragging behind it comes to him for comfort, tail wagging slightly, uncertainly. But he can do nothing. If he were to try to save every damaged dog he'd be doing nothing else, but it makes him sad. The only reason he's in Wrexall at all is to pick up some lengths of batchboard. The carpenter is the only one on the island who won't charge him white price. Shake completes his business as quickly as he can, pays the man, loads the bare, intricately patterned boards in the jeep, sweat staining his T-shirt. It's searingly hot and the wind drops suddenly, the palm and ficus leaves falling silent. Shake drives out of town, trying not to look at the tail-wagging puppy and failing, as butter-ball rain begins to spatter the windscreen. Even Saltbag seems cowed by the experience that is visiting Wrexall, her ears lying flat. It's as Shake strokes her head that he sees Bap sitting by the side of the road, and he stops the vehicle, winds down the window.

'Whey yuh goin'?' Bap's voice sounds quiet and broken. His eyes are still shot through with blood and Shakes notices a filthy bandage tied around Bap's upper arm.

'Why aren't you in Sansobella?'

'Why I go to Thanthobella?' Bap can't remember what day it is, can't remember what happened the night before. He knows he went to some house in Paria and had himself some crack but then the night falls away from him like a landslide.

'To get some teeth.'

Bap nods. 'I had wath to do it,' he says, thinking this confession would cover a multitude of sins, and he's pretty sure he must have sinned. 'Yuh len' me twenny dollah? I thucker-guts.'

'I think I already gave you enough, don't you?'

Bap screws up his eyes against the rain, trying to think. Shake already gave him money? 'Jus' twenny dollah? I wuk it off.'

Shake hates this. 'No, Bap. No. And don't come back to work until you're cleaned up. You look like shit. Go home, get yourself sorted.' And he engages the gears and drives off, leaving Bap whining in a storm.

There are small waterfalls running by the side of the road as the rain hardens, gets angry. Shake drives slowly, jouncing in and out of potholes hidden by puddles, trying not to splash the worshippers walking home from their churches in a deluge. The woman and children, dressed in finery, white satin and black patent shoes, peach dresses and jackets with alarming hats, are picking their way through the detritus of leaves and branches washing down from the hills, some with umbrellas, some with sodden newspapers drooping over their heads. The men, in white shirts, black ties and trousers, holding Bibles and hymn books, step out, heads held high, being purified by God's water.

The goat, when Shake finally gets to Liberty, is very wet, very big and very bad-tempered. Shake does not like goats, doesn't like the feel of their hide, like hard, prickly grease, doesn't like the way their bones move and the awful bleating that he can hear at night, the loneliest sound in the world. But Mister Jeremiah's goat is a racing goat, it must be treated with care. So Shake and Cussbud Perky prod it and shove it, lose it time and again. Eventually the goat is standing on the expensive batchboard, chewing grass and staring at Shake with its demonic eyes. Mister Jeremiah is pleased to see it back but he's wearing his church clothes, so Shake is left to haul the goat out of the jeep and drag it to its tethering spot.

'I t'ank you.' Mister Jeremiah smiles. 'I got yuh sometin'. If yuh lookin' for beer, don' bodder.' And he goes into his teetering house to reappear with a six-pack of Arawak. 'The minister selling his supply. For the church him say.'

'You sure?'

'Sure, man.'

By the time Shake has fed Saltbag and put out some fish for the two feral cats who live in the bush in the back of his yard, he's ready for a drink, and then remembers he has none, other than the warm six-pack of Arawak, which he puts in the fridge. Turning on his computer, he taps in his password and the electricity dies. Using his lighter, Shake searches for his torch, burns his thumb and cusses. No electricity means no phone line, no water, no light. He decides to go to bed, although it's not yet seven, but the noise on the tin roof is deafening, so he gets up, hunts down a candle. Tries not to think that he can feel his loneliness like an ulcer. By candlelight he finds his cell phone, thinking to call Rajiv and sees he has voicemail. Above the din of the storm he can make out Mr Westmore's voice, thanking him for bringing Leanne home and asking if they can meet. He tries Rajiv's number in Sansobella but there's nothing but static in his head as thunder rolls across Gilbey beach.

Shake crawls back under his sheets, blows out the candle and lies on his back, looking into nothing as the wind rattles the windows. The love of a good woman? He can't do that, can't do that again. Because he doesn't deserve it – he's not careful enough with love, not *vigilant* enough. Maybe it's the rain, maybe the thunder or the wind tearing the banana leaves, but it takes Shake a long, long time to fall asleep, to dream once again about tending the bar at El Floridita. The cowgirl comes back in, demands a mint julep and this time he holds on the sugar.

17 June

Shake wakes at five-thirty to the sound of drops of water falling on paddle leaves, the gurgle of a hundred tiny streams draining the hills above. The heavy rain of the night before has driven even the cocricos to ground. Shake lies in his bed, watching the sky change through the slats of his ill-fitting shutters, moving through shades of grey and he knows, even without going out-side to look east from his porch, that there are clouds on the horizon, blocking the sun's rays. He also knows that these clouds will soon clear and the sky will be scrubbed as clean as if Miss Lizbeth had scraped it across her washboard, knows that the sea will be a deep, rich blue, that the line between sea and sky will be sharp as a razor. Shake, after a decade of living beneath alien skies, is no longer fooled by the quality of light.

Later, as he wades through shallow sea water, made murky by the sediment run-off, carrying iceboxes and bait to load on *Ribailagua*, Shake keeps looking along Gilbey beach, hoping to see Stumpy but the only other people he sees are two tourists, white as fresh linen sheets, holding hands as they walk the water's edge. They wave to Shake and mouth a greeting, and he nods, smiles. For half an hour Shake sits and waits, checking his watch, tapping his feet, watching the sun moving over the headland and the clouds burning away, as Shake had known they would. Stumpy does not appear. Stumpy may like money, but he likes sleep more.

'Shit,' mutters Shake at quarter to seven. He fires the boat's engines and races out of the bay, heads west, round to the

Tradewinds hotel on Grand Anse, where he ties up, then jogs along the jetty to the lobby. The three Germans are slumped on rattan chairs, all of them blond and bulky, dressed in Polo shirts, shorts and Birkenstocks. Shake notices the empty beer bottles in front of them – still sweating, froth running slowly down the inside. As Shake greets them, apologizing for his lateness, a waiter appears with a tray of three more Arawaks and the Germans down the beers, apparently in one swallow and then follow Shake out to the boat. The tallest of them unties the painter, pushes the boat out, comes aboard and pulls in the fenders without being asked, and Shake begins to think that maybe the Stumpy-less trip won't be so bad. As it turns out, the Germans speak English, are all experienced fishermen and want nothing more than a rod, some bait and a beer. Shake cruises east along the north coast of St George as the Germans stand with rods slotted in fighting belts, drinking Shake's precious six-pack of Arawak, supplemented with glasses of rum punch Shake has added in to make up for the shortfall of beer.

Ribailagua rides the moderate swell, passing the Killdevill peninsula, and Shake can make out John Dory and Liberty, can spot the villages he passed through the day before, sitting at the backs of the bays, shaded by a canopy of trees. Drawing level with Jacamar Island, Shake tells his passengers to reel in and sit on the stern bench.

'We cannot fish any more?' asks one of them.

'On the way back we can do some trolling, but we're running a little late and I need to be at dock by nine-thirty for you to meet the limo.'

'Ah, OK.'

The three men sit dutifully and Shake opens up the throttle, pulling back the Morse Control lever, and the prow of the Bertram rises as the stern dips and *Ribailagua* begins to motor. Shake still gets a hit from this, even after all his years of crossing the Dorado Passage, he still gets a buzz from pushing the Bertram to its limits. Glancing back from the flybridge, he sees the Germans are laughing, even as they're spattered with spray, and Shake begins to aquaplane as the swell narrows, gliding from one crest to another. It's possible to see the peak of the volcanic island of Dorado from the east coast of St George and as they speed towards it, the mountain seems to grow, shakes off its dull, green-grey and begins to coalesce into forest and treeline, distant beaches, valleys, gullies and a flat, palm-covered coastal strip. From Jacamar Island to the dock at Baccarat is eighteen nautical miles and *Ribailagua* covers the distance in fifty minutes. Once again, the tall man helps out, tying up at a bollard and pulling in. Shake accompanies his passengers to the stretch limousine waiting at the end of the jetty, and arranges to meet them at the same spot in five hours. This gives them time to have a tour of the island, peering at stars' villas and have lunch at Coconut Grove, the only hotel.

'You are not accompanying us?' asks the tall man.

'No. I'll wait here.'

'We are happy for you to come with us.'

'No, thank you.'

'I think you have seen the island too many times?'

'Maybe. Enjoy your trip.'

Shake walks back to the boat, sits in the cockpit, fills in the log and prepares to wait. There's no point in heading back to

St George; the journey would use too much fuel and there would be no time to do anything but turn around and head back. He goes below and cleans the head. Tidies the piles of charts and fish recognition cards on the shelves. Fixes a broken catch on a cupboard door. Goes back on deck, plays with the fish-finder, which still malfunctions. Checks the safety gear. Fiddles with the Garmin Depth Sounder. Spends a while trying to turn a rope on the deck in a perfect circle, but, like Giotto, like Sammy in the classroom, he fails. He finally runs out of things to do, cannot distract himself any more.

Shake lies on the stern bench, which is in the shade, puts a hand on his heart and tries to sleep. 'I think you have seen the island too many times?' He'd only been ashore on Dorado once, many years before, in a different life. He has sepia memories of one of the villas, on the leeward side, he thinks. A week spent there in a drugged haze, a week of tequila and cocaine, bowls of the stuff left out for the guests like ashtrays, on tables and cabinets, by the bathtub, by the jacuzzi. A long, long week of talking bullshit, of shagging some woman who had been nominated two years before for best supporting actress, shagging her whenever he could, whenever he was able, doing lines so he didn't notice the pale scars under her breasts, the thinning of the skin on her neck, the incipient double fold under her muddy eyes – which weren't green at all. Hoping all the time Emma wouldn't find out, wouldn't find them. And then someone giving him a tab of something new, something they called ecstasy and he didn't care, then, whether Emma found him or not. All he could think of was his prick and the actress with the muddy eyes. And when it was over, when the long week was over, the light plane came in and flew the two of them, Shake and Emma, to Sansobella, and they caught a flight to LA. One of the worst flights of his life: his hands shaking, his heart flapping like a wind-blow pennant against the muscles of his chest as the air crew, one after another, sidled up and asked Emma for her autograph and, sitting next to her, he discovered he couldn't raise the glass of tequila to meet his lips. Stumbling to the toilet, unwrapping a foil wrap of powder, which only saw him as far as the skies over Texas or Nebraska or one of those shitty states that you'll never visit. And when the hit passed, taking hold of the glass with both hands and forcing it to his mouth, drinking until he passed out, snoring, dribbling, in the wide, leather first-class seat. Scoring in the VIP lounge in LAX, and knowing, then, that he was home, that he'd be OK, as he slid onto the seat of the stretch limousine, which looked exactly like the chauffeured vehicle the Germans had just taken from the end of the pier.

Shake won't go ashore on Dorado because he doesn't want to be reminded of the man, the husband, he had been. Shake doesn't leave the road any more, does not go where he should not be. Shake thinks, in a drowsy, painful way, that his mother might be proud of him now. He rolls on his side on the short bench, draws his legs up and falls asleep.

He is woken by the insistent ringing of his cell phone, and as he answers it, he realizes the Germans are clambering onboard, having had their trip around Dorado and their lunch at Coconut Grove. It is Mr Westmore on the phone and Shake, his mouth treacly with sleep, is short with the American, arranges to collect him the next morning and shuts off the phone. The Germans, he realizes, are pissed as parrots. They won't be wanting to troll for grouper or tarpon, they'll be wanting to get to their rooms, wanting to escape the stunning heat of mid-afternoon and so he cruises slowly back to St George, not rocking the boat, saying nothing. When they reach the jetty of the Tradewinds, late in the afternoon, Shake has to deal with the painter as the tall man is asleep, his head resting on a life jacket. He wakes the Germans gently, tapping their beefy arms, and helps them negotiate the gap between the boat and land. The blond men, still half-asleep, slap Shake on the back, grip his hand and disappear, stumbling slightly on the uneven wooden boards. Shake waits until they are out of sight and then he goes to reception to collect the cheque – minus commission – for the trip. The local woman behind the desk is beautiful, even in her cheap uniform of dark suit and grey shirt. She smiles at Shake, tells him to wait. As he waits he plays with a wad of notepaper on the desk, flipping the corner with his fingers, remembering how his father used to draw scenes of stickmen bouncing balls, or little Scottie dogs pooing, scenes which seemed to move when he flicked the paper with his thumb and it's as he smiles at this memory that Shake hears it.

'Don' stand near whitey.'

Shake turns his head in time to see a well-groomed black woman pulling her young daughter towards her and away from him. The young girl shrinks back from Shake, staring at him the meanwhile, and before he can think of what to say the beautiful receptionist returns with his cheque as the woman is given her room key and she sweeps her daughter in front of her, as if protecting her from the rapacious white man.

*

That evening, sitting on the sandy boards of his porch, dressed in vest and shorts, eating a plate of crab and dumplings brought down to him by one of Miss Avarice's many grandchildren, Shake stares out over Gilbey beach as he sips rum between mouthfuls. Shake is thinking of many things as he chews. When he got back from the Dorado trip, tired after a ten-hour day, Dragon had been waiting for him, pleased as punch, to say that the flag would be raised on the roof of the concrete house – if everything went well – the next Friday. This means Shake has to get in beer and rum and meat for a cook-up for all the boys who've been working on the house. Where's he going to get beer? The Germans drank all the beer he had. And where's he going to get the money? It will take thirty days for the German's cheque to clear. Maybe Mr Westmore will pay cash again? May tip generously? This thought reminds Shake of Bap and he wonders how his toothless crew is doing. He has never seen Bap like this before, blames the puncheon rum Bap's drinking. Shake slips Saltbag a dumpling as he tries to shimmy away from the thought that it's more than rum that's doing Bap in.

'Don' stand near whitey.'

Shake sips rum and shakes his head slightly. That was new – he'd never heard it before. And in the lobby of the Tradewinds hotel? The woman's obviously Sanso – on holiday from the main island, he's sure. Her clothes and jewellery, her carefully styled hair, give her away. Is that what they say, these days, on Sansobella? Don' stand near whitey? Jesus. Shake yawns, strokes his dog, smoothes the hair between her eyes, as he thinks an early night would be a good idea after the rainstorm of the night before. It's been one of his good days, when panic, when drifting have been kept at bay and he wants to wrap it up in a sheet. His cell phone rings and he sighs, pulls it out of his pocket, checks the name of the caller.

'You have to come.'

'Susannah – I've had a really, really long day. I need to get some sleep.'

'Shake, please come by.'

He has never heard Susannah's voice, unpredictable and elastic as it is, like this before: supplicant. 'You OK?'

'Just come by.' Susannah hangs up.

'Shit.' Shake mutters his favourite word as he hauls himself to his feet, crocked knee cracking.

The infinity pool, which runs ninety-eight feet from the middle of Susannah's living room, to the lip of the hilltop, is looking very different from the last time Shake saw it, only two nights before. Floating in the cool, pristine, chemically balanced water, underlit with twinkly halogen lights which emphasize the mosaic-work of the tiles, is a huge, dark brown and tan ridgeback. As Shake stares at the dog's body, spinning so slowly, spun by the flow of the computer-controlled jets, Susannah smokes, her fingers trembling.

'He was poisoned. He must have managed to make it to the pool and then he must have collapsed or something.'

'How d'you know he was poisoned?'

Susannah beckons and Shake follows her, along an artfully designed path, discreet uplighters showing the way, and there, by a clearing in the manicured gardens, is a heap of brown and tan bodies – the three other ridgebacks who didn't make it as far as the pool. Susannah pushes back the undergrowth with her foot and Shake sees a mess of meat – goat, chicken, belly pork, tied with twine, weighted with a trolling cannonball strung with nylon filament. He reckons a strong man could hurl the bundle thirty metres or more; the wall of Susannah's property is maybe twenty, twenty two metres away at this point. The meat has an oily, greenish sheen; as do the gums and open mouths of the dogs. They had been beautiful dogs – Shake doesn't know their names because they had been working dogs. He doesn't even know if they had names; he had trusted them and not trusted them. Trusted them to guard Susannah and yet he always made sure he released the gate of their pound from the reverse side of the fence. Shake sighs, blows out his cheeks, glances at Susannah, who looks old and small and vulnerable and he suddenly wants to go home, back to his shack or somewhere he can call home because his little world, his little *fenced* world seems to be under attack. Susannah smokes and trembles and Shake says, in a small voice which blankets the dead dogs, 'I was in the Tradewinds today and a black Sanso woman told her daughter to stay away from me. "Don't stand near whitey," she said.'

'Can you stay here tonight? Please, Shake? Security hasn't turned up for two nights now. Can you stay? Please?'

And here it is, what he knew would happen from the moment he arrived at the security hut at the gate to Mojito to find it empty. He knew then he was going to be asked to guard someone as they slept.

'Come on.' Shake motions with his head, ushers Susannah in front of him and the two of them make their way back up to the villa, where they re-encounter the slowly spinning corpse in the pool. 'I have to do something about this. Why don't you go to bed?'

'Are you going to stay?'

Shake thinks of his own black and tan dog down in the shack by the beach. 'Yeah, I'll stay. But I have to tell you something.'

'What?'

'I can't lock the doors.'

'What are you talking about?'

'I can't lock the doors. I can close the windows and put the alarm on in all the zones, but I can't lock the doors.'

Susannah frowns, lights another cigarette. '*I'll* lock the fucking doors.'

'No. If I stay here tonight, you can't lock the doors. I'll sleep downstairs on the couch or something but you have to keep the doors unlocked.'

Susannah walks over to the pool bar and pours herself a few fingers of rum, downs them. 'Shake, now is not the time to indulge whatever repressed childhood memories you have. I don't have time to sit here and listen about when your daddy locked you in the fucking cupboard under the fucking stairs or whatever it was that triggered this. I don't have time. *We* don't have time for this crap. Live with it and lock the fucking doors.'

'No.'

Susannah turns and walks away, walks into the living room, slumps on one of the many sofas and punches the button on a remote. A fifty-eight inch plasma flatscreen glides down from the ceiling. Shake assumes this means she's accepted his condition for staying and he sets about hauling the dead dog from the pool. He strips down to his shorts and jumps in, setting the corpse swaying, the long legs, which are dangling down limply, begin a slow dance. Shake pushes the body over to the steps and tries to pick it up but the waterlogged beast, awkward and unhelpful in death, weighs more than a hundred and sixty pounds. Shake ends up dragging it out unceremoniously by two legs, bouncing it on the travertine steps, and the pool water rolls back and forth, rippling angrily. Panting, he finally pulls the body onto the side, and the dog's tongue lolls, grey and green, its eyes covered with a chalky film. Shake pads damply to the open doors of the living room.

'What do you want me to do with them?'

Susannah doesn't look away from the screen. 'Burn them.'

'*Burn* them? I can't burn them, it'll stink. Anyway, the one out there is soaking. It won't burn.'

'Put them in the incinerator.'

Shake has forgotten that Mojito was designed with its own waste disposal system, which includes a furnace, and the energy from this fuels the pool pump and irrigation lines for the gardens. He wheels the bodies, one by one, in a barrow, down to the incinerator, and on each journey he passes the empty guard hut, finds himself looking up the spotlit drive, looking for what, he isn't sure – maybe the snaking black beast from Jungle Jam? He can barely cram the ridgebacks through the hatch, has to shove them in with his foot. He leaves the drowned one until last and it nearly breaks his back, lifting the dog and balancing it until he has enough leverage and all the time trying not to breathe the foul fumes of burning fur and soft tissues. The flames leap in the dark night, framed by concrete, sputtering and hissing with the burning fat of the dogs' soft tissues. Shake slams the hatch and spins the wheel for the last time, then retches into a stand of majestic, pendant heliconia, tasting Miss Avarice's offering and he thinks how much the long, thin dumplings remind him of the dog's poisoned tongues and he retches again.

The length of the pool running through the living room is flat as glass by the time Shake walks in, having showered and changed into a borrowed pair of shorts. Susannah pushes a tumbler across the marble table and gestures to a bottle of Huggins' eighteen-year-old rum, already open, already breached. She must have raided the cellars whilst he laboured. Shake picks up the glass, feels its weight, the balance of the base when he turns it in his palm – Murano or maybe Urbanbar. Why does he give a shit what the glass is? He pours an inch of the rum and drinks, not tasting the smoke, blackstrap and voodoo hues, not noticing the rasp on his tongue like the drag of a coconut husk, he's unaware of the sensation of the rum (paid for with blood) running like molten copper into his belly. Shake sits, bareback, on a fine, leather sofa, in one the most expensive slices of real estate in this world, a virtually priceless drink settling in him, and he begins to wonder what's happening to paradise. As the rum weaves its magic in the cage of his ribs, Shake watches the plasma screen.

'What's this?' he asks Susannah.

'"This" is Darfur.' Susannah says.

Shake, who finds watching television difficult because he so seldom does it, frowns and concentrates on the images: pickneys who should look like Jeremiah Roberts' great-grandchildren, looking instead like death, lying on filthy scraps of cloth, their eyes covered in flies. Women in rainbow cloth walking through a sandstorm carrying firewood, women running pell-mell through gusting sheets of rain. Uniformed men carrying rifles, balancing themselves carefully, yet confidently, as the camels they ride rise to their unlikely feet.

'Who are they? Who are the soldiers?'

Susannah takes a sip of rum, inhales, exhales a drag on a cigarette. 'Arab militiamen. Employed by the government.'

'Which government?'

Susannah looks over at Shake, sees how hard he is trying. 'The same government which is supposed to look after the women and children. The Sudanese government.'

Shake hears that the women have to collect the firewood early in the day (where from? he wonders, looking at the sandy desolation around the refugee camp. Where do they get the wood *from?*) to minimize the risk of rape.

'Mimimize?' Shake repeats, looks at Susannah.

'It's the BBC,' she says, with a thin smile, a smile like a flick knife blade.

'The Arab militia are raping, killing and displacing the black Africans of the country,' remarks the BBC reporter, not without emotion.

'Shit,' says Shake. 'But it's their country.'

This time, Susannah doesn't even bother to smile, however thinly.

Before Shake has time even to begin to deal with this, with these pictures that show him in awful clarity those things he has pushed to the edges of his mind, he is transported to another land by the flick of an editor's switch and he sees colossal blocks of concrete being manoeuvred by heavy plant in yet another sandy desolation. Again, he looks at Susannah and before he asks, she says, 'The Israelis are building a wall, to keep out the Palestinians, the Arabs. The wall will run for seven hundred kilometres.'

Shake drains the drink from the exquisite glass he is holding, because he doesn't know what else to do, because he was going to say of these Arabs, 'But it's their country.' Susannah punches the mute button and their conversation is accompanied by a montage of gaunt faces and desolations.

'So,' she says, 'what do we think so far?'

'Looks like the world's going mad out there.'

'No, Shake, it's just the same as it ever was.' Susannah settles herself in the cushions and Shake knows then that she's not going to bed, that she's going to stay wherever he is. 'I get the sense we're ignoring the elephant in the living room here.'

'Eh?'

'Do you think it was aimed at me or at rich bastards in general? The dogs being poisoned?'

'I don't know.' Shake thinks of how unpopular Susannah is and he imagines that many people would like to have tossed the contaminated bait into her garden. But so much meat – that was expensive. 'There are ex-pats all over Killdevill, why don't you call someone, see how they're doing?'

Susannah calls the white people she knows in Du Bouchett, Polonaise and Margarita. Looks over at Shake. 'All of them. Same thing everywhere.'

Shake thinks of Saltbag inside the shack. The door's shut, so she should be OK. Besides, Saltbag is a beach dog, a smart dog, she didn't get to be ten years old here in St George, by trusting strangers. 'What're they going to do?'

'Bury them.'

'I mean, what are they going to do, about all of this?'

'"They"? Who are "they", Shake? You white too, or you t'ink because you spend time mixing with dada heads yuh safe?'

Shake shrugs, pours himself a little more rum. He doesn't answer because he had, in fact, thought that. On the television screen more uniformed soldiers patrol rubble-filled streets – US marines in Baghdad, the caption informs him.

'We've known each other long time now, Shake, and yet we don't know each other at all. Do we?'

'No.'

'I don't know anything about you, really. Don't know where you come from, where you grew up, who your family are. And what's more, you're in no hurry to tell me. I like that. I've always liked that. Yuh watch yuh content. Most people, they fall over themselves to let you know how important they are, or how happy they are, or how hard done by they feel. Like I give a shit.' Susannah laughs. 'I don't know how you ended up here; why you chose to end up here. I don't think I want to know. Maybe I could guess.'

No, thinks Shake. You could never guess.

'Did I ever tell you I went to Cambridge University? Well, you probably know that anyway. People round here don't like to work but they do like to talk. I went to Girton and studied maths. Sometimes I think I should have stayed there. Y'know, sometimes during wet season when the storms come in and the days are dark, I think I should have stayed. Then the sun comes out. Yuh don' ko ko bruck, does yuh?'

'What? I don't what?'

'You don't tell secrets, you don't gossip. You haven't told anyone about the time we met in Florida?'

'No.'

'I didn't think so. I just wondered. I know people t'ink many t'ings but dey's a difference between t'inking and knowing. I din' stay in Cambridge because I don' belong there. I could pretend enough to get by but I don' belong. You and me both, Shake, you an' me both.' Susannah's beginning to croon a little, her dialect sliding in and out of the portal of language. 'You wan' know somt'in? It piss me off that people look at me and t'ink I don' should be here. My family been here longer than mos'. Longer than some of the niggas who look at me like I shit.'

'Susannah, can you go away for a while? For a few weeks?'

'I can go away for a lifetime. I can go anywhere in the world for as long as I want but I'm not going to.'

'I think it would be a good idea if you did.'

Susannah smiles. 'I know it would. But I'm not leaving. This is my place, my home. And I know that you're too polite, or too scared or too something to say so, but I do realize that I'm the focus for a lot of resentment. That I'm the embodiment of everything some people despise. But I can't help my past, Shake. I can't erase it. And neither can you. Every race has been enslaved. Your ancestors and mine were sold in the streets of Rome. There have always been traders and merchants, some sold cloth and metals. Some sold spices and glass. Some sold rum and molasses.' Susannah shrugs. 'Some sold bodies. Kouranis the Greek – he's nothing but a fucking Phoenician trader, it's in his blood. He's doing what he knows best. Have you thought about what I said? About the change in temperature?'

'A little bit.'

'Well, you need to think about it a lot, Shake. I'm going to tell you something. The blacks in Sansobella and St George are lashing out at the most visible target: whitey. But for once, whitey isn't the problem.'

'What is? What is the problem?'

'It started in Sansobella. It's to do with Kouranis and the East Indians. Think about it. Did you hear what happened in Queenstown last week?'

'Something about a march. Bap told me.'

'Bap told you – that well-known social commentator. The Indians took to the streets in their thousands to demonstrate about the crime levels, the murders, the killings and kidnappings. They were calling for UN peacekeepers to be sent to Sansobella.'

'The UN?' Shake frowns. 'The UN? That's nuts.'

'Not really. Five hundred murders so far this year and it's only the end of June. Fifty-seven kidnaps that they know about – the victims all Indian. Ransoms are paid, bodies are found, body parts arrive by DHL delivery.'

'But it's the Indians who have the money, they're the ones who own the businesses. They're bound to be the target.'

'T''ink about dat: the Indians own all the businesses. The blacks are saying the demonstration was illegal and the ringleaders should be locked up. They say it was mass intimidation. And on top of all dat there's Kouranis and his family and their Phoenician guard.'

'I still think you should go away for a while.'

Susannah doesn't reply for a while, looks, instead, at the

light-speckled view of the moon over the Caribbean Sea. 'Isn't it beautiful? The moon – bright enough to cast shadows. I read a short story once, years and years ago, and it's always stayed with me. About a young boy on a cruise ship somewhere and he's very bright, some kind of genius. And at some point he says to someone, very calmly, that it will either be today or in ten years' time. And you don't know what he means. And then he dives by mistake into a pool that's been emptied and he's killed. And you realize then that he knew it was going to happen – either that day or in ten years' time. But he was very calm about it. Philosophical. Phlegmatic. Resigned. Whatever.'

'It's a Salinger story, in *For Esme, with Love and Squalor.*' says Shake. 'It's called "Teddy" I think, I'm not sure.'

Susannah looks at Shake and laughs, raises her glass. 'You're right. Goddammit, you're right. I've been trying for months to remember where I read it but it never occurred to me to ask you.'

It's Shake's turn to smile. 'I have a degree in English Lit.'

'Well, my, my. Anyway – that's why I'm not going away. It will either be today or in ten years' time. I nearly forgot, there's something for you in the garage. A present.' And Susannah falls suddenly asleep.

Shake watches her for a while as she shifts a little, snuggles into the deep pile of cushions. Only Susannah could sashay from badmouthing to geopolitics and back again without drawing breath and then fall asleep as swiftly as someone falling down a well. He picks up the remote and before he turns off the television, he sees the infants of Darfur yet again, trying to move, trying to live.

The house is silent, too silent, as he walks through the rooms, checking windows, closing – but not locking – doors. Before he sets the alarm system, Shake goes into the garage, large enough to house six cars, and there he finds a massive box covered in the chevrons of a Fed Ex delivery. Is this the present? He checks the label; the package has been sent from West Marine, Bonita Springs, Florida, so it must be. Shake slashes the nylon binding with a Stanley blade and the cardboard falls away to reveal a Pompanette Tournament fighting chair: four thousand American dollars' worth of leather, springs and high-spec steel. Only Susannah could do this – locate, purchase and arrange for forty-eight hour delivery. Shake is stunned, is not sure if he can accept this bribe. Because deep down in the jumbled space where Shake keeps his instincts, he realizes that Susannah needs him to stay on the island; that's why she wants him to build his concrete house, why she wants his boat to be well-fitted, because then he will stay, not leave, whether it's tomorrow or in ten years' time.

With the alarm set, Shake pads through the house, barefoot, back to the living room. Susannah is still asleep and he tries to stay awake, tries to guard her, but he, too, falls asleep, falls back on the plush sofa, seduced by its softness, and puts one hand on his heart, flings the other above his head. He dreams of sand-storms blowing across angry, open seas, in which dogs are swimming, paddling furiously, just trying to stay afloat. It's the blat of the alarm which wakes him, as the housekeeper arrives, a local woman, dark and surly, who looks at the white man and sucks her teeth.

18 June

It turns out that Mr Westmore doesn't want to go out fishing again; he wants Shake to take him on a tour of the island and he wants to do it alone.

'Leanne is still feeling very shabby,' he explains as he walks up to Shake's Land Rover in the car park of the Oriole, 'and since we're flying out tomorrow, my wife wants to top up her tan.' In fact, what Mrs Westmore wants to do is lie on the beach, eyes shaded by dark glasses, and watch the men-boys playing football, their black bodies muscled and loose.

'I could rent a vehicle if you want,' says Shake, as Mr Westmore brushes ash, dog hairs and sand off the passenger seat. 'I'd have cleaned it if I'd known, but I thought you'd want to go out in the boat.'

'No problem. This is great. Can we take off the rag top?'

'Of course.' Shake strips off the tattered roof, stuffs it under the rear seat. 'So, what would you like to do?' he asks Mr Westmore as the American shifts his feet around in the footwell, pushing aside empty plastic bottles, crushed cigarette packs, lengths of rope and a half-eaten roti in a paper bag. Shake leans over, picks up the garbage and puts it in a bin. 'Sorry about that.'

'I really don't mind. You know the island – you call the shots. I want to see as much as I can. Take as long as you want. I've got all day.'

'OK,' says Shake, driving out of the hotel, turning right. 'This is what we'll do. We'll drive right around the island, via the rain-forest. Have you been out on the reef yet?'

'No.'

'We'll see if we can get out there too.' Shake slips on a baseball cap against the glare of the sun.

'I'll pay for all the gas and lunch and drinks, plus whatever your daily rate is. And I insist I take you out for supper. If you hadn't been there Saturday night . . . well, it's good that you were.'

'How is Leanne?'

Mr Westmore shrugs. 'She's very quiet. Says she still feels nauseous. Since that night she's stayed with us all the time, y'know, won't go anywhere on her own.' Mr Westmore drums his fingers on the jeep door. 'Thing is, Shake, Leanne thinks she's all grown-up. Back home, she has a car, her own apartment in our home, a separate phone line, all the things they have now – cell phone, iPod, Wi-Fi, what all. And she's queen bee, y'know, in her friend-ship group. But I wonder sometimes if we've done the right thing. I guess every parent feels that way, I guess everyone thinks kids grow up too soon. Leanne spends five minutes on her math and two hours getting ready to party. She goes out looking like she's twenty-five and I know she knows nothing. She knows less than I did when I was ten years old, living in Hicksville. But y'know, when Marcia and I left the beach that night, the atmos-phere was real nice – lots of dancing and music. We left her with a group of other kids from the hotel and they said they were all getting a cab back. People were just having fun.'

'The later it gets, the more people's idea of fun changes.'

'Yeah. Anyhow, tell me about what we're seeing.'

'OK.' They're passing a long, golden sand beach, on the

leeward side, facing the Caribbean, palms waving in the breeze, a few large, discreetly hidden hotels lining the road. Each has a security gate and guard outside, securing the entrance to exquisite gardens. A well-tended golf course runs along the opposite side of the road. 'As you know, this is Grand Anse. There's one seven-star hotel along here – the Oriole, where you're staying. The five-stars are Tradewinds, the Kiskadee and the Royal. They're all top end of the market, and you get the usual crowd there – celebrities, politicians, rich Sansos, that sort of thing. The government owns sixty per cent of the Kiskadee and all the flight crews and visiting politicians are supposed to stay there. Y'know, all the conferences are supposed to be held there too, so the St George House of Congress can make some money. But that doesn't happen. They all stay at the Oriole, where you are. You might be interested to know that the beach outside isn't real. The sand was shipped in from Guyana, because it's whiter. Gets washed away in storms. They all look out on Midori reef, over the sandbanks and lagoon, so they all have seabreezes.'

'Well, you know what they say – the rich breathe different air.'

Shake glances at Mr Westmore then back to the road. 'All the hotels have their own jetties and restaurants and bars and they're all all-inclusive. If you don't want to walk out of the gates and spread your money around, you don't have to. Only black faces you're going to see will be in uniform.'

'Who owns the Oriole?'

'A man called Kouranis.'

'Is he a local businessman?'

'No, he's Greek. Moved to Sansobella maybe thirty years ago. Anyway, the highway runs along Grand Anse to Pillikin, which is more down-market, smaller hotels, a few holiday apartment blocks. But I think the beach is nicer, the water seems clearer.'

'Maybe the air's better too,' says Mr Westmore with a smile.

Pillikin is a long, less-manicured beach, dead palm leaves, green coconuts and driftwood littering the sand. Sea grape, sea almond and cherry trees spread their roots through the sand, holding the beach together. The hotels are small and unassuming, painted yellow-green, pale blue and pink. Tourists sit on their balconies looking out over the bay, and they can see the shades of blue captured in the lagoon. Men in green overalls rake the sand, collecting small piles of vegetation, piles which are dotted along the roadside, awaiting collection as blue painted fishing pirogues bob on the water, some weighted down by hosts of pelicans.

'Is that where the name comes from? Pillikin, pelican?'

'No, strangely enough. Pillikin is a local name for a tern. Someone told me recently that the name for a group of pelicans is a scoop.' Shake smiles.

'That's neat.'

The early morning clouds are floating out to sea and the sky is clearing. Shake rarely drives with the top off and he looks up to see arching palm trees waving above him. Points suddenly. 'See that bird? It's a rufous-browed peppershrike.' But Mr Westmore misses it. 'Don't often see those. OK, we're coming up to a fork in the road, where the highway ends. If we turn right, we carry on across the island, through Paria, where you went to Jungle Jam and on to the east coast. If we go left, we can drive around Killdevill, which is the name of the peninsula that sticks out off the north coast. You'll have seen it on a map. I got one in here somewhere – have a look on the shelf.'

Mr Westmore rummages about amongst the spark plugs and oily cloths, jabs his finger on a fish hook and pulls out a creased and torn map of St George, studies it. 'We're here?'

'Yeah, that's right.'

'Where d'you live, Mr Shake?'

'Just Shake, please. I live here.' He points to Gilbey beach to the north of the small peninsula. 'Place called Tom Collins.'

'That's the name of a cocktail in the States.'

'I know.'

'Can we go there? I'd like to see where you live.'

Shake makes the turn and soon the two of them are driving along a well-maintained road, the verges clipped, gardens flourishing, towering bougainvillea covering walls and leaning over picket fences. Between the settlements of Sangaree, Polonaise and Fleischmanns, the road is green and empty, long grasses growing beneath a verdant tree canopy. They glimpse the sea, waves breaking on Lanesborough Bay. Most of the villas are hidden by towering mango and breadfruit trees, grown behind tall walls, but occasionally they pass a house owned by a local, set in the trees, concrete steps leading to a wooden structure set on pilings, a couple of chairs set out on a small porch.

'This is beautiful,' says Mr Westmore.

'If you turn up one of these tracks,' Shake waves to the right, points to dusty, rutted traces, 'you climb up to the hills that run down the middle of Killdevill. They're not very high, maybe two, three hundred feet. But the views from up there are spectacular – you can see the reef and sandbanks one way and the mountains in the north of Sansobella the other way, and Dorado, too on a clear day, out to the east.'

'Can we go see?'

'No. It's all privately owned. There are places up there you never even dreamed of. Frank Gehring designed one of the villas. They reckon the hills of Killdevill are the most expensive parcels of land in the world.'

'More than Mustique?'

'Yeah. Even more than Dorado. It's cheaper down around the coast, which is weird.' Of course, Shake could take him up to Mojito, introduce him to Susannah Huggins. But he doesn't think he will, what with the stench of singed fur and bundles of poisoned meat lying around.

'How did you end up here?'

'By which you mean, how can I afford it? Well, for a start I bought my plot years ago, and it's a small one, just under seven thousand square feet. And it's not next to the road, which makes it cheaper. It's taken me seven, eight years to get enough together to finish the building. I lived in an apartment in Du Bouchett before, but now I live in a shack on the site to save money. Plus I do most of the construction myself, to save on labour.'

'But why here? I mean, there must be other pretty places.'

'Why didn't I buy somewhere less expensive? It sounds nuts, but I always wanted to live here. Not because of the status or anything but because of the place names.'

'I'm sorry?'

'Killdevill is an old, local name for rum. There was a sugar cane plantation around here and that's how it got its name. Then in the twenties and thirties, y'know, during Prohibition, St George and Killdevill in particular was really popular with rich

Americans. The Fairbanks and Chaplin often stayed here, and Cecil B. de Mille, Dietrich and all that lot. There were a few hotels right on the beaches then – you can still see some of the ruins in places – and they'd spend the winter here, getting drunk. They basically took over the place and the price of the land went up, or they bought out the locals for enormous sums of money. And then they started to build villas and hotels and small villages. If you look at the place names and villa names, you can see they're all something to do with booze or cocktails.' Shake leans over and points out the names on the map. 'Gilbey and Greenall for gin, Margarita, Mojito, Myers, which is Jamaican rum, Sangaree, which is sangria, Vampiro, which is a Mexican cocktail. Craddock is the surname of the guy who made cocktails in the American Bar in the Savoy in the twenties.'

'I see what you mean – Rickey Point, Curacao, Julep Bay. Shit, I never seen anything like that before.'

'Anyway, I have a thing about cocktails and so when I came here and saw Killdevill, I promised myself I'd live here. Didn't know then how expensive that promise would turn out to be. Have you noticed the vintage Rolls Royce outside the Oriole?'

'Yeah. Hell of a car.'

'Apparently it belonged to Clark Gable. Or Errol Flynn, or Valentino, depending who you talk to.' And now it belongs to Kouranis the Greek, thinks Shake. 'Well, this is it – Gilbey beach. My place is down this track.'

As Shake slows to turn onto the potholed trace, Mister Jeremiah waves from his porch, waves for Shake to stop.

'You want to meet Mister Jeremiah?' asks Shake, and he sees a flicker of panic in Mr Westmore's pale blue eyes as the American looks over at the old black man, sitting bareback on a chair outside his rundown wooden house.

'Sure,' Mr Westmore says.

By the time the two of them get to the porch, Mister Jeremiah has slipped on an immaculate short-sleeved shirt and a pair of sandals. Shake makes the introductions and Mister Jeremiah beckons them into the house.

'Come to meet my wife.'

Miss Avarice is cooking up green sauce in a pot and the air is rich with the scents of shadon benet and scythe. She's wiping her face with a sweat cloth when she looks up and sees the men, and she smiles broadly.

'Miss Avarice, this is a friend of mine, Mr Westmore.'

'Well I please to meet yuh, Mr Westmore.' Miss Avarice wipes her palm before shaking his hand. 'Yuh t'irsty? Yuh wan' a drink?'

'We got no beer,' says Mister Jeremiah. 'But we have a little rum, some mauby, some juice I tink. Or maybe yuh like tea?'

'Tea will be fine for me,' says Shake, glancing at Mr Westmore, who gets the message.

'And for me – tea will be just fine.'

A tall, young black girl walks out of the bedroom, dressed in jeans and a white T-shirt.

'Hello, Ayninka – how you doing?' asks Shake, as he fondles the floppy ear of the Roberts' dog.

'Good morning, Mr Shake. I very well, thank you.'

'Ayninka, this is Mr Westmore.'

'Good morning, Mr Westmore.' She walks over to the only table, which is covered with books, and sits, picks up a pen.

'Are we disturbing you?' Shake asks.

'No – is fine.'

'What're you doing? School's finished.'

Ayninka smiles. 'I know. Is the Heritage Festival nex' week. I making a speech. My own speech.'

'Her makin' speech at openin' of Ole Time Weddin' ceremony. Her won a comptishun.' Miss Avarice smiles even more broadly.

'That's great. What's your speech about?'

Ayninka looks down at the paper in front of her. 'I not decide yet,' and Shake knows she's not being truthful.

'Less go out and take some air.' Mister Jeremiah leads his guests down the back, to a spot in the yard, from where they can look down to Gilbey beach.

'Hey – you got some view here,' says Mr Westmore, settling himself and looking out over the reef.

Miss Avarice appears with tea and coconut cake she made that morning.

'Shake, yuh know what take place las' night?' Mister Jeremiah does not take tea, does not eat cake.

'Yeah.'

'Is bad.' Mister Jeremiah puts his gnarled hands on his knees, looks up to the sky. 'Is very bad.'

'I know.' Shake glances at Mr Westmore, to find the American studying the distant reef intently, so intently he has lost the power of hearing. Shake thinks how he has underestimated the man.

'Miz Susannah OK?' asks Mister Jeremiah.

'I don't know. I think she should go away for a while.'

'I t'ink we should all go away a while.' The old man rubs at his face. 'Yuh remember Sheldon?'

'Josie's son? Yes, I do. Joined the army, didn't he?'

'He come by us las' night, passing t'rough. He say there trouble deep down. He no say why, but Sheldon no happy. Reckon he might caship.'

Shake knows what this means: jump ship. 'Right.'

'Him say officers turning bad, and de boys are sharing licks for no good reason.'

'D'you know who was responsible for last night's happenings?' Shake is reluctant to speak of details.

Mister Jeremiah shrugs. 'I could say the beach boys. I could say the rum boys. Or mebbe,' and the old man turns his dark eyes full on Shake, 'I could say Kouranis. I could say de army. Dey too many damn choices. I don' want Miss Avarice upset. Her feets not good and she don' need upset. And she can' run nowhere.'

'The meat thrown into Susannnah's place was expensive.'

'OK.'

'Your dog's still here.'

'My dog still here. *I* still here. Too many damn choices. Yuh know de elections in t'ree weeks time?'

'No, I didn't know.'

'Jus' som'ting I adding in.'

Miss Avarice labours her way down the back steps to collect the cups and plates, and Shake stands and gathers them together, motions that he'll carry them.

'Thank you, Miss Avarice. That was delicious. And thanks for the crab and dumplings yesterday – they were good.' He looks over to Mr Westmore. 'We better get going. Lots to do.'

Mr Westmore is the first whitey to have been in Shake's shack, and it is as he watches him looking around that Shake becomes aware of how disordered his life appears. Mr Westmore looks around the single room, takes in the pile of books, the beer crates, the mattress on the floor, rumpled sheets piled in a heap, the bin bag of clothes in the corner. Through the gently swaying bead curtain Mr Westmore can see the teetering gas ring, a quarter of pumpkin waiting to be made into soup, the box of empty S&G beer bottles, the small fridge, rusted by seablast. There are no pictures, no photographs, there is no evidence of a life having been lived.

'How long d'you say you lived here?'

'Two years.'

Mr Westmore whistles, raises his eyebrows. 'Show me this place you're building.'

Mr Westmore admires Shake's plot of land, examines the structure of the concrete house and nods as Shake explains what the finished house will be like. As they stand in the shade of a mango tree, looking down at the beach, hummingbirds, butterflies and batty damsels flit and hover around the two men.

'What're you going to call your place?' asks the American.

'I'm not sure. I thought I might call the house Beatrice but it doesn't seem like a house name. Or I might call it Daiquiri.'

'I think you'd better call it that. Daiquiri. It fits in. You're going to have a hell of a place here, Shake.'

'Hope so.' Shake jangles the vehicle keys. 'C'mon. Lots more for you to see.'

As they turn out of the rutted track back onto the Killdevill pass road, a bulky, black 4x4 shoots past them, the white lettering a blur.

'SWAT team?' asks Mr Westmore. 'You have a SWAT team here?'

'It's a private company – a lot of the residents here pay into a fund to have protection.' And where, Shake wonders, had it been the night before?

Shake takes the Paria road, follows the same route he had driven on Sunday, when he went to fetch the batchboard but it looks different now, beneath clear skies, a hundred different shades of green fluttering in the trees as the leaves move in the breeze, dancing in sunlight. Goats and their kids graze in the shadows on the verges, some tethered, some not; occasionally two or three burst, gambolling, into the road, and trot in front of the jeep, long tails flapping. Long-horned cattle chew ruminatively, their brown eyes following the car as white egrets perch on their backs. Men walk along the roadside, shouldering bundles of long grasses, the sheaves brushing the tarmac, as women stand in the shade of umbrellas, bags at their feet, waiting for a drop or a bus. Shake points out the paw paw and breadfruit trees, the wild banana plants, some with huge hands of yellow fruit standing proud, others with the curious red-pod heart dangling down, waiting to ripen. To the north they catch glimpses of curved, moon-sliver beaches between the stands of palms and ficus trees and all around and above them is the canopy. Mr Westmore hardly speaks, and when he does it's to ask a question – the name of a plant, the purpose of various structures – and he's content with Shake's short answers. He asks why there's miles of road with nowhere to stop to buy anything, and then they'd see two shacks next to each other by the roadside, both painted pastel, covered in small, metal signs for Tampico, Miss Tubby, Breeze soap powder, Clorox bleach, Supligen, S&G beer and Wild Boar, selling sweets and cakes, fruit and soda drinks, loose flour and sugar, rice, spices, cigarettes and half-bottles of puncheon rum.

'The locals don't really cooperate with each other. It's difficult to explain. One family will build a little shack and buy in some provisions to sell, and their neighbours think, well, who they? If they can do it so can we. So eventually both shops fail, whereas maybe they could have survived as one shop. Or maybe not.'

'I'm surprised they don't have donkeys. I'd have thought there'd have been lots of donkeys – save these guys doing all the carrying.'

'There is a donkey in Liberty. And there used to be one in Wrexall, but they ate it.'

'Oh.'

Shake slows as they swoop round a hairpin bend and down below them is Buccaneer Bay, the town of New Georgia strung along the large, horseshoe beach.

'You hungry?'

'I could sure eat something.'

Shake parks in the shade of a flaming flamboyant and buys each of them a plate of buss-up shot from a stall.

'What's this?' Mr Westmore looks at the mess of food.

'It's a torn up roti skin, with a potato sauce. You just wrap the food in the little bits of roti instead of using a fork.' Shake looks at the American. 'It's OK. The food's good. It will have been cooked fresh this morning.'

'OK, if you say so.'

The two men sit on a wall, eating in the shade and watch the yachts bobbing on the waters, moving slowly, majestically almost, with the current, turning and turning again. They watch dark, slight children kicking around a ball on the beach, twigs jammed in the sand for goal posts, yelling and screaming, each of them peeling away from the game every now and then to hurl themselves into the sea. They watch two fishermen re-stringing their nets, working silently, sometimes pausing to slurp from bottles of Miss Tubby. Beyond them a young man sits behind a small stall made from a mess of tarpaulin strung across the lower branches of a sea almond, and he's whittling the dried half-shell of a green calabash, scoring and picking at the surface with a blade. In the stall carved calabash bolies hang by leather straps, turning in the breeze, like trophy skulls. It's nearly midday, the shadows beneath people walking on the street are pitch black, tiny, look like wells of loneliness, and the locals are resting beneath trees, or on their porches, dozing, long black legs swinging. A lone, dark grey cloud passes slowly overhead and as the sun blazes once more on the beach, the cloud's rain falls, fine and unexpected, and a rainbow arches over the town. Mr Westmore frowns and smiles, holds out his hand to catch the drops.

'They call it liquid sun,' says Shake.

'Figures.'

The two men say nothing more, they just sit and watch the world.

Eventually Shake stands and tosses the paper bag in a bin and Mr Westmore follows suit. The seats of the Land Rover burn the backs of their thighs as they get in and drive up and out of New Georgia.

'How old is Mister Jeremiah's granddaughter?' Mr Westmore asks out of the blue.

'Eighteen, I think. Yes, she must be, she just finished school.'

'Just about the same age as Leanne.'

'Right.'

Mr Westmore looks up at the blue-blue sky, framed by verdant hills, terns, tropicbirds and frigate birds wheeling above him. 'She seems like a good girl. A happy girl.'

'She is. She got a scholarship to study at UWI and she's going to the Barbados campus in September. I've known Ayninka since she was a little girl – she deserves it. She works hard.'

'Didn't seem like the family have much money.'

'No, they don't but it doesn't seem to bother them.'

'You could fit that whole house into Leanne's room back at home and then some.' Mr Westmore is still looking at the sky, his face turned to the sun. 'Leanne flunked math and English, she can't graduate high school for a year.'

'OK.'

'It's not OK. It's not OK. You have any family, Shake?'

'No. Look, I was just thinking – you know I said we could maybe do the rainforest and get you on a glass-bottomed boat, well, I don't think we've got time. Which would you prefer to do?'

'I like just doing this – driving along, looking at everything. I can pass on the boat ride.'

They drive on, through Lebe Lebe, into Wrexall and out again as fast as Shake can. The people there stare at them with hollow eyes, mouths set, and by the side of the road Shake recognizes the mashed puppy, dead now, just another roadkill. The road rises out of the town, leads up to the southern ranges and then narrows, the potholes become deeper and the storm drains wider. As they climb the temperature drops and the vegetation changes – lianas trail from tall, broad-leaved trees, parrot apples lie on the road and in the litter, their geometrical pods snapped open, and wild orchids bloom shyly, difficult to see in the undergrowth. The shower that has passed through makes music as it drips from the tips of waxy, variegated leaves. There are houses, but very few. Some are derelict, their pilings covered in strangler vines, epiphytes and vines climbing through broken shutters. The buttress roots of cottonsilk trees have pushed the tarmac aside in places, raising it like a cotton sheet, an afterthought of no consequence. The quality of the air, of the silence, is different from that of the lowlands; it's an alien, patchy silence, broken by falling branches and leaves, by the rush of small waterfalls. A primeval silence. Shake thinks of Miss Lizbeth up there in the hills somewhere, sucking on her chicken bones as she watches the moon rise. Thinks of her walking down to the potholed track, hoping for a drop every early morning.

'Have you been in there?' Mr Westmore points into the forest.

'I did a bit of walking when I first came, y'know, bird watching and all that. But I haven't been in there for years. Scares the shit out of me, actually. I don't know why but I know I shouldn't be there or something.'

'Yeah – I can imagine.'

Once across the pass at Beaulieu, Shakes stops at a roadside fruit stall, buys a pineapple and a couple of cut, cold coconuts, shows the American how to cut a pineapple in four strokes, how to drink the purest water on earth and then scoop out the jelly with the tongue of the shell. They've nearly completed the circuit of the island now, as the road begins to drop and widen and the temperature rises. The verges reappear, and groups of old boys sit on the hairpin bends, talking and watching the traffic, playing desultory games of dominoes. Shake stops at a turn before Torpoint and parks the jeep, walks along a manicured, signposted path, cut through bush, the American following. The bush clears, the ground falls away and Shake opens his arms.

'The best view in St George.'

'Shit,' says Mr Westmore, 'that's quite something.'

Looking east they can see the tropical forest, the hills rising and falling, dotted with flamboyants on the lower slopes, yellow pouis flaring orange almost in the afternoon sun. To the west they can see Grackle Bay and the white finger of Coral Strand pointing at the turquoise lagoon. Below them the turbulent waters of the Sansobella Passage churns up the sediment and nutrients floating in the deep submarine trench. Shake knows there are giant mantas and hammerheads down there, barracuda and kingfish, dolphins, moray eels and sea snakes. In front of them, looking due south, they can see the tall peaks of the northern range of Sansobella, rising above the curve of the horizon, made dark grey by distance, by rain and salt spray. As always, when he stands there, Shake thinks of Rajiv, looking at the mountains and wanting to be on Sansobella. How both of them had changed since that day; how they had both been changed.

As they walk back to the jeep, a man appears from nowhere, sees Shake and raises his fist for a knuckle hit.

'How you, man?'

'I'm fine – how're you?'

'Whey yuh goin'?'

'Bridgewater.'

'Dat's good.' The man puts his foot on a rear tyre of the Land Rover, begins to clamber into the back seat.

'Hey – wait a minute, Bluebottle. Mr Westmore, d'you mind if we carry Bluebottle to Bridgewater? It's not far, maybe five miles.'

'Sure, it's not a problem.'

Bluebottle doesn't look much like the poster in Redpath any more; twenty-five years down the line, Bluebottle is thin and wasted – a long streak o' misery, as the Georgians would say. Twenty-five years later and Shake has never mentioned how Bluebottle had scared him, how he still owes Shake sixty-three dollars. Bluebottle's dreads have turned a rusty black, as has the small, tangled goatee he's toying with as he sits in the back of the vehicle.

'Yuh Merican?' he asks.

'Sure am. From New York City.'

Bluebottle nods, turns his back on Mr Westmore and begins to talk to Shake in an accent thick as maple syrup, about a friend of his, Redman, who'd appeared in court because he stole an onion from his mother's garden.

'So what happened?'

'Him apologize to he mother. Him say her his slave when she ketch him and she no like that. So him apologize in front of de judge.'

'Excuse me,' says Mr Westmore, 'sorry to butt in, but you're saying a man has been in court because he took an onion from his mother?'

'That's right,' says Shake.

'An *onion?*'

'Yes – it's praedial larceny, whether he takes it from his mother or anyone else. Very serious.' Shake glances at Bluebottle, sees him staring intently at Mr Westmore.

'What happened?'

Bluebottle clears his throat, hawks. 'Redman say he cookin' trotters an' got no green seasonin' so he wen' up an' took de onion. De way it was, her was sleepin' an' she woke by noise. She look out an' see Redman with a flashlight in her yard, holdin' de onion. Her go out an' tell he put it back. But Redman? Him been smoked some weed and maybe had a bit o' rum, so he no t'inking too good. He yell an' den her shout and de people around wakin' too. Him jumpin' up an' down, sayin' her his slave, sayin' her should be pleased for he to have de onion, dat her should feed him. Then her hit him. Her a big woman and her put he in de dirt.'

'But surely if she's his mother, it doesn't count? I can't believe a mother would take a son to court over an onion.'

'Yuh cyar t'ief a man's coconut or banana. Yuh cyar climb his paw paw tree an' strip it. Man spen' long time tendin' dose things, yuh cyar take dem. Dey no belong to you. Jus' like de onion no belong to Redman. If her turn away from dat and what nex'? Maybe nex' time Redman got de onion an' no chicken claws, so what he do? Go take de claws from she chicken?'

Mr Westmore frowns. 'Perhaps it's different here but in America we wouldn't take our sons to court over an onion.'

Bluebottle looks at the American and sucks his teeth. 'Lebe lebe. Seem to me yuh right – in America modder no take son to court. More likely shoot him. Him no in de dirt, him bury in it. Seem to me 'Merica use guns instead of judges, an' yuh no like it when people start to fight back.'

'Where you want to be dropped?' asks Shake.

'Right heah.' Bluebottle climbs out of the car and begins to walk along the verge in a slow lope, his height making him appear majestic, unworldly.

'That guy seems to have a problem,' says Mr Westmore, taking off his cap and resetting it. 'I mean, you can't take someone to court over an onion.'

Shake says nothing. There is a lot he could say but he says nothing.

'So, where would you like to have supper?' asks Mr Westmore. 'I've booked a table at the Oriole but I can always call Marcia on my cell phone and we could eat somewhere else, just you and me.'

Shake thinks of the dining room at the Oriole – ersatz colonial rattan chairs and sofas. Starched linen and silver service, the waitresses dressed in immaculate white shirts, looking annoyed, defiant almost. Bowls of polished fruit and bottles of bad French wine at extortionate prices. The guests dressed for dinner, a hollow hush hanging over everything.

'I'd rather go somewhere local, if you don't mind? My favourite place is Avril's Kitchen, the food's really good.'

So Mr Westmore calls his wife as Shake parks at the foot of a trail of uneven concrete steps on the outskirts of Bridgewater. They climb up to a rickety gallery where there are seven or eight tables with mismatched chairs, and the roof is a tangle of goosefoot and vines and banana leaves. The menu is scrawled on a blackboard – callaloo soup, crab and dumpling, dasheen, fried cassava, macaroni pie, spanish rice, provision, red bean stew, fish in creole sauce. The other customers, mainly white tourists, with a few Sansos, are leaning towards each other, cupping ears against the calypso which is playing loudly. A short, dark woman emerges from the kitchen, dressed in long skirt and blouse, spotless white turban shrouding her hair, and serves callalloo before she notices Shake.

'Shake, baby!' She comes to the table and the two of them hug. 'Where you been? You not been here for weeks-too-long, ent?'

'Been busy making money, busy building my house. Mr Westmore, this is the lovely Miss Avril. Miss Avril, Mr Westmore. I brought him here to taste some good food before he leaves.'

'Well, you don' wan' to be eating this shit. Seat yourself and I'll bring you out som'ting good. But first I wan' you to make me a Shake special.'

'No problem.'

As Avril disappears into the kitchen, Shake steps behind the bar and begins to fill a shaker. One shot Sauza silver tequila, one shot Southern Comfort, quarter shot J&B whisky, quarter shot Tanqueray gin, dash of grenadine, measure of orange juice. He fills a towel with ice and crushes it with a heavy spoon, pours the cocktail over the ice in martini glasses, sends one to the kitchen for Avril.

'Hey – this is really good,' says Mr Westmore. 'This one of your own?'

'Yeah.'

'What's it called?'

'Is It Tuesday Yet?'

'Huh?'

'That's what it's called – Is It Tuesday yet? Long story behind *that* name.'

A waitress begins to load the table with dishes – round, flat garlic bread, minted pork, lime fish, salsa shrimps, bollo con carne, baby squid in garlic, mozzarella and tomato salad, seafood in hot sauce. The dishes keep coming and the men keep eating, Mr Westmore wiping the sweat from his face as he eats the seafood, the heat of which hovers at some point between pain and pleasure. Bottles of Corona beer (and just how did Avril get hold of those? Shake wonders), necks stuffed with lime slices, wash the food down. As they finish, having cleared the plates, Avril reappears, comes to sit at the table, leaving the waitress to deal with the other customers – who have been eyeing the spread with some envy. Avril has showered and changed into a knee-length burgundy dress which fits close and tight. Her hair is cornrowed, her lips dark red. She sits next to Shake.

'So, baby, you been busy, nuh?'

'Yeah. That was great. The squid were really good.'

'All the way from sunny Venezuela, frozen in blocks. So how you like St George, Mr Westmore?'

'I think it's great. Shake has been kind enough to take a day showing me around. It's very beautiful.'

Avril nods slowly, watching him. 'Where you stayin'?'

'At the Oriole.'

Again she nods, but slowly, very slowly. 'You like it?'

Mr Westmore shrugs. 'It's fine but it's like a lot of places. Could be anywhere. Almost like it's in a different country, not in St George.'

'Yuh said it.'

'Mr Westmore asked me today, y'know, when we were out driving, what's changed in the years I've been here.' Shake turns the ice-cold, sweating Corona bottle in his tanned hand. 'Funny, all I could think of were little things.'

'Like what, baby?'

'Like the way everyone used to use scythes not long ago and now they all use petrol strimmers. And you don't see so many old boys having sea baths, or fishermen cleaning their boats with wet sand. And the kids don't fly the kites any more, the ones made of sticks and coathangers and plastic bags. Fewer sous stalls, fewer old girls selling their stuff by the roadside. Now you see cell phones everywhere, flash cars and guys who look like drug barons or something. And you know what I really miss? The way everyone used to drive with their hand hanging out the window, and you could tell what they were saying by the way the hand moved. You could tell whether they were having an argument or not, or laughing. But now a lot of the cars have air con and you don't see it.'

'Pimp vehicles and whores' chariots.' Avril laughs, stops. 'Sometime I t'ink all the bad t'ings stay the same – landslides, garbage everywhere, mashed dog, mosquitoes, men no showin' when they say they comin'. But the good t'ings on the way out. You right, though, Shake, you t'inkin' of the small t'ings.'

'Excuse me, where's the bathroom?'

'Down out back.'

Mr Westmore walks uncertainly down the side alley as Avril asks, 'What happen at Killdevill?'

'Dogs were poisoned.'

'All the dogs?'

'No. Only whiteys' dogs.'

Avril sucks her teeth. 'This ain't a small t'ing.'

'Avril, do you know what's going on?'

Shake leans towards her, speaking softly and Avril falls a little more in love with him, drops another love bead in an already bulging bag, knowing it's pointless. Shake never sees anyone, seems to need no one. In all the years he's been on St George, Avril's never heard of him stepping out with anyone. She knows she can ask him for anything, ask him to do anything for her and he'll oblige. Everything except the one thing she wants.

'To say the truth, I worried. Somet'ing up but no one know what. People gettin' very hot and boddered. I hear Jungle Jam no fun any more – too many choppings and ruckshuns. Part of me t'ink maybe it's the rum instead of beer, but I not sure. There a lot of anger out there but what is the anger? I don' t'ink whitey the problem but whitey easy to see. Even in the dark. People in the market, in the stores, they keep saying there's a storm coming an' I look at de sky and I see nothin'. But maybe I look in the wrong place.'

'Susannah says the same. She says the temperature's dropping.'

Avril smiles with one side of her face. 'Susannah? Hmmm.' She half-smiles again. 'Huggins not a good name to have right now. Never was, nuh? Hear me now, Shake, baby – she right. She a smart woman and she right. But she in the eye of the storm. Right or wrong. And t'ing is, Shake, I t'ink you are too, in the eye of the storm.'

'What do you think's going to happen?'

Avril shakes her head, chews her lip. 'I dunno. Elections comin' soon, maybe that will sort it out.'

'Sort what out? I don't get it.'

'Shake, baby, I t'ink you got to be black to get it.'

Mr Westmore reappears, having paid the bill. Shake pushes his chair back and stands up, and Avril follows suit.

'Thank you, Miss Avril, that was very good.' The American shakes Avril's hand and heads for the door.

Avril stands on tiptoe and wraps her arms round Shake's neck and he hugs her tightly. 'Don' stay away so long, Shake. You know I like to see you roun'.'

'I promise I'll come lime by you soon.'

'I don' suppose I got me any chance of a poke in the whiskers?'

And Shake laughs, laughs deep down, from his full belly, like he hasn't laughed for a long, long time. 'That's a new one.'

'No, it not. Maybe new one for you, but for me it an old one. So old I nearly forgot me how to do it.' But Avril's laughing too.

'I got to go, have to take Mr Westmore home. I'll see you soon.'

'Promise me, baby. An' don' forget durin' your lonely nights – de blacker de berry, de sweeter de juice.'

'I won't.'

Mr Westmore falls asleep in the Land Rover on the short journey back to the Oriole, his gingery head nodding, his pale eyes closed. Before he wakes the man, Shake looks at him for a moment, thinks he's a nice guy, a *soft* guy. Thinks it's a good job he's flying out the next day, taking his sex-starved wife and feckless, airhead daughter with him. They're too vulnerable, too pale, to survive a storm, if survival is about the colour of your heart. The Westmores' hearts are beige, mint, magnolia, when they need to be blood red. Mr Westmore wakes at Shake's first nudge, wakes with a start and looks around with bleary eyes.

'Hey – sorry about that. Must have slept for a while there.' Mr Westmore bundles himself out of the jeep and stretches. Reaches for his wallet. 'I had a great time, Shake. Can't thank you enough, you made my vacation – well, and, y'know, Leanne and all that. Like I say, can't thank you enough. Now I can go home with something to remember, somewhere to think about when the winter snows are coming through. Here – I want you to get something for your house – I dunno, a tree or something. Maybe a royal palm – is that what they're called? The ones I really like? Then maybe you'll think of me sitting in my office some days when the sun's shining and you're swinging in your hammock.' Mr Westmore holds out a wad of notes and Shake smiles, takes it and shakes the empty hand. 'Here's my card – if you're ever State-side, call me up.'

'And if you're ever in St George again, make sure you get in touch.'

'Will do. Bye, Captain.' Mr Westmore salutes and walks slowly into the hotel, flattened by exhaustion.

Shake finds Saltbag sleeping on the porch when he's mounted the steps up to his shack, and the old dog hauls herself to her feet and wags a tail when she wakes and sees him. He fills her bowl with chow and fish and pours himself a couple of fingers of rum before sitting on the top step and counting the bills Mr Westmore gave him – five hundred US. Shake raises his eyebrows. Bloody ridiculous. But he has the feeling the man is generous, that he is not braggadacious but quietly generous. At least now he knows he can pay for the raising of the flag party. Shake sips at the rum as he watches the ocean move, and is glad he spent the day as he had. Sometimes he knows he forgets to look up at the sky, forgets to look at the island, forgets how beautiful it is. Memories of sun-light on palm leaves, of the distant smoky peaks of Sansobella, push thoughts of the impending storm out of his mind. As always, Shake checks his cell phone before he goes to his bed. There's an SMS message from Rajiv – he's to meet him at the Kiskadee Hotel the next day for breakfast. Typical of Rajiv – the Kiskadee is the most expensive of all the hotels on Grand Anse, the most expensive and the only one owned by a Sanso. Shake whistles the dog inside and shuts – but does not lock – the shack door.

19 June

Shake still wakes, some mornings, with a weight on his chest, fearful that no one knows where he is; all these years later he sometimes wakes feeling as he did the morning of the boat race when he was sixteen – compressed by panic, as if he is lost. But now he knows how to deal with these loose, baggy jitters. He lies in his bed and thinks of those people who do know where he is – they may not much care but they could point to a map and say, 'Shake is there'. He lies in his makeshift shack in St George, watching gaps in the louvres lighten, and he tries to relax his muscles, starting with his toes and moving up his body as he makes plans. Thinking of the future, puncturing it with the pinpricks of decisions, seems to help.

The morning Shake is due to meet Rajiv in the Kiskadee he wakes with this familiar sense of the leaden, as his ribs fail to rise and fall. He forces himself to breathe as he considers the weeks ahead. First there is the red flag party and yet there is still no red flag; the work on his concrete house has ground to a halt. He must track down Dragon and find out why the roof isn't rising. And then there is the matter of his vacation. It's June and he should start to think about booking his flight to Miami, start thinking of where he'll stay and whether to hire a car for the two weeks. Every year he travels to Miami, with a near-empty holdall and a long list of marine boat parts. For two weeks he sleeps as long as he wants in air-conditioned rooms, spends the afternoons visiting chandlers and boatyards up and down the coast, collecting together the parts which are impossible to find in Sansobella or St George and arranging shipping. Some years he drives all the way down the Keys, spends a few nights in Key West if he can afford it. He likes it there: not too American, some European streaks colouring the streets and bars. In the evenings he may drift along the strip on South Miami Beach, maybe having a beer in every bar; or he finds a bar in one of the one-horse towns on the Keys, and sits out on the deck, watching the sun set as men tinker with the engines of their trucks or boats and women cook up some mess of food and try to call their raggedy children back to the trailer to eat. If he's in Key West, Shake visits Sloppy Joe's, where Hemingway drank his days away, and he tries all the cocktails, tries to follow the movements of the bartender as he muddles and blends. If Joe's is too crowded, he moves on to the Green Parrot Bar. And every year, if he's in Key West, he visits Hemingway's house and tries to imagine the writer there, in the dark, ugly building, surrounded by his six-toed cats. Before leaving Miami to fly back to St George, Shake buys two dozen dark navy Fruit of the Loom T-shirts, has them imprinted with his Dream Catcher logo, and half a dozen pairs of O'Neill shorts, which just about solves his clothing problems for the year. When he packs to fly home, each of the T-shirts are wrapped around a bottle of liquor, cushioning the contents as they fill the holdall: Opal Nera, Chambourd, Midori, Buffalo Trace, Aba Pisco, Zubrówka. Every year Shake hunts down a few bottles of Passoã, and carries the black bottles in his hand luggage, the passion fruit liqueur too precious to be entrusted to baggage handlers. He smuggles the booze into St George, prepared to pay duty if caught, but he never has been. It seems to Shake a negligible vice.

Then there are the women he meets as he drifts around Miami, or motors slowly south along the Marine Highway, coasting over the sweeping bridges of the Keys. Shake might be sitting at a bar, turning a frosted beer in his tanned hand and a woman slides onto the stool next to him; a woman from one of the frozen northern cities, Chicago or Boston or Milwaukee or somewhere, out to have a good time during her week in the sun, her skin smarting a little, feeling alive for the first time in months. And maybe there's something about the set of Shake's shoulders, or the way he moves, or the way his long fingers play with the beer mats and napkins, or the challenge of scaling the fences he has built around himself, because all of them, once they hear his accent and discover where he lives and how he lives that life, fall a little in love with him. Not with their hearts but with that part of their bodies that lies between their hips and thighs. And they all know that he's safe because of the way he thanks the bartenders and the way he waits for the women to step out first and then gently places his hand in the small of their backs as the two of them leave together. Shake sometimes smiles when he thinks of these women, as he stands on the flybridge of *Ribailagua*, spray spattering around him, in search of kingfish. He thinks of them fondly and he smiles.

But maybe this year he'd pass on his annual trip, thinks Shake, as he climbs out of his bed, ribs moving easier now. Maybe this year, what with the unfinished roof and the bundles of poisoned meat flying around and the falling temperature, he'll stay here. Keep an eye on what is his. Shake fills Saltbag's bowl and strokes the old dog as she lumbers over to eat. Out of habit he turns on his laptop and checks the weather, even though he doesn't have any trips lined up for a few days. Zooming out of the forecast for St George, enlarging the map until it takes in the Windwards and northern Venezuela, he sees a spiral of dark cloud spinning west, across the Atlantic, spinning slowly, gathering fury in its eye. It's June, it's the beginning of hurricane season, the tropical storm should move north, passing, with luck, between the islands. Sansobella and St George are way south, out of the usual path of catastrophe. Shake throws on old shorts and a stained vest, and steps out with a cup of coffee to inspect the shell of his concrete house in the pale early morning light. The footing, pillars and concrete floors are all in place; the timbers of the roof are angling skyward but they've not been tied. The site has the air of having been abandoned, as if tools were dropped and left where they fell, a hardboard spot lies twisted by the pull of sunbaked, dried concrete. Shake tries not to think about this as he looks at the footings and pictures where his kitchen will be and the tiles he'll have as a splashback. He narrows his eyes as if by seeing less he will see more, and he tries to imagine a wardrobe in the corner of his soon-to-be bedroom, where he can hang his clothes and he laughs. Hang his clothes? He hasn't done that since he went to Redpath College.

Shake sees Rajiv before his old friend sees him. Rajiv is sitting in the restaurant of the Kiskadee, a newspaper folded neatly in quarters at his elbow, ignoring the black waitress as she pours coffee from a silver pot into his cup. Beyond Rajiv, through the closed plate glass windows, is a view of the tranquil waters of Midori reef, which Rajiv also ignores. Shake shivers in the air-conditioned air and watches Rajiv for a moment. They haven't met for a few months and Shake is surprised, as he always is, by how like his father Rajiv has become. The beautiful slim, brown boy, whose shoulder blades were like nascent angel's wings, whose eyelashes were long and straight, who wore creaseless silk suits and looked ready to wield a knife, has disappeared. In his place there is a plump, middle-aged man, paunch straining against a Jermyn Street shirt, thinning hair brushed over his crown, squinting at the newsprint. Shake walks towards Rajiv, weaving between tables busy with groups of Sanso businessmen and families eating their breakfast, all of them ignoring the distant, unheard braiding of water beyond the plate glass. A black waitress stands aside to let him pass and he smiles, thanks her. She stares back, unsmiling.

Don't stand near whitey.

The Sansos glance at him as he passes, take in his shorts and T-shirt – all clean and pressed, fresh back from the laundry – and they purse their lips, raise their eyebrows and look away.

'Hello, stranger.' Shake holds out his hand as Rajiv stands, takes his hand and then hugs Shake, before motioning to a chair and beckoning over the waitress.

'Would you like coffee? Or would you like a full breakfast? The saltfish is good.'

'Just coffee would be great.'

They watch the waitress clear the glasses, plates, cutlery and soiled linen napkins.

'You staying here with the family?' asks Shake, noticing the number of settings.

'No, I am here alone. I came in last night and I had an early meeting with some people over breakfast.'

'You're a busy bunny.' Shake smiles up at the waitress as she pours him a coffee but, yet again, he gets no response.

'As you say, a busy bunny.'

'What we going to do today? You want to go out on the boat? Some guys pulled in some kingfish out by Frigate Island a couple of days ago. And I was wondering, if you're here for the day, if maybe you could lend me a hand doing something. Won't take long. How long *are* you here?'

Rajiv lights a cigarette and leans back, rubs his curving stomach. 'How are you, Shake.' It's not a question.

Shake feels that he has stretched out his hand only to meet the age-old invisible carapace, the sheet of glass between them. 'I'm OK. The island's busy so I'm busy. The Oriole and Tradewinds are full next week and I already had a few enquiries about trips.'

'The Oriole is not full next week.'

'That's not what I heard.'

'One of the people I shared breakfast with this morning is the manager of the Oriole. He tells me that he has had forty-two per cent cancellations for the next two weeks. The same with Tradewinds. The Americans and the Europeans will not be coming.'

'What're you talking about?'

Rajiv says nothing. Instead he unfolds the paper and refolds it in half, holds the front page headline out for Shake to see. Shake looks at the masthead. The paper is the Trinidadian *Guardian* and yet the front page is devoted to the state of Sansobella. '378 in 100'. Three hundred and seventy-eight murders in one hundred days. '58 in 100'. Fifty-eight kidnappings in one hundred days. There is a separate piece about the multiple rape of two white tourists on Saturday night, in St George, at an event called Jungle Jam Bow Wow. Shake reads the articles and looks up at Rajiv.

'What's this mean? Rumours of a military coup?'

'You know what it means, Shake.' Rajiv grinds out his cigarette, takes a small, silver cylinder from his trouser pocket, removes a toothpick and begins to root out white flecks of saltfish.

Shake looks out at the reef, where waves break silently and roll to shore. 'There are always rumours. Rumours about everything. You know that. About the ferry, about Kouranis, about Coral Strand and drugs and guns and corruption and . . . shit, there are always rumours.'

Rajiv sucks his teeth, replaces the pick and leans forward on his elbows. 'You ask how long I am here for. I am here until this afternoon, when I am flying back to Sansobella. And on Friday I am flying to Frankfurt with my family.'

'How long for?' But Shake thinks he knows the answer.

'For a long, long time, Shake. Perhaps for a lifetime. My lifetime, perhaps. Last month bandits attempted to kidnap Ramesh as he returned home from school. The chauffeur was shot but Ramesh, luckily, managed to escape. I have had enough of living like this. If you remember, I went to a gymnasium in Germany and so I can speak the language. I am going back where I can conduct my business and my family can live unmolested.'

'Was the chauffeur killed?'

'Eh?'

'The chauffeur – did he die?'

'Yes.'

'Was it the same guy you always had?'

'Yes.'

Shake thinks of the tall, Gujarat warrior, reduced to wearing a suit and tie, ferrying two young, arrogant men around Sansobella that distant, innocent summer. The man who had looked at the pictures in the paper because he couldn't read. 'I don't remember hearing anything about that.'

Rajiv shrugs. 'Why would you? He was only one of three hundred and seventy-eight.' Rajiv gestures for the bill and Shake notices the young black waitress pause for a moment before stepping forward and he could not say for whom she registers the most contempt: himself, in his shorts and T-shirt, or the sleek, fragrant (Shake can smell Rajiv's eau de cologne like a heavy, briny mist) East Indian Sanso with the winking pinkie ring. 'What is the thing you wish me to do? You said you have a favour to ask me? My flight leaves at three, so perhaps I can help?'

'Um, I need to pick something up from Susannah's. She said she'd like to see you again anyway, so I thought we could kill two birds with one stone.'

Rajiv smiled. 'Kill two birds with one stone? If anyone could do that it would be Susannah. Shake, I want you to leave here.'

'What?'

'I want you to leave. This is not the place for you now. Go home. I am leaving and I think you should too.'

Shake stares at Rajiv as the waitress puts the bill, hidden within a black leather folder, in front of Rajiv, who fusses with a wallet and shoves in a credit card without checking the price.

'Shake, I am happy for you to come with me and my family to Germany. Come with us and we can work together again. Come with us.'

'Germany?' Shake shakes his head. 'I can't do that.'

'Why not?'

'I can't speak the language. And anyway, my house here is nearly finished. Well, it's getting there. Just takes time here.'

Rajiv signs the chit for the breakfasts and Shake's coffee. 'They will take your house.'

'Who'll take it? Who will take my house?'

'The military.'

'Oh, fucking bollocks. No one's going to take my house. It's a fucking shell. Who's going to take my house? Get a fucking grip, Rajiv. You're telling me rumours and that's all they are, fucking rumours.'

'You seem very angry, like you running scared.' Rajiv is aware of the other Sansos who have turned from their lavish, half-finished breakfasts to look at the loud white man.

Shake lights a cigarette and runs his hands through his thick, greying hair. 'Well, shit, I am angry. All I hear is crap and I look around myself and everything's the same. The sun and moon rise, the waves break and the fish jump or get shy. That's life.'

Rajiv stands, brushes crumbs from his lap. 'Let us go to Susannah's and do whatever it is you have to do.'

Shake waits for Rajiv to leave the table, checks the bill and folds a twenty S&G dollar note into the wallet because he knows Rajiv never leaves a tip.

'I'll take you to the airport later,' Shake says, as he drives along Grand Anse, and that is all that is said during the ride to Susannah's because the two men can think of nothing else to say.

Shake stops his jeep by the gates of Mojito, steps out to open them. It's as he's yanking at the heavy padlock on a thick chain that he hears a strange sound and then Rajiv's shout. Looking up he sees three Rottweilers hurtling towards him behind the fence.

'Shit!'

Shake whips his hand away just as the lead dog throws itself at the gates, which bulge outward. Shake looks at the maddened, furrowed brow of the animal, the blood-red glint in its eyes and he thinks of *The Omen*, the pierced priest and the ravens picking out eyeballs. 'Shit.' Shake shivers, moves away. The dogs keep howling and hurling themselves at the fence, never once looking away from Shake. He walks to the empty guard hut, which is also padlocked, and presses the intercom but there is nothing but static. Fat, buttery rain begins to spatter on the pale herringbone bricks of the driveway as Shake stares at the mirror-like surfaces of the windows of the main house. He trots back to the jeep, takes out his cell phone and dials. The phone rings and rings. He tries again and on the third ring Susannah answers. Shake breathes out long, relaxes his shoulders and only then does he realize what he's been thinking.

'Susannah – it's Shake. I'm here with Rajiv.'

'Come in.'

'How *can* I come in? You've got the Hounds of the sodding Baskervilles out here, baying for my blood.'

'I'll open the garage.' Susannah rings off and soon the rolling doors of the garages begin their smooth ascent. Rajiv and Shake run across the drive but by the time they reach the shelter of the garages, their shirts are soaked. Shake laughs and wipes his face, then points to the Pompanette.

'That's what I wanted you to help me with. I need to get it in the vehicle.'

'No problem,' says Rajiv, smoothing his wet hair.

The door at the rear opens and Susannah walks away, back into the house. Shake admires, as he always does, the gleaming burgundy Aston Martin DB7 which should be under dust sheets, it's so rarely used. He leads Rajiv through the marble mansion, and finds Susannah punching out numbers on the keypad of the alarm.

'Just closing the garage again.'

Shake can smell the sweet, mahogany scent of rum on Susannah's breath. He notices her skin is grey-white, as if she has not seen the sun for weeks.

'Susannah, you remember Rajiv?'

'Why, of course I do. How nice to see you again, Rajiv. Do come in and sit down.' Susannah smiles and extends her hand to shake Rajiv's. 'Heavens, what a rainstorm.'

Behind her, Shakes half-smiles. Mercurial as ever – who's Susannah being today? Not the rum-pickled, foul-mouthed slave-driver, that's for sure. Shake stands by the infinity pool running through the main living room, watches the rain slapping down plants and trees, snapping fragile blooms. He can't even make out Gilbey beach below. Later he'll have to check on the boat, bale out if he has to. He hates being penned in behind glass by the rain; feels twitchy. 'There anything you want me to do?' he asks Susannah.

'The pool man hasn't been for a while.'

'OK, I'll check it when the rain eases off. Anything else?'

'Well, you could make Rajiv and me a drink.'

Shake turns around to see the two of them lounging on the leather settees, Rajiv looking right at home in the stark opulence, all ready for his time in the Bauhaus settings of the Fifth Reich.

Shake, finding thick cream and milk in the bar fridge and knowing Rajiv's sweet tooth, knocks up a Velvet Nut for them, regretting that he doesn't have frozen six ounce sauce flutes in which to serve the muddy mixture.

'What d'you do about the dogs? I can't do the pool with those hounds on the loose.'

'I'll show you. Excuse me, Rajiv.'

Rajiv smiles urbanely and extends a manicured hand as if conferring a blessing.

Susannah leads Shake into the utility area. 'I had it modified. I can't deal with the fucking dogs, they're fucking psychotic. So look.' Susannah slides back a metal hatch in the wall, lobs three shanks of meat out into the yard, takes a whistle from the shelf and blows hard, making no sound. Nothing happens and then a lot happens as she nods to a closed circuit television and Shake watches the Rottweilers sprint towards the meat. As the dogs begin to bolt down the bloodied piles, Susannah points a remote control, presses a button and the cage door slides shut behind the beasts.

'There, that's them dealt with. This,' Susannah waves the remote and slips it into a pocket, 'works from anywhere within three hundred yards.'

Shake fights a sense of fury that Susannah can arrange for this work to be done in a day and he can't even get his roof finished. It's just money, he tells himself. Just money talking loud as ever.

'So if I'm by the pool and something happens, I can let them out. Mind you,' Susannah laughs her odd, rasping laughter, 'I'll have to run like fuck and get me inside. Like I said, they're deranged.'

'Where d'you get them?' he asks, watching the dogs, still standing as they eat, front legs splayed, eyes moving, licking at sanguine puddles.

'Sansobella. A man out near San Bernadino. Don't know what he does to them. I think they're crossed somewhere. With what, I can't imagine. Fucking caiman by the looks of it. He's a smooth little bastard, isn't he?'

'Eh?'

'Rajiv – he's a smooth bastard. Sitting there like butter wouldn't melt.'

'He's alright.' Shake watches the dogs growling at each other, circling as they prepare to scrap.

'He's fucking East Indian Sanso. How can he be alright?' Susannah flicks a look at the screen and turns to leave. 'Thinks he's God, or that God is East Indian Sanso. Don' matter which. Check the pool, Shake. Like I said, pool man hasn't arrived. Neither have the housekeeper or gardeners. And I haven't seen security since before the dogs got poisoned.'

'How you managing?'

'I can cook, mix a drink and wipe my own arse. So I'm managing.'

The rain has eased and Shake strips to his shorts and goes outside, opens the pool pump house and finds the net and telescopic pole. Walks back and forth along the edge of the pool, turning the handle, slowly gathering the debris of leaves and petals in sweeping figures of eight, so familiar a movement. Shake thinks of the hundreds of pools he has cleaned, under a different sun, in a different country, and he thinks this pool, marking the spine of the mansion that is Mojito, is the most beautiful he has ever seen. He looks north and sees the rain clouds moving away, trailing net curtains of showers which break up the distant sea, mottling it. Wet season won't be long now, he thinks, days of thunderous downpours followed by steam and heat. He likes wet season until it gets to October, November, when clothes grow mould, paper sticks together and cutlasses seem to get sharper as they cut through skin. Tolerance falls, tempers rise and even the goats get antsy. But by October he should be in his house, surely? Shake stops moving the pole, counts on his fingers – four months. Maybe it won't be finished but he'll be in it. There'll be painting to do – he needs to get himself down to the Benjamin Moore shop and look at some colours. That'd be good – get down there and choose some colours whilst the light is clear; if he waits until wet season he'll choose blues, greys and greens. Shake cleans out the net with his hands, finds tan and brown hairs from the ridgeback in the water and he tosses the wet muck in the bushes. Then he kneels by the filter outlet and unscrews the lid – no tablets in the basket. He rummages in the pump house for a testing kit, scoops out some of the liquid and calculates bromide and chlorine levels, pours in liquids, fills the basket with tablets and seals the outlet. He looks up and sees Rajiv and Susannah talking in the living room, looking like they're getting along. Shake looks at his good friend's face as he listens to Susannah, and he remembers Rajiv chewing the yellow jelly of coconut and pointing up to the Huggins' old estate house as he said he didn't understand how people could have so much to say to each other every evening. Remembers floating in the old pool out by the bungalow at the Samaroo mansion in Queenstown, floating there with Rajiv, smoking and laughing and thinking life would be good; remembers Rajiv at university, when he would lend Shake a tenner for a night out; remembers Rajiv coming to Bridgewater and staying with him long enough to put him back together again. That was more than ten years ago, when Rajiv had a young family and a business to run and yet he left them and came to put Shake back together again. Shake is surprised to find himself swallowing, his eyes filling, as he thinks that his friend is leaving on Friday. Rajiv is leaving Sansobella. Shake turns away from the sight of Rajiv, looking like his father, drinking with the last of the Huggins' dynasty, turns away and watches as the clouds move and the sun suddenly blazes.

'Rajiv tells me he thinks you should go to Germany,' remarks Susannah conversationally when Shake eventually joins them. 'Why don't you?'

'Because I live here,' says Shake, looking at the colour of the drink Susannah now has in front of her. Single malt whisky or seven-year-old rum, he knows.

'You can live with us in Frankfurt. I have been explaining to Susannah that there are many opportunities for import and export now, in Europe. I shall need someone I can trust. The trade barriers are falling and the American dollar is very volatile. The opportunities are endless.'

Shake stares at the infinity pool, follows it to its inconclusive conclusion. 'I live here.'

'Butcha no black, nuh?' says Susannah, smiling.

'Neither are you. Either of you.'

'Lebe lebe, but I Georgian.'

Rajiv places his glass carefully on the travertine table and smoothes out his cheeks. Shake knows his old friend does this when he's buying himself time to think. Rajiv doesn't know about Susannah's lack of a mother tongue, doesn't know how the black-strap molasses wraps itself around Susannah's words and pulls them hither and thither.

'Why yuh not go, Shake? Yuh say yuh live heah butcha don'. Live here, I mean. You do just enough to keep body and soul together.'

Shake takes his sunglasses out of his pocket, cleans them with the hem of his shorts. It is what he does when he's buying himself time to think. Both of them, Shake and Rajiv, know they're in a room with a woman who is smarter and more malicious and more powerful than either of them will ever be and they buy time, bank it.

'I know what your life is like, Shake. I can imagine every detail,' croons Susannah, dragging out every word, making it elastic.

Shake walks to the bar and begins to mix himself a drink as Susannah carries on crooning. He tries not to listen as he pours a double measure of Havana Club Tres Años into a shaker over a mound of ice, a dash of bitters, five centilitres of lime juice and then the opening of the black bottle, the scent of passion fruit rising as he dribbles in a double of Passoã. And all the time Susannah's talking.

'Some early mornings, when the rains come in, you lie in your shack, on your hard bed, and you stare at the ceiling and wish you were with someone. And maybe you have a wank because that makes you feel better, for a couple of minutes at least. And then you feel ashamed, because you're Shake, some kind of fucking saint from what I hear. And I expect you've got some kind of shower or bathroom and you get in there and wash yourself clean because soon you'll be being nice to all the old girls and boys on the beach or on the road. And maybe you pick some of them up and give them a drop into Bridgewater and you don't take any money, wave it away with that smile of yours when you only use one side of your mouth. Yuh payin' penance with deed and I dunno what fuh. And you walk around Bridgewater with your cap and shades on, looking handsome and clean-cut and obviously you live here and the women from the cruise liners look twice and the locals don't quite know how to treat you, so they're kind of pleasant but say things behind your back, maybe about the fact you know me. That queer rich bitch on the hill.'

Shake picks out the Hawthorn strainer from a drawer and, having shaken the drink so long and hard that he almost drowned out the account of his life, he pours the orange liquid into a chilled old-fashioned and then grinds a few specks – no more – of black pepper on the filmy surface.

'Saturday nights you come here and fix up a few things and that's supposed to be payment for . . . what? My protection? The umbrella of my name? Access to my bathroom suites? You think of us as friends but don't forget where you come from, how we met. You just a handyman. You shower yourself and then head off to Jungle Jam and because you're a walking fucking cliché, with your tan and your ponytail and your look-at-my-working-hands-and-scratched-up-jeep, greeting the locals with a lazy wave of the hand and a few phrases you picked up from me, you think you're part of the fucking furniture. And you sit there, sucking on a beer or a rum, looking at the whiteys, like you ain't one of them, looking at them like they som'tin yuh foun' on yuh shoe. Maybe other nights the loneliness gets too much but you put it down to a sunset or a rush of blood to the head and you take yourself to a bar where you'll find the surfing boys or the divers.'

Shake rotates the drink in the glass, watching the film of the pulpy passion fruit juice move. He draws the scent deep into his lungs. This is a cocktail he never makes for anyone but himself. Shake has named it 'Mama's Dream' because that is what is it is. It is a refinement of the drink he never bought from a stall twenty-five years before, when the scent of passion fruit snagged him.

'And you sit there, at the bar, all hunched over, playing with a bottle of beer and talking to wide-eyed boys about how you live and they think you're a fucking god or some kind of hero or something.'

Shake sips a little of the nectar and feels his mother's long fingernails scraping across his forehead.

'And then you go back to your lonely bed and wonder why things ain't moving along so well, maybe on your house, or why boys ain't turning up to work. You sit there in the near-dark and play with your cell phone and think about how things might have been. I mean, fuck it, you must look in the mirror and wonder? And you call your dog over and scratch her head because it's better than thinking you're on your own. And yuh call dat livin' heah. Yuh paying penance, Shake – like I said, I dunno what for – and you call dat livin' heah. I make no excuses for my perspicacity.'

'Shake, you can come with me to Frankfurt. It is not too late – I can arrange everything.' Rajiv can't even look at Susannah.

Shake drinks the nectar that he believes would have transported his mother to a place where there were no urchins. He wonders what happened to Adonis, that thick-lipped monster, wonders if he has a family, if he has children. Hears the creak of a cart's wheel, the silence of falling snow.

'Shake, I think it would be a good idea to leave. If you will not come with me then at least go home.' Rajiv stretches his cheeks again.

'I live here,' Shake says. 'I don't have anywhere else to go.'

Susannah clicks on the television and there are the women of Darfur, running through sandstorms, hoping to escape rape.

The airport, when Shake and Rajiv arrive, is bedlam. Shake drives into the departure area, parks in the lane that always has notices saying 'no parking' where everyone always stops but a soldier toting a machine gun waves him on.

'Shit,' says Shake, 'what's going on?'

Rajiv shrugs. 'It is what I said.'

Shakes drives on and parks on the dusty verge of a road running alongside the terminal and the two men walk back, Rajiv wheeling a small case. Usually Shake likes visiting the airport, likes to sit in the bar sipping a freezing S&G beer as he waits to pick someone up, maybe Susannah or a customer flying in to take a Dorado trip. He likes to watch the beach boys as they lounge on pillars and walls, waiting for the arrivals to come through, white and flustered. The beach boys lounge there and check out the women, watch out for the pasty, middle-aged English and Germans, in new, garish T-shirts and tight jeans, their feet puffy in sandals, tattoos revealed on fat arms and shoulders. The women sweat and look about themselves, confused by the humidity and the noise of taxi horns and plane engines roaring and men shouting and moving them on. Eventually a white woman, a tourist rep, approaches them, holding a plastic folder emblazoned with the Thomas Cook logo, or Golden Caribbean, and the frowns clear, smiles are exchanged. The women begin to think that maybe there will be good times ahead. What they don't know is that the beach boys are checking out which hotel their chosen victims are staying at, which beach they'll be lounging on soaking up the vicious rays of the sun. The beach boys have learned that these women are a better bet than the groups of young girls, with their washboard stomachs and blonde ponytails. The older women are richer, lonelier – they don't make such a pretty picture hanging on your arm but they might be good for a car or a new boat engine or a fridge before they leave. And they certainly guarantee two weeks of beers and food. Shake likes to sit in the bar and watch the local women selling benay balls and coconut cake from the stalls, likes to watch the Sansos waiting for the short hop plane to Queenstown, strutting around, talking on cell phones. And in the bar there are the dive masters and hotel reps, dressed in chinos and hot shirts or smart skirts and blouses, standing in groups, drinking neat rum or gin and tonics. Everyone knows each other, everyone knows Shake, and chitchat is swapped back and forth about how busy the island is, the new petrol station, the food poisoning at the Royal, the reclusive stars staying on Dorado. There's a loose, fluid bonhomie between these drifters, these people who find themselves where they did not expect to be.

Rajiv checks in and looks at his watch, suggests they have time for a drink. But today the bar is quiet, the reps and divers are there, but they're sitting at tables in small groups, leaning in close, glancing up every time the door opens. Through the tinted windows Shake can see another soldier with a machine gun, looking bored, standing by the domestic gate. He orders two fruit punches because he knows there's no point in asking for a beer, and a woman he's known slightly for years comes to stand next to him. She's worked out of the Oriole for as long as he can remember and what's weird about her is that she never has a tan; Shake often jokes with her about it, calls her a vampire. What's her name? Maureen or something?

'Hi,' the woman says. Shake notices she's not carrying her clipboard. 'Glad I caught up with you to say *adios*. I've got a new job in the Canaries; I'm flying out on Virgin this afternoon.'

'You're leaving?'

'Yeah.' The woman, whatever her name is, sips neat white rum and Shake notices she has bitten her nails down to the quick.

'Why?'

She looks around herself, speaks quietly. 'Oh, you know. I've been here a long time. It'll be good to have a change of scene. Rolling stones and all that.'

'Well, good luck.'

'Thanks,' she says, and drifts off, still looking like she hasn't seen the sun for years.

Rajiv is talking on his cell, and Shake waits until he flips it closed before asking Rajiv why he hasn't imported foreign beers. 'I mean, you could have made a mint. Just bring in some Banks or Carib or Red Stripe or something. You had the license.'

'I *have* imported Carib from Trinidad. I imported two containers of Stag and Carib three weeks ago.'

'Well, we haven't seen any of it here and we're getting thirsty. You could charge what you wanted and people would pay.'

'The containers are sitting on the dock in Queenstown, as well as many others. The Haraksinghs brought in five containers of Heineken and Guinness and they are sitting there too. Customs will not clear the papers.'

'What's the problem?'

'The same problem as there always is – Kouranis. He has bought the customs men. They will not clear any imports of beer which means Kouranis will be able to break the brewery strike.'

Kouranis. Shake thinks of Mister Jeremiah, thinks maybe the time has come to visit Wrexall and find some commanding powders. The tannoy blares a muffled message and Rajiv picks up his briefcase. 'I have to go.'

'I'll come to the gate.'

'Shake, I am sorry Susannah was so abusive.'

Shake looks away. 'It's not your fault. Not hers either. Just the rum talking. Come on, you'll miss the plane.'

The soldier's interest is snagged by the sight of a white man and a Sanso standing near each other, saying nothing. He stares at them and is surprised to see them hug, long and hard. The Sanso breaks away, walks to the gate, turns and walks back to the white man, hugs him again, says something and then walks quickly through the gate. The soldier watches the white man walk away, shifts his gun strap, which is digging into his shoulder.

The steps up to his plot of land seem steeper than usual, longer than usual, and Shake puts this down to the weight of Rajiv's leaving. He wants to shower and lie in his hammock for a couple of hours, drinking rum and watching the sun set. That's all he wants to do. But when he reaches his porch, Shake sees the door of the shack is open. Bones must be in there, searching for tequila or whatever he can get his skinny hands on. Shake steps inside quietly, making no sound on the boards and he sees someone rummaging through his kitchen, turning over bags and looking under the sink. It's not Bones.

'Bap – what're you doing here?'

Bap swings round, locks bloodshot eyes on Shake. Bap's hands are working, fingers flipping over and over and Shake can smell him even from where he's standing, by the door: a jumbled stink, redolent of sweat and blood and fear. The chop on Bap's arm hasn't healed, it glistens in the afternoon light.

'I come by yuh to thee if yuh got wuk for me. I hungry, man, I need thome money. I broken to t'ief but I only takin', not thtealin', I no sell anyt'ing on.'

'I'll give you some food but I can't give you work. There isn't going to be any. But I can give you some potatoes and eggs.'

'I need money.' Bap's raddled mind recalls something that seems like a long time ago but was a good idea then. 'I got to ketch Thanthobella ferry, get teefs. I need thome money.'

'I'll give you food. You say you're hungry.'

'I thucker gutth.'

Shake looks at Bap's eyes and skin, looks at the bones showing through the dull, matte black. He's seen this before, seen it in the men who sit in the scrubland behind the port. Seen it in himself. Bap's doing crack and he's been doing it some time.

'I'll give you food but I'm not giving you money.'

Bap's hands begin to work furiously. Shake walks past him warily, smells the sweet, fermented stench of puncheon rum and digestive acid on Bap's breath, fills a plastic bag with provisions.

'There you go. That'll keep the wolf from the door.'

Bap stares at him, breath whistling between the gap in his gums. Eventually, he takes the bag. 'Who doh hear go feel,' he says and walks out.

Lying in his hammock, a bottle of Huggins' seven-year-old rum resting on his stomach, Shake tries to empty his mind, tries to drift away and not think. He swigs from the bottle, thinks he should check on *Ribailagua* but he can't be bothered. Frigate birds are skimming low over the headland and Shake watches them as they cruise the thermals, rising slowly, forked tails jerking as they adjust their flight. The Welsh guy who had told him about the pelicans had also told him that frigate birds never catch their own fish, instead they steal fish from other birds. Shake pictures the white and pale grey tropicbirds flying over the lagoon, or round Frigate Island, fish dangling from red beaks, imagines what the birds must feel as the huge, black, jagged Men o' War swoop on them and snatch the fish away. Pissed off is how they must feel, Shake decides. He re-corks the bottle, puts a hand on his heart and throws the other above his head.

He must have slept because the next thing he knows, a hand is tapping his shoulder and a voice is saying, 'Mister Shake, Mister Shake.' He opens his eyes and there's Ayninka standing above him. Shake feels vulnerable, dressed in his old shorts, dead to the world.

'Hello Ayninka. What's the problem?' Shake sits up, balances on the edge of the hammock.

'It's Mama, Mister Shake. Her not good. Daddy wondering if you could carry her into the hospital.'

'Your mama? What's wrong with her?'

'She say she can' breathe and her feets are all swollen up.'

'Of course I'll take her. Wait a minute and I'll be right there.'

Shake throws water on his face, shoves into a T-shirt, grabs his jeep keys whilst trying to ignore Susannah's voice: 'because you're Shake, some kind of fucking saint from what I hear . . .'

Mister Jeremiah says nothing when Shake and Ayninka appear, just beckons to Shake and leads him into the listing, wooden house, balanced on pilings, and there is Miss Avarice, lying on her bed, a fan playing over her. Miss Avarice's feet are the size of pawpaw and her breath sounds like a labouring water pump, yet still she raises a smile for Shake, pulls a little at her nightdress, ashamed by the intimacy of the moment. She tries to speak but nothing happens.

'Her not good.' Mister Jeremiah's face is grave. 'It start las' night. Her cookin' up some callalloo and her say she have to get in her bed and der her stay.'

'Well, let's get you to hospital.'

'Ayninka, sort mammy, nuh, an' call we when her ready.'

Mister Jeremiah and Shake leave the room, go outside to wait for the call, standing in the early evening sunlight in the yard. Mister Jeremiah clasps his hands over his stomach, lowers his head.

'We pray for she.'

Shake catches a glimpse of someone down below by the vegetable garden and is saved from the act of having to pray.

'Isn't that Sheldon?'

Mister Jeremiah snaps his head up, looks at Shake. 'Yes, that he.'

'Is he on leave?'

'Nuh – he desert de army. Came here t'ree nights back, in de dark. No one know he here. He say a lot of black boys caship.' Mister Jeremiah watches Sheldon as he squats on his haunches in the shade of a breadfruit tree, pulling on a cigarette. 'Shake, Sheldon need to leave heah, need to leave de islan'. Der a ferry leavin' tonight for Port o' Spain. Miss Avarice got family in Tobago an' Sheldon need to go there for a spell.'

Shake knows that Mister Jeremiah won't ask, so he says, 'I could drop him on the way to the hospital.'

Some kind of fucking saint.

The sun has set and the evening sky is grey and torn by the time Shake and Mister Jeremiah have carried Miss Avarice to the jeep and laid her in the back on a mattress. Miss Avarice tries to smile but Shake can see she's in pain. Sheldon crawls in next to his grandmammy and holds her hand. Mister Jeremiah sits in the passenger seat, muttering his prayers as Shake drives out of Killdevill and turns onto the Grand Anse road, heading for Bridgewater. On the way he passes Bap, standing by the roadside, pointing west, yelling for a drop. Shake sees Bap no longer carries the plastic bag of provisions and he wonders what happened to it. He drives into Bridgewater, crawls through the traffic, aware of Miss Avarice's labouring heart just behind him, and Sheldon jumps out at the dockside, melts into the crowds there, just another local with no luggage. Shake negotiates his way through the trucks and cars, flicks on the headlights and drives up the back way, to the hill behind Bridgewater where the hospital sits on a rise. The headlights pick out goats and sheep by the road, old men sitting on walls, swinging their legs.

'De British build de hospital,' says Mister Jeremiah, as they drive past red brick barracks and old colonial houses. 'Dey built all of dis many years ago an' it still standin'.'

'I know,' says Shake.

'Yuh built all de bridges too, before yuh lef'. Before independence dat is. Now no one build anyting, unless to make money. De Sansos build der villas and hotels and de roads and bridges fallin' into de sea. What good a hotel if yuh cyar drive der? What good a hotel if yuh cyar drink beer? Yuh could build. Nutting de same now. It better when yuh was heah. Now it all choppin' and drugs and rum.'

Shake pulls up in front of a dilapidated whitewashed building – the barrack hospital of the eighteenth century, built within the walls of the British fort. Shake sometimes wonders if it's been decorated or cleaned since then. He's had to go there a couple of times – for a bad cut on his arm and once for a fishbone jammed in his throat which the nurse loosened by making him eat a cottonwool sandwich – but anything else, he's promised himself, and he's on the first flight to Miami. Shake and Mister Jeremiah gently lift Miss Avarice from the jeep, set her on her poor feet as Mister Jeremiah yells for a chair. There is no triage nurse; instead, propped up at the entrance to A&E is a large sheet of hardboard listing, in handwritten white letters, the order in which patients will be seen: choppings, stabbing, shark bite, scorpion sting, snake bite, broken bone, poisoning, stonefish. Seems like people still did more damage to each other than the natural world contrived. No chair appears, and so Miss Avarice begins to shuffle towards the door, helped by the two men. Nowhere, thinks Shake, does the list mention heart attack, appendicitis, aneurysm, nitrogen bends, and that's why he'll be heading for Miami should the need arise.

Shake helps lower Miss Avarice into a chair and waits beneath flickering neon lights as Mister Jeremiah talks to the nurse. The old man seems older when he returns. 'Dey don' know how long before doctor come. Her say to wait heah. Lots of trouble at de docks, t'ree or four choppins. Dey sewing people up.'

'Well, that shouldn't take too long.' Had enough practice, thinks Shake.

Miss Avarice groans.

'Yuh go home, Shake. T'ank you for dat. Yuh a good man.'

'Shall I check on Ayninka?'

'Her be OK. Her a big girl now an' she sensible.'

'Right, well, good luck. You call me anytime if you need a pick-up to go home. Look, here's my home and cell numbers.' Shake gives Mister Jeremiah a business card. 'Anytime.'

Miss Avarice touches his hand, strokes the back of his hand with her tough fingertips.

'You be good, Miss Avarice – no jump-ups on the ward tonight.' Shake squeezes the dying woman's fingertips.

Miss Avarice smiles and Shake leaves the two of them there, waiting for the doctor who may never come.

20 June

Jesus Christ, what a day, Shake thinks the next morning as he's sluicing off the deck of *Ribailagua*. Where have the quiet days gone? Days of driving slowly along empty roads with the sun shining and the icebox full of beers in the back; days of fishing out above the trench, long-lines straining as the trophy fish bite? Days of running the Dorado trip, trousering hundreds of dollars for nothing, just dropping the star-struck on a jetty built on the lip of an active volcano? Where have the they gone, those quiet, easy days? Now it's all about the colour of your skin, the malevolence of your dogs, all about not standing near whitey and keeping your head down. Shake sits on the gunwale when he's finished cleaning the boat and lights a slightly damp du Maurier cigarette, not enjoying the first drag. All he wants to do is fire the engines and set off for the Five Sisters or Frigate Island, strap himself into the fighting chair and see if he can pull something in. Instead of which he knows he has to trawl the beaches, fish the sands, using himself as bait. Because Rajiv had been right – the hotels were emptying. Already his inbox was full of cancellations.

Shake climbs back up to his shack, stands by the collapsing hole that will be his pool, and watches the tiny cascades of soil that are falling, tumbling into the pit, waterlogged particles. Thinks of the physics of the event – gravity, mass density and kinetic energy. Fuck it. Soon it will all have to be back-hoed again. He needs to find Dragon and get his house finished, get the pool lined.

The water pressure has dropped and Shake is forced to stand under his shower head a while before he feels damp enough to soap up. He wonders about Miss Avarice and her feet, wonders about her heart and whether it kept pumping during the night. He hopes it has. As water drips on his hair the picture of a white leather Pompanette fighting chair appears in Shake's mind, wrapped and ready to go in Susannah's garage. He and Rajiv had left under something of a cloud and the chair was still up in Mojito. Maybe he didn't want it any more, the Pompanette? But if he wasn't going to Miami, then should he fetch it down and fix it on *Ribailagua*'s deck? On the other hand, Shake doesn't much feel like talking to Susannah. Shampoo sits in Shake's eye sockets as he thinks of what it's like to be a walking fucking cliché. Because what he can't even begin to think about is the fact that Susannah was right. As shampoo sluices slowly down a reluctant drain, Shake shaves himself close in the fragment of a mirror he has stuck to the shower stall door with mastic. Then he pulls on his last pair of unworn O'Neill shorts and a new Fruit of the Loom T-shirt, the logo 'Dream Chaser' still sharp above his heart. And he knows, he just knows, as he trots down the steps to the Land Rover, cell phone in his pocket, clipboard and cards and flyers in his hand, that he looks like the kind of man that divers and fishermen think is God.

Shake drives down to the Pillikin Road and cruises along, checking out the beach, but there's no one out there. Maybe it's too early for the tourists who cook their own breakfasts in the guest houses: Shake checks his watch – eight-thirty. Coral Strand won't start for a while, so he heads south towards Grackle Bay, near the airport, where the guest houses and apartments have burgeoned. A woman is pointing down the road, waiting for a drop, waiting for someone pulling bull, but she's lucky because good old Shake slows for her and throws open the passenger door. She's dressed in some kind of uniform – the Nation Bank maybe? – and she's real careful about folding her skirt beneath her so it doesn't get creased.

'I can drop you at Grackle Bay. I'm not going any further.'

'Dat's fine.'

Shake drives on, along a road that's lined with old-style houses falling into dilapidation because there are no papers relating to the land and the sub-divisions, houses with beautiful, rotting batchboard falling into long savannah grass and galvanize peeling back from the roof because there are no papers, no cadastrels. Houses being strangled with vines as the heirs – who live in New York, Toronto, Munich, Sansobella, Trinidad, Barbados, London – have their lawyers and solicitors write letters to illiterate great-aunts and uncles, who gaze with amazement at the stamps and place the unopened documents under elaborate paperweights. Shake, driving barefoot, hating the thought of what he has to do, is about to comment on these houses, when he sees the woman dig in her handbag. She has three fingers on her left hand. Shake glances at the woman, charts her profile and he wonders if it is indeed Ruby, who sat on a wall drinking beer with a sixteen-year-old boy twenty five years before. He thinks of how he threw up on her feet and he smiles, thinking that he really can't ask this apparently respectable middle-aged woman any questions about that afternoon. He drops her on the main road – not taking the few notes she offers – and turns down to the beach. The wall is still there, repainted in white and red squares, and the wide bay beyond is already busy with tourists and beach boys. Shake sighs as he collects together his stuff. He hardly ever visits the beach, never spends days lying on a towel sunning himself, because it's too hot and uncomfortable. He'll take Saltbag for an evening walk, or maybe sometimes he'll sit in the shade for a while and watch the surfers on those rare days when the waves are coming in at the east end of Pillikin near Sangaree. He likes to sit and watch them paddling out beyond the surf, then sitting astride the boards, talking to each other, yelling over the sound of the water breaking, waiting for the long rollers and he can remember how that feels, that rocking motion, the fleeting camaraderie. Shake doesn't surf now, can't surf because of the time he wiped out and his board slammed into his knee, wrecking it. He sometimes thinks of that morning, out of his head on coke, thinking he could do anything, thinking he was Jan Michael Vincent in *Big Wednesday* or something, shooting the twenty foot tube. Shit, what had he been like?

Walking along Grackle beach, Shake can feel the heat rising up from the sand, as sweat begins to trickle down his spine. He knows his best bet are the slightly older couples for the fishing trips, or maybe a small group of youngsters who can split the cost. Shake scans the beach, selects a few hopefuls, turns on his lopsided smile and heads their way. He knows to greet them when still a few feet away, giving them time to register that he is white, giving the women time to adjust their straps or pull on a T-shirt, knows it is best to half-kneel next to them, on their level, as the man sits up, then ask them how they're doing, where they're staying, if they're having a good time. Recommend a few restaurants and bars. Then suggest a trip to catch some fish, or just to see some of the island, visit a few beaches inaccessible by road, maybe do some snorkelling. Flirt a little with the women but talk to the men, look them in their nervous eyes. He knows the men are nervous, edgy, because of their office-white hands, their sloping, pink shoulders and sad, apologetic paunches, looking at Shake's tanned, tall, muscular body, wishing their wives or partners were Shake-blind. Hand them a flyer and a card, don't push it, suggest they give him a call on his cell. Smile as he stands up, shake the man's hand with a strong, virile grip which will make him feel like an equal and then move on. Remember to wave to them as he leaves the beach. Shake works Grackle for an hour, thinks there are two couples who might be interested but he can never be sure.

It's gone eleven o'clock when he pulls up at the guard hut at Coral Strand. Shake hasn't been to Coral Strand for more than a year; he hasn't had to solicit for trade since that time because business hasn't been this slow for a while, since 9/11 now he thinks about it. Shake waves at the woman in the hut and waits for the barrier to be lifted but it stays right where it is.

'Twenny dollah,' says the woman, holding out a limp hand, staring straight ahead and not at Shake, chewing gum.

'What?'

'Twenny dollah.' She points at a sign on the side of the hut.

For years there's been a tacit agreement that local traders – the sweet sellers, glass-bottomed boat operators, fishing charter men, jewellery makers – could all enter and do their business as long as they did it quietly. Kouranis has obviously noticed this loophole and closed it. The guard standing by the barrier, unbelievably dressed head to foot in black trousers, black cable jumper with epaulettes and black beret, comes over to Shake, holding a electric pink strip of paper which he fixes around Shake's wrist.

'It's not my colour,' says Shake, trying to raise a smile and failing. He hands over twenty dollars and eases the jeep along the mile-long track leading to the clubhouse, cabanas and bars, bouncing over ramps. He has always loved this drive, through the old coconut plantation, dotted with flamboyants, the lagoon on his left, mangrove swamp in the distance on his right. But now he sees a tall diamond link fence has been built along the shore, along the high tide line and he remembers Bap shouting about this one morning, shouting about how his brother, who lives in Zabico, could no longer cross the land to reach his fishing boat, how none of the fishermen were allowed through. Shake thinks of a guy he got drunk with one day, a tourist who took a fishing trip and they got along so well Shake invited him to stay on the boat and share his beers. The guy had taught college kids about tourism, something Shake couldn't quite understand – did he teach the kids how to get to distant places and buy too much booze? Apparently there was some theory about paradise and the way it was created. Shake can't remember much of it – something about paradise controlled, contrived and contained and one other thing. Coral Strand now seemed to be all three.

The beach is packed, and Shake drives right down to the far end, parks in the shade and steels himself for another uncomfortable couple of hours. First he strolls around, checking out the families and groups in the cabanas and on the sunbeds under umbrellas. He sees that it costs fifteen dollars to hire a bed, ten for an umbrella, fifty for a cabana for a day. There are notices everywhere, instructing the merrymakers not to sit on tables, not to move tables or benches, not to litter, not to bring in their own food or iceboxes, disclaimers announcing that the management would take no responsibility for either injury or loss of property. And everywhere the black-clad guards loll against posts or walk slowly along the back of the beach, watching the white girls as they smear sunblock on their thighs and stomachs. Where there had once been a hut selling fried shrimp, shark and bake, rotis and provision, there now stands a concrete and glass outlet, selling donuts, Chunky Chick, KupKakes and burgers, milkshakes, Miss Tubby and Diamond Falls water – all the franchises owned by Kouranis. Shake's hungry but he decides to wait until he gets home. He sits for a moment on a bench, watching the glass-bottomed boats filling with tourists and he notices a green truck parked by the fence. Dragon's truck. Shake knows if his truck is here, Dragon is here and he finds him working on the foundations of a small bar being built down the beach.

'Hey, Dragon, how you doing?'

Dragon, his shirt soaked in sweat, takes off his trademark red cap, wipes his forehead.

'My roof is waiting for you. It misses you and looks forward to seeing you tomorrow.'

Dragon sighs, replaces his cap. 'I workin' here.'

'I can see that. You did say the roof would be tied by tomorrow.'

'Kouranis want new bar. He want it now-now, like I work-jumbie.'

Shake looks at Dragon, who he's known a long time, who he's sat in bars with, lamenting the state of the weather, the state of the cricket, the state of Lara's bat. 'When will you be able to get to my place?'

'Shake, I workin' mi' liver string. Kouranis he wan' dis to jus' dey by Sunday. Den I coming by you jus' now. I goin' so fas' I giddy rong.'

Shake knows he can't say anything because there's no point. If Kouranis wants Dragon, he gets Dragon. 'Don't kill yourself, I can wait a while.'

Shake begins to work along the beach, trying to sell the Dorado trip to the wealthy Germans and English, trying to interest the Sansos – who are sitting on the tables in the cabanas, drinking their own rum from their own iceboxes – in trips to other beaches. He has the sense he's doing fine; a lot of people are asking all the right questions and nodding in all the right places. He sees two attractive women sitting in the shade of a sea almond, reading, and heads slowly towards them. He knows they've got money to burn; even when people are nearly naked on a beach there are still enough signals flashing to pick up who they are: jewellery, tattoos, hair cuts, sarongs, the cut of a bikini, the cover of a book, the logo on a beach bag, the label on a T-shirt, the way they move their hips and hands. Turns out Shake's right about the English women, who are well-groomed and articulate, self-assured. The three of them talk for a while and he discovers they've visited the island before a few times, that their husbands are playing golf at the Royal but they're staying at Tradewinds. The dark-haired one is looking at Shake in that way he recognizes and he knows it wouldn't take much to tip her over, to tip her into his bed but he's not even thinking about that. As they're all laughing about the road signs that hang upside down or point the wrong way, he's thinking they'd be good for a Dorado trip and the commission he gets from the limo company and the restaurant on the island where they'll have lunch.

That's when it happens – the noise. A flat, stifled crack, like a bullwhip snapping but, strangely, more threatening. Shake stands up as everyone on the beach falls silent and looks in the same direction as he is. The tinny music of the Sansos' boom decks is left running on the air as Shake shades his eyes and tries to make out where the noise came from because he knows it was gunshot. There's no echo because the bougainvillea and hibiscus and paddle leaves and frangipani soak up the sound as they move in the breeze. The groups of Sansos, who've heard the same sound many times and recognize it for what it is but who have never heard it in St George before, begin to pack and move towards their cars, already chattering on their cell phones. The English women are shading their eyes, looking up at Shake.

'What was that?' asks the woman with the dark hair and hot blood.

'Um,' Shake chews his lip. 'I'm not sure.' But he is.

'I think it was a gunshot,' says the other, older woman. 'I don't know why but I think it was a gunshot.' She stands and folds her towel, closes her book. 'Come on.' Her friend gathers together her things and the two of them stand, bags packed, next to Shake, as if he is suddenly responsible for them. Which, perversely, he feels he is.

'I'll take you back to your hotel.'

The two women cram into the cab, not wanting to ride in the open bed of the jeep, and Shake begins the slow crawl back along the sandy track. He sees a taxi driver he knows loading his car with anxious tourists.

'Hey! Beardy!' Shake stops the jeep, opens his hands, lifts his shoulders, the universal gesture of noncomprehension. Beardy looks left and right, comes over to the window.

'Dey shot Carlisle. He come onto de beach, start mixin' wid some people and the guards tell him to go an' Carlisle start to run. One security guard, he call him, tell him to stop but Carlisle keep runnin'. That's what I hear.'

'But Carlisle's deaf. He's harmless, everyone knows that.'

'Ever'one *here* know but the guard's Sanso.' Beardy walks away, climbs in his over-burdened taxi and joins the slow exodus.

'Shit,' says Shake. 'Shit.'

'Has someone been shot?' asks the dark-haired English woman, her eyes locked on Shake.

'Yeah.' Shake eases up the clutch as two workers ask if he can give them a drop on the highway. Shake nods and the men climb in the back, soon joined by three more. 'Apparently a local called Carlisle was shot by a guard. Thing is they yelled to him to stop but he's a deaf mute and he wouldn't have heard. Anyway, Carlisle wasn't all about, y'know, he was a bit simple. Everyone knew that. He's lived in Zabico all his life and everyone knows him. There are quite a few deaf mutes here and all over the Caribbean. Here they say that Carlisle's daddy must have killed songbirds and cut out their tongues. That's what they say and I think he has lots of brothers and sisters and they're all deaf mutes. Except maybe one who can hear but she can't talk, which is odd.' Shake knows he's rambling now, just talking to cover the slow mile of track back to some kind of reality. Police cars are passing the other way, and the jam slows to a halt, pulls over to let an ambulance by, paintwork being scratched by bougainvillea thorns.

'Is he dead?'

'I don't know,' says Shake.

The workers jump out of the jeep at the junction with the highway and Shake drops the tourists at the entrance to Tradewinds. It's gone two when he pulls into the car park of the Royal and Shake does something he hasn't done for years – he visits the tourist shop in the reception area and buys every paper he can see: the Trinidadian *Guardian*, the *Sanso News*, *USA Today*, *Herald Tribune*, *Daily Mail*, *Sunday Times*, *Sunday Telegraph*, *Daily Express*. Some of them are a few days old but Shake doesn't care. He drives through the searing heat back to Tom Collins, climbs the steps to his shack, showers, throws on his usual dress of tatty shorts and T-shirt. Then he sits on the step of his porch with a bottle of water, an ashtray and his cigarettes and he begins to read. He reads about a country, a republic that he doesn't even recognize.

When Susannah opens the rear door in her garage it is to find Shake standing in the harsh neon light, holding out a sheaf of newsprint, articles torn from papers.

'OK,' Shake says. 'I give in. What's going on? I don't understand.'

Susannah walks away, back to her cavernous marble living room, and Shake follows, sits opposite her as she sips at her rum.

'What don't you understand?'

'I don't understand any of it. I've read all these,' Shake throws the articles on the travertine table top, 'and I can't make any sense of it. I mean, these all talk about protests, coups, civil unrest and all that shit. And I go down to the beach and people are lying in the sun or napping in the shade and it seems I'm supposed to be living in the middle of a fucking revolution.'

'Well, Georgians always did know how to relax themselves.' Susannah smiles.

'It's not funny.'

'What *is* it then, Shake? If it's not funny, what adjective would you use to describe the situation?'

'Snafu would just about cover it.' Donald had often used the expression and Shake hadn't thought of his father's saying it for years.

'Get yourself a drink and I'll tell you all about it.'

'I don't want a drink.'

'Get one.'

So Shake rummages in the bar, pours himself a couple of fingers of single malt and sits.

'The PDM, the governing party, is black African West Indian. The ministers are black, their henchmen are black. They sit in Parliament House in Queenstown in Sansobella and they pass legislation or they try to. The government is given vast amounts of development money by the Europeans and Americans, although the Americans are more concerned with stopping the drugs trade in the Caribbean than building hospitals and schools. Where the money goes is anyone's guess because it never seems to be spent on visible impovements. Yet the ministers drive around in limousines and live in villas on the outskirts of the city. The opposition, the NMDC, is East Indian. The opposition is essentially comprised of the heads of the families of five Indian dynasties. Between them they probably have a collective fortune worth more than the aid money given by foreign governments. They, too, drive around in limousines and live in villas on the outskirts of the city.

'There is a House of Congress here, in St George, as you well know. The job of the First Minister here is to represent the PDM on the island and to legislate according to the particular needs of St George, regarding health, education and transport. The First Minister lives, as you also know, in Government House up in the hills behind Bridgewater. An old colonial estate house, where he is catered for by an army of lackeys and local workers. It is the second most desirable residence in St George, after, of course, my own, and I am sure that if he had the balls, if he had the fucking guts, the First Minister would live here, in Killdevill, in this house. Because, as we know, he doesn't like mixing with his people. No, he want to mix with whitey, want to have his picture taken glad-handing businessmen at conferences. He want to stay at the Oriole and negotiate with ministers about projects that will never begin. He like wearing suits and driving round in a limo, a limo with windows tinted so dark he never have to look at what happening.'

Shake hasn't touched his drink, his hands are wrapped around the glass but he hasn't taken even a sip. He's just watching Susannah's lips move in her ugly face.

'So – this is St George, land of sun and sea, where life is easy, so they say. Where life is black and the soil is black and there's always breadfruit and mangoes and fish. In Sansobella, life isn't black, it's a fucking mess. It's not a melting pot it's a boiling pot. There are blacks, there is a black government. The blacks outnumber other races but the margin is getting slim. The black party won the last elections because of weight of numbers. They'll win the next one, in two weeks' time. Numbers win elections but they don't mean anything. The blacks are the underclass. They are, on the whole, undereducated, unskilled and poverty-stricken. The majority have little hope that anything will change because they don't know how to act, how to demand that things change. Yuh listenin' to me, Shake? They see the Chinese, the Koreans, the East Indians building houses, buying cars, opening shops, setting up businesses and they're resentful. Some are resourceful. They steal cars and kidnap the children or the scions or the heads of the powerful Indian families. Ransoms are paid or a body is found. But most are resentful and so they drink puncheon rum and they chop at each other because they're so blind drunk they can't see the enemy. And the ex-pats watch them from their gated communities, the Venezuelans, the Brazilians, Trinis, English and Americans drink their cocktails on their balconies and count the money flowing into their bank accounts from the oil and the natural gas and the drugs and then they pour themselves another cocktail. But the East Indians, who are boastful, who like to display wealth and power, who have politics in their blood, who are *born* into a political party, are themselves resentful. Because it is their babies, their wives, their husbands, who are car-jacked and kidnapped. So they protest. They take to the streets and protest, walk in their thousands down Champs du Ciel to the parliament buildings and they say they've had enough. It's a barely veiled threat because the Indians own the businesses. They down tools and Sansobella grinds to a halt. Get me a drink.'

Shake pushes his tumbler across, the whisky still intact and Susannah drains the glass.

'The blacks, those few who have any power in their hands – and you have to ask yourself at this point, what is the definition of power? – check the finer points of the constitution and announce that the protests are illegal and the ringleaders will be arrested. The ringleaders, of course, are the heads of the five Indian dynasties. These men find the situation laughable. They trot off to the bank, return with suitcases of cash and they are not arrested. The bluff of the government is, shall we say, called. There are more protests, more threats. Perhaps the government, sitting in Parliament House, is watching CNN, or reading accounts of Mugabe's actions in Zimbabwe because then there are calls for repatriation and the confiscation of land. Perhaps the Indians are watching CNN too, because they stop handing out bribes and start to mobilize opinion instead. But the numbers don't add up. They can't win the election.'

Susannah stands, walks to the bar and slops rum into her glass.

'You heard of General Ramprakesh?'

Shake shrugs, shakes his head.

'Yuh playin' do'tish? Lord, boy, how can you not know he? Three days ago the general's eldest son was found dead on a road out by Pitch Lake. The boy not like his pappy and never went into the army. He run a business in San Bernardino and he kidnapped. The police runnin' giddy rong, the army out in the bush and cane looking for the boy, the papers screaming and carrying ons. Turns out, a ransom had been paid but he was still found dead. The Ramprakesh family run the military, everyone knows that.'

'I didn't,' says Shake.

'Well of course you didn't. You know fuck all, as I've always said. End of lesson. QED. Book close.'

'There's someone you haven't mentioned.'

'Who?'

'Kouranis.'

'Ah, Kouranis.' Susannah stares at the pool running through the room. 'Why don't we step outside? Get some air as you English would say? Lock the dogs in and I'll refresh the glasses. Don't forget to use the whistle.'

Shake finds Susannah standing on the lip of the pool, the Caribbean Sea glittering below, spreading north and west, rippling towards the shores of Mexico and the Caymans and Cuba and Belize and and and . . . Shake recalls reading Jean Rhys when he left university, thinks he should re-read *Wide Sargasso Sea*, now that it might mean something. Susannah wordlessly hands him a tumblerful of Huggins Estate eighteen-year-old.

'Feels like the end of the world, doesn't it? So I thought we might as well open the finest in the cellars and sup from the irreplaceable.'

'What d'you mean? The end of the world?' Shake asks as his stomach chills.

'Yuh askin' all night. It might only be the end of *this* world, Shake. People think there's only one world, one big grapefruit, one fucking enormous pamplemousse as Otty used to say, but it isn't like that. There are lots of little worlds, lots of little pamplemousses and maybe this one has had its day. Maybe it's going to explode or implode and be a red dwarf or a black hole or whatever the fuck it is. Maybe this place, this country, this *idea*, grew too quickly. Maybe it's like a young child given a bank account and a candy store and a temper and a long lead and it all went wrong.' Susannah shrugs, drinks a mouthful of the analgesic she was given in her dummy by Otty, her black nanny.

'Kouranis.'

'Kouranis.' Susannah smiles in the darkness. 'You know, sometimes I lie in bed and wonder whether he's richer than me.'

'Sometimes I wonder whether he's richer than God.' And Shake smiles too, because he can remember sitting in the cabana at Coral Strand listening to Rajiv's father. But then he remembers Carlisle and it's not funny any more and Shake stops smiling.

'Kouranis. Part of me admires him. The merchant's blood in my veins makes me admire him. You have to think what he's done is extraordinary and yet I despise him.'

'Why?'

'Because he blow in the wind. Monkey eye deep all about *an'* know tree to climb.'

'Don't talk in riddles. You know I don't get it.'

'Ah Shake. What am I going to say? I'm just an old lady living out her days.'

'Susannah.'

'It's company law and regs that are to blame. If Kouranis could move about, he would. But he can't. If only he could move about on a schooner, skimming the waves, moving from island to island, jus' takin' a little bit here, a little piece there. But he forced to stay somewhere and he get rotten. Phoenician trader should move about. Every Caribbean island has its own Kouranis, a hog who lay in dog manger. Every island in the whole pamplemousse will have a Kouranis. Every island has gaps and the traders worm into them but worms have no soul, no conscience, no sense of *comme il faut.*' Susannah's beginning to lose the thread, beginning to weave a little, standing on the edge of infinity, weaving.

'Kouranis,' Shake says again. 'How does he get away with it?'

'What yuh got to understan', Shake, and listen to mi nuh, is that every mind has a set, every mind has a way of being. You an' me – us not so differen'. Not really. We t'ink de same. Essentially you and I are the products of the same culture, to a point. But Kouranis' mind is something we never step on an' if we did, we wouldn't know what to do with the shoe. Burn it or frame it. Maybe Kouranis is driven by memories of his daddy and his daddy's wealth, maybe he feel he got to do even more damage than his daddy did. I don't know. What I do know is that I donated three million dollars to the fund for the new hospital in Bridgewater and Kouranis upped the ante and said he'd give four. There's still only three million in the fund eighteen months later.'

'Right.'

'No, it's not right. Because there should be nearly three point two million with interest. And the First Minister's being driven in a new limo these days, a nice, long Mercedes. Kouranis waiting to see what direction the flag flapping. I trying to fight him, Shake, with the only t'ing he understand.'

'Did you hear what happened at Coral Strand?'

Susannah nods in the darkness. 'Carlisle's mammy worked in our kitchens. Yuh tell people dat woman set a canary in a cage in de kitchen and de bird sang. Dat bird wag its tongue. Yuh know in New York when the whiteys started building de city dey had butterfly men? Men to ketch butterfly to feed to canaries. Goddamn Victorians. Barking fucking mad'

'Is Carlisle dead?'

'Yes.'

'Susannah, I'm going to go now. D'you want me to get you inside and let out the dogs?'

'Shake, I'm sorry I was so rude to you the other night. I didn't want to be. It was that friend of yours – Rajiv – he annoyed me. I didn't mean it. Well, perhaps some of it. But I don't want you to go. I want you to stay here and build your house and all this will blow over. Like a storm it will pass. It just that the landscape might be a little different afterwards.'

Shake helps the drunken last vestige of the Huggins' line back into the house, onto the sofa, and then he releases the Rottweilers, wondering, yet again, what happened to paradise, contrived or otherwise.

Avril is sitting alone in her restaurant, beneath the goosefoot plants threading across her canopy. She sees Shake climbing the steps and smiles. 'Hi, baby. How you doin'?'

Shake pulls out a chair, sits at the table. 'You don't look too busy.'

'No customer all night. Even the new girl I hire no turn up. She be no good I begin to think. The tourist stay in hotels tonight. After what happen at Coral Strand, they go back to they hotels and they stay there. Maybe they feel safe.'

'Are they safe?'

Avril shrugs. 'Shake, baby, a lot happenin' but nuttin' goin' on but I don' think it stay that way.'

'Why not?'

'On Tuesday it's Carlisle's funeral.'

'OK.'

Avril laughs suddenly. 'You know what I hear? Kouranis, he give in to the beer workers so the strike over. Say we have beer in two days. His guards shootin' at Georgians and he think a crate of Essangee beer will close the cut.'

Shake watches Avril's petite, jet-black hands play with a lighter. 'What do you think is going on? I've just been up to Susannah's and she told me a lot of stuff, a lot of politics but I still don't get it.'

'I told you, Shake, I think yuh got to be black to get it. I black, but I black Sanso, a black Sanso woman. I live on St George because I love the islan', I love the sea and the hills. I come here an' I set up my bu_iness but I can't get good help. They lazy, they don' want to work. You remember Marianne?'

Shake thinks of the big girl who always had a smile for him, who used to wait at the tables moving like she was wading in water. 'Yeah, I remember.'

'She and me – we had a revolution. She getting too comfortable, too relax. She sittin' and I runnin'. So we had a revolution and she gone. See, Shake, the young Georgians, they have it easy but they still want more but they don' want to work. Not all of them, there are a lot o' locals who work hard, who try to make something of themselves, maybe start a business or something. But, yuh know, it strange. Lots of people they say to me that if they do well, they cut down. If they succeed then they vex their friends an' they lost. An', like me, they say they can't get good help. The young Georgians, they wan' cell phones and foreign used vehicles and DVDs but they don' want to work. Las' week I have a delivery of gravel for my pathways out back. The truck man dump the gravel in the road an' I arrange for a boy to come an' carry it up. I give him fifty dollar, say he get another fifty when he finishes. So he move half the load then he say he going for fetch a roti. He not come back so I move the rest of the gravel. Fifty dollar was all he wanted. He don't think maybe soon he need another fifty dollar and maybe he have to come by me but he can'. They jus' wan' to lime and ramcram. I go into people's houses and they have no water inside but they got a television and a boom box and they both playin'. You can' hear youself t'ink for the noise and it like they want it all all the time but they don't wan' to work. But the Indians, they wan' to work, ent? They work but they wan' too much, they wan' it all and until there nothin' lef' for anyone else.' Avril fingers her cornrows, smoothes down her shirt. 'You ever hear about God and his gingerbread men?'

'No.'

'God make up a whole batch of gingerbread men and then he decide to cook them. So he put some in the oven and he wait an' he take them out but they all white, undercooked. So he throw them away an' put in more gingermen an' this time he wait longer, let the fire play on them. But when he take them out they all black, cook too much. So he throw them away an' the next time he put in his gingermen he leave them just right, and when he take them out dey all yellow and God is pleased. He call his gingermen Asian.'

Shake smiles, thinks of the gingermen and this reminds him of the gingery Mr Westmore and he wonders how he's doing.

'Shake, baby, I can't tell you how to think, what to feel. You know it all deep down. You recently been to Jungle Jam?'

'Yeah, but I'm not going again.'

'You been to Fiddla's or Block Seventy-Seven or Mistah Tom's?'

'No.'

'You going to Carlisle's funeral?'

'No. I'd like to but . . .' Shake shrugs.

'You see? You know it.'

Shake sits back in the chair, looks up through the canopy and sees the moon, looking like it's hanging upside down, yellow as an Asian gingerman. 'I've been here ten, nearly eleven years. Longest time I ever spent anywhere. And, you know, I've always felt conspicuous, because I am. I used to sit in Mistah Tom's and be the only whitey there, or I've been invited to Mister Jeremiah's kids' weddings and I've been the only whitey there. I've always felt conspicuous but never uncomfortable. I've never felt uncomfortable in my skin before.'

'If it help, I black and right now I feel uncomfortable in my skin, too. Not because of its colour but because it was made in Sansobella. I going to say something I never said to anyone else. This for you, Shake.'

'What?'

'I glad my ancestors did the middle passage. I glad they were brought here because if they hadn't come here I be in Africa now. You know what I'm saying?'

Shake thinks of the women of Darfur and he nods; Shake nods reluctantly because he knows now what the Atlantic Triangle means, but he nods even though it seems wrong. He lights a cigarette and stares over the lights of Bridgewater.

'You wan' me to cook something? I got some king, I could throw together lime fish.'

'That'd be great.'

Avril disappears into the kitchen and Shake busies himself behind the bar, making a pitcher of weak planters' punch, squeezing in fresh lime juice and stirring in a mound of fresh ground nutmeg. Then he helps Avril, washes the salad and prepares it, heats up some rounds of garlic bread. Shake hasn't eaten all day and he's got sucker guts.

'You know the phrase "my stomach feels like my throat's been cut"?' he asks Avril.

'No.'

'It's what we say when we're hungry.'

'Well, baby, I make you a whole heap of fish.'

'Where d'you buy it now?'

'I used to go by Greenie in the market, but she gone. Now I go to the stalls on Sangaree.'

'I remember Greenie. She had a moustache. Went to England or something.'

'Thass right. Went for two weeks and never came back. Her husban' take a new woman.'

'And d'you remember Rack and Ruin? They had that weird place outside the market? In the car park?'

Avril shrieks with laughter, puts down the knife. 'I ever tell yuh I sole a car to them once and the nex' day Rack or Ruin, I dunno which person, they call me an ask if I ever clean my car, because there a snake in the boot!'

Shake laughs, too, then, puts down his drink and laughs out loud. 'Did I ever tell you about a time, years ago, must be eight years ago, when I bought my first jeep? I took it down to the beach one early morning and when I came back, it had gone. So

I went into Bridgewater to the insurance place and told the girl, and she just looked at me like I was crazy. "*What?*" she said. "*All of it?*" Turned out it was the first whole car that had been stolen on the island. Those days they usually just took the spare or the seats or the radio.'

The two of them sit under the canopy, eating lime fish and drinking rum, under a cheddar moon with the paddle leaves of tall heliconia moving around them and they swap stories of the past decade, helping each other to remember events and people they had forgotten, people who'd moved on or died. Reminding themselves of when times were different, when they had both felt easy in their own skins. Once the pitcher is empty, Shake collects together the plates and glasses, washes them and cleans the kitchen. When he's finished he finds Avril sitting with her feet up on the rail, looking out at the lights of Bridgewater, smoking.

'You see that?' Avril points out to the horizon, where the sea glitters with moonlight.

'What?'

'There, straight in front. An orange light.'

Shake shades his eyes and stares, finally spots the distant glow. 'What is it? Looks like a fire at sea.'

'That right. They exploring for oil and burnin' off gas.'

'I read in the papers today that the oil companies are pulling out all their workers. And some embassy staff have left.'

'That so?'

'One of the English papers mentioned Grenada. Remember Grenada?'

'Who forget?'

'Maybe the Americans'll come.'

Avril sucks her teeth and shrugs. 'Well if they do they won't be getting a welcome. But,' she shrugs again, 'we got oil, so maybe they will. Only reason they ever shift they backsides.'

Shake puts his hands on Avril's shoulders, kisses the crown of her head. 'What you going to do?'

'I goin' to ask you to stay the night. Stay here with me tonight, Shake.' Avril reaches up and touches his hand.

'I can't. I got to get home to my dog, got to check my place.' Shake moves away, picks up his car keys and cell phone. He'd like to explain about how he's not vigilant enough to stay, but Shake can't think of the words. 'I'll see you soon. Thanks for the fish, it was great.'

Avril says nothing and Shake walks off, begins to descend the steps to his jeep. Stops. 'Hey – Avril, be careful.'

'I will, Shake baby.'

'Lock your doors.'

As Shake turns off the Paria road, north into Killdevill, the widely spaced street lamps flicker and fade and the few lights in the windows of the villas snap off. Shake drives slowly, strains to spot the potholes, aware of verges, knowing a local walking or cycling along the road will be nearly impossible to see. As he reaches the turn off to the trace leading down to Gilbey beach, the headlamps flare against the side of Mister Jeremiah's house, lighting the clapboard and galvanize, and Shake catches a glimpse of someone sitting on the porch. He stops the jeep, turns off the engine but leaves the lights on. He sees it's Mister Jeremiah, sitting out under the stars.

'Good night,' the old man says as Shake sits on the porch step. 'How's Miss Avarice doing?'

'Her OK. Her got som'ting wrong wid blood pressure. It too low and her having trouble pumping it round. Her need to lift de pressure.'

'Is she still in hospital?'

Mister Jeremiah nods his greying head. 'De bed feel hollow and I cyar sleep. Fifty-t'ree years I share Miss Avarice bed. But her in bes' place. De problems we havin', the ruckshuns right now, her in bes' place.' Mister Jeremiah squeezes his knees, rolls his shoulders and neck. 'Lebe lebe us all be der soon.'

'You heard about Carlisle.'

'Dat I did. Fust ting I hear der ten people shot down Coral Strand, bodies ever'where. But dat's St George. Yuh hear and yuh wait, yuh hear and yuh wait. Like de time woman in Wrexall had she arm chop off in de morning an' by night her got a scratch on back of hand. So, by evening der's t'ree people shot at Zabico. Now it night an Carlisle dead.'

'I was there when it happened. It was one of Kouranis' security men.'

Again Mister Jeremiah nods. 'De funeral Tuesday an dey say der a march down to Coral Strand. De minister, he say us all go, after service we all go. Ever minister telling his congregation de same, so I goin'. But I worry, I t'ink der be bashment crew and bad boys makin' commotions. I tole Ayninka she stay home.'

'Is there anything I can do to help?' asks Shake, but the old man's not listening.

'De world change. De islan' change. Used to be we was quiet people, better people. Der was order and de young, dey stay home. When I was a boy, up in Woolly Coom, up in de hills, men look out for each other, dey have der goats and der yard, and dey fishing if dey like. It a quiet life. Den men start talking about independence and yuh lef and der parties and celebration and then come the hurricane and took all the cane plantations and us have nuttin'. Us like pickneys widout pappy. When I live in Woolly Coom, der forty-one plantation and estate on de islan'. After hurricane der were t'ree. Den the palm grease start an de government sit on its hands, fill dey own belly. So what we do? We ask yuh all to come back, but dis time yuh come to party an' us haf to build de roads an' bridges an' de guest houses an' de reservoir. Whey de sense in dat? It better before, ent?'

'What do you think will happen?'

Mister Jeremiah scratches his bare chest and shakes his head. 'I not know. Only God know. We a small islan' and lebe lebe we be forgot.'

'Funny, I've lived on islands nearly all my life. I lived in Cyprus when I was boy, and then England and now here.'

'Der two way yuh look at islan' life. Yuh can t'ink yuh safe because yuh don' haf vexing neighbour. Or yuh can t'ink yuh got no place to run.'

'Which do you think?'

'I t'ink yuh better watch yuh content. Yuh asking fuh answers and de bush have ears.' Mister Jeremiah stands slowly, hands rubbing his lower back. 'I try to sleep. I tole Miss Avarice I be by to see her early.'

'Do you need a drop?'

'No, tank you Shake. De minister say he come by.' Mister Jeremiah shuffles to his door, opens it. 'Pray for Carlisle.' And he disappears into the listing house.

Shake keeps a torch in his jeep and he uses it to negotiate the rickety steps up to his shack. When he reaches the porch, he finds Saltbag waiting for him, wagging her bushy tail, ears cocked for sound. Shake fetches the old dog some biscuits and treats her to a can of mackerel, sits with her as she eats. When she's finished, Saltbag flops down next to him and, as he rubs the dog's furry neck, Shake switches off the torch and he's wrapped in black velvet, so dark is the night. After a while his eyes adjust and he can make out the waters of Gilbey beach glittering in the weak moonlight. The nearest light pollution is on the burning oil rig, on the south side of the island, and the stars are so bright, spread like thick paste on an obsidian plate, that Shake can't make out any of the constellations. He knows Scorpio is on the horizon but he can't pick it out. In the bush, fireflies flitter, flashing their white electricity. The outage means there are no generators humming, no distant televisions or music playing, no pools pumping, and the stillness is like a thick blanket, silencing the world, as the air-conditioned rooms all over Killdevill begin to warm up, their occupants stirring in sleep. Shake sits on his porch, scratching his dog, staring at the stars and building another of his fences, outside which lies Carlisle.

21–23 June

Shake lives the next three days as he wishes he could live every day. He's busy, out on *Ribailagua* in the early mornings and late afternoons, with four fishing trips and a Dorado run, thanks to his trawl of the beaches. He's too busy to think of what Susannah, Avril and Mister Jeremiah have told him, too busy to think of any impending storm. Coral Strand is closed, roped off by the police, and the tourists and Sansos are fanning out over the island looking for distraction. Shake leaves messages with Stumpy to get down to Gilbey beach at six if he wants work but all that happens is Stumpy's brother scuffs his way through the sand one early evening to explain that Stumpy didn't show up because he has a beetle in his ear.

'He what?' asks Shake, wiping the sweat from his face with the hem of his T-shirt.

'Him haf beetle in he ear.'

'Why can't he get it out?'

'It too deep in. Stumpy go to hospital.'

'OK. Well, do *you* want some work? I need someone for a while. I'll pay a hundred and fifty a day.'

Stumpy's brother looks perplexed, annoyed, almost. 'Wuk?'

'Yes. You have to be here by six and we finish about five.'

The boy looks out to sea, scratches his stomach through a stained T-shirt. 'I busy,' he decides and scuffs his way back to road.

Shake works the boat on his own, paddling out, humping

iceboxes, cutting bait, untangling lines, fixing trolling balls, cleaning the decks, filleting and gutting, keeping the customers happy,
plying them with beers (crates of S&G, Wild Boar and Arawak
are piled up, now, in Top-Mart and Cruickshank's, the two main
supermarkets, as Kouranis pours beer on troubled waters). The
fish are jumping and he returns from his trips with iceboxes full
of tarpon, bonefish, shark and – trophy indeed – a small marlin.
He takes photographs and poses with the pink-faced hunters. All
this, as well as fielding email enquiries, arranging the limo pick-
ups in Dorado, checking the satellite weather reports on the net,
planning the trips, filling in the log, banking the cash and cheques.
Shake's so busy he doesn't have time to think of fences and
people not standing near whitey, too hot to feel the temperature
dropping. The only reminder of change is the sound of whining
jet engines overhead, late Friday, as he stands on the rocking deck
of the boat, sluicing down with buckets of water. Shake stops,
shades his eyes against the glare of the setting sun and watches
the 737 bank as it turns north, heading for Frankfurt, lights visible against the darkening sky. Shake sees the blue and yellow
livery: the Condor flight and onboard is Rajiv, taking his family to
some kind of safety. Shake follows the path of the rumbling
plane until it disappears behind a cotton wool roll of pink-shot
cumulonimbus.

Late afternoon on Saturday, Shake drives up to Mojito, checks the
pool, carries a few crates of beer and mineral water into the
kitchen and then has his soak in a hot tub. He's finished work
early because Susannah has asked him to drive her up-country, so
Shake changes into clean shorts and shirt and rather than heading

for the pool bar, he heads for the garage, swinging the jeep keys on his little finger.

'If you imagine, for one moment, that I'm travelling in that vehicle of yours, you're crazy,' says Susannah.

'OK. Which car d'you want to take?'

'This one.' Susannah throws him the keys and climbs into the passenger seat of the Aston Martin. 'The only reason I'll even contemplate you driving is because you have just completed your ablutions.'

Shake slides in the driver's side, smiling, adjusts the seat, pressing buttons until his knees, his back, his shoulders are snugly supported and comforted by soft leather. He turns the key, has to check the revs to establish if the engine is turning over, it's so quiet. He adjusts the air con and sits back, snuggles down. 'Mmmmm,' he hums.

'Have you driven one of these before?'

'Oh, yeah. I took my test in one. Of course I bloody haven't.'

'Well, take it easy, nuh? Some of the roads rip to hell.'

'Where are we going?'

'Up through Castries and then Williamsville. Take the highway and then the back road from Bridgewater. I'll tell you where when we get to Woolly Coom. Track's shit but I might have to play Lady Bountiful, so I need the comfort of my Aston.'

The garage doors roll up, the Aston whispers out onto the herringbone driveway, and the doors shut, as caiman-crossed hounds hurl themselves at the gate. Shake, who normally rolls with the potholes, one wrist resting on the wheel, as he eats a roti or drinks an S&G, finds himself inching forward, driving like an old maid. Even the dust settling on the gleaming bonnet upsets him.

'Shake, we hopin' to reach Williamsville some time today. Gas up.'

By the time Shake has negotiated the track and reached the coast road, he's feeling fine, feeling relaxed as shadows lengthen across the tarmac, and he puts his foot down on a long, empty stretch, feels the automatic gears moving, sliding and gliding through the ratios, and the car rockets forward, as if unaware of the friction of motion.

'Sorry, couldn't resist it,' he says, taking his foot off, touching the brake.

'If de pries' could play, who is me?' Susannah smiles. 'It what it for, Shake. This car should be driving the autoroutes and boulevards of the Med. Poor thing.'

'Why are we going up to Woolly Coom?'

'I got to check on something. Saw something in the paper I need to check on.'

Shake slows as they approach the traffic lights in Bridgewater. 'Lot of cars around. I don't drive round much this time of day, hardly ever come into Bridgewater.'

'It the same every day now. Too many cars, too little road.'

Empty trucks heading back to the quarry surround the Aston, 4x4s queue to turn into town, saloons ramcrammed with passengers – the drivers illegally pulling bull – inch forward as jalopies, tied with rope and nylon fishing lines, hare down the shoulder, shuddering with the bass beat of reggae.

Once they are up in the hills, the traffic falls away, and Shake slows again, to a near-crawl as the potholes deepen and lights flicker on. In the dusk he can make out men sitting on their porches, sitting on the walls of bridges, drinking in the bars and rum shops, playing cards. And all of them stop and stare at the vehicle as it passes, children run after it, waving, as goats' eyes flare on the verges. By the roadside taps, women wash clothes in buckets, shouting to each other as they wring and scrub, sharing the water with children and men soaping themselves down.

'Up here, turn right opposite the church. Careful of the storm drain, it's deep.' Shake slows to a halt, bumps into and out of the drain. 'OK – carry on and turn left into the next driveway. There's a sign outside.'

'You still haven't told me what we're doing.'

'Dat, Shake, is because I not sure, yet, what I have to do. We coming to see Merle, she a daughter of mih nanny, Otty. A fine woman, an upstanding, decent woman. I hesitate to say Christian but no doubt that's how she would describe herself. She runs a hospice for AIDS sufferers. In the paper this week, I read that Rome sent a monseigneur here to visit Merle. I need to see what happened. Merle run this place for ten years, maybe, and she still don' have hot water inside, still don' have an emergency generator. Let's go see what largesse Rome has bestowed upon her.'

The Aston squeezes through a pair of rusted gates and comes to halt in front of a run-down, half-concrete, half-board building. Outside, beneath a bare bulb, a woman is wringing out a mop in a bucket.

'You want me to come in with you?'

'I don't need you to come in but I think you need to come in.'

Shake follows Susannah inside, where he is introduced to Merle, a tall, skinny blue-black woman with greying hair. Shake takes her hand and is aware of how dry the skin is, how powerful Merle's hand feels.

'Shake, Merle and me going to her room to take tea. I won't be long,' and Susannah disappears, leaving Shake in the middle of a desolation of a different sort to those he's become accustomed to lately. The room is long and bare, concrete floor, concrete walls. The windows are louvred, some louvres missing or cracked, and four neon strips, one flickering wildly, light the room. Two fans spin above the twelve beds, beside each of which there is a chair and a bed pan. A third fan turns slowly in the breeze, its motor broken. In each bed lies a wreck of a man, some elderly, most young. Their cheeks are hollow enough to hold salt, their wrists skinny as a horse whip. A few are turned on their sides, frowning even in sleep; one is coughing feebly, drooling blood into a plastic bowl. Shake feels his ribs compressing as the woman with the mop reappears, shoving the bucket with her foot, the metal scraping on concrete. She shuts the door behind her, begins to swab down the floor, and Shake has to walk, walks to the end of the room and turns, sees a man motioning to him with a hand seemingly made of black ball bearings and string. Shake glances at the woman mopping, but she ignores the patient and so he goes to him, leans over and tries to make out what the man wants but his voice is as faint as a bananquit's heartbeat. Eventually, Shake realizes the patient needs the bed pan and he panics.

'Excuse me,' he says to the cleaner. 'Um – this man needs help.'

'I told he afore to make use but he hard ears.' She leans the mop against a wall and shuffles over, slippers dragging. 'Din' I? Eh? Ole Halter Neck – I tole yuh. Now look, I got to hot foot.' The woman lifts the sheet and slides in the pan, makes sure the patient settles. Then she strokes his forehead, croons a little, singing a bush song as Ole Halter Neck relieves himself.

'Shake, we goin'.' Susannah motions with her head and Shake follows, wanting nothing more than to be outside, away from smell of ordure, Gersol and despair. Susannah climbs in the Aston and slams the door, sits staring straight ahead as Shake negotiates reversing out of the drive. He knows better than to speak.

'Man, I head-hot,' Susannah says, thumping the dash with her fist. 'That Merle she have it to do for ten years now. She hecrie of the Church, a fine mother, a woman who done nothing but give all her life. And what happen? What happen when Rome come? What happen when fancy Dan in his robes come all the way to poor little St George so Merle can kiss his pinky ring? She whose ass he not good enough to wipe? Yuh know what he give?'

Shake shakes his head, turns onto the Williamsville Road, swerving to avoid a trotting dog.

'The powers that be in the Vatican saw fit to give Merle, not a hot water tank, sinks and plumbing, nor a cheque for medicines, nor a generator. The monseigneur gave her a medal. A fucking medal. And you know what? Merle has it hanging on the wall. She's proud of it. That priest come with his han's hangin' and she proud of her medal.' Susannah stares out into the night, chewing her lip. 'What hope we got if we don' know how to play de game? Play jackass, dey go ride yuh. Shit.'

The lights flare against cottonsilk and board houses, catch the glitter of a waterfall as they drop down back towards Bridgewater and still children chase the car as it passes through villages strung out on ridges, houses teetering over deep valleys and gorges. Once on the highway, where the road is wide, where there are no potholes, where lights dispel the gloom, Shake speeds up, overtakes the jalopies, until he slows for a crossroads. As he waits for the lights to change, he notices blue police strobes in his mirror. Four outriders on BMWs pull up next to him, two policemen dismount and stop the traffic, blowing whistles and raising their hands. The other outriders wait for the long, black Mercedes to catch up with them. For a moment, the Mercedes stops next to the Aston, the pennant on the bonnet fluttering, and for that moment it is possible to see the lit interior of the Mercedes, despite the tint of the glass, and there is the First Minister in the rear seat, laughing at something his companion has said. His companion looks at the Aston, stares into it, locks his eyes on Susannah, who stares right back and it is Kouranis who looks away first. The Mercedes, its path cleared, swings in front of Shake, and accelerates away as Susannah lights a cigarette. The lights change and Shake heads towards Killdevill.

'I have often wondered,' Susannah remarks calmly, but Shake isn't fooled, 'as I am forced to pull over and stop in order to allow his motorcade to speed by, with its outriders and sirens and lights, what, exactly, the First Minister makes of the pickneys he passes, dressed in rags, standing by a tap in the street because the shacks where they live have no water inside, or outside come to that. I wonder what he makes of the homeless, the new homeless, a state of affairs which never happened before because people lived with family, even if it meant living on the floor, they lived with family. But now there's AIDS and family don't care, family is ashamed. I wonder what he makes of the crackheads living in Independence Park. What he makes of the increase in the price of land as the foreigners and Sansos flood in and the locals sell up. What he makes of the choppings and the rapes and the incest up in the hills, up-country where things haven't changed that much. Where a man lives with his daughter and boasts of having had thirty-eight children. Where the men sit at tables playing dominoes, looking like good ole boys clacking the ivories, perhaps talking about the good ole days – you saw them tonight up in the villages. Those men are playing dominoes and explaining how sex with a child or a baby cures AIDS, or how fucking a virgin cures AIDS or laughing about how anything after twelve is lunch. And just in case you're wondering, they're not talking about dining out. I sit in my Aston Martin watching the First Minister pass and I wonder what he makes of these things.' Susannah falls silent and watches the moon light the passing land.

The dogs snarl their greetings as Shake parks the car in the garage, its bodywork spattered with mud and dust, and he finds Susannah in the living room, talking on the phone. She breaks off long enough to ask for a daquiri, and then picks up the conversation and Shake can hear enough to know she's pulling strings. When she's finished, Susannah joins Shake out by the pool, sits on a lounger and takes in the balmy, breezy night. The air in Mojito, Shake thinks, is indeed different from the air in the hospice.

'So what do we think, eh, Shake? What do we think of the underbelly of paradise?'

'Grim.'

'Yuh said it.'

'I couldn't help overhearing. You're having the hot water put inside? At Merle's?'

'In the absence of Papal charity, I felt it was the least I could do. There will also be a generator and a fully qualified nurse. You going to Jungle Jam?'

'Nope. I'm going to have an early night. Got a Dorado trip tomorrow and I have to do it myself.'

'Don't I know it – you just can't get good help these days, can you? Thanks for coming with me, Shake. I don't like driving back hills on my own at night.'

'That's OK. I'll come by you soon.'

24 June

Monday morning Shake doesn't have a trip and yet he still wakes early, before dawn. He lies on the mattress in the gloom, planning: he needs to catch up on paperwork, pay the electricity company – although why he should when the power's always going down, crashing his laptop? Then he must find Dragon and hound him into finishing the roof. Shake doesn't bother showering, just slips on some shorts, makes a coffee in the disaster that is his kitchen, then tries to access emails but the machine tells him his password is invalid. He tries again and again, restarts because that sometimes works but has no luck. He tries to call S&GTS but no one answers the phone and then the phone line dies. Shake's wasted an hour and a half and his pulse is beginning to tick in his wrist. He digs out a beer, even though it's only eight o'clock, swigs down half of it, spreads butter and Marmite on a piece of bread, wolfs it down, makes another and then picks up his cell phone, redials the phone number. Eventually, after the polar ice caps have melted, someone answers.

'Good mornin', yes?'

'Good morning. I'm having trouble with my internet connection. Essangee TS keeps telling me that my password is invalid.'

'The offices are suffering an infestation.'

'*What?*'

'The Essangee TS offices currently suffering an infestation and services may be interrupted. Essangee TS apologize for any inconvenience.'

'An infestation of what?' Probably bloody paperwork, thinks Shake.

'I not at liberty to disclose. The offices have been fumigated and just as soon as practicable my colleagues will return to their desks.'

Shake cuts the connection, finishes the beer, considers a rum and opens another S&G instead. What to do? He could try to find Dragon, who can't be working at Coral Strand because it's closed, or maybe spend time visiting the hotels to ask if there have been enquiries. Or he could take some time out and have a few beers and games of poker in the bars around Grackle Bay. Maybe the roof's more important? Shake bites into the Marmite sandwich and there's a knock on the door.

'S'open!' he shouts, his voice muffled by bread, before he realizes that no one knocks at the door, no one ever has. He pushes aside the bead curtain and steps out of the kitchen as Emma steps through the door. Saltbag lumbers in behind her, sniffs at Emma's calves, at her fingers, tail wagging. Shake swallows the half-chewed Marmite sandwich. 'This is the Saltbag,' he says, thinking that for all the speculation he has indulged in down the years about what he would say to Emma should he see her ever again, this is not a sentence he ever anticipated uttering.

'Hello, the Saltbag.' Emma scratches the dog's thick ruff. Looks up. 'Hello, the Shake.'

'Hello, Em.' Shake realizes he's holding a half-finished bottle of beer, puts it on the jumbled table. Realizes he's bareback and takes a T-shirt from the back of the chair, slips it on. Realizes that his yard, his shack, his life, look a mess and he can do nothing about these things. 'How did you find me?'

'By accident, Shake, by accident. I've been staying at the Oriole for a couple of days and last night I was in the lobby, waiting to meet someone and she was late. So I was flicking through some leaflets and things and I came across this.' From the pocket of her close-fitting, linen capri pants, Emma pulls out a flyer for Dream Chaser fishing trips. There, on the first fold, is Shake's smiling face, standing next to some guy who'd caught a thirty-pound tarpon.

'OK.' Shake had forgotten how the sight of Emma made him want to smile.

'Y'know, I spent all night wondering whether to phone you but I thought if I did, you might run away again. So this morning I asked at reception and it turns out everyone knows Shake, the dream chaser. The receptionist, the bell-hop, the gardeners. The taxi driver who brought me here knows Shake. Even the old black guy at the top of the lane, sitting out on his porch, who the taxi driver asked for directions, knows Shake.'

'Mister Jeremiah,' says Shake needing to block out the sound of Emma's voice for a moment. Emma's voice: if Shake can string together a trolling bait ball, Emma can string together a sentence. Her voice – that honed, trained, modulated instrument – sounds like Huggins' eighteen-year-old single mark would sound if it could sing and Shake hasn't heard that music for a long, long time.

'Well, Mister Jeremiah obviously thinks you're the cat's meow.' Emma takes off her hat, her shades, pulls the band out of her short ponytail and shakes it loose, runs her fingers through sweaty hair. Looks, now, like Emma Beckworth, Oscar winner. Her eyes scan the shack, take in the mattress covered in rucked sheets, the inverted beer crates stacked as a table, the sand-crusted wooden floorboards, the earth below visible through the cracks, the busted, rusted fighting chair in the corner, the bead curtain, clinking quietly in the breeze from the ill-fitting shutters. 'Say it ain't so, Joe.'

And Shake's stomach flinches, feels as if it has been brushed with a feather, because that's a phrase he and Emma used to use when they saw something sad, unfit. 'Would you like a coffee or something?'

'I'll have one of those, please.' Emma points to the half-finished S&G beer.

Shake pushes aside the bead curtain, stands for a moment in his kitchen, stands still as a rock, trying to think of what to do next, what to think next, and then he reaches into the fridge, pulls out an S&G, cracks the cap, walks back into the other room, which is empty, both of ex-wives and old dogs, and he walks out onto his shambolic porch to see Emma standing by the pit which will be his swimming pool but which looks, right now, like the site of a soon-to-be mass grave, and Shake trots down the few steps to give his ex-wife the beer because he can't bear the thought of her standing by a grave, examining it, he needs to draw her way from the lip of that slowly eroding bowl because everything is physics and he owes Emma too much and the microcosmic land slips of the muddy bowl could carry anyone away.

Emma swigs from the bottle, gestures with it. 'So, what's going on here? Looks like you're having a pool built.'

Shake takes Emma on a tour, shows her his incomplete con-crete house, shows her the land he's cleared, explains that the wooden shack is where he lives whilst his house is built, describes the view he will have from his tiled gallery when it is finished, shows her where the air bricks will be, how he will be able to watch sunset through the bricks as he showers at the end of the day. Describes to Emma all the cuttings he's potted up and where they will be planted out. But all the time he's talking and pointing and describing, Shake can feel his sternum growing, the last bone in the human body fully to form, and it feels like it's pressing against his sense of what is right. He's looking everywhere but at Emma, because he can't look at her, can't look at her familiar face, hardly changed by years. But Shake knows that Emma is watching him, scrutinizing his face as he talks and he wonders what she's looking for and if she finds it.

'Well,' says Emma, taking a mouthful of beer, 'seems you landed on your feet, Shake. I can't get over the fact you like gardening. Shake, gardening.' And she barks out a laugh. 'It's a very beautiful place, it really is. What a view.' Emma shades her eyes and looks out over Gilbey beach down below.

'That's my boat.' Shake points to *Ribailagua* moving about lazily on the line. 'That's what I work with, y'know, the fishing trips. Just around the island. Sometimes I run people out to Dorado. I've even taken trips to Grenada and Trinidad but I stopped doing that because I took one couple who never came back. Y'know, I took them to Grenada, arranged to meet them four hours later and they just disappeared. No stamp in the passport, no one knew they were there. I thought it seemed a bit dodgy so I came back and kept my mouth shut.'

The sun's climbing high in the sky and the breeze has dropped. On the far horizon a bank of dark cloud appears. A smooth, rolling bank which is moving slowly west, heading straight for them.

'Looks like we'll be in for some rain later,' says Shake. They stand in silence, despite having so much to say.

'Could we go out in the boat? I saw in the flyer that you do snorkelling trips. I'd like that. Then maybe I can buy you lunch somewhere. That is, if you'd like to. I've kept the taxi waiting. I can leave if you'd prefer.'

Shake considers this possibility – of Emma leaving, packing up her voice and leaving. 'We could go for a trip on the reef.'

'Have you got a costume I can borrow?'

'There are a couple of spares on the boat. I'll get you a towel.'

Ribailagua slices through the slight swell, leaving a bubbling twin wake, as Shake motors around the headland, heading for the reef off John Dory, aware of Emma stripping and changing behind him and again he can't look, even though he wants to see if she has changed, wants to see if there is somewhere a mark, a sign of all the damage that's been done. Nearing the reef, Shake slows and the boat drifts, as Emma slips on fins. He hands her a fish identification card and a mask and she drops into the water, fixes the snorkel and swims lazily, confidently away. Shake sits on the gunwale, lights a cigarette and watches his ex-wife moving back and forth over the reef, shimmering in hatched light, moving carefully in the shallow waters covering the coral. What, Shake wonders, is she doing here? What does she want? He watches Emma and he sees her body has been toned and honed, refined like sugar cane; each muscle peeps through skin that looks too young to have lived as long as it has. Why has she come? What can they possibly have left to say to each other? The silence has been too long, too sterile, to breed words.

Emma splashes up by the boat, tugs off her mask and snorkel and Shake hauls her in, holding her hand, gripping her arm.

'It's bloody marvellous down there,' Emma says as she towels down her gym-trim body. 'I saw an octopus hiding in the rocks and a barracuda, about this long.' She holds out her tanned hands. 'Do you ever do it? You know, for pleasure?'

'Haven't done it for years. I rarely go in the sea. Because it's like my office, I suppose, all about work. If you see what I mean.' Shake busies himself at the controls, turning his back to her, not wanting to see the familiar movements that are Emma dressing. 'I sometimes do some wind-surfing but it can do my knee in.'

'Oh, yes. Your knee. How is it?'

'Older. It's OK. Plays up in the cold.'

'Yes, well, I suppose it would. In the cold.'

Shake senses other conversations taking place, unheard, ghost-like, beneath these polite exchanges. Webs of gossamer words, trails of strung-out phrases, like cirrus cloud, that he and Emma have spoken in the past, some so faint they are hard even to imagine; more a cadence than a spoken word and he wonders if Emma, too, can sense these fragments of the past.

'I'm starving. Where we having lunch?' Emma towels her hair.

'There's a place on the beach at Liberty, just over there.' Shake points to a small village further east. 'A guy I know has a restaurant there, and he's built a platform up in the trees. Serves up excellent local food.'

'Can I have a coke?'

'Help yourself. Take anything you want.'

Shake motors slowly over the reef and eases the boat into the cove at Liberty. As he's throwing out the anchor line, he hears a muttered 'bugger' and turns around to see Emma wiping at a splash of brown liquid on her cropped T-shirt, dabbing at a dribble on her bare skin. She slips on her hat and shades, ties up her hair again, and Shake knows she's trying to hide herself, trying to look like everyone else. But Emma fails because she cannot look like everyone else around her. In the midday sun Shake sees that her cascade of glitter is still there, shimmering, just as it had done around his father.

'I just want to show you something before we eat,' says Shake.

'Will it take long? I'm bloody ravenous.'

'No – it's a five minute walk.'

Shake leads the way across the beach, crabs scurrying into their holes as he passes, to the mouth of a narrow river running across the sand, the water stained coffee colour with sediment, and he leads Emma along the bank.

'There,' Shake says.

Before them stands an emerald cathedral, one graceful, towering, vaulted arch leading to another as far as they can see.

'Wow – that's beautiful.' Emma shades her eyes.

Sunlight barely breaks through the delicate mass of bamboo leaves and the air is still, the light dim. Ecclesiastical almost. A parakeet, short, stubby wings flapping, labours through the nave and disappears.

'It's bamboo. I know it's beautiful but it's not indigenous. It's taking over everywhere, killing off other plants, even in the rainforest. I just wanted you to see this.'

'It's lovely.' Emma looks up, gazes at the intricate ceiling, and

Shake steals a glance at her. She seems hardly to have aged at all.

Sitting under the rustling palm fronds of the restaurant in the sky, beastly cold beers on the table, the only people in the place, Shake, finally asks his ex-wife, 'So, what are you doing here?'

'I've been on Dorado for a week.' Emma looks down at the beach, watches two young children playing in the waves with coconuts, throwing them and racing to fetch them. 'On honeymoon. I got married there, to David Sterne.'

'OK.'

'Obviously, the name means nothing to you?'

Shake shrugs, toys with his beer bottle.

Emma rummages in her tote bag, pulls out her purse, flips it open and hands it to Shake, and he notices that each nail on her hand has been sculpted and polished, artfully painted. As he reaches out he sees the oil ingrained in his own fingerprints, the cuts and nicks from the fish hooks and lines, the skin leather-cured by sun and salt. His hands look old. He looks old. Shake looks at a photograph of the happy couple, standing beneath a bower of bougainvillea, deep blue sea captured in the background. 'David's a very successful film producer. Which suits me because I never want to be married to another actor. This, I'm afraid, is my third marriage. My second, to Michael Bailey, and even *you* must have heard of him, was a disaster, only lasted six months.' But Shake's not listening to Emma, he's staring at the photograph, surprised, because David Sterne is black. Not passing white, not café au lait, not mixed, but black black. 'David had to go back to LA early, but I wanted to stay on, finish my holiday.'

'When're you going home?'

'I'm flying out this evening, on the six o'clock to Miami.' And

Shake is relieved by this. He doesn't want Emma on St George for many reasons.

Two plates of fish, spinach rice, fried plantain and red beans arrive.

'What's the fish?' Emma asks the man.

'Dolphin, very good.'

'Dolphin?'

'It's not dolphin,' says Shake, 'it's just a name. It's mahi-mahi. Thanks, Bevon.'

'No problem.'

Emma tries the fish, chews and swallows. Nods. 'It's good.'

'So how are you?'

'I'm just the same, Shake. Life is just the same as it always was. You know what it's like. House up in the hills, early morning pick-up, day in the studio. Home late enough to not want to eat, just have a few drinks and then bed. And the same again the next day and the next. The only difference now is that I have to fit in the bloody personal trainer and the five-mile runs. Plus I'm supposed to eat some kind of macrobiotic diet which might as well be served up in a nosebag. And all the time the house is being cared for, the pool cleaned, the gardens clipped and the fridge filled by people I never see. And sometimes I sit and wonder why I bother having the bloody place.'

'You're still busy then?'

'Which is a polite way of asking if I still get work even though I'm forty-four. Yes, I do. But it's beginning to dry up. Just like me, I suppose. I'm not going to have the nips and tucks, so I guess I'll have to wait for twenty years until I can play the grandmother or something. In the meantime I suppose I'll do all the art house stuff, you know, the *worthy* movies and get glowing reviews and win a few prizes at Toronto and Sundance and everyone will wonder what happened to me.' Emma delicately pulls a bone from between her whitened, straightened teeth, places it on the side of her plate. 'But what I really want to know is what happened to *you*, Shake? What happened to *you*? I had to wait five years to get my divorce papers because no one could find you. It was like you fell off the edge of a cliff or something.'

Shake pushes away his half-eaten lunch, lights a cigarette. Thinks that that was how it had felt all those years ago, that day when Emma had gone to the studio and he lay in their bed, staring at the ceiling, listening to the air conditioning drip. Then he got up, showered, packed a holdall with a few clothes, walked out of the house and fell off the edge of a cliff.

'I stayed in San Francisco for a while and then went to Florida. I can't really remember, it was a long time ago.'

'But what did you do for money? I'll give you that – you walked out on me and left me alone when I needed you more than any other time but you never took any of my money.'

'I got a job as a handyman for a while and then I went to Florida, and I was a pool man there. I used to look after the hotel pools around West Palm Beach, Palm Springs and Lake Worth. I lived in a shitty little apartment in Delray and I spent my days cleaning other people's pools.'

'And all the time you were cleaning these pools, you never thought you should pick up the phone and speak to your wife?'

Shake frowns, picks at the red and gold label on the S&G bottle. He tries to think of that time when he has spent years trying *not* to think of that time, trying not to think of the memories that compress his ribs most mornings. 'I don't know. I'm sorry. I'm sorry about all of it.' Months of days spent working and then lying in his room every night, fighting the desire for cocaine, drying out, hanging himself out to dry, to blow away the lint and dust of the white powder. His mind narrowing to a tunnel inside which there was Shake and his nets and brushes and chlorine and ray vacs and outside of which was everything else.

'I thought you'd come back. I thought you'd come back after a few months. I kept thinking I'd come home and find you sitting in your chair, or by the pool. I *wanted* you to come back.'

'I'm sorry,' Shake says again.

'And all the time you were up the road in San Fran.' Emma takes one of Shake's cigarettes. 'Haven't had a fag for months. So what happened next? How long have you been living here?'

'Ten years, just about.'

'Why here?'

Shake shrugs. 'I came here when I was a boy for a summer, with Rajiv. I always liked it.'

'Shake, this is like getting blood from a stone.' Emma draws smoke deep into her lungs, expels it as a flume. 'Look, I didn't come here looking for you but when I saw that flyer I thought I'd come and talk to you. Ask a few questions. I just want to know what you've been doing, that's all. I haven't come here to have a go at you. And I haven't come here to forgive you. I just want to tie up the loose ends. I just want to know what happened to you. Don't you understand? Because then I can forget about you. You owe me that, Shake. Why do you think my second marriage failed? The arguments and the egos didn't help, but I think one of the reasons was because I hadn't finished with you. I was still thinking you might come back. I don't want to keep on thinking I'll walk in and you'll be sitting out by the pool.'

Shake knows that he does indeed owe Emma this, this and so much more. He feels dislocated, feels as if the sea and sky are merely backdrops, sets almost, against which he is playing a scene with a now-flawless Emma, who *has* changed, who, he now realizes, seems finished, complete and undiminished. As if nothing will hurt her again, nothing will penetrate beneath that faultless skin. And so, sitting beneath the shifting canopy of palms, the torn combs of banana leaves rustling, a breeze flapping the tablecloth as puddles form under the beer bottles and cigarette ash whirls away out of the ashtray, Shake tells Emma what he has been doing since he fell off the edge of a cliff.

He tells her about the hostel he stayed in San Francisco, surrounded by crackheads and whores, people dying of AIDS all over the city, apartments closing down because the owners had died. How he had counted the bills in his wallet and knew he had to find work, move away from the urban nightmare. He found work as a live-in handyman for a family out near Larkspur, tending the grounds and pool, maintaining the property. Then in the autumn, as the rains began, the family announced they were moving east, to Denver, and Shake imagined being able to see snow covered peaks and he packed his holdall and moved on, spent three days on a Greyhound, three days from hell. Arriving in Miami, feeling the sun on his skin and deciding to stay, he ended up in Delray, cleaning pools, watching other people having fun around those pools, on the beach, in bars, in restaurants, and Shake feeling like he'll never have fun again. Then he gave up his job, bored with staring at mad, turquoise water and met a guy in

a bar who turned out to be looking for crew to sail a yacht down
to Puerto Rico but it was leaving that night. Shake didn't care. He
drove to his apartment, fetched his passport, his mother's cocktail book and filled the holdall again. Drove to the marina, left the
car on the dock, with the keys in the column and sailed into the
night. Shake hadn't told the man he knew nothing about sailing
and he spent his days learning quickly. Spent months moving
around the Bahamas, anchoring at Freeport, Nassau and Five
Cays, and December, when hurricane season was over, the yacht
docked at San Juan and Shake collected his worn clothes together
and stepped onto dry land. Soon he was twitchy again, found
another yacht, a different crew, and headed south along the chain,
leaving one island and sailing towards another, the peaks of the
volcanoes appearing and disappearing on the ever-shifting horizon. And then he disembarked in Queenstown, Sansobella,
where he found the familiar, decided to stay for a while.
Sometimes he considered visiting Rajiv, but the weeks passed and
he was still living in a room in a house near the docks. Everything
was too easy, the money in his wallet, the wages from his sailing
days, stretched a long, long way and there were many bars where
he made friends for an hour, for a day, drunkenly imagining it
would be for a lifetime. There were the white women, who came
to the island looking for something and found Shake; there was
the camaraderie of displacement in the beach bars; there were
rum shops in the back of Snake Alley where the air roiled thick
with weed smoke and Shake began to slip and slide again.

One day he woke up in his rented room to find a dead roach
between his fingers and a scorch mark on the sheet and the
wooden board house was rotten, nothing more than a pile of

kindling, and he realized it was time to halt the slide. So he took a bus up to the hills behind Queenstown and he walked the streets until he saw the gates of the Samaroo mansion and the guard stopped him entering and he had to wait for Rajiv to come home from the office. Lying in the shade of a stand of banana plants, his small, worn backpack – all he owned – acting as a pillow, Shake finally admitted to himself that it had been shame that had kept him from his friend. Late that afternoon Rajiv arrived in a limo and saw Shake lying in the shade, looking nashy, razzled, and the gates were opened. The house was the same, only the people had changed, grown older, died or left to be replaced by other tanties, nanas and baboos. And Mr Samaroo was old now, thin and wizened, his hair white, so Rajiv was king of the Samaroo castle.

Rajiv put Shake in the old bungalow, let him sleep for a day, and then he woke him with fruit and tea and cold water, and he sat with Shake by the old, square pool where they floated as boys, knowing they were young and they could be unhappy later. Rajiv sat and listened to Shake as he told him everything, told him what he'd told no one else and when Shake had finished speaking, when he had fallen silent, Rajiv said he needed to think. Shake was to stay in the grounds of the house, sleep in the bungalow and Rajiv was going to think. When Rajiv had thought and made his plans, he took Shake to St George, because he knew that Shake always wanted to be there and he knew Danny Kyow would be safe there. He loaned Shake the money to buy a boat, found him a place to live and introduced him to all the hotel managers and resort staff, took him to meet the owners of all the Sanso businesses he knew. Rajiv stayed with him for a few days, made sure that Shake stayed on course, that he got cards printed, that he ordered the equipment he needed, made sure Shake had insurance, the official licences. Then Rajiv flew back to Sansobella, leaving Shake to fill the empty corners of his life.

There had been one international flight a week out of St George when Shake first arrived, ten years before. Every Friday evening at five-fifty, he'd stand on the collapsing porch of the rented house in the Willbyn area of Bridgewater and listen for the roar of an engine, scan the darkening sky to the east, searching for the winking lights on the wings. He'd watch the plane dip, bank, head north towards the Florida Keys and it reassured him, this roaring and banking because he knew, then, that it was possible to leave. It was possible to catch a flight and disappear. Shake stood on the rotting boards, swigging from a bottle of S&G beer, occasionally slapping at mosquitoes, and followed the red pinpricks of lights until they either faded or were shrouded by clouds. Shake doesn't tell Emma this last part of his story; doesn't tell her about his further contemplation of disappearance.

Emma's beer is untouched, lukewarm now, bleeding water onto the table. The story she has heard, the history she has been in search of for more than a decade, is not what she expected it to be but it fits Shake, it fits her ex-husband like a tailored coat, like a glove. Her eyes have been locked on Shake's face for the duration of that history and she has, more than once, glimpsed a gesture, a look, that reminds her of the man-boy he was when they married. Listening to his voice, she has been surprised to hear that the cadences, the rhythms of it have changed slightly, as if his accent has been smudged.

'And that's it, really. The tourism here began to take off and the deep sea business did very well. The only blip was around nine eleven but it's not too bad now. Rajiv suggested to me that I buy the plot of land in Killdevill and I wasn't sure at first but I did it.'

Emma, who is smoking another cigarette, still watching Shake's face as he talks, says nothing, looks out to sea, watches the pickneys playing. Eventually she asks, 'Is Rajiv still here? On Sansobella, I mean?'

'No. Strange you should ask, because he left on Friday. He's taken his family to Germany because of all the violence on Sansobella. There's a bit of trouble between the blacks and Indians and he thinks they'll be safer there. I miss him already.'

'Safer in Germany?' Emma stubs out the cigarette, grimaces. 'Maybe. Personally, I think he's gone to the wrong place. Perhaps he hasn't read the papers but Europe's not exactly the place you want to be if you have brown skin. And if you have, you sure as hell don't want to be in the States.'

'Did your husband enjoy his time here?'

Emma shoots a look at Shake, shoots it across the table like a dart. 'Because he's black, you mean? Is that why you're asking?'

'I suppose so.'

'It was fine on Dorado. But I don't think he wanted to come here. He's been here before and I think it made him uncomfortable. I got the sense that he could have stayed, that he didn't have to rush back. I don't know. Maybe I'm talking bullshit.'

'Surely not.'

Emma half-smiles at the reference to another old saying they had shared in their past life and checks her watch. 'I'd better get going,' she says but doesn't move. She sits in the sun and turns Shake's history over and over in her mind, finds she is disappointed by it, by its lack of drama, by its lack of any reference to her. 'So that was it, then? You just drifted down here all those years ago and stayed?'

'Yes, that's all I did.'

'Don't you miss home?'

Home? 'No.'

'Did you miss me?'

Shake fiddles with the peak of his cap. 'Yes. But I couldn't afford to think about it. I didn't . . . deserve to think about it. I can't explain, I'm sorry. I didn't realize you had so much trouble with papers and all that. But I did miss you.'

'You know, Shake, you could have done this in LA. If this was what you wanted to do, the deep sea fishing gig, you could have done it there. I wouldn't have stopped you. I'd have encouraged you. I'd have bought you a boat. I'd have bought you a fucking fleet of boats.'

Shake thinks of the thin, silvery days of his life when he was married to Emma and living in LA, thinks of the way the memories seem blurred, hazy, as if they had been left out in a snowstorm. 'I didn't know what I wanted back then.'

'And now you do?'

Shake touches his ear, runs his finger along the tiny bumps there. 'I think so.'

'And what is it that you want?'

Shake stares at the children playing on the beach, frowns. It is, after all, a simple question. 'I want to finish my house, I want to finish it and sit on my gallery and watch the sunset.'

'And are you planning to do this with anyone?'

'Sorry?'

'Will you be doing this alone? You haven't mentioned any girl-friends or lovers.' Emma's voice has an edge to it, a razor-sharp blade mounted on her words, like a shark's fin in water.

Shake swallows, lays his palms flat on the table. 'I expect so.'

'So that's how you're punishing yourself, is it, Shake? Is that what you're doing? Hiding away here, all on your lonesome? Is that your penance?'

Shake says nothing, just sets his ageing, handsome face in such a way Emma knows he will say no more, will not be goaded.

'I'm sorry.' Emma glances at the bill, opens her purse and leaves too many notes under her plate, then shoves her purse back in her bag. 'I said I hadn't come here to have a go at you. I came here to see how you are, and I find you running a business, building your own house. Shake – all grown up at last.'

'We'd better go.'

Hardly a word is exchanged between them as Shake cruises *Ribailagua* round the headland to Gilbey beach, anchors and fetches the jeep keys. They drive in silence to the hotel, their throats dammed, jammed by the flotsam of all the things they could say to each other but as the triangle of their time together narrows to a point the excess of memories leaves them mute.

The question Shake has been dreading isn't asked until Emma is standing by the open window of his jeep, in the driveway of the Oriole, ignoring the whispers of other guests and their point-ing fingers. Emma has rediscovered her voice, finally asks the question.

'*Did* you lock the door?'

Shake closes his eyes, bites his lip. 'I don't know. I can't remember.'

'Did *you* lock the door? Shake?'

'I can't remember. I can't remember. I'm sorry. I can't remember.'

Emma Beckworth stares at her ex-husband's bowed head and then walks away, brushing aside requests for autographs, and steps from the dazzling light of the afternoon into the shade of the foyer and disappears.

The rain arrives as Shake drives home from the Oriole, back to Killdevill. The rag top is off and he's getting soaked but Shake doesn't care. He wants to close the shutters and lie down in his room and sleep, sleep so he doesn't have to think. He tosses his sodden cigarette out of the window and a blue light begins to turn. Glancing in his mirror, Shake sees a police car flashing him.

'Shit.' He's really not in the mood for this. Shake sits in the downpour as the police officer shrugs on a waterproof and then slowly walks to Shake's door. Looks at him, looks at the vehicle.

'Licence and other document.' The officer holds out a black hand.

Shake rummages in the dash, pulls out an envelope, hands it over. The policeman takes a long, long time to check the vehicle plates, the validation dates on the papers, the rain pouring down the meanwhile, beginning to puddle in the footwells. The officer returns the wet papers, stares at Shake with black eyes.

'Do yuh know why I have stop you?'

Shake tries to think if his backlights are working, if he failed to indicate. Shrugs. 'No.'

'Perhaps, in yuh country, it is legal but in dis country litterin' is a criminal offence.'

'What?'

'As I follow your vehicle, I see you t'row a cigarette out of your vehicle. On dis island we have a serious problem with fire.'

Shake wipes the rain from his face and knows he has to sit and listen, to not speak.

The officer steps nearer, leans towards Shake. 'I could take you to de station and charge you wit' a criminal offence.'

'I'm very sorry. I wasn't thinking. I won't do it again.' Shake thinks this is not the time to mention the piles of garbage rotting on street corners in Bridgewater, the bottles and plastic bags and beer crates floating in the river, the fridges and cookers dumped by the beaches in Wrexall and Torpoint.

The officer walks to the front of the jeep, looks again at the number plate, returns to say one more thing, leaning in close, his face blank as a carnival mask. 'Why don' yuh go back to yuh own country and litter it up? Why don' yuh leave mih country alone?' Then he jogs back to the police car, slipping off the waterproof. Shake waits until the policeman has reversed and driven away before starting the engine and driving on.

Lying on his bed, his fingers laced in Saltbag's ruff, Shake tries to sleep. Rolls into a ball and tries to sleep as the rain hammers on the tin roof sounding as if it's raining all over the world. Above the din he hears the rumble of a jet heading for Miami passing over the island, another fragment of his past in flight, leaving him behind. Shake dips into sleep but each time he drifts away, he can see them, the bodies outside his fences. They're moving, like the walking dead, the bodies are moving.

25 June

By the next morning, the morning of Carlisle's funeral, the sun
has batted away all the clouds, cleared the rags of rain, and steam
is rising from the wet soil as the sun clears the horizon. Shake –
standing on his porch with a coffee, feeling unravelled, tender, as
if his heart and mind have been beaten – knows this is merely an
intermission, that the storm is gathering energy out at sea. He has
an early morning trip, out of Tradewinds, three Englishmen, and
a late afternoon trip to the trench with two Americans. Shake
doesn't know if he can drag himself through this day. The pool
pit, he notices, has collapsed at the north end. It's only six o'clock
yet Shake picks up his keys and trots down the steps to the jeep,
drives up the hill and parks by Mister Jeremiah's tumbledown
house. He knocks at the door and Mister Jeremiah opens it at
once, as Shake knew he would.

'Good mornin', Shake.'

'Good morning. I just wanted to ask how Miss Avarice is. I'm
sorry I haven't been around before.'

Mister Jeremiah spreads his huge hands and Shake notices he
is holding a tie. 'Her still wid us, tank de lord. But I go to bed las'
night an' I t'ink her lookin' coffin-ripe.' Shake sees a movement
behind the old man, and Mister Jeremiah turns quickly, motions
at his granddaughter. 'It only Shake. Get yuhself ready, Ayninka.'
The shadow disappears.

'Is there anything I can do?'

Mister Jeremiah looks at Shake, stands tall, straightens his shoulders. 'I tole yuh, yuh can pray for she.'

'I can't do that, Mister Jeremiah. I can't pray.'

'Yuh *can* pray. De Lord will hear yuh.'

'Are you still going on the march?'

Mister Jeremiah sighs and shifts his aching, yardie feet, the flat toes splayed on the splintered wooden floor. 'Yes, I goin' on de march. An' Ayninka persuade me to let she go too. Dey say it a peace march, so we go. Us have to be in church by seven so we mus' move. Yuh goin' out on de boat today?'

'Yes.'

'Mr George, him say a storm comin' an' him know de skies. Maybe late today or in de night. Yuh be careful.'

'I will be. Mister Jeremiah?' Shake stares at the ground, the fertile, blood-soaked earth under his feet.

'Shake, nuh?'

'If . . .' Shakes stops himself, thinks he can taste electricity on the air as a towering, blue-white cityscape of cumulonimbus clouds blocks the sun and the temperature drops. 'If anything happens. If . . .' Shake scuffs the blood-red earth with his toe. 'If anything happens and I'm not here, will you take Saltbag in?'

Mister Jeremiah's cloudy blue-black eyes fix on the white man. He sees the white man is stretched thin, thin as one of the strange nylon lines he uses to fix fishing hooks. But Mister Jeremiah's not surprised. Shake has no family, no church, no God. What is it with whitey? They all the same, with their big, empty houses and small, empty lives. But Shake not so bad, really. He good when he remembers. 'What yuh t'ink happen? Shake? What yuh t'ink happen?'

'I don't know.'

Mister Jeremiah folds his tie over and over in his hands. 'I know what yuh mean. It like dey beer, now, on de islan' but ever'one still drinkin' rum. Like ever'one got hot head when de sun hidin'. Us will take yuh dog. Don' worry 'bout Saltbag. She a fine dog.'

'Thank you.' Shake feels like crying. 'Thank you.'

'Us haf to go now.'

'Be careful on the march. I might swing by, say goodbye to Carlisle.'

'If yuh do dat, stay yuh distance, Shake.'

'I know.'

Shake drives down to the beach, parks up and then paddles out to *Ribailagua*, brings her in, loads her up, hands shaking, and roars around the headland to the jetty at Tradewinds. The three Englishmen are colleagues and they talk about the office, compare notes about a lazy manager, a seductive secretary, as Shake watches the towering rain-laden cityscapes pass overhead. He listens to their talk and wonders if they ever look at the sky, if they ever notice the path of the sun and how it changes, or the time the moon rises as it waxes and wanes. Wonders if they've otherwise been outside the gates of Tradewinds, or if the all-inclusive diet of booze and food has kept them there, safe from three-fingered women selling benay balls and the beast that dances on the sand. The three men manage to catch a mere two bonitos between them, argue with Shake about the cost of the trip, and walk off from the jetty, feet splayed, slope-shoulders working as they agree that Shake is a charlatan.

Shake thunders *Ribailagua* back to Gilbey beach, paddles the

board to the shore, runs up to the shack to change into dry
clothes and then drives out of Killdevill, turns right onto the
Pillikin road, which will take him to Coral Strand. As he drives, he
passes long crocodiles of Sunday-dressed people, the women
holding newspapers above their elaborate hats to ward off the
sun as pickneys, in dazzling taffeta or pressed shirts, walk behind
them, looking solemn. The men, grave and laden, walk ahead,
their heads held high. And everywhere there are ministers leading
their flocks: the Moravians, the Baptists, the Anabaptists,
Pentecostals, Seventh-Day Adventists, Methodists, Catholics and
Anglicans. Nearing Coral Strand, the crocodile begins to bulge as
the road narrows at the entrance to the sandy spur of land. Shake
crawls along in his jeep, not knowing what else to do. The silence
of the marchers, their finery in the harsh midday sun, the sheer
fucking dignity of what they're doing – walking for a dead man
who could not speak for himself, who has come to represent an
island which cannot speak for itself – leaves Shake confused. He
knows he can't join them because of the colour of his skin but he
wants to watch over them because he can feel the temperature
dropping. The head of the march reaches the gates of Coral
Strand and its progress is halted by black-clad guards and blue-
uniformed police. Behind this knot of people, the crowd grows,
bellys out, trampling on the bougainvillea and banana plants
Kouranis has shipped in from Sansobella, which he has had
planted by the nephews, sisters and sons of the marchers. Shake's
jeep is surrounded by bodies and he gets out, leaves it, walks to
the edge of the march, walks along the limits of the crowd. He
reaches the end of the track where the diamond link fencing
stretches, reaches the barrier and sees that Coral Strand is open,

that there are white tourists inside, who have paid their twenty dollars to relax in the sun as thousands of marchers mill about at the gates. Shake squats in the shade of mangrove, unmindful of the mosquitoes, and watches closely. Sees Miss Lizbeth at the barrier, bony fingers jabbing at a guard's chest and he wonders how early she had to leave her hillside house to get there, how the bush telegraph had got the word to her. He sees Redman loping through the crowds, and Cussbud Perky standing with his family, looking worried. There's Dragon, wearing his red cap, and behind him is Bluebottle, looking raggedy but still carrying shoulders like boulders. Even Stumpy has managed to drag himself from his bed and is waving his arms and shouting at the guards. Squatting in the shade, making himself as small as possible, Shake watches the guards finger their guns, watches the police, who have family out in the crowd, trying to make sense of the jumble of bodies. Shake's scanning the crowd, looking out for Mister Jeremiah and Ayninka, when he notices the crowd begin to behave oddly, cleaving itself into two and then coalescing, like a herring bait ball parting in the presence of a white shark as a hush falls over them. And then he sees the reason for this cleaving – the passage of Susannah Huggins.

Shake stands up and watches Susannah – white woman, queer woman, Billy-no-mates, plantation woman, estate owner, cane sucker, rum boo boo, slave trader – walk to the barrier to remonstrate with the guards, who begin to shuffle, who mutter into the radios pinned to their black cable-knitted jumpers.

'Shit.' Shake's hands begin to prickle because he knows he should be doing something and he knows – as always – he won't.

The crowd starts to shift on its well-shod feet, begins to lose patience. Shake can see the white tourists standing, brushing sand off their legs as they look towards the gate, some acting leisurely, taking photographs, some rushing to pack their bags and leave. Susannah turns, pushes her way to the fencing on the shoreline, begins to claw at it, trying to pull it down. The black crowd watches her for a while, an old white woman pulling at some wire. And then, person by person, piece by piece, the crowd fragments and strings itself out along the fence and the posts are uprooted, thrown aside, wire trampled. Shake sinks back down on his haunches, watching the fence come down, crushed as the crowd spills onto the beach, to begin its slow, patient march along the shoreline – where they have the right to walk, where the fisher-men and their pickneys, where the locals and the crafts people have the *right* to walk, up to the high tide line, because no one, *no one* can buy the sea, no one can buy the sand. Not even Kouranis the Greek, with his fleet of oil tankers can buy the air that is dif-ferent. The crowd regroups on the beach, fills it, spills into the water, the exquisite skirts of the Sunday mamas floating in the salty water. And they're shrieking and laughing, because they haven't been to Coral Strand for years, because they haven't seen the waves breaking on the reef and the flying fish leaping, for years. The ministers ensure the crowd stay below the high tide mark, ensure the letter of the law is not broken and then they lead the crowd in their singing. The singing of gospel, deep and slow, hot as the sun, gospel which is blown across the lagoon by the breeze. And there, in the middle of them, is Susannah Huggins, singing her blood-red, deep magenta heart out.

The white tourists shake their towels, pack their books and leave, confused by the sense of joyous threat. The Sansos on the beach, sitting in the cabanas, drinking rum, shake their heads and jabber, pointing at the guards and the crowd. The Sanso guards and the Georgian police mill about uncertainly, not knowing what to do as they listen to the music of their youth. Shake senses that the moment for danger has passed, that the guns and batons will not be used, and he walks back to his jeep, reverses and drives away.

The swell, late that afternoon, is running high and *Ribailagua* bounces and yaws, making the work of hooking the bait, setting the line, difficult. The wind picks up and tears Shake's words from his mouth as the spray flies. Overhead the clouds begin to spill over each other, as if they're boiling, racing for the horizon, and below them a slow moving, solid bank of black clouds moves towards the island. Mr George had been right, thinks Shake, the storm is coming. The Americans begin to look worried, edgy, and Shake decides to call it a day, hauls in the lines and tells the men to sit on the stern bench, hold on to something. *Ribailagua* skids and thuds as Shake opens up the throttle and races for the shelter of Grackle Bay. Once they reach the headland, Shake eases off and follows the coast, passes Zabico. Through gusting curtains of rain, Shake can just make out the beach at Coral Strand, empty now, the palms bending before the wind, the grass thatch of the cabana roofs being whipped away, bowled along the sands. He drops the Americans at the Royal's jetty and waves away any offer of payment, says he'll rearrange the trip for later that week. Hugging the coast, motoring slowly in the lee of the hills, he sees locals huddled under tarpaulin on the beaches and in their yards, trying to keep alight the candles they have lit for Carlisle. Hundreds, thousands of them burning, flickering and each time one is extinguished, another is lit as sulphur flares.

By the time he's tidied the boat, moored it up and paddled back to shore, Shake is exhausted, wrung out. He trudges up the steps, thinking of dry clothes and a cup of coffee with a shot of rum. He feeds the Saltbag, feeds himself, checks the satellite pictures on the net and the weather station. There are no hurricane warnings but a tropical storm, TS3, is coming through. Rain is being dumped on the islands as the clouds, having left the coast of west Africa and spun west across the Atlantic, head for landfall in Mexico. Shake tidies up the kitchen, empties his fridge and wipes it out. Puts the empty S&G bottles in a crate. Packs his work clothes in a bag to take to the laundry the next day. Checks his diary. Then, bone-weary, he does what the locals do when the rains come: he sleeps.

26 June

Shake wakes early, in pitch darkness, the rain still dinning on the galvanize. He gropes on the floor for his cell phone and switches it on: 01.04 a.m. He lies back on rucked sheets and thinks about Emma, imagines her house in the hills above LA, pool glinting, fans turning, machines buzzing, the rooms waiting for someone who is never there. One o'clock – she'll be in Miami, or boarding another plane to head west. Not wanting to think about the manner of their parting, Shake considers the march at Coral Strand, glad it was peaceful, that the bad boys stayed away so that Mister Jeremiah and his like could sing and be heard. Remembers the way the singing and the joy discombobulated the police and guards, disarmed them. And maybe that singing, that joy, would make a difference? Perhaps it would wrong-foot Kouranis, make him realize that he already had enough, that he could allow them all to breathe different air? The rain, Shake thinks, sounds heavier, it's beginning to drum out a bass rhythm. As he lies on his damp mattress, Shake listens in the darkness, sits up and listens. Because it's not rain drumming, it's an odd, chattering boom that's snagged his attention. Hidden behind the sound of the rain is another sound – chopper blades churning air. Shake throws back the sheet, steps outside and stands on his porch, looking into the night, not caring that he is soaked. But he can't see anything, he can still hear the sound, faint now, but he can't see anything, no lights. Did he imagine it? As water boils, Shake thinks. There are two helipads on Killdevill, Susannah has one at Mojito, and there's another at a house in Craddock. Some filthy rich English guy who sometimes flies in from one of his other houses in Sansobella. Maybe it's that? Shake drinks his coffee, thinks that he should get some more sleep but he can't settle. He tries to get online, but the phone is out, which may be from the storm dropping a tree on the line. He decides to drive to Bridgewater, go to the airport, where the bush telegraph is loudest.

The roads in Killdevill are deserted, the only movement the tethered sheep and goats trying to huddle under trees in the flare of his headlights. Shake drives through Myers, Vampiro, Fleischmanns, Polonaise and Sangaree and doesn't pass another car or a person. It's the middle of the bloody night, Shake reasons, trying to dampen down rising, indefinable panic. He negotiates the sharp bend before the road joins the highway and it's there that he sees the roadblock, manned by armed soldiers. Shake slams on the brakes, realizes he's breathing hard and he hears the drumming again, as a military helicopter flies low overhead, tilting like a batty damsel. A soldier strolls over in the glare of a spotlight, fondling the magazine of his machine gun. Holds out his hand and Shake, unbidden, gives him the sodden mass of papers that are his documents. Unlike the policeman a couple of days before, the soldier simply glances at the licence and hands the papers back. His young, Indian face is unreadable.

'We ask dat yuh go back home and stay on yuh premises. Doh try to leave as der is a curfew.'

'A curfew?'

The soldier looks at Shake's white face and nods. 'Yuh will be tole when de curfew finish. Sugges' yuh lissen to yuh radio.'

'OK,' says Shake, and he reverses, drives back into Killdevill, keeps driving until he can no longer see the soldier in his rearview mirror. Shake can feel his sternum again, as if it's still growing, still pressing against his chest. What the fuck's going on? Back through Sangaree and Polonaise and now the dark, empty roads look different, look abandoned, hopeless and menacing. Hands jumping, he lights a cigarette, draws on it and stops the jeep. He throws the gearstick, shifts into four-wheel drive, and, checking the mirror, turns off the road, because if he remembers rightly, beyond Polonaise is the track the contractors forced through the bush when they built Mojito. It will be overgrown but only with grasses and stinking susan, perhaps a few saplings but the Land Rover can deal with those and Shake needs to see Susannah, needs her to explain everything because once it is explained to him then he can deal with it.

Shake hates the bush, always has; even in a vehicle, he hates the darkness, the wildness, the *chaos* of it, which make him feel trapped, claustrophobic. But right now it seems like the place to be. He's sweating as branches and paddle leaves beat on the wind-screen, slap at his face, and he closes the window, even though the cab is steamy, humid. His lights are on because he calculates that the bush is so dense he won't be seen. Shake finds he is on the track, that he found it without realizing, and the Land Rover begins to grind over packed earth, crushing the new growth. It's a slow, rolling ride and Shake can feel he's being bitten by mos-quitoes, but he can't take his hands from the wheel to slap at them. The ground rises steeply, and even with the four-wheel drive, the tyres are beginning to slip, beginning to slide away a little, and Shake is glad to see the piles of rubble which were never cleared from the land out back of Mojito, glad to see the bush thinning. He parks beneath the cover of a breadfruit tree, the vehicle hidden by tall, savannah grasses and then, taking his torch, walks slowly along the edge of the bush, ignoring the scratches and the sodden leaves brushing his face and legs. Mojito is set in a vast parcel of land and it takes Shake time to work his way around to the gates, making sure he stays under cover. When he finally reaches the security hut he finds it empty. He plays the torch over the driveway and sees the dogs lying behind the gate, lying in puddles of blood thinned by rainwater, staining the blond brickwork. The gate is open, the chain cut, lying on the ground. Shake stands in the rain-filled night and he knows, he's not sure how, but he knows that there is no one there, no one in Mojito. He pushes open the gate, steps over the crazed dogs, whose furious psychosis could not stop bullets. Walking round to the pool, Shake is surprised to see the pool is lit. He is not surprised to see one of the plate glass doors leading to the atrium is shattered, the shards lying on the patio, in the living room and, Shake notices with a professional eye, in the pool. He steps through the jagged hole and sees signs of a small, hopeless struggle, the struggle of an old, white woman. The travertine table has been cracked, a chair lies on its side. It would not have taken the soldiers long to restrain Susannah, to slap her around a little before bundling her out of the house and into a van.

Shake wipes his face with his filthy, torn T-shirt then spins around, heart lurching, as a blade of glass falls from the doorframe like a guillotine and diamonds scatter over marble. The television is turned on, the sound muted, and Shake stares at the screen, at the pictures of Sansobella being beamed around the globe on BBC World, picked up by the satellite dish in the grounds of Mojito. The camera is scanning the skyline of Queenstown and the city is burning as military vehicles roll along the boulevards. There is shaky, stuttering footage of looters smashing shopfronts, of soldiers beating civilians, batons crashing into black skulls and black ribs, children crying as they are dragged into doorways, into cars by shouting, weeping parents. Shake searches for the remote, finds it on the floor, turns on the sound and the reporter's clipped tones inform him that a military coup has occurred in the Republic of Sansobella, St George and Dorado.

'It is believed that the coup, led by General Jamini Ramprakesh, has been relatively successful. The former President and Prime Minister were, apparently, arrested just after midnight and the entire cabinet, including the First Minister of the St George House of Congress, is now under house arrest. General Ramprakesh has installed his headquarters in Parliament House in the Champs du Ciel, in Queenstown.'

As he speaks, images of a military motorcade arriving at Parliament House appear on the screen, and Shake recognizes some of the faces of the civilians who are greeted by the General and then led inside – the heads of the five Indian families.

'The reports here are still very confused, as the telephone exchange is occupied by military and in many places the lines are down. The state television station is also under military control and is not currently broadcasting. The pictures you're seeing were filmed by a Trinidadian crew, about an hour ago. There were elections scheduled for next week, here in the Republic, and some commentators believe that the growing tension between the black community and the minority East Indian community has boiled over. The leadership of the military is essentially Indian and there is speculation that it anticipated that power would be returned to the black majority. There has been considerable violence here in the past few months, indeed, the UN had been involved in talks with the now-deposed government about deploying a UN Peace Corps on Sansobella.

'Some people have been speculating that the kidnapping and subsequent murder of General Ramprakesh's son earlier this month, who was found dead on an oil field, even though a ransom was paid, contributed to the decision to mount the coup.

'However, most commentators agree that is far more likely to be the events that took place yesterday on the sister island of St George, which is predominantly African black, that triggered the overthrow. There were riots and civil unrest in the west of the island, where the majority of European and American tourists take their holidays.'

Shake watches in growing confusion as the BBC shows a clip from a tourist's digicam, blurred images of the peace march shudder across the screen, then the lens focuses, brings Susannah into sharp relief as she pulls at the fence. The crowd – looking vast and black and angry, looking like the beast of Jungle Jam Bow Wow – spills through the gap and, in the background, Shake can see his yesterday self, crouched by the mangrove swamp, watching events unfold. 'But it wasn't like that,' Shake says to the empty room.

'There has been considerable concern about the safety of those tourists staying on Dorado, the smallest of the islands, which is essentially a luxury resort. Feverish speculation is taking place about who, exactly, is staying there as it is an exclusive retreat favoured by the rich and famous. No names have yet been issued but we would expect some information soon.'

The images of the peace march are replaced by the bland studio in London. 'Thank you, John,' says the presenter. 'We talked to a spokesperson from the Foreign Office earlier, about the concerns of those who have friends and family on holiday in the republic at the moment. The phone number issued by the Foreign Office for those who need information is at the bottom of the screen.'

Lightning forks into the hillside below Mojito, crumpling a towering mango tree, and the thunder which follows reverberates around the valley, as another jagged section of glass in the door frame slumps and shatters. Shake is oblivious to this pandemonium. A reed-thin man, with pale, dry skin, appears.

'The Foreign Office is, naturally, concerned about the situation and recommends that anyone planning to travel to the area, for business or pleasure, cancels those plans. As for those British nationals already there, we have reliable manifests from the airline companies and we think there are roughly four hundred and ten British citizens currently holidaying on the islands. However, there is no reliable source of information for those British people who either live there or work there for foreign companies. There were no contingency plans in place for this type of emergency.'

'Shouldn't there have been contingency plans?' asks the interviewer.

The official clears his throat, narrows his eyes. 'We had been monitoring the situation and felt that the tensions would evaporate after the elections. The coup was completely unexpected. We cannot plan for the unexpected. At the moment we are working with the Americans, and planes are already scheduled to pick up those stranded there.'

'The Foreign Office spokesperson,' says the presenter. 'We are getting reports that General Ramprakesh, who led the coup, is about to broadcast a statement via Sansobella state television. John?'

The burning city of Queenstown appears again on the screen, and the reporter's voice is near-drowned by the sound of sirens and gunshots, rain and thunder. 'Yes, there are rumours that a statement is about to be made in Parliament House. I'm currently in the southern part of the city and, as you can hear, the situation is very volatile. The military have met no ordered resistance but there are bands of looters and pockets of fighting taking place. This is now live feed and as you can see and hear, there's a lot of activity on the streets. The coup was obviously well-planned as the military now control all communications and transport. The airport in Queenstown is being used by the military and the international airport on the island of St George, near Bridgewater, has been closed. Not many reports are available for St George but it would seem a curfew has been imposed there too. Also, the oil wells have been sealed off and are being guarded. The few workers left out on the rigs have been arrested and brought back to Queenstown. The impact of this on the already struggling oil industry is yet to be seen but I've been told the Americans are monitoring the situation closely. One has the feeling that this isn't over yet, that it's going to—'

'John, I have to interrupt you there. General Ramprakesh is about to speak.'

The images change yet again, and a shot of a long, highly polished desk appears, set in a high-ceilinged, ornate room. General Ramprakesh, a slim, elegant East Indian Sanso, appears and sits in the high chair in the centre of the table. A group of men file into shot, stand in a line behind the general, dressed in suits, hands crossed demurely. All of them East Indian, all either related to the general or to the five families. All of them except one, who stands immediately behind the general, looking down at him, looking down at the man whose son was found dead on an oil trace.

'Kouranis,' mutters Shake. 'Kouranis the Greek.' Shake had seen him only two days before, laughing with the First Minister of the St George House of Congress.

General Ramprakesh taps a sheaf of paper on the table, clears his throat and begins to speak. 'At eleven o'clock last night, twenty-fifth of June, the Army of the Republic removed from power the government of the People's Democratic Movement. The islands have suffered for too long as a result of the incompetence and endemic corruption of the PDM. I have been asked to act as temporary president for an interim period, until such time as elections can be called and I reluctantly accept this invitation. I have appointed a cabinet, also a temporary measure, until elections are called. I ask the people of Sansobella, St George and Dorado to respect the curfew and to stay in their homes.'

The general has more to say, much more, but Shake doesn't wait to hear it. He runs out of Mojito, cutting his arm as he flies through the broken glass, sprints down the driveway and hurdles the dogs. He's still running even as he makes his way through the bush to his jeep, not thinking of snakes and scorpions, thinking only of safety. He drives back down the track, easier to see now the Land Rover's already cut through it once, but he drives too fast, too fast, slithering this way and that, having to reverse out of dips and holes. He has to stay in the bush because now he knows the the track from Mojito is too exposed, too open and Shake doesn't want to be seen. He has diesel, in his cage on the beach, he can load it on *Ribailagua* and make it to Grenada. Shake can hear his breath rasping, above the sound of the engine and the trees slashing at the rag top, which is leaking. He slows to a halt, turns off the lights and lowers his head to the wheel. On the dash, the compass stops spinning as Shake thinks. Thinks of Avril feeling uncomfortable in her Sanso skin. Thinks of Rajiv. 'That is doing nothing, running away. The way you speak of it is as an end and it is not, running away is not an end. You think that if you run then everything will be alright.' But, thinks Shake, that is what Rajiv has done; Rajiv has run all the way to Frankfurt.

Shake raises his head, wipes the rain from his face, and he turns on the torch once more, yanks open the glove compartment, throws the contents into the footwell, until he finds what he's looking for – an old British army OS map of the island. He opens it and spreads it on his lap. The colours have leached away, paled to pastels, but the information is there: the old estate roads and tracks, the old borders are still on the map. Shake traces the hatched lines with a trembling finger. Apart from perhaps five hundred metres on the Pillikin Road, when he'll be out in the open before he can turn onto the Huggins' Estate Division Two boundary, he can work his way to the Willbyn area of Bridgewater entirely off-road. Shake glances at the compass, knows he must keep heading south. He engages the gears and, hoping the old Land Rover can do what is about to be asked of it, he rolls forward.

The most dangerous part of the journey turns out to be the last section, when Shake has to crawl through the empty streets of Willbyn, lights off, unable to see storm drains and potholes, looking out the meanwhile for patrols and helicopters. He can see fires burning, lighting the streets two blocks away; remembers the tinder box of a house he had lived in when he arrived. These streets could explode despite the drenching rain. Dark figures dart between buildings, trying to outrun a military jeep, which races past the junction ahead, spotlight sweeping the street, flaring on shutters and balconies. Shake brakes and ducks beneath the dash. When the spotlight has passed, he switches off the engine and freewheels to a halt in the cavernous carport of a tyre shop. In the back of his vehicle he has a dark blue waterproof and he puts it on to cover his pale clothes, takes the torch and his cell phone – it's now 3.07 a.m. – and weaves an unlikely route through yards and alleys. Shake knows Willbyn, the old section of Bridgewater, like the back of his hand, it hasn't changed in a decade. It has rotted, been abandoned in places to the vines and lianas, but the geography remains the same.

The sirens grow loud and fade, as Shake makes slow progress, crouching behind a rusting wreck of a truck as a car screeches to a halt on the street and three locals fly out, leaving the doors open, and scramble over fences. The sound of breaking glass distracts Shake, until a patrol turns into the street and Shake flattens himself into the storm drain, which is flooded, tins, shit and vegetation swirling around him. He can see the boots of the soldiers, milling around the abandoned car, can hear the soldiers talking, their voices loud, high-pitched with fear. A gunshot, another, and the boots turn in the same direction, begin to run.

'Shit.' Shake lies in the drain, counting, and from the vaults of his memory an image of Adonis, with his ugly face and wet lips presents itself. The sound of splintering wood and a dog howling and Shake lurches out of the drain, water and detritus sluicing from him. As he runs to the junction, on the corner of which he knows is a derelict rum shop, he hears the blatting of a bullhorn, the words indistinct but Shake can imagine what the good citizens of Bridgewater are being told. He reaches the corner, breathes deep, pulls up the hood of the jacket, and peers around the corner. No lights, no movement at all. There is someone but he's not moving. He's lying in a muddied rut, limbs tangled, face down in a puddle. Next to him are the shattered remains of a television, but Shake knows the man won't be needing it. He won't be needing it because he is dead.

Shake kicks at the rotten door of the rum shop and it caves in, hardly making a sound as termites scatter. He waits until he is in the room at the back of the shop before turning on his torch, sees the empty bottles, the filthy counter top, climbs over it, through a door and into the kitchen. The door there is barred. Shake snatches up a metal bin and beats at the shuttered window, the rusted bars giving way, springing free of salt-eaten screws. He scrambles over the sink, out into the yard and switches off the torch. He clambers up a wall, grazing hands and knees, drops down the other side, hoping there's no guard dog. There is – a large, pale hound, which races at him, looms out of the darkness, teeth bared. Shake presses himself into a corner as the dog yelps and howls, throwing itself at him time and again, jerked back by a length of chain. Shake looks up, sees black faces watching him from a window. The shutters slam shut. Shake edges to the next fence, drags himself over it to the flat, mechanical sound of semi-automatics.

Accustomed to the darkness, he covers his eyes against the thunderous rain and sees the rear of a familiar two-storey board house and climbs the outside steps, pressing himself against the wall, to a small porch. Tapping lightly on the door, Shake keeps checking the yards and houses around but nothing is moving except the dog still spinning and yelping. 'Come on,' he mutters, tapping again. A dog begins to yap inside and he keeps tapping to keep the dog yapping. He hears movement, a rustle, and senses someone breathing on the other side of the door.

'It's me, Shake.'

The door opens a sliver and Shake shoves it, pushes Avril, who is dressed in pyjamas, back into her kitchen. They look at each other as the dog sniffs at Shake's calves, tail wagging. Shake glances at his cell – 4.03 a.m., one and a half more hours of darkness. In the corner, the television is playing a loop of the general's speech, Kouranis looking straight at the camera.

'The storm come finally,' says Avril

An explosion blows in a glazed window and April ducks, covers her head. Shake crosses the kitchen, opens the door to Avril's bedroom, and he can see a blaze out towards the docks, thinks a gas tank may have been hit.

'I'm going to Grenada.' Shake takes a towel from the rail and wipes his face and hands, not noticing the blood that stains it. 'I want you to come with me. I've got more than enough diesel to get there. But we need to go now.'

Avril looks at Shake's bloodied face. 'I can' go to Grenada.'

'Why not?'

'This mih home, Shake. What about mih place? Mih dog?'

'We'll come back when it blows over. We can come back. St George is not a good place to be right now.'

The chuttering sound of helicopter blades grows, and a beam of light plays over the house, along the street, blazing in the now-unglazed window.

'I staying. This will pass. Troubles come and troubles go.'

Shake stares at her. He doesn't have the luxury of time, doesn't have an excess of darkness to fritter away on persuasion.

'Avril, please.'

'What I do in Grenada? I live here. Maybe in Sansobella things will be bad. But here? People forget soon. Shake, I live here.'

Shake frowns, wants to shout, wants to drag her out of the titling frame house and out to the Land Rover. Wants to take her away from men lying in puddles and storms and growling batty damsels but knows that he can't. Hears himself talking in the Kiskadee with Rajiv.

'Shake, baby, you want to go, you go. These not yuh people, not yuh troubles. But you have to tell me you come back.'

Shake nods as Avril comes to him, holds him tight, not minding the blood and sludge and rain on his jacket. Shake kisses Avril's forehead, picks up his cell phone and torch, and steps back out on the porch.

'Hey, Shake, thanks for coming for me. I so sorry.'

Shakes waves a hand and he steps back into darkness.

The sky begins to lighten, a grey smear on the horizon, as

Shake pushes the Land Rover to its limit, following the track he made for himself across the Huggins' estate. He bounces out onto the road above Tom Collins by Mister Jeremiah's house, rainwater sloshing around his ankles, sweat dripping inside his jacket. He doesn't want to see the old man, doesn't want to involve him, so he drives past and down the trace to Gilbey beach, the trees and bushes turning white and grey as the rain drowns the rising sun. Shake has the key to the cage on the jeep's keyring, and he paddles the board out, brings the boat in, his heart hammering, and loads the diesel onboard, watching the skies, watching the track, the beach for movement. He sprints across the sand, to the back of the beach where there is some cover, and makes his way to the steps leading to his shack. His breathing is ragged, he's blowing as he searches through crap-filled drawers in his kitchen for his passport, smearing the blood on his arm and hand. He finds it, stuck to the *Savoy Cocktail Book*, stuffs both of them into a plastic bag which he forces into a deep pocket of his combat shorts. He looks around the shack but there's nothing else to take, there's no *time* to take anything else. His book and his cell phone and his passport and his boat keys – that's all he needs. Shake pours three bowls of chow for Saltbag, and fills bowls and calabash with water, spilling it with his shaking hands, because he doesn't know how long it will be before Mister Jeremiah comes to get the old dog. Shake kneels and strokes Saltbag's head, rubs the fur between her eyes. Saltbag sits up, begins to bark huskily.

There are four of them, looking jumpy, looking young and trigger-happy, climbing the steps. Behind them is the long streak o' misery that is Bap. The lead soldier points to Shake.

'Dis he?'

Bap nods. 'Dat he.'

The van is sweltering, thick with sweat and damp, mosquitoes swimming drowsily in the fetid air. Shake can't sit down easily because of the handcuffs, so he stands, tries to catch the breeze from the barred, unglazed window set high in the van's sides. He sees Bap talking to one of the soldiers, sees something change hands and then Bap saunters off, disappears into the bush behind the beach as the engine turns over and the van begins to crawl up the hill. Three of the soldiers are in the cab; the youngest has been detailed to sit with the prisoner in the back. The soldier raises his weapon, motions for Shake to sit on the wooden bench. Shake can hear the rain growing heavy again, hammering on the van's roof, as he shifts uncomfortably, wrists aching. He tries to imagine the route the van is taking, tries to follow the turns, guess how far they are travelling, and all the time he's doing this, he's listening. Because he cannot see anything, he listens and behind the curtain of rain he hears sirens and, growing louder, another faint sound, which he recognizes as the bullhorn. He knows, then, they're probably heading for Bridgewater. The docks? The airport? Sweat is pouring from him, but he can't wipe it off; it stings his eyes, blinding him, and he squeezes them shut, concentrates on sound. He hears the commonplace, now unearthly, trilling of a green light on a pedestrian crossing and he knows they're in the centre of town. But there are no other cars, the van keeps moving, so there are no pedestrians either. Thunder blasts overhead as the interior of the van flashes ultra violet. The engine begins to labour as they climb a hill, so the docks are not an option. All Shake can pick out now are distant shouts, dog barks and the bullhorn muffled by rain. The van lurches to a stop, reverses as Shake hears metal dragged over concrete, stops again. The doors open and Shake squints, sees a red-brick quadrangle, the bricks soaked dark by rain, the cobbles swimming in puddles. The young soldier, who has slept for the duration of the journey – being a local, that is what he does when it rains – jumps to, grabs Shake's arm and hauls him out of the van. Shake slips on the cobbles, nearly falls. The four young men look around, seem as surprised as Shake to find themselves standing in the middle of a tropical storm, standing in the middle of a revolution. A sergeant opens one of the many doors lining the quadrangle and shouts an order, and the soldiers half-heartedly push Shake around the edge of the cobbles and eventually open a door – marked 'laundry' in faded, stencilled letters – and shove him into a room bare but for a table and two chairs. The four of them stand by the open door, one leaning against the jamb, talking, but Shake can't hear what's said with the rain beating down. The soldiers laugh, then assemble themselves as the sergeant appears. He walks in to find Shake slumped against a wall.

'Sit.' The sergeant motions to a chair.

Shake looks at the man. 'Where am I?'

'Sit.'

'Don't talk to me like that. I'm asking you where I am.'

'Sit.'

Shake stares at the sergeant, shrugs.

The sergeant, who is short and plump, a pale-skinned Georgian who likes his fried chicken and Kup Kakes, who lives for Miss Tubby and Ponche Rum, who doesn't know what's going on and wants to be at home, watching WWF, waddles over to Shake, looks up at him and shouts, 'Sit!'

Shake looks down at the man's shiny, sweating face. Shrugs again and the sergeant, who is tired and confused, turns and walks away out into the rain.

The soldiers at the door laugh, the youngest looking in at Shake, smiling shyly. Shake sits, then, sits and waits, imagining he is out in the open sea, out in *Ribailagua*, heading for Grenada. The boat is aquaplaning, dancing across the swell, heading for Grenada, and soon he'll catch sight of the tip of Mount St Catherine appearing over the curve of the earth.

The soldiers at the door suddenly leap to, polished boots and magazines snapping sharply, and Shake stands, faces the door. An officer walks into the room, an East Indian officer, tall and thin, his immaculate uniform tailored to his frame, dapper, almost.

'Please take a seat.' The officer motions with one hand as he lays a notebook and pencil on the table with the other.

Shake looks at the officer, who seems familiar for some reason. 'I would, if these were taken off.' Shake turns and shows the cuffs.

'Of course.' The officer shouts an order and a soldier strides in, turns the key in the lock and Shake rubs at tender, abraded skin. 'Please, take a seat. But, before you do, can I ask that you empty your pockets?'

Shake considers this; looks at the guards at the door, looks at the hooded eyes of the man opposite, and empties his pockets of keys, cell phone, cocktail recipes, cigarettes and passport. Then he sits.

'Thank you.'

As the officer looks through his effects, Shake can see the peak of Mount St Catherine growing larger, changing colour as the gullies and valleys appear.

'The name in your passport is given as Samuel Henry Andrew Knight. Is that correct?'

Shake nods.

'Is that correct?'

'Yes.'

'Allow me to introduce myself, Mr Knight. I am Major Ramprakesh.'

Again Shake nods. Must be a brother or cousin of the general, that's why he looks familiar.

'And you are a British citizen, Mr Knight?'

'Yes.'

'You have residency here, however?'

'Yes.'

'How long have you lived in St George, Mr Knight?'

'Nearly eleven years.'

'I see. Can you tell me why you think you are here?'

'I have no idea. Come to that, I don't even know where I am.'

'You are in prison. Have you been offered any refreshment?'

Shake stares at the man.

'I see.' An order is shouted once more and Shake and Major Ramprakesh wait in silence until a bottle of water is brought.

'So – where were we? Oh yes – can you tell me why you think you have been arrested?'

'I have no idea.'

'Oh, come, Mr Knight. Surely you have some idea?'

'No.'

'Well,' the major settles back a little in his chair, 'let us see, shall we?' He picks up the notepad and refers to it as he speaks. 'There is the matter of certain trips you have made to Grenada without collecting visas or clearing trips with immigration. On one occasion you ferried an English couple there with whom you did not return. There is also the matter of aiding and abetting a deserter from the Republican Army.' Bap had seen him that night, as he drove Miss Avarice to the hospital, Bap had been standing by the road, and would have seen Sheldon in the bed of the jeep comforting his grandmammy. Bap was with him, too, when he made the Grenada run – spent the four hours in rum shops and got himself cut up. 'And only two days ago, I see from police records, you were cautioned by the police. Also, you were discovered violating the rules of the curfew.'

Shake says nothing.

'You are, I believe, an associate of Miss Susannah Huggins of Mojito, Killdevill.'

'I'm a friend of hers, yes.'

'How good a friend?'

Now there's a question, thinks Shake. For where had he been when gunshots rang out and dogs fell, when glass shattered and soldiers burst in? 'A close friend.'

'I have seen video pictures, Mr Knight, incontrovertible evidence, that show that you were part of the crowd that rioted at Coral Strand. That you were part of an illegal demonstration against the government. There were two white people there. Yourself and Miss Huggins. Miss Huggins was the ringleader, and now you say you are a close friend of hers. Are you a member of any political organization, Mr Knight?'

'No.'

'Are you a supporter of the PDM?'

'No.'

'Thank you, Mr Knight. We shall be investigating these matters in due course. In the meantime, as a potential enemy of the state, you will be required to remain here. Unfortunately, the facilities are extremely crowded at the moment, due to the lawlessness of citizens in St George. I apologize for the cramped conditions.'

'I want to speak to a lawyer.'

'I am sure you do, but as yet you have not been charged.' The major smiles. 'Why would you need a lawyer?'

'I'm entitled to a phone call. I want to make a call.'

'Unfortunately, the lines are down and no calls can be made. Even I am reduced to two-way radio.' The major smiles, raises his shoulders and turns his coffee-coloured hands to the sky. 'But what can you expect, Mr Knight? I am sure you have often been thus inconvenienced as you go about your business. We are a backward nation, we are nothing but the sons of slaves. I apologize. Now, please excuse me.'

Shake's ribs are beginning to shrink. 'You can't keep me here without charge. It's illegal. You can't keep me without charge.'

'You are, I believe Mr Knight, referring to the principle of habeas corpus. And, of course, in the normal run of things, I would be in complete agreement with you. Before I joined the military, I had the pleasure of studying law in your country, in London, in fact. Indeed, it was a necessity to study in England, since our legal system was, and still is, ultimately under English jurisdiction – a curious state of affairs, I grant you. However, those studies enable me to tell you with some authority that the

English legal system allows for the suspension of habeas corpus in times of war or other extraordinary circumstances. In short, suspect people may be detained without the legality of that detention being determined before a court. And, unfortunately, given your actions over the past few months, Mr Knight, you are a suspect person.'

'But all you have, all you've talked about is hearsay, it's bullshit. You have no evidence because there *is* no evidence because I didn't do anything. OK, I was at Coral Strand, but it wasn't a riot—'

'Mr Knight, Mr Knight, quiet, please.' Major Ramprakesh stands, and even in the grey, lumpen light in the room, his Indian features are sharp – he looks handsome, he looks dangerous, he looks like he could wield a knife. 'You talk of habeas corpus. Have you never heard of Guantanamo Bay? After all, just a few islands away.' Major Ramprakesh walks out and the soldiers walk in.

Shake starts to back away from them, but where does he have to go? There is nowhere to go, nowhere to run, so he stands still, just as he had when the marshal at Redpath found him, and allows himself to be cuffed again. He's dragged across the quadrangle, through an archway, into a smaller, gloomier courtyard. The rain is still lashing down, beating on his skull, but Shake looks up, blinking furiously, looks up to capture a last look at the grey, lowering sky. He's shoved against a wall, pinned there, as a steel door is unlocked. As he stands, ribs contracting, the breath squeezed from his lungs, face pressed against a red brick, he feels something being shoved in the pocket of his shorts, looks as well as he is able at the young soldier, who brushes his lips with his fingers. The steel door clangs open and Shake's cuffs are removed before he is spun around, then shoved into the cell as the door is slammed shut behind him. Then he hears the sound he's been trying not to think about: the sound of a key turning, the sound of the tongue of a five lever lock sliding into a recess. Shake knows the prison is part of the old British fort, not far from the hospital, and the walls are British-built, built from the red bricks used as ballast in the slave ships, built to withstand cannon fire, revolutions and insurrections, thick as oak trunks. Shake leans against the steel door, closes his eyes and tries to breathe but his ribs are squeezing him too tight.

'Shake?'

Shake swivels, peers into the gloom, the cell lit only by the light from a tiny unglazed, barred window, set high in the wall. He sees a body sitting on one of the two hard beds. 'Susannah?'

'Yuh OK?'

'I don't like being shut in.'

'No, well, it's not what we used to.'

Shake stands by the door, trying to breathe, fearful of time being made dense, thick and paste-like so it can be squeezed into the cell, layer upon layer.

'How they ketch yuh, baby?' Susannah's face is grey in the light seeping through the window.

'At home.'

'Me too.' Susannah watches Shake, watches him straining to breathe, becoming strung out like wire, like cat gut. 'Yuh look like yuh havin' a night-fright when the sun out.'

'I can't stand being locked in, it makes me feel claustrophobic.'

'Well, why don' yuh lie yoursel' down, close yuh eyes and tell me what happen?'

Shake tries this. He lies down and tries to tell Susannah about the backstreets of Bridgewater, about men lying in puddles and sirens blaring, but his jaws feel rusty, his tongue is grinding against his teeth. Susannah eventually stands and crosses the tiny cell, makes Shake lift his head and then she lays it in her lap, tells him to close his eyes, and in her odd, deep crooning voice, she tells him he'll be alright, that he'll be fine, over and over as she strokes his head, singing almost, almost singing him a lullaby. Shake is rigid, unyielding, at first, his neck knotted and his breath jumping, never finishing itself, but eventually he softens a little, begins to soften at the edges and then, abruptly, without warning he falls asleep.

It is the sound of the door being opened that wakes him. For a moment Shake thinks he is in his shack, rain beating on the tin roof but then the red-brick walls move closer. He sits up, realizes it is night, because the cell is lit by a single, fly-blown bulb. His mouth is foul and sticky, his neck aches but the panic has abated enough for him to stand and breathe deeply. Susannah, whose legs have been dead a long time, crushed under Shake's weight, cannot move. The guard pushes in two plates and two bottles of water, slams and locks the door.

Shake picks up the plates, gives one to Susannah, who looks at the offering and repeats, 'Well, it not what we use to.'

Shake pokes about in the food, which is mashed mush, some boiled pumpkin and peas with a few rice grains. 'How are we supposed to eat this?'

'With your fingers. Like we all did before you Brits came along and taught us manners.' Susannah picks up a mouthful, tastes it and spits it out, rinses out her mouth with water.

'How long have you been here?'

'Shake, not entirely unsurprisingly, they took my Rolex. I don't suppose they think we have much need for one in here.'

'You know what I mean.'

Susannah stares up at the filthy ceiling. 'They came in the middle of the night. Must have been about one in the morning.' Shake wonders if that's what woke him. 'I heard gunshots and then the glass breaking downstairs. I tried to argue with them but it didn't do much good.'

'I went up to Mojito this morning.' Shake tells Susannah what he had found, what he had seen on the television. 'They all came in and stood behind the table – all the Indian bigwigs. And then Kouranis walked in, stood behind Ramprakesh. He stood there looking down at him, like he was shit. Like he was nothing. And two days ago we saw him in the car with the First Minister, and he's been arrested too.'

'Kouranis, nuh? Like I say, he see which way flag flap.' Susannah sucks her teeth. 'I in trouble.' She rubs at her legs, wiggles her feet. 'So Ramprakesh has done it? I didn't think he would, I didn't think yalla belly had the guts. And him sayin' the PDM corrupt? T'ief from t'ief does make God laugh. Why you here Shake? I know why I here, because Kouranis want it so. But why you here?'

Shake lists the allegations and again Susannah sucks her teeth. 'It doh look good. You should be fine because you are a subject of her Majesty, the Queen of England, and Ramprakesh won't want to fuck with her. Kouranis won't care but Ramprakesh just might t'ink twice. International goodwill and all that shit. I don't know. Dog cyar see cat in de dark. How many people you know outside?'

'What do you mean?' Shake pushes aside the food, feels something in his pocket. They have taken his passport, his book and cell phone and keys but the young soldier had slipped him his cigarettes and lighter. Shake looks in the packet – he has eighteen. He lights one and the first drag leaves him light-headed.

'How many people do you know off the islands? I don't mean the dada heads yuh hang with here. They won't give a shit. What about your family? Friends in England? The more people you have outside, the better. The more people who realize you're missing, the greater the chance someone will contact the authorities, asking questions.'

Shake thinks of the people who could point to a map and say, Shake is there. That is where you will find him. 'I have a sister, Diana, who lives in Slough, in England, but we haven't spoken for years. I don't know her, really. I never did. I have the feeling she never really approved of me. And anyway, she may not know what's going on. It's not exactly news, is it?' Shake draws smoke into his lungs, holds it there, as he thinks of his sister. 'I mean, obviously it's news but I'm not sure that Diana will make the connection. There's Rajiv, of course, but he's in Germany and he'll be worrying about his family in Queenstown.' Shake thinks of Queenstown burning, thinks of the smouldering cityscape. 'And I have an ex-wife in the States. She knows I'm here. But she just got re-married.' Shake elects not to tell Susannah that Emma's purpose, when she came to see him, was to erase her memories of him. She had come not to forgive but to forget. And Avril? Avril will imagine him escaping to Grenada, crossing stormy, white-capped seas in *Ribailagua*, as oil tanks blow and windows shatter.

'Dat it?'

'Yes.'

Susannah stands up to stretch her legs, looks with disgust at the toilet bowl in the corner, the bucket and tap next to it. Dat it? Susannah has often wondered about the whiteys who come to the island, wondered why they come. They arrive and build their houses and live tiny lives, driving the same roads, visiting the same shops and market stalls, lying on the same beaches, as if they're trying to cram their lives into the smallest possible place. And behind them they have left galleries and theatres, libraries and universities, to come to an island where there isn't even a bookshop.

'A whitey woman I once knew, who came to St George about fifteen years ago, we were talking one day and she told me that she'd come here on holiday with her husband and she like it so much, she want to live here. She tried to persuade her husband to come but she say he didn't want to. So she leave him and come alone. Yuh know what she say to me? "I left him for an island". Never forgot that. "I left him for an island", like the island a lover or a glad-hand-Dan. If yuh lucky, maybe Rajiv will try to do somet'ing. But like yuh say, he got all his own family on Sansobella to worry about. You OK? I going to try to sleep.'

Shake stubs out the cigarette on the floor, tosses the butt in the toilet. 'I'm fine.'

But Shake is not fine, he's feeling the walls too thick around him, feels constrained by the immobile heat, wearing it as if it's a straitjacket. He paces the cell for hours, five paces to the wall, five paces to the door, stopping occasionally to sip at the water, rubbing at the cables in his neck, fighting the desire to smoke. At some point the light is switched off and Shake has to lie down, then. He tries to sleep but his breathing is breaking up again. He closes his eyes, puts one hand on his heart, feels it pulse-jumping, throws the other above his head and he hauls himself onto the deck of *Ribailagua*, races away, dancing on the swell, heading for Mount St Catherine.

The rain is still hammering on the cobbles and shingles of the prison the next morning; it pours into Shake's dreams and he wakes, imagining *Ribailagua* is flooding, capsizing. In the gloom he sees Susannah squatting on the toilet and turns away, feigning sleep, pretends to wake when the cell door opens. He wolfs down the breakfast of paw-paw and naked rice, washes it down with water, partly smokes another of his precious cigarettes, offers Susannah a puff.

'No, thank you.'

'You're not eating yours? Aren't you hungry?'

Susannah frowns, pushes at the plate with her foot. 'I not know whey dis come from. How they wash it, how they cook it. But, yes, I hungry.'

'What time d'you think it is?'

'Wet season.' Susannah half-smiles.

'Eight o'clock? Seven?'

'Why yuh ask? Yuh haf an appointment?'

'It's Thursday, isn't it?' Shake calculates backwards, finds his memories already jumbling.

'Shake, you have to let go of time. Drop the leash and let time run free, because yuh can't control it.'

But Shake can't do this, can't ignore the passing of time as Susannah is able to; he can't catnap and snooze as she does.

Susannah is Georgian – for Susannah the sound of rain is a metronome, a heartbeat; it is the sound of her mother's pulse in the womb and she can slip away without warning. Shake spends the day lying on his damp bed, or pacing the room, obsessing about time and space, remembers standing in Avril's kitchen, where he did not have the luxury of time nor an excess of darkness and now he has both. Sometimes, Shake lies down on the creaking steel bed and half-sleeps, half-dreams of Donald sitting at the table in the house in Limassol, pulling his son to him and explaining how everything was physics. Time and space – physics indeed. Behind these dreams, Shake is aware of every variation in sound and light, is aware of Susannah shifting, of the clang of distant doors, of the night creeping through the barred window. As the cells grows dark and the light bulb flickers, the door opens and more mush and water arrives.

The storm abates, the rain lightens, becomes a quiet, arhythmic percussion on the slick cobbles. Susannah wakes, asks if she can share a cigarette with him. Shake watches her as she smokes, notices the grime beginning to gather in her corners, her crevices, notices her hair is greasy, plastered to her skull.

'So, what you think happens now?' Susannah hands him the near-finished butt.

'What d'you mean?'

'We've been here a while. I'm trying to calculate what their next move might be. Interrogation, maybe.'

'What's to interrogate about? We haven't done anything.'

Susannah stares at the wall, chews her cheek. 'That, Shake, depend on whether yuh look at mama or pappy. Incitement to riot isn't a pretty thing.'

'That's not what it was like.'

'They be up there now.'

'Where?'

'In Mojito. I been lying here thinking about what they doing. They be up there, going through mih papers, mih computer, lying on mih beds and drinking mih rum. God – I could do with a deep glass of seven-year-old.'

'What do you think they'll do with us?'

'I think they make us wait while they deciding. Like I say, you a British citizen, yuh may be fine. But I don' reckon they do anything until someone make a fuss. Like I also say – who know you here?'

And the walls seem to inhale, seem to expand like a puff adder's throat, expanding until they could swallow Shake.

The cell begins to stink, as the two of them, Susannah and Shake, begin to stink, as the toilet bowl refuses to empty, no matter how much water Shake pours down it. He runs out of cigarettes on the third day. On the fourth morning, the two of them are escorted to a shower stall where they are given a bar of blue soap but no towel and Susannah washes in her clothes because she isn't going to remove them in front of the guards. Shake spends the rest of the fourth day in a delirium, his guts rumbling. There is no longer the pretence of politeness, no longer any attempt at personal dignity. Susannah helps Shake to the toilet bowl, holds him as his bowels void, pulls his soiled sheet from his bed, tries to sluice out the cell. She hammers on the door until a guard arrives, demands a doctor, a clean cell and is given a mop. Flies zoom in lazy, deliberate patterns around the light bulb and the mosquitoes hover under the bed, in the dank corners, and for the first time in years Shake is bothered by the bites, scratches at them as he worries about dengue. On the fifth morning – or is it the sixth? Seventh? – they are allowed out, one after the other, to walk in the quadrangle for half an hour. Shake drags himself from the cell, joints aching, mouth drowning in foul spit, so he can see the sky. His eyes pain him as he looks up to the square of blue-grey sky, his pupils contracting too slowly, and the after-image of a purple patch burns on his retinas, stays with him for a long time. He stumbles often, weak, now, his stomach long-empty.

Every night, as Susannah sleeps, Shake takes a trip, perhaps drives around the island, stopping at the beaches to wade into the deep, cold water; or he takes the boat to Dorado; or fishes the trench, imagines the hammerheads and giant mantas moving lazily in a bottomless cavern. Sometimes he floats in the infinity pool at Mojito and the water stretches forever. These trips are taken to the accompaniment of Susannah's quiet, rhythmic snores.

And every day, as the small rhomboid of light moves around the cell, Susannah makes Shake talk, makes him listen, strokes his head when the walls grow too thick, when the rasping of distant keys is too loud. 'Yuh remember one Saturday you came by Mojito and I say I always liked yuh because yuh watch yuh content, because yuh don't ask about my life? I t'ink it was the night the dogs were poisoned. That seem like years ago, but it only a couple weeks. T'ing is, Shake, we got nothing to do here but talk. We got all the time in the world.'

So Shake lies on the bed, his head in Susannah's lap, and he tells her his life, describes his mother and father, talks about leaving Cyprus and going to Redpath.

'I went to a boarding school too,' says Susannah. 'I had a governess until I was seven and then I was sent to a convent in Sansobella. I hated it but I liked the lessons. It was a nun there who persuaded mih daddy to let me go to England. She tell him I could get into Cambridge and mih daddy like that, so he let me go. I wanted to be an engineer. I wanted to build things, leave something behind. I was a woman but I was a fucking good mathematician.'

'My father was an engineer. I think you two would have got along.'

Susannah laughs. 'Well, it a shame we never met because most t'ink I a quenk, gambage.' Susannah sighs. 'When I neither of those t'ings.' She stares at the wall, scratching Shake's filthy head. 'I had a brother, Cyrus, who was older than me. He drown in Guachara Bay when he twenty six. I hate him for that. I still do. Because I had to come back, leave England and come back to work with mih daddy. There was no one else, yuh see? I was the only Huggins' chile left. So I never was an engineer. I never build anything.'

Even in his muzzy state Shake has noticed Susannah's voice, her language, her accent still changes, slips about. It is not rum that causes it, he realizes. It is her many selves speaking.

Sometimes Susannah talks about how the island was years before, before whitey came. 'I born in 1940, here on St George, in mih mummy's bed in the estate house. Yuh got to understand, Shake, how rich we Huggins were. We could do anything we want. But you a baby, money like the clock, it mean nothing. I was loved by mih nanny, mih black nanny. It was she washed me, fed me, held me when me cry. Yuh t'inking of big black mammy, I bet, like *Gone With the Wind*? Mih nanny not like that. She thin as a horse whip, pale like café au lait, like storm stream on sand. Her called Otterley, but I call her Otty. Otty had lots of pickneys, all black as hell because Otty's man was black like night and we all play together. Me and Merle use to play in the cane fields, hide and seek, or make-believe pirates, or marbles, zop and X. Or us fish with hook and line. And Otty, she know all the bush medicine and when we sick, she boil up shandilay for fever or stew pain bush leaf for lay on cuts. And if I evil, Otty would pepper mih tail and sen' me home. It was Otty who taught me how to eat, how to wash, how to speak, how to dress meself. Mih mummy never did. Then, I sent to Sanso school an' when I come back, I not allowed to play with pickneys. Have to stay up at the great house and dress proper, dress frou frou. I look like a jackass. I lost all my friends, the children who didn't care if I was white and ugly, because mih daddy want me be a lady. That was cruel.

'It a different world, Shake. We owned everything we could see, all the land, all the houses, all the people. The cane fields spread all over, round Pillikin, up through Killdevill and down to Zabico and Coral Strand, south to Bridgewater. Four divisions we owned. Plus land down to Batteau and Woolly Coom. That was where we had our vegetable gardens and cattle and sheep and goat. Mih gran'daddy, he keep horses in stables up at an estate house near Polonaise, and I used to ride them on Lanesborough Bay, before anyone had built there. Early mornings, just as the sun lighting the hills of Killdevill, I used to take out a horse and ride from one end of Lanesborough to the other and see no one. I like that – I see no one and no one see me. Then all the film stars come back with they money and t'ings change. Mih gran'-daddy start to sell off plots to Americans and other whiteys and the world change. Petit bourge everywhere.

'Mih gran'daddy, before he die, he give Coral Strand to the nation. He love it there, and he haf a beach house built and he live there mos' of the time. Before he die, he leave it to the people, he want it to be a park, like a reservation, where no one ever build.' Susannah laughs, startling Shake. 'And everyone thought he was marvellous, just *marvellous* darling, to bequeath such a jewel. Fact is, he was a selfish fucking bastard. Lounged about on Coral Strand on his lonesome all his life, and only when he's dying does he think maybe it's time for others to have the chance to do the same.'

Susannah falls silent and Shake wonders whether the past is galloping along Lanesborough beach, catching up with her. 'I t'ink of mih gran'daddy and mih parents and what we were like. When I was young – what we was like. We was like the world frozen. Even when I come back from Cambridge with mih head hot, angry with ever'ting, hating ever'one, I'd dress for dinner and stand out on the gallery drinking mih cocktails as someone played piano. Like we was in Nice or Monte Carlo. All these whiteys, and I including mihsel' in dis, standing there, bein' waited on by Otty's children, the pickneys I play wid when I young, like we own the land, the sea, the air itself. An', of course, we did.' Susannah sighs a shuddering sigh, as if that past has now lodged itself in her polyglottal throat. 'I think of that, and I am ashamed. I have always been shamed, Shake, by my history. I stood on that gallery and I drank rum as Gershwin played and I vowed I would drink myself to an early grave and, given the chance, I will. I vowed I would never have children and I haven't. I vowed I would commit genetic suicide, and I have. Although I may yet be denied that luxury by the powers that be. The Huggins will die out with me, and that is how it should be. We had our time.

'But what shames me most is that I never told my parents of the vows I made. I never told them about my lovers, I hid my drinking, I always spoke my lines in the script that was the Huggins' life. I never had the guts to tell them what I was going to do. I built Mojito as an indulgence – Lord, listen to me. As an indulgence. At least it is a temporary indulgence, because I have left my entire estate – my land and property, art collection and other assets to the state. I have left it where it might do some good. That's one of the many reasons I hate Kouranis. My grand-daddy gave Coral Strand away, gave it to the people, and Kouranis bought it.'

'Well the government must have sold it to him.'

'The bloody NMDC sold it. The bloody East Indian Sansos sold it. And Carlisle's dead and he should be lying in the shade on the beach at Coral Strand. That's why I went to the march, why I pulled down the fence, because dat land was mine before Kouranis even heard of fucking Sansobella. Now I pay de cake.'

There are times when Shake's hands flutter and his legs jig, when his breathing is so difficult that he can't listen and then Susannah makes him talk, talk about anything. Asks him to describe how to make cocktails, challenges him to come up with ten cocktails beginning with the letter 'w', with the letter 'j'. Asks him to list the names and places of the famous bartenders.

Susannah doesn't know if he's right but Shake concentrates so hard she thinks he must be trying.

'Giuseppe Cipriani – Harry's Bar, New York; Fernand Petoit – Harry's Bar, Paris; John Collins – Limmer's, London; Don Beach – Beachcomber, Hollywood; Ngiam Tong Boon – Raffles, Singapore; Victor Bergeron – Emeryville Bar, Hinky Dinks; Constante Ribailagua – el Floridita, Havana. Ribailagua – e*l rey de los coteleros*. The king of cocktails.'

Sometimes Susannah fantasizes aloud about food or cars, hoping to draw Shake out of himself, trying to stop him disappearing into the acid depths of his guts. 'Mih mout' shape up fuh a ches' provoker – an Angus steak, a bowl of Kenyan fine beans, wid maybe some sautée Idahoes on the side. I'd be insistin' on a fine bottle of Pouilly, a little Muscat wid some mille-feuilles, an' a thick Java coffee to finish. An', of course, a glass of brandy. What yuh t'ink, Shake?'

All Shake can dream of is space and cold water, so he remains silent as Susannah composes her elaborate menus.

This talking and listening, the listing of cocktails, the dredging of memories from the monochrome past begins to falter. No amount of cajoling and questioning, can hide the fact that Shake is fading, literally fading. His tan is fading, the colour leaching away in the dark cell – he's now house colour. The food makes Shake sick, and Susannah suspects the water does too. Shake has let go of the leash of time and time has bolted. He no longer cares which day it is, can no longer measure the passing of the day by the light seeping into the cell. They don't talk about outside, don't mention Rajiv or Shake's sister, because every day that passes shunts the outside further away, makes outside more distant, as if the moat of time between then-and-now grows wider. Susannah had thought Shake, with his dark red and gold passport, would have been out of there in a day. After the first week, she begins to wonder, but she says nothing, as Shakes slips in and out of wakefulness.

There is one break in the monotony, when Susannah is taken away and returns some time later with her left eye blackened and her lip split.

Shake, the loner who is no longer used to being alone, who has been pacing the floor, asks, 'What the fuck happened?'

Susannah sits on the bed and smiles, flinches as her lip splits again. 'I was questioned by a charming man who didn't like my answers.'

'What happened?'

'You don't know the man himself, but you *know* him. The kind of policeman who's getting heavy, beginning to press against the buttons of his well-pressed uniform. He can remember a time when he was a beach boy, when he was lean and black and handsome but he's not any more. What's the English phrase?' Susannah frowns, clicks her fingers. 'He's poacher turned gamekeeper. He loves his gun and hates whitey, hates dada head, hates Sansos, hates his boss, hates his wife. But he loves driving round with the white women, loves sitting in their sleek, expensive vehicles, pretending like they're his. And he sits in the cars and he fingers his gun like he playing pocket billiards. Yuh *know* he.'

Shake nods.

'Well, that's who questioned me, about the march, about my politics, about Mojito. Who he t'ink he is? Dog among doctors. Anyway, he leaning right heah, right close, so close I can see de hair in he nose. He say, "Why doh yuh take yuh white skin back home?" I point out, firmly but politely, that my family have lived here since 1753. I also point out that means the Huggins have been here longer than his family. Then I offer to buy a ferry and leave it at dock in Bridgewater and everyone who wants to go home, everyone who wants to go back to the Congo, or Benin or Togo or wherever it is the fuck they come from, can have free passage. I opine that the ferry would remain empty because no one in their right mind would want to experience libera*shun,* emancipa*shun* or revolu*shun* in the lawless, starving, fucking *hellhole* that is their homeland. I give he the length of mih tongue, and then he hit me.' Again, Susannah smiles.

That night, when the key rasps in the lock as the door slams, Shake begins to whimper. He feels hollow, undone, he can think of no more trips to take in his mind. Susannah strokes his head, tries to calm him but nothing works.

'Shake, hey, Shake, remember that night when you came by because the dogs were poisoned? I ask you to stay and you say you will but only if the doors not locked? What's that about? Maybe if yuh tell me it, it will pass, eh baby? Maybe if yuh chuchoter me what it is, the soucouyant that trouble you go leave yuh, nuh?'

Shake waits to speak, curls up and waits until the light fades, waits until he is lying and dying in the dark.

Shake stood in the white marble hallway of the house in the hills, shivering slightly in the heat of a late-afternoon Californian summer's day, as he watched the chauffeur carry in the cases from the trip to Dorado. The lines he had taken in LAX were still stringing Shake – tanned marionette – together, stringing him into one long piece, as Emma walked by and climbed the stairs to the mezzanine floor. Shake could see himself dancing a little involuntary shimmy in the plate glass mirror opposite. Saw the mirror image of the chauffeur, who had finished his task, slow as he passed Shake, his hands open, palms waiting to be greased. Shake patted his pockets, which were empty. He signalled to the chauffeur to wait, walked through the swing doors to the kitchen, rummaged in the drawers for a twenty dollar bill, searched through tins, fury rising as he found each tin, each drawer, empty. Shake sprinted up the stairs, saw Emma's purse, blood-red Mulberry, lying on a cloud-white sofa, and tore it open, found a few bills, and trotted down the stairs. He held out the money, which the chauffeur flattened and folded carefully, before slipping it into a billfold. Shake knew he was supposed to say something but he couldn't remember what it was; besides, his jaws appeared to be wired.

Back in the kitchen, Shake pulled open the fridge door,

cracked open a bottle of Beck's Dark, drank it down, opened another. Already he felt trapped – by the opulent, by the bland, by calico and linen, by travertine and ivory. He slammed open the sliding doors leading to the pool, doors which whispered to a stop, controlled by hydraulics, and stepped outside. The land beyond the pool, which was artfully designed to appear larger than it was, surrounded by grey and beige pots prickly with ferns and cacti, dropped away to the distant Pacific shore. Between Shake and the ocean was the tumorous, grey cancer of Los Angeles, blossoming in its secondary state, unstoppable. Shake finished his beer and set the bottle down pool-side, where it tilted and toppled, rolled to a stop against a sunlounger. As he flicked through his mental Rolodex of contacts, calculating the best score, Emma came to stand next to him, her arms folded, looking out at the same smoking, choking vista.

'I'm pregnant,' Emma said.

Shake imagined his wife standing in their bathroom, afternoon sun slashing the tiled floor white and grey through the blinds, waiting for a needle-thin cobalt line to appear. Still his jaws felt wired.

'I said, I'm pregnant.'

Shake knew what happened to mothers.

The slap made Shake's skin fizzle, made it twitch, beneath his week-old beard. He stood by the pool and watched for hours as a sickly, pale sun dropped towards an unseen horizon. Then he went back to the kitchen, picked the phone from the wall and began to make his calls. When he was done, he climbed the stairs and walked the long, slate-floored corridor to the bedroom, where he found Emma asleep. Shake showered, slipped into clean clothes – there were always clean, pressed clothes hanging in the dressing room – struggled with the buttons on his shirt as his fingers became sausages and grew cold. Those same fingers searched through the blood-red purse, fumbled with notes and car keys. The drive down to the strip, the turning of sharp, tree-lined bends, occupied Shake's mind, leaving no room for the contemplation of fatherhood and guilt, boredom and addiction, no time to consider bodies lying outside fences.

Ten weeks it took Shake to dry out, ten weeks to disjoint the marionette he had become and reassemble the man he had been. After three weeks, Emma visited the clinic, bringing him English papers and videos of Chelsea's games. She sat with him in the manicured, fenced grounds, her face tilted to the sun, a hand on her still-flat belly, and waited for Shake to speak. When six weeks had passed, Emma brought papers, videos, Marmite and wine gums. She sat with him in the manicured, fenced grounds, and she talked about the nursery, about schools and her new car – a station wagon had replaced the Porsche. After nine weeks, Emma brought papers, videos, Kit-Kats, wine gums, Shake's cell phone, Filofax and wallet. Emma sat in the manicured, fenced grounds with Shake, her face tilted to the sun, eyes closed, her fingers laced over the tiny mound of her belly, and she said, 'I could sit here and ask that you delete every entry, tear out every page that has the numbers of those people who sold you what you wanted. But the way I look at it, that's your prerogative. It's up to you. In the wallet you'll find a card with twenty thousand dollars credit and five hundred dollars in cash. I'd really like it if you used the money to come home, to come back. But, again, that's your prerogative. I miss you. I sleep alone every bloody night, feeling myself grow, and I miss you.'

Shake looked at his wife and saw she was crying. Her eyes were closed and she was crying. Perhaps she had cried during each visit? He cleared his throat. 'I miss you, too.'

Emma opened her eyes and looked at Shake, wondering if he would ever grow up, wondering if she was the one who didn't want him to – this man who had careered around London in a rusty van, music blaring, giggling and cuddling, yodelling and partying, mixing cocktails. This man who had cleared drains, built stud walls, who had had a life, a way of luring her into fun. A man she had ripped untimely from the womb of the familiar. Emma rubbed her belly. 'Good. I have to go now.'

Emma made sure, once Shake had returned to the house in the hills, that he never walked two steps behind her again. Always, when they were out and about, Emma linked her arm with his, hugged him close rather than flit away to talk to people she barely knew. Even when she went into labour, Emma kept him close, clamped him to her side in case he flew away. Shake held her as she laboured, wished himself in her place as she screamed, cried as their son slipped into the hands of the doctor, cried because his wife was now a mother. Photographers were waiting for them as they came out of the hospital, crouched like crabs at the foot of the steps, and Emma took hold of Shake's hand as if she'd never let it go. Shake looked at the predators, Kodak crustaceans scuttling for better shots, and he shook himself free of Emma's hand, wrapped his arm around her shoulders and pushed the photographers aside as the limo arrived.

*

Christopher, who had a sleek blanket of black hair when he was born, wrestled with his own hands and feet, groping at the un-understood. He gurned with spittle-pink gums, charming his parents, as he tried to come to terms with dimensions and perspectives. He drooled white spittle, excreted yellow faeces and looked proud of these offerings. Shake laughed, cleaned his son up, and bought him gifts – vast, spidery, multi-coloured mobiles which he suspended over Christopher's cot and huge, stuffed animals. But the toy Christopher loved the most, the toy he chewed as he teethed, the toy he waved his marshmallow-soft hands for, was a scrap of a thing, a scrawny grey rabbit, which was eventually named Bedtime Bunny since Christopher would not sleep unless Bedtime Bunny had kissed him goodnight. Shake fed his son Emma's expressed milk, changed his nappies, powdered the pale rolls of his fat thighs and buttocks, and counted his son's toes and fingers. Later Shake took Christopher for walks on the beach, holding Christopher's hands as he balanced on his father's feet, learning to move his pudgy legs one in front of the other, wobbling, swaying like a web in a wind. Shake looked down at his son and marvelled that the straight black hair had fallen away to be replaced by pale blonde. Shake and Emma wondered who, in their collective pasts, had slept with a Viking, a Norsewoman, wondered whose misdemeanour was being repaid in gold.

Emma, who was working full-tilt, who slalomed between parts, her voice and accent, her posture and attitude changing over and over, reinvented herself every morning before stepping out of her door and into a limousine, leaving Shake and Christopher to bumble through their days. She would return, late at night, to find all three of them asleep on a sofa, Christopher's cheek, his ear, pressed against the skin over Shake's heart, drooling on his father's chest as he dreamed and Bedtime Bunny kept watch over them. Sometimes Emma wondered what it was her son might dream about, wondered if Christopher already understood about what ifs. Emma would pour herself a drink, carefully, quietly, cushioning the ice cubes' fall into glass, and then sit on the floor, watching her family. As the months passed, became years, Emma gradually – without noticing she had – ceased to check the ashtrays, the wastebin, the last number dialled, the mileage on the car, the cash in her purse, the balances in the accounts. The mirror in the bathroom.

When the cameras stopped rolling and Emma was released for a week, for a month, there were trips to Venice, Cannes and London for the festivals, there were holidays on crewed yachts, in cabins in the mountains, in villas in the Virgins. The three of them would go bowling, or horse riding or perhaps stay by the pool in the house in the hills overlooking LA, and Shake would play with Christopher as Emma read and marked scripts, learned her lines, smiling absently when asked to watch Christopher jump from the board into Shake's arms, or kick a ball, or run through the sprinkler spray. Sometimes, rather than smiling absently, Emma watched husband and son intently, protected by the bland barrier of her shades, watched the way Shake anticipated Christopher's every move, anticipated every potential death. His hand or body was always between his son and danger: a table corner, a diving board, a horse's hoof, a car door, a stranger. Sometimes Emma wondered if Shake was hovering, waiting to step even between mother and son, when she scooped Christopher up and covered his white-blond head with kisses,

when she swayed her hips and held him close and crooned lulla-
bies and nonsense verses about blue eyes and red-breasted
robins.

There were arguments, there were tantrums but they were like
lens clouds, northern lights, double rainbows – memorable but
rare and remarkable. The three of them fashioned a groove,
seamless and smooth, along which they slipped, their passage
eased by the emollience of money. Promises were made and
broken, about bedtimes, about candies and cookies, about cleaning out toy cupboards. The larger, weightier promises were never
voiced but neither were they broken.

And then they went to Aspen.

A donkey scream. A pair of blue eyes. The strange, silver silence of falling snow. Shake shivers in the fetid, humid cell and Susannah rubs his arm.

'What happened in Aspen? Shake, what happened in Aspen?'

'We rented a lodge up in the mountains, and we spent a few days skiing, making snowmen, hiking. When Christopher got tired I carried him in a kind of backpack thing on my back so he could see over my shoulder.' The weight of that sturdy three-year-old body on Shake's back. The heat of it radiating through his parka. 'It was beautiful up there, like no one else had ever been where we were. Just fir trees and snow and spruce. We had a hot tub outside, and when Christopher was asleep, Em and I would sit out there, looking up at the night sky, not talking much, and it was like you could hear the steam freeze. Then Em had a call from the editors saying she had to do some dubbing because the sound technician had messed up. She didn't want to go but it was in her contract. So she flew back to LA for four days and was coming back for Christmas Eve. I had a ball with Christopher. Every day we made breakfast and then we'd go into town and buy some papers and groceries, and we'd have hot chocolate and ice cream. One afternoon we went sledding, you know, just outside the lodge. There were sledges there, those old-fashioned wooden ones, and Christopher loved that. I remember he had this ridiculous hat, like a jester's hat, with bells on the tips and ear flaps. It was red and blue and orange. Another afternoon we tried skating, down in a rink in the town. They had these dinky little boots you could hire and Christopher managed to stay up after a while, if I held his hand. I wasn't very good at it and I slipped and fell over and Christopher kind of wobbled on, laughing at me, until he bumped into the side. Then we drove back to the lodge and we fell asleep, both of us, on the sofa and I was woken by someone hammering on the door.'

Shake remembers moving his son gently away, lifting him and then putting him back on the sofa, still sleeping.

'It was some friends of mine from Santa Monica, they'd flown in that day and they wanted to party. Christopher woke up and I made some pasta stuff and everyone was happy, bottles of wine going round the table and Christopher sat at the head of the table and people were playing with him. I can't remember what – snap, I think. One guy could do magic tricks and he was pulling money and cards and balls out of Christopher's ears and hair. It was late when Christopher fell asleep, on the sofa again, and I thought, that's fine, I can keep an eye on him. And I fetched Bedtime Bunny and he slept all through the party, through the music. Then the wine was gone and out came the cocaine and the poppers and the uppers and the downers and the dope. And this time, I don't know why, after all those years, I joined in. I don't know why. Because I was happy – I don't know why I started taking that stuff again.'

Susannah's fingers have stopped moving but Shake doesn't notice.

'When I woke up, Christopher was gone. I woke up lying face down on my bed, still dressed in my jeans and sweater, and when I went downstairs, Christopher wasn't on the sofa any more. The kitchen and living room were trashed and everyone had left. I looked in Christopher's room, in the bathrooms, in the spare rooms, in the den. I looked everywhere and I started to panic because he wasn't in the house. I checked the car in the garage, looked everywhere until there wasn't anywhere else to look but outside. It was snowing but not heavily, just enough to dust the old snow. First thing I did was look in the hot tub. It looked like it was smoking, it had been on for so long, and there were bottles and clothes and tin foil and syringes all round it. I didn't want to look in but when I did the only things floating there were cigarette butts and roaches.

'So I started to look around, in the woods. I wanted to run, I wanted to run all over as fast as I could, but I knew the best thing was to look for marks in the snow. There were some tyre marks, where people had driven off, and a lot of footprints. But they were all big prints, grown-up foot prints. It was so cold and I only had my sweater on but I couldn't go back, I had to keep looking, and I was shivering so hard I could hardly think. I saw deer prints. They were small, like fairy prints, very fresh. And I saw a pair of eagles overhead. It took me a long time to find Christopher because the snow had covered his footprints. I saw Bedtime Bunny first.' Shake remembers seeing the grey, stuffed animal, one ear already covered in snow, and then catching sight of a splash of scarlet. 'Then I saw Christopher. The cover of snow was so thin, like gauze, not like a blanket more like a film. It was nothing, it was so thin. I picked him up and tried to run back to

392   Jules Hardy

the lodge but the snow was nearly up to my knees and I had no shoes on and I couldn't go any faster but I knew already, because he was so cold. So cold.

'And then there were police and ambulances and choppers everywhere. And Em came back and I couldn't speak to her, I couldn't say anything to her. She kept screaming at the police and she kept screaming at me. She couldn't stop screaming at me because when I went to look for Christopher outside, outside the lodge, the door had been locked. Christopher must have woken up and gone outside and the door must have locked behind him and he couldn't get back in. And Em kept screaming at me, asking if I'd locked the door and I couldn't remember because I'd been out of my fucking head, I couldn't remember.'

The childless, genetically suicidal Susannah strokes Shake's head, tries to imagine the thoughts trapped inside his skull. 'Ah, Shake, Shake, baby,' she says, 'God does fit back fuh burden.'

Susannah hears the lock turning as Shake sleeps. It must be the middle of the night and Shake has finally fallen asleep. Susannah blinks as the light is switched on, taps Shake's shoulder to wake him and he sits up slowly, shielding his tired, watery eyes.

Two white men, tall and thickset, dressed in black suits, black ties, are standing in the door, the hawk-eyed Major Ramprakesh standing beside them.

'Mr Knight, follow me please,' says the major, and walks away.

The two white men stand aside, waiting for Shake, who is confused, who stands by Susannah's bed, reluctant to leave her.

'Mr Knight?'

'Yuh go, Shake. I see yuh in time, nuh.' Susannah, in the dim light, looks feral, her ugly face battered and bruised, her skin sallow.

'Mr Knight? We must hurry.'

Shake shakes his head. 'I can't go. I can't leave you here.'

The taller of the white men steps into the cell, reaches out to touch Shake's arm, thinks better of it. 'Mr Knight, we don't have much time.'

Shake looks at Susannah, who smiles her half-smile, touches his hand. 'Yuh look for yuhself, Shake. Doh worry bout me, I be fine. And doh worry bout cuchuments – remember, it's jus' a different pamplemousse. Go now. I be fine. I call yuh and we will drink ourselves some Snake Bites by de pool. Go now, baby.'

Major Ramprakesh is waiting in the main building, where he had questioned Shake weeks before. He hands Shake a bag, in which is his passport and the *Savoy Cocktail Book*, but Shake's too bleary, too confused to realize what's happening. He sees a clock, a white clock with black numbers and it looks odd. Sees the big hand is on the twelve and the little hand is on the two. The white men lead Shake outside and the night air feels cold, feels so cold it's like it might snow and Shake begins to shiver. He's put in the back of a black 4x4 with tinted windows, and the taller white man gets behind the wheel, drives fast, wordlessly, along deserted roads and Shake can't see anything except the startled eyes of goats on the verges because there's an outage and Bridgewater is drenched in pitch.

At the airport, where there is power, where the lights hurt Shake's eyes, there are soldiers milling about, some lounging on benches, feet up. They stand up when the black vehicle squeals to a halt, some raise their guns but the white men ignore them. They drag the fading, shivering Shake from the back of the car as an officer signals to the soldiers to stand down, and Shake is half-carried through the departure lounge, watched by silent, sullen soldiers, out through a door to the apron and there is an unmarked Gulfstream jet, no livery breaking the blank fuselage, its engines roaring. Shake is dragged to the plane, helped up the steps and once he's inside, inside the clean, cool interior, he's put in a wide, white leather seat and the seat is soft, comfortable. Shake is given a bottle of water and two small, white pills, told to drink and swallow. A blanket is put over Shake as he falls, not for the first time, off the edge of a cliff.

It's the change in the pitch of the howling engines and the pain in his ears that wake Shake. He looks around himself, stunned by grogginess, the sleeping pills leaving him slow and stupid. He doesn't know where he is.

'Where am I?' he asks no one.

'We're approaching New York, sir. Should be landing in around fifteen minutes. Here, let me help you with that.'

The man in the black suit leans over Shake, gently moves Shake's hands which are fumbling with the blanket. His seat is straightened, the blanket removed and his seat belt fastened and then Shake closes his eyes again, begins to drift. Emma must have forgiven him enough to save him, must have forgiven him enough to think he is worth saving and he whimpers a little, too tired to cry.

The jet lands untidily, throwing Shake against the small, misty window as concrete flashes by. Shake stares at the buildings, hundreds of them, pale and cuboid in the early morning light. The jet taxis to a distant, nameless building and glides to a halt. The black suit unbuckles Shake's belt, advises him to be careful when he tries to walk as he may be a little unsteady. Shake's legs are water-filled, wavering, and he's helped down the steps, into a car which drives him the few hundred yards to the doors of the building. The two men stay with Shake as he stumbles along a long, white corridor, lit by neon, the walls and floor gleaming and spotless. Shake tries to order his thoughts but they keep leaking away; he's trying to work out how to greet Emma, how to say sorry yet again for not being able to remember.

The three men turn a corner and there is a man sitting at a desk, a man in uniform, and behind him there are two guards, dressed in dark blue, wearing caps. Shake doesn't like uniforms now. He is suddenly aware of his own stench, of the dirt under his nails, the grime on his bare feet, the stains on his sweat-stiff-ened T-shirt and shorts.

'Passport?' says the seated man and Shake stares at him. The black suit reaches out and gently pulls the plastic bag from Shake's hands. Shake has been holding it so tight, for so long, he has forgotten it. The black suit takes out Shake's passport, hands it to Shake, who hands it to the man in uniform. The man flicks through the pages, picks up a rubber stamp, inks it, slams it on the page and initials the imprint. Hands the passport back to Shake.

'Welcome to America. Have a good day.'

Shake is led to the frosted, automatic doors at the end of the corridor, trying, still, to work out what he is going to say. But when the doors slide back, with a rush of air, he realizes he is still unforgiven, because it is not Emma Beckworth he finds waiting for him. It's Mr Westmore, the gingerbread man.

A DIFFERENT PAMPLEMOUSSE

It's the end of summer, the tail-end, the raggedy first week of September; the air coming in off the sea has a zing in it, as if soon it will be bringing rain and sleet, eventually snow, and this worries Shake. All around, people are packing their bags and leaving the beaches as if for the last time. All over America, all over the northern world, people are folding their towels and standing, hands on hips, to look out over the oceans for the last time. Preparing their memories to help them get through winter. Sand has worked its way into the corners of the rented beach huts and seaside homes; the paint has dulled in the glare of the sun; doors and catches need fixing; windows need replacing. The dunes have shifted a little and the dry river beds are beginning to fill. Sag Harbor, Long Island, moneyed as it is, looks battered, too, as the summer visitors pack their cars and MPVs and leave, drive back to their places in the city, or catch planes to fly to the landlocked mid-west.

Shake has said he'll drive Leanne and some of her friends to the last of the summer fairs, over Riverhead way, around the bay, and then take them onto a beach party at Luce Landing. But he won't stay, he's going to drop them at Luce Landing and come back to Sag Harbor. Leanne is waiting at the door, nearly naked as always, looking out for Shake and when she sees his truck coming up the drive, she smiles. As always, she comes up to him, winds her arm through his, practically rubs herself against him, like a needy feline. Shake knows Leanne has the hots for him, as do all her friends and he plays along but he's not interested because she has nothing to say that he wants to hear. Mr Westmore comes to the door as Shake's car fills with bare flesh.

'I want you back here by midnight, Leanne. You hear?'

'Yeah, Dad. Maybe one o'clock?'

'No, midnight. You got a ride back because Shake's not going to be there? You got a designated driver?'

'Yeah – Brad said he'd bring us.'

'OK. Make sure he's not drinking. Thanks, Shake. See you later.' Mr Westmore disappears back into the clapboard mansion that is his summer home on Long Island.

Shake doesn't listen to the girls yabbering around him, instead he watches the coastline pass as he drives around the bay. Such a mild, milky coastline, pale and uninteresting. The fair, it turns out, is set up a couple of miles south of Riverhead, a mess of trucks and cables set in a circle, inside which were the usual rides, the waltzer, dodgems, spiders and a small, sad roller-coaster. The fair is on its last summer stop, hoovering up the remains of the money the tourists have in their pockets. Leanne and her friends set off, giggling behind their hands, pierced belly studs flashing, heading for the pockets of boys hanging round, who are trying to look hard, trying to look cool, like street kids, although they've arrived in daddy's Porsche and they're spending daddy's money, wearing eight hundred dollars worth of Animal, Aloha and Ray-Bans. They see Shake and straighten their shoulders, spit expertly on the ground, flex their arms and look away as Shake smiles. He buys himself a hot pretzel and wanders around the rides, watches girls screaming and the boys trying to look unconcerned, as if hanging upside down experiencing the disorienting effects of centrifugal forces were a normal, everyday event. Trying to ignore the effects of physics. Again, Shake smiles. In the centre of the fair, he finds the main attraction – a small rodeo. He pays and sits in the bleachers for an hour or so, watching cowboys and cowgirls being thrown in the dust, slapping at chaps and hamming it up for the kids in the crowd. And again, everything seems so mild, milky, as if Shake is seeing it through a smeared lens. More families start to arrive, filling the bleachers, and he wants to leave, then, because there are too many little blond boys with blue eyes cheering the cowboys. He looks around the fair and finds Leanne, talking to a feckless youth, playing with her hair as she talks, and it's OK because the boy is short and swarthy, not quite as ugly as Adonis but getting there.

'Come on, Leanne. Get your mates and let's go. I need to get home.'

And because it's Shake, tall, tanned, sexy Shake who's asking, Leanne rushes off and herds her friends to his car. Mr Westmore often remarks that he wishes Shake was Leanne's teacher at school because then she might actually learn something since he's the only one she'll listen to. Shake – Leanne's hero, the man who saved her from the black beast that was Jungle Jam Bow Wow a million miles away.

Shake drops the girls at the beach party, and swings by a pharmacy on the way back to Sag Harbor. As always, he's stunned by choice. Racks of gleaming white, blue, yellow and red goods spread out under halogen. Shake stands in front of the shelves of toothpaste for a while, feeling as he did when he was a child, when he was Sammy and he looked at jars of sweets and needed to pee. Shake grabs the nearest tube and pays.

Driving past the mansion, Shake waves to Mrs Westmore as he passes her out in her garden deadheading roses and she waves back, returns to her clipping. Shake's bungalow is way down the back of the Westmore's land and Shake's grateful that it's screened from the house by a stand of pines and bushes. He's grateful because he likes to sit out on the porch, with a beer, likes to sit out and watch the stars and he wouldn't feel comfortable being watched, doesn't like being watched. Shake's not due at the bar until nine so that's what he decides to do – sit on the porch and drink a beer. He has to pull on a sweater because the zing in the air is sharp tonight; the evenings are beginning to draw in, like the neck of a purse seiner net, drawing in, capturing daylight. Shake fetches a beer from the icebox in the kitchen, which is white and clean and functional, which has running hot and cold water and a phone which always works hanging on the wall. The bungalow, as Mr Westmore calls it, is enormous, twice the size of the concrete house Shake had been building. It has three bedrooms, three bathrooms, two living rooms, a study and a two-car garage. Sometimes Shake thinks he might get lost in it, snow-blinded by white walls.

Shake sits on the step of the porch and, unthinking, reaches out for the Saltbag but of course the old dog isn't there. She's on St George and Shake wishes he was too but he can't ever go there again. In his passport is an angry red stamp: Republic of Sansobella, St George and Dorado: undesirable alien – entry barred. Shake sits on the porch of the Westmore's bungalow in Sag Harbor and he wonders about this, about this being an undesirable alien because sometimes he thinks that's what he's been all his life, on one island or another and now he's living on another one but it's not really an island because it has bridges and if he drove over those bridges he'd find himself in New York City and Shake could keep driving, drive across a continent and if he drove for long enough, if he drove far enough, he'd reach LA, reach Hollywood.

Shake sips the beer and worries about winter, worries about the snow coming because he hasn't seen it for years. The last time he saw snow it was shrouding Bedtime Bunny. He considers, as he always does, running away to Florida, where the sun always shines and there are hundreds, thousands of swimming pools. But he can't do that, he knows he can't do that because he can't abandon Mr Westmore, can't disappoint him because Shake owes him too much. It turned out that the price Mr Westmore paid for Leanne's intact hymen was high, very, very high.

Mr Westmore had tried to contact Shake when Queenstown went up in flames, had called Shake's cell and landline as he watched the tourist videos replaying again and again on CNN, of the apparently angry crowd at Coral Strand on St George. But Shake hadn't answered the calls because the lines were down and anyway, he wasn't there, he was rotting and turning house colour in a cell in Bridgewater.

'It took me a while,' Mr Westmore had said to him. 'I'm sorry but it took me a while to realize that Samuel Henry Andrew Knight was our very own Captain Shake. But once I got that, I moved as fast as I could. I contacted everyone I knew in shipping and oil and the information started coming back. I used the same channels to make an offer they – in the end – couldn't refuse. It was that guy Kouranis at the end of the chain. I remember you mentioned him.'

'What kind of offer?'

Mr Westmore shrugged. 'Money. What else?'

'But Kouranis is richer than God.'

'Men like us are never rich enough.'

Shake wanted to ask but he couldn't.

'You want to know how much?'

Shake didn't know if he wanted to be told the figure. 'OK.'

'Two hundred and fifty thousand dollars.'

'Shit.'

'Plus I had to pay for the company plane and the goons. But that's fine, Shake. I owed you one. Every time I look at Leanne I think I'd do it again if I had to. The way I look at it, I don't think Kouranis thought you were important enough to bother with. Maybe I should have offered less, maybe negotiated?' Mr Westmore laughed.

Kouranis the Greek at the end of the chain. Susannah had been right – he wanted it all. He began by buying Coral Strand twenty-five years before and he ended up with an entire nation. Shake often thinks of the days when he first arrived in Sag Harbor, when he sat in the bungalow, recovering from dengue, eating and drinking, sometimes walking out to stand in the sun because he could and no one would stop him. Watching the news channels, watching General Ramprakesh making his speeches, watching the soldiers patrolling the boulevards and traces of Queenstown and St George. Watching Kouranis, aptly titled Foreign Minister, because he *was* foreign, because he was where he shouldn't be, an undesirable alien. Watching Kouranis making a statement announcing that Susannah Huggins, heiress to the Huggins' fortune, had died unexpectedly whilst in custody, pend-